PENGUIN BOOKS

LONDON KILLS ME

Hanif Kureishi was born and brought up in Kent, England. He read philosophy at King's College, London, where he started to write plays. In 1981 he won the George Devine Award for his play *Outskirts*, and in 1982 he was appointed Writer in Residence at the Royal Court Theatre. In 1984 he wrote *My Beautiful Laundrette*, which received an Oscar nomination for Best Screenplay. His second film was *Sammy and Rosie Get Laid*. *London Kills Me* is his third film and his debut as a director. Kureishi is the author of a novel, *The Buddha of Suburbia*. His short stories and nonfiction have appeared in *Harper's*, *The Village Voice*, and *The Atlantic*. He lives in London.

Hanif
ureishi

London
Kills
Me

3 Screenplays &
4 Essays

Penguin Books

PENGUIN BOOKS
Published by the Penguin Group
Viking Penguin, a division of Penguin Books USA Inc.,
375 Hudson Street, New York, New York 10014, U.S.A.
Penguin Books Ltd, 27 Wrights Lane,
London W8 5TZ, England
Penguin Books Australia Ltd, Ringwood,
Victoria, Australia
Penguin Books Canada Ltd, 10 Alcorn Avenue, Suite 300,
Toronto, Ontario, Canada M4V 3B2
Penguin Books (N.Z.) Ltd, 182–190 Wairau Road,
Auckland 10, New Zealand

Penguin Books Ltd, Registered Offices:
Harmondsworth, Middlesex, England

Published in Penguin Books 1992

LIBRARY OF CONGRESS CATALOGING IN PUBLICATION DATA
Kureishi, Hanif.
London kills me: three screenplays and four essays/ Hanif
Kureishi.
p.   cm.
ISBN 0 14.01.6831 1
1. London (England)—Drama.   I. Title.
PR6061.U68L6   1992
822'.914—dc20   91–39236

Printed in the United States of America

Set in Simoncini Garamond
Designed by Brian Mulligan

2008-AU

Contents

Introduction

A friend of my father's had laundrettes in West London and he was happy for me to visit them with him. It was 1984 and I was trying to write plays. Unfortunately, I was discovering that this was a form I found difficult—too difficult, in fact. I didn't know what to do. Whether to persist, perhaps eventually breaking through the block; or whether to circumvent the block, trying something new, in writing or another field. To escape this struggle with words that refused to come, I would go with my father's friend to look at his laundrettes. These places were, inevitably, dirty and too brightly lit, and usually flooded with water.

I wasn't making much money from writing but there was money to be made, we were told, in the service industries. Everything was falling apart, but small businesses that didn't actually make things but made things run were going to be the future in the new, stream-lined, Thatcherite Britain. Looking at these laundrettes, I decided that the washing business was not my vocation. But I kept notes of my friend's laundrette stories. And instead of running a laundrette, I went back to my desk and imagined what running one might be like.

The resulting film, *My Beautiful Laundrette*, changed my life and had a great effect on many of those involved in it: Stephen Frears, Daniel Day Lewis, Roshan Seth, Saeed Jaffrey, and the producers Tim Bevan and Sarah Radclyffe. It was made cheaply and quickly, out of love and without the expectation of reaching a wide audience, or even of receiving theatrical distribution.

"It's our turn in the sun," Frears used to say. "It's just our turn —so don't expect it to last." This was the mid-1980s—that fevered time, when to make it in that most bullish of industries, the media, was to be guaranteed a high time. In London new clubs and resturants were opening to sell-out crowds. Soho was full of people making pop promos and commercials. Good newspapers and magazines were being started. Parts of London seemed gripped by money madness. Insane ambition blossomed in the mediocre, and Ecstasy and cocaine were frantically indulged in. There was all the febrile confusion that accompanies lives whose pace outstrips people's ability to understand.

For a time we were caught up in this. The trips, awards, festivals, the acceptance and opening of doors where once there had been indifference, was disturbing and exhilarating. I was looking miserable somewhere when someone said to me "make the most of it." I decided she was right.

The London cinema mostly consisted of big American films—Sylvester Stallone vehicles and the like. And there was English nostalgia, often set in India—the cultural analogue of Thatcher's grandiose idea of Britain's place in the world, culminating in the Falklands. (A war that Borges characterised as "two bald men fighting over a comb".)

Television in Britain had been financing films since the 1960s but forbidding them from being shown in the cinema. The new Channel Four invested in cinema films by pre-buying showings on TV and taking an equity stake. So there were, at this time, a number of singular British films that looked at the world from unexpected angles: *Mona Lisa, My Beautiful Laundrette, The Ploughman's Lunch, Letter to Brezhnev, Caravaggio, Wish You Were Here, A World Apart, The Draughtman's Contract*. They were not necessarily oppositional, but they represented a creative and sceptical spirit; they were small in scale but not necessarily in resonance. Their success helped illustrate that it was possible to make films about non-traditional subjects and reach large audiences. For a time in London there was a sense of community in this area of the film industry.

Coming from the suburbs, I'd always desired and feared the city. By 1986 I was less intimidated by London, and as I came to know it I was excited by its variety. I knew I'd discovered both a place to live and inspiration for my work. I couldn't write fast enough to net all the stories that were being suggested to me.

Sammy and Rosie Get Laid was an attempt to reflect the fragmentation of that time: a young affluent middle class with 1960s values gentrifying working-class areas; riots and the creation of an unemployed and alienated underclass, necessitating the growth and increasing empowerment of the police; and a Third World Muslim whose country was being Westernised, coming to the West and being bewildered by the spiritual chaos he discovers. Later, *London Kills Me*, which is set at the end of the Thatcher dream, was another look at the city, from the point of view of those who hadn't made much out of the forced and artificial boom of the mid-1980s. The kids in it thought they too could be entrepreneurs—except that they were dealing not in junk bonds but in LSD.

Strangely, around the time of *Sammy and Rosie Get Laid*, when Thatcher and the Tories were at their most invincible and triumphal, there were a number of attacks on writers. The *Sunday Times*, being the lair of the new, non-traditional, lower middle-class ideological right, especially fostered this hostility. So writers as diverse as Ian McEwan, Salman Rushdie, Angela Carter, and Margaret Drabble, film-makers like Derek Jarman and Stephen Frears, and I, playwrights like David Hare and Caryl Churchill, found themselves being abused and lectured by a part of the media that normally would have ignored them.

Interestingly, none of us could be said to be particularly radical, though Thatcherism tended to push people that way. The slurs resembled nothing so much as the right's desire to construct dreadful enemies against whom it could prove itself. And being concerned liberal artists wasn't really bad enough, though for some conservatives it was pretty bad. In "The Meaning of Conservatism," Roger Scruton wrote: "There is no greater bigotry than the bigotry of liberalism."

We were attacked for complaining, for whinging, for the hypocrisy of being successful but wanting to defend the poor. And mostly for not celebrating Thatcher's achievements at a time of censorship, attacks on the unions and the welfare state, increasing poverty, escalating redistribution of wealth from poor to rich, and the creation of thuggish yuppies. In place of genuine ideas about fairness and opportunity was the elevation of certain entrepreneurs whose self-interest was supposed to benefit everyone else.

Most of us were surprised by these articles and editorials. After all, in post-war Britain, outside literary and theatrical circles, writers had never been important as public figures, as moralists, as takers of the social temperature. Until Rushdie wrote *Midnight's Children* and refused to see writing as a purely private activity, there was no one with the moral stature of Sartre or Grass or Gordimer or Baldwin, and not even contraversialists like Mailer or Vidal.

It was puzzling, hard to see why the Tories and their press supporters were getting so bad-tempered and frustrated, so angry even, and why these writers mattered to them. The Tories had won three elections, and the Labour Party, though gaining in coherence, was not a substantial threat. Much of television and the press was owned, controlled, or intimidated by the ruling ideology.

But I realise now that all this underlined their fear. The Tories must have panicked, realising that time was running out, that they had to move faster. They had to transform everything—now—before their era inevitably passed and the mood of the country swung against them for good.

This row between us and them was also an argument about language and representation. These people wanted to control the freedom of the imagination. They were afraid of anyone who saw Britain as a racially mixed, run-down, painfully divided, class-ridden place. For their fantasy was of a powerful, industrially strong country with a central, homogenous, consensual culture. There necessarily would be hinterlands, marginals, freaks, perverts, beggars, one-parent families, and dissidents. But these didn't matter. There could not be other versions of reality escaping into the world, poisoning the purity of their vision. It was a threat, it created confusion, it wasn't the image of Britain that others should be allowed to see.

These attacks were helpful. They enabled us to see the uses of writing and film-making as a challenge to the ruling world-view. Writing could undermine assumptions and undercut authoritarian descriptions. Writing mattered.

The Rainbow Sign

My Beautiful Laundrette

The
Rainbow
Sign

'God gave Noah the rainbow sign,
No more water, the fire next time!'

ONE: ENGLAND

I was born in London of an English mother and Pakistani father. My father, who lives in London, came to England from Bombay in 1947 to be educated by the old colonial power. He married here and never went back to India. The rest of his large family, his brothers, their wives, his sisters, moved from Bombay to Karachi, in Pakistan, after partition.

Frequently during my childhood, I met my Pakistani uncles when they came to London on business. They were important, confident people who took me to hotels, restaurants and Test matches, often in taxis. But I had no idea of what the subcontinent was like or how my numerous uncles, aunts and cousins lived there. When I was nine or ten a teacher purposefully placed some pictures of Indian peasants in mud huts in front of me and said to the class: Hanif comes from India. I wondered: did my uncles ride on camels? Surely not in their suits? Did my cousins, so like me in other ways, squat down in the sand like little Mowglis, half-naked and eating with their fingers?

In the mid-1960s, Pakistanis were a risible subject in England, derided on television and exploited by politicians. They had the worst jobs, they were uncomfortable in England, some of them had difficulties with the language. They were despised and out of place.

From the start I tried to deny my Pakistani self. I was ashamed. It was a curse and I wanted to be rid of it. I wanted to be like everyone else. I read with understanding a story in a newspaper about a black boy who, when he noticed that burnt skin turned white, jumped into a bath of boiling water.

At school, one teacher always spoke to me in a 'Peter Sellers' Indian accent. Another refused to call me by my name, calling me Pakistani Pete instead. So I refused to call the teacher by *his* name and used his nickname instead. This led to trouble: arguments, detentions, escapes from school over hedges, and eventually suspension. This played into my hands; this couldn't have been better.

With a friend I roamed the streets and fields all day; I sat beside streams; I stole yellow lurex trousers from a shop and smuggled them out of the house under my school trousers; I hid in woods reading hard books; and I saw the film *Zulu* several times.

This friend, who became Johnny in my film *My Beautiful Laundrette* came one day to the house. It was a shock.

He was dressed in jeans so tough they almost stood up by themselves. These were suspended above his boots by Union Jack braces of 'hangman's strength', revealing a stretch of milk bottle white leg. He seemed to have sprung up several inches because of his Doctor Marten's boots, which had steel caps and soles as thick as cheese sandwiches. His Ben Sherman shirt with a pleat down the back was essential. And his hair, which was only a quarter of an inch long all over, stuck out of his head like little nails. This unmoving creation he concentratedly touched up every hour with a sharpened steel comb that also served as a dagger.

He soon got the name Bog Brush, though this was not a moniker you would use to his face. Where before he was an angel-boy with a blond quiff flattened down by his mother's loving spit, a clean handkerchief always in his pocket, as well as being a keen cornet player for the Air Cadets he'd now gained a brand-new truculent demeanour.

My mother was so terrified by this stormtrooper dancing on her doorstep to the 'Skinhead Moonstomp', which he moaned to himself continuously, that she had to lie down.

I decided to go out roaming with B.B. before my father got home from work. But it wasn't the same as before. We couldn't have our talks without being interrupted. Bog Brush had become Someone. To his intense pleasure, similarly dressed strangers greeted Bog Brush in the street as if they were in a war-torn foreign country and in the same army battalion. We were suddenly banned from cinemas. The Wimpy Bar in which we sat for hours with milkshakes wouldn't let us in. As a matter of pride we now had to go round the back and lob a brick at the rear window of the place.

Other strangers would spot us from the other side of the street. B.B. would yell 'Leg it!' as the enemy dashed through traffic and leapt over the bonnets of cars to get at us, screaming obscenities and chasing us up alleys, across allotments, around reservoirs, and on and on.

And then, in the evening, B.B. took me to meet with the other lads. We climbed the park railings and strolled across to the football pitch, by the goal posts. This is where the lads congregated to hunt down Pakistanis and beat them. Most of them I was at school with. The others I'd grown up with. I knew their parents. They knew my father.

I withdrew, from the park, from the lads, to a safer place, within myself. I moved into what I call my 'temporary' period. I was only waiting now to get away, to leave the London suburbs, to make another kind of life, somewhere else, with better people.

In this isolation, in my bedroom where I listened to Pink Floyd, the Beatles and the John Peel Show, I started to write down the speeches of politicians, the words which helped create the neo-Nazi attitudes I saw around me. This I called 'keeping the accounts'.

In 1965, Enoch Powell said: 'We should not lose sight of the desirability of achieving a steady flow of voluntary repatriation for the elements which are proving unsuccessful or unassimilable.'

In 1967, Duncan Sandys said: 'The breeding of millions of half-caste children would merely produce a generation of misfits and create national tensions.'

I wasn't a misfit; I could join the elements of myself together. It was the others, they wanted misfits; they wanted you to embody within yourself their ambivalence.

Also in 1967, Enoch Powell—who once said he would love to have been Viceroy of India—quoted a constituent of his as saying that because of the Pakistanis 'this country will not be worth living in for our children'.

And Powell said, more famously: 'As I look ahead I am filled with foreboding. Like the Roman, "I seem to see the River Tiber foaming with much blood".'

As Powell's speeches appeared in the papers, graffiti in support of him appeared in the London streets. Racists gained confidence. People insulted me in the street. Someone in a café refused to eat at the same table with me. The parents of a girl I was in love with told her she'd get a bad reputation by going out with darkies.

Powell allowed himself to become a figurehead for racists. He helped create racism in Britain and was directly responsible not only for the atmosphere of fear and hatred, but through his influence, for individual acts of violence against Pakistanis.

Television comics used Pakistanis as the butt of their humour. Their jokes were highly political: they contributed to a way of seeing the world. The enjoyed reduction of racial hatred to a joke did two things: it expressed a collective view (which was sanctioned by its being on the BBC), and it was a celebration of contempt in millions of living rooms in England. I was afraid to watch TV because of it; it was too embarrassing, too degrading.

Parents of my friends, both lower-middle-class and working-class, often told me they were Powell supporters. Sometimes I heard them talking, heatedly, violently, about race, about 'the Pakis'. I was desperately embarrassed and afraid of being identified with these loathed aliens. I found it almost impossible to answer questions about where I came from. The word 'Pakistani' had been made into an insult. It was a word I didn't want used about myself. I couldn't tolerate being myself.

The British complained incessantly that the Pakistanis wouldn't assimilate. This meant they wanted the Pakistanis to be exactly like them. But of course even then they would have rejected them.

The British were doing the assimilating: they assimilated Pakistanis to their world view. They saw them as dirty, ignorant and less than human—worthy of abuse and violence.

At this time I found it difficult to get along with anyone. I was frightened and hostile. I suspected that my white friends were capable of racist insults. And many of them did taunt me, innocently. I reckoned that at least once every day since I was five years old I had been racially abused. I became incapable of distinguishing between remarks that were genuinely intended to hurt and those intended as 'humour'.

I became cold and distant. I began to feel I was very violent. But I didn't know how to be violent. If I had known, if that had come naturally to me, or if there'd been others I could follow, I would have made my constant fantasies of revenge into realities, I would have got into trouble, willingly hurt people, or set fire to things.

But I mooched around libraries. There, in an old copy of *Life* magazine, I found pictures of the Black Panthers. It was Eldridge Cleaver, Huey Newton, Bobby Seale and their confederates in black vests and slacks, with Jimi Hendrix haircuts. Some of them

were holding guns, the Army .45 and the 12-gauge Magnum
shotgun with 18-inch barrel that Huey specified for street fighting.

I tore down my pictures of the Rolling Stones and Cream and
replaced them with the Panthers. I found it all exhilarating. These
people were proud and they were fighting. To my knowledge, no
one in England was fighting.

There was another, more important picture.

On the cover of the Penguin edition of *The Fire Next Time*,
was James Baldwin holding a child, his nephew. Baldwin, having
suffered, having been there, was all anger and understanding. He
was intelligence and love combined. As I planned my escape I
read Baldwin all the time, I read Richard Wright and I admired
Muhammad Ali.

A great moment occurred when I was in a sweet shop. I saw
through to a TV in the backroom on which was showing the 1968
Olympic Games in Mexico. Thommie Smith and John Carlos
were raising their fists on the victory rostrum, giving the Black
Panther salute as the 'Star Spangled Banner' played. The white
shopkeeper was outraged. He said to me: they shouldn't mix
politics and sport.

During this time there was always Muhammad Ali, the former
Cassius Clay, a great sportsman become black spokesman. Now
a Muslim, millions of fellow Muslims all over the world prayed
for his victory when he fought.

And there was the Nation of Islam movement to which Ali
belonged, led by the man who called himself the Messenger of
Islam and wore a gold-embroidered fez, Elijah Muhammad.

Elijah was saying in the mid-1960s that the rule of the white
devils would end in fifteen years. He preached separatism, separate development for black and white. He ran his organization
by charisma and threat, claiming that anyone who challenged him
would be chastened by Allah. Apparently Allah also turned the
minds of defectors into a turmoil.

Elijah's disciple Malcolm X, admirer of Gandhi and self-confirmed anti-Semite, accepted in prison that 'the key to a Muslim is submission, the attunement of one towards Allah'. That this glorious resistance to the white man, the dismissal of Christian meekness, was followed by submission to Allah and worse, to Elijah Muhammad, was difficult to take.

I saw racism as unreason and prejudice, ignorance and a failure of sense; it was Fanon's 'incomprehension'. That the men I wanted to admire had liberated themselves only to take to unreason, to the abdication of intelligence, was shocking to me. And the separatism, the total loathing of the white man as innately corrupt, the 'All whites are devils' view, was equally unacceptable. I had to live in England, in the suburbs of London, with whites. My mother was white. I wasn't ready for separate development. I'd had too much of that already.

Luckily James Baldwin wasn't too keen either. In *The Fire Next Time* he describes a visit to Elijah Muhammad. He tells of how close he feels to Elijah and how he wishes to be able to love him. But when he tells Elijah that he has many white friends, he receives Elijah's pity. For Elijah the whites' time is up. It's no good Baldwin telling him he has white friends with whom he'd entrust his life.

As the evening goes on, Baldwin tires of the sycophancy around Elijah. He and Elijah would always be strangers and 'possibly enemies'. Baldwin deplores the black Muslims' turning to Africa and to Islam, this turning away from the reality of America and 'inventing' the past. Baldwin also mentions Malcolm X and the chief of the American Nazi party saying that racially speaking they were in complete agreement: they both wanted separate development. Baldwin adds that the debasement of one race and the glorification of another in this way inevitably leads to murder.

After this the Muslims weren't too keen on Baldwin, to say the least. Eldridge Cleaver, who once raped white women 'on principle', had a picture of Elijah Muhammad, the great strength-

giver, on his prison wall. Later he became a devoted supporter
of Malcolm X.

Cleaver says of Baldwin: 'There is in James Baldwin's work the
most gruelling, agonizing, total hatred of the blacks, particularly
of himself, and the most shameful, fanatical, fawning, sycophantic
love of the whites that one can find in the writing of any black
American writer of note in our time.'

How strange it was to me, this worthless abuse of a writer who
could enter the minds and skins of both black and white, and
the good just anger turning to passionate Islam as a source of
pride instead of to a digested political commitment to a different
kind of whole society. And this easy thrilling talk of 'white devils'
instead of close analysis of the institutions that kept blacks low.

I saw the taking up of Islam as an aberration, a desperate fantasy
of world-wide black brotherhood; it was a symptom of extreme
alienation. It was also an inability to seek a wider political view
or cooperation with other oppressed groups—or with the working
class as a whole—since alliance with white groups was necessarily
out of the question.

I had no idea what an Islamic society would be like, what the
application of the authoritarian theology Elijah preached would
mean in practice. I forgot about it, fled the suburbs, went to
university, got started as a writer and worked as an usher at the
Royal Court Theatre. It was over ten years before I went to an
Islamic country.

TWO: PAKISTAN

The man had heard that I was interested in talking about his
country, Pakistan, and that this was my first visit. He kindly kept
trying to take me aside to talk. But I was already being talked to.

I was at another Karachi party, in a huge house, with a glass of whisky in one hand, and a paper plate in the other. Casually I'd mentioned to a woman friend of the family that I wasn't against marriage. Now this friend was earnestly recommending to me a young woman who wanted to move to Britain, with a husband. To my discomfort this go-between was trying to fix a time for the three of us to meet and negotiate.

I went to three parties a week in Karachi. This time, when I could get away from this woman, I was with landowners, diplomats, businessmen and politicians: powerful people. This pleased me. They were people I wouldn't have been able to get to in England and I wanted to write about them.

They were drinking heavily. Every liberal in England knows you can be lashed for drinking in Pakistan. But as far as I could tell, none of this English-speaking international bourgeoisie would be lashed for anything. They all had their favourite trusted bootleggers who negotiated the potholes of Karachi at high speed on disintegrating motorcycles, with the hooch stashed on the back. Bad bootleggers passed a hot needle through the neck of your bottle and drew your whisky out. Stories were told of guests politely sipping ginger beer with their ice and soda, glancing at other guests to see if they were drunk and wondering if their own alcohol tolerance had miraculously increased.

I once walked into a host's bathroom to see the bath full of floating whisky bottles being soaked to remove the labels, a servant sitting on a stool serenely poking at them with a stick.

So it was all as tricky and expensive as buying cocaine in London, with the advantage that as the hooch market was so competitive, the 'leggers delivered video tapes at the same time, dashing into the room towards the TV with hot copies of *The Jewel In The Crown*, *The Far Pavilions*, and an especially popular programme called *Mind Your Language*, which represented Indians and Pakistanis as ludicrous caricatures.

Everyone, except the mass of the population, had videos. And

I could see why, since Pakistan TV was so peculiar. On my first day I turned it on and a cricket match was taking place. I settled in my chair. But the English players, who were on tour in Pakistan, were leaving the pitch. In fact, Bob Willis and Ian Botham were running towards the dressing rooms surrounded by armed police and this wasn't because Botham had made derogatory remarks about Pakistan. (He said it was a country to which he'd like to send his mother-in-law.) In the background a section of the crowd was being tear-gassed. Then the screen went blank.

Stranger still, and more significant, was the fact that the news was now being read in Arabic, a language few people in Pakistan understood. Someone explained to me that this was because the Koran was in Arabic, but everyone else said it was because General Zia wanted to kiss the arses of the Arabs.

The man at the party, who was drunk, wanted to tell me something and kept pulling at me. The man was worried. But wasn't I worried too? I was trapped with this woman and the marriage proposal.

I was having a little identity crisis. I'd been greeted so warmly in Pakistan, I felt so excited by what I saw, and so at home with all my uncles, I wondered if I were not better off here than there. And when I said, with a little unnoticed irony, that I was an Englishman, people laughed. They fell about. Why would anyone with a brown face, Muslim name and large well-known family in Pakistan want to lay claim to that cold little decrepit island off Europe where you always had to spell your name? Strangely, anti-British remarks made me feel patriotic, though I only felt patriotic when I was away from England.

But I couldn't allow myself to feel too Pakistani. I didn't want to give in to that falsity, that sentimentality. As someone said to me at a party, provoked by the fact I was wearing jeans: we are Pakistanis, but you, you will always be a Paki—emphasizing the slang derogatory name the English used against Pakistanis, and therefore the fact that I couldn't rightfully lay claim to either place.

In England I was a playwright. In Karachi this meant little. There were no theatres; the arts were discouraged by the state—music and dancing are un-Islamic—and ignored by practically everyone else. So despite everything I felt pretty out of place.

The automatic status I gained through my family obtained for me such acceptance, respect and luxury that for the first time I could understand the privileged and their penchant for marshalling ridiculous arguments to justify their delicious and untenable position as an élite. But as I wasn't a doctor, or businessman or military person, people suspected that this writing business I talked about was a complicated excuse for idleness, uselessness and general bumming around. In fact, as I proclaimed an interest in the entertainment business, and talked much and loudly about how integral the arts were to a society, moves were being made to set me up in the amusement arcade business, in Shepherd's Bush.

Finally the man got me on my own. His name was Rahman. He was a friend of my intellectual uncle. I had many uncles, but Rahman preferred the intellectual one who understood Rahman's particular sorrow and like him considered himself to be a marginal man.

In his fifties, a former Air Force officer, Rahman was liberal, well-travelled and married to an Englishwoman who now had a Pakistani accent.

He said to me: 'I tell you, this country is being sodomized by religion. It is even beginning to interfere with the making of money. And now we are embarked on this dynamic regression, you must know, it is obvious, Pakistan has become a leading country to go away from. Our patriots are abroad. We despise and envy them. For the rest of us, our class, your family, we are in Hobbes's state of nature: insecure, frightened. We cling together out of necessity.' He became optimistic. 'We could be like Japan, a tragic oriental country that is now progressive, indus- trialized.' He laughed and then said, ambiguously: 'But only God keeps this country together. You must say this around the world: we are taking a great leap backwards.'

The bitterest blow for Rahman was the dancing. He liked to waltz and foxtrot. But now the expression of physical joy, of sensuality and rhythm, was banned. On TV you could see where it had been censored. When couples in Western programmes got up to dance there'd be a jerk in the film, and they'd be sitting down again. For Rahman it was inexplicable, an unnecessary cru- elty that was almost more arbitrary than anything else.

Thus the despair of Rahman and my uncles' 'high and dry' generation. Mostly educated in Britain, like Jinnah, the founder of Pakistan—who was a smoking, drinking, non-Urdu speaking lawyer and claimed that Pakistan would never be a theocracy ('that Britisher' he was sometimes called)—their intellectual men- tors were Tawney, Shaw, Russell, Laski. For them the new Islam- ization was the negation of their lives.

It was a lament I heard often. This was the story they told. Karachi was a goodish place in the 1960s and 1970s. Until about 1977 it was lively and vigorous. You could drink and dance in the Raj-style clubs (providing you were admitted) and the at- mosphere was liberal—as long as you didn't meddle in politics, in which case you'd probably be imprisoned. Politically there was Bhutto: urbane, Oxford-educated, considering himself to be a poet and revolutionary, a veritable Chairman Mao of the sub- continent. He said he would fight obscurantism and illiteracy, ensure the equality of men and women, and increase access to education and medical care. The desert would bloom.

Later, in an attempt to save himself, appease the mullahs and rouse the dissatisfied masses behind him, he introduced various Koranic injunctions into the constitution and banned alcohol, gambling, horse-racing. The Islamization had begun, and was fervently continued after his execution.

Islamization built no hospitals, no schools, no houses; it cleaned no water and installed no electricity. But it was direction, identity. The country was to be in the hands of the divine, or rather, in the hands of those who elected themselves to interpret the single divine purpose. Under the tyranny of the priesthood, with the cooperation of the army, Pakistan would embody Islam in itself.

There would now be no distinction between ethical and religious obligation; there would now be no areas in which it was possible to be wrong. The only possible incertitude was of interpretation. The theory would be the written eternal and universal principles which Allah created and made obligatory for men; the model would be the first three generations of Muslims; and the practice would be Pakistan.

As a Professor of Law at the Islamic University wrote: 'Pakistan accepts Islam as the basis of economic and political life. We do not have a single reason to make any separation between Islam and Pakistan society. Pakistanis now adhere rigorously to Islam and cling steadfastly to their religious heritage. They never speak of these things with disrespect. With an acceleration in the process of Islamization, governmental capabilities increase and national identity and loyalty become stronger. Because Islamic civilization has brought Pakistanis very close to certainty, this society is ideally imbued with a moral mission.'

This moral mission and the over-emphasis on dogma and punishment resulted in the kind of strengthening of the repressive, militaristic and nationalistically aggressive state seen all over the world in the authoritarian 1980s. With the added bonus that in Pakistan, God was always on the side of the government.

But despite all the strident nationalism, as Rahman said, the patriots were abroad; people were going away: to the West, to Saudi Arabia, anywhere. Young people continually asked me about the possibility of getting into Britain and some thought of taking some smack with them to bankroll their establishment. They had what was called the Gulf Syndrome, a condition I recognized from my time living in the suburbs. It was a dangerous psychological cocktail consisting of ambition, suppressed excitement, bitterness and sexual longing.

Then a disturbing incident occurred which seemed to encapsulate the going-away fever. An eighteen-year-old girl from a village called Chakwal dreamed that the villagers walked across the Arabian Sea to Karbala where they found money and work. Following this dream the village set off one night for the beach which happened to be near my uncle's house, in fashionable Clifton. Here lived politicians and diplomats in LA-style white bungalows with sprinklers on the lawn, a Mercedes in the drive and dogs and watchmen at the gates.

Here Benazir Bhutto was under the house arrest. Her dead father's mansion was patrolled by the army who boredly nursed machine-guns and sat in tents beneath the high walls.

On the beach, the site of barbecues and late-night parties, the men of the Chakwal village packed the women and children into trunks and pushed them into the Arabian Sea. Then they followed them into the water, in the direction of Karbala. All but twenty of the potential *émigrés* were drowned. The survivors were arrested and charged with illegal emigration.

It was the talk of Karachi. It caused much amusement but people like Rahman despaired of a society that could be so confused, so advanced in some respects, so very naïve in others.

And all the (more orthodox) going away disturbed and confused the family set-up. When the men who'd been away came back, they were different, they were dissatisfied, they had seen more, they wanted more. Their neighbours were envious and resentful. Once more the society was being changed by outside forces, not by its own volition.

*   *   *

About twelve people lived permanently in my uncle's house, plus
servants who slept in sheds at the back, just behind the chickens
and dogs. Relatives sometimes came to stay for months. New bits
had to be built on to the house. All day there were visitors; in
the evenings crowds of people came over; they were welcome,
and they ate and watched videos and talked for hours. People
weren't so protective of their privacy as they were in London.

This made me think about the close-bonding within the families
and about the intimacy and interference of an extended family
and a more public way of life. Was the extended family worse
than the little nuclear family because there were more people to
dislike? Or better because relationships were less intense?

Strangely, bourgeois-bohemian life in London, in Notting Hill
and Islington and Fulham, was far more formal. It was frozen
dinner parties and the division of social life into the meeting of
couples with other couples, to discuss the lives of other coupling
couples. Months would pass, then this would happen again.

In Pakistan, there was the continuity of the various families'
knowledge of each other. People were easy to place; your grand-
parents and theirs were friends. When I went to the bank and
showed the teller my passport, it turned out he knew several of
my uncles, so I didn't receive the usual perfunctory treatment.
This was how things worked.

I compared the collective hierarchy of the family and the per-
manence of my family's circle, with my feckless, rather rootless
life in London, in what was called 'the inner city'. There I lived
alone, and lacked any long connection with anything. I'd hardly
known anyone for more than eight years, and certainly not their
parents. People came and went. There was much false intimacy
and forced friendship. People didn't take responsibility for each
other.

Many of my friends lived alone in London, especially the

women. They wanted to be independent and to enter into relationships—as many as they liked, with whom they liked—out of choice. They didn't merely want to reproduce the old patterns of living. The future was to be determined by choice and reason, not by custom. The notions of duty and obligation barely had positive meaning for my friends; they were loaded, Victorian words, redolent of constraint and grandfather clocks, the antithesis of generosity in love, the new hugging, and the transcendence of the family. The ideal of the new relationship was no longer the S and M of the old marriage—it was F and C, freedom plus commitment.

In the large, old families where there was nothing but the old patterns, disturbed only occasionally by the new ways, this would have seemed a contrivance, a sort of immaturity, a failure to understand and accept the determinacies that life necessarily involved.

So there was much pressure to conform, especially on the women.

'Let these women be warned,' said a mullah to the dissenting women of Rawalpindi. 'We will tear them to pieces. We will give them such terrible punishments that no one in future will dare to raise a voice against Islam.'

I remember a woman saying to me at dinner one night: 'We know at least one thing. God will never dare to show his face in this country—the women will tear him apart!'

The family scrutiny and criticism was difficult to take, as was all the bitching and gossip. But there was warmth and continuity for a large number of people; there was security and much love. Also there was a sense of duty and community—of people's lives genuinely being lived together, whether they liked each other or not—that you didn't get in London. There, those who'd eschewed the family hadn't succeeded in creating some other form of supportive common life. In Pakistan there was that supportive common life, but at the expense of movement and change.

In the 1960s of Enoch Powell and graffiti, the Black Muslims and Malcolm X gave needed strength to the descendants of slaves by 'taking the wraps off the white man'; Eldridge Cleaver was yet to be converted to Christianity and Huey P. Newton was toting his Army .45. A boy in a bedroom in a suburb, who had the King's Road constantly on his mind and who changed the pictures on his wall from week to week, was unhappy, and separated from the 1960s as by a thick glass wall against which he could only press his face. But bits of the 1960s were still around in Pakistan: the liberation rhetoric, for example, the music, the clothes, the drugs, not as the way of life they were originally intended to be, but as appendages to another, stronger tradition.

As my friends and I went into the Bara Market near Peshawar, close to the border of Afghanistan, in a rattling motorized rickshaw, I became apprehensive. There were large signs by the road telling foreigners that the police couldn't take responsibility for them: beyond this point the police would not go. Apparently the Pathans there, who were mostly refugees from Afghanistan, liked to kidnap foreigners and extort ransoms. My friends, who were keen to buy opium, which they'd give to the rickshaw driver to carry, told me everything was all right, because I wasn't a foreigner. I kept forgetting that.

The men were tough, martial, insular and proud. They lived in mud houses and tin shacks built like forts for shooting from. They were inevitably armed, with machine-guns slung over their shoulders. In the street you wouldn't believe women existed here, except you knew they took care of the legions of young men in the area who'd fled from Afghanistan to avoid being conscripted by the Russians and sent to Moscow for re-education.

Ankle deep in mud, I went round the market. Pistols, knives, Russian-made rifles, hand grenades and large lumps of dope and opium were laid out on stalls like tomatoes and oranges. Everyone was selling heroin.

The Americans, who had much money invested in Pakistan, in this compliant right-wing buffer-zone between Afghanistan and India, were furious that their children were being destroyed by a flourishing illegal industry in a country they financed. But the Americans sent to Pakistan could do little about it. Involvement in the heroin trade went right through Pakistan society: the police, the judiciary, the army, the landlords, the customs officials were all involved. After all, there was nothing in the Koran about heroin, nothing specific. I was even told that its export made ideological sense. Heroin was anti-Western; addiction in Western children was a deserved symptom of the moral vertigo of godless societies. It was a kind of colonial revenge. Reverse imperialism, the Karachi wits called it, inviting nemesis. The reverse imperialism was itself being reversed.

In a flat high above Karachi, an eighteen-year-old kid strung-out on heroin danced cheerfully around the room in front of me and pointed to an erection in the front of his trousers, which he referred to as his Imran Khan, the name of the handsome Pakistan cricket captain. More and more of the so-called multinational kids were taking heroin now. My friends who owned the flat, journalists on a weekly paper, were embarrassed.

But they always had dope to offer their friends. These laid-back people were mostly professionals: lawyers, an inspector in the police who smoked what he confiscated, a newspaper magnate, and various other journalists. Heaven it was to smoke at midnight on the beach, as local fishermen, squatting respectfully behind you, fixed fat joints; and the 'erotic politicians' themselves, the Doors, played from a portable stereo while the Arabian Sea rolled on to the beach. Oddly, since heroin and dope were both indig-

enous to the country, it took the West to make them popular in
the East.

In so far as colonizers and colonized engage in a relationship
with the latter aspiring to be like the former, you wouldn't catch
anyone of my uncle's generation with a joint in their mouth. It
was *infra dig*—for the peasants. Shadowing the British, they drank
whisky and read *The Times*; they praised others by calling them
'gentlemen'; and their eyes filled with tears at old Vera Lynn
records.

But the kids discussed yoga exercises. You'd catch them standing on their heads. They even meditated. Though one boy who
worked at the airport said it was too much of a Hindu thing for
Muslims to be doing; if his parents caught him chanting a mantra
he'd get a backhander across the face. Mostly the kids listened
to the Stones, Van Morrison and Bowie as they flew over ruined
roads to the beach in bright red and yellow Japanese cars with
quadrophonic speakers, past camels and acres of wasteland.

Here, all along the railway track, the poor and diseased and
hungry lived in shacks and huts; the filthy poor gathered around
rusty stand-pipes to fetch water; or ingeniously they resurrected
wrecked cars, usually Morris Minors; and here they slept in huge
sewer pipes among buffalo, chickens and wild dogs. Here I met
a policeman who I thought was on duty. But the policeman lived
here, and hanging on the wall of his falling-down shed was his
spare white police uniform, which he'd had to buy himself.

If not to the beach, the kids went to the Happy Hamburger
to hang out. Or to each other's houses to watch Clint Eastwood
tapes and giggle about sex, of which they were so ignorant and
deprived. I watched a group of agitated young men in their mid-
twenties gather around a 1950s' medical book to look at the female
genitalia. For these boys, who watched Western films and
mouthed the lyrics of pop songs celebrating desire ('come on,
baby, light my fire'), life before marriage could only be like spend-

ing years and years in a single-sex public school; for them women
were mysterious, unknown, desirable and yet threatening crea-
tures of almost another species, whom you had to respect, marry
and impregnate but couldn't be friends with. And in this country
where the sexes were usually strictly segregated, the sexual tension
could be palpable. The men who could afford to, flew to Bangkok
for relief. The others squirmed and resented women. The kind
of sexual openness that was one of the few real achievements of
the 1960s, the discussion of contraception, abortion, female sexuality and prostitution which some women were trying to advance,
received incredible hostility. But women felt it was only a matter
of time before progress was made; it was much harder to return
to ignorance than the mullahs thought.

A stout intense lawyer in his early thirties of immense extrovert
charm—with him it was definitely the 1980s, not the 1960s. His
father was a judge. He himself was intelligent, articulate and
fiercely representative of the other 'new spirit' of Pakistan. He
didn't drink, smoke or fuck. Out of choice. He prayed five times
a day. He worked all the time. He was determined to be a good
Muslim, since that was the whole point of the country existing
at all. He wasn't indulgent, except religiously, and he lived in
accordance with what he believed. I took to him immediately.

We had dinner in an expensive restaurant. It could have been
in London or New York. The food was excellent, I said. The
lawyer disagreed, with his mouth full, shaking his great head. It
was definitely no good, it was definitely meretricious rubbish. But
for ideological reasons only, I concluded, since he ate with relish.
He was only in the restaurant because of me, he said.

There was better food in the villages; the new food in Pakistan
was, frankly, a tribute to chemistry rather than cuisine. Only the
masses had virtue, they knew how to live, how to eat. He told
me that those desiccated others, the marginal men I associated

with and liked so much, were a plague class with no values. Perhaps, he suggested, eating massively, this was why I liked them, being English. Their education, their intellectual snobbery, made them un-Islamic. They didn't understand the masses and they spoke in English to cut themselves off from the people. Didn't the best jobs go to those with a foreign education? He was tired of those Westernized elders denigrating their country and its religious nature. They'd been contaminated by the West, they didn't know their own country, and the sooner they got out and were beaten up by racists abroad the better.

The lawyer and I went out into the street. It was busy, the streets full of strolling people. There were dancing camels and a Pakistan trade exhibition. The lawyer strode through it all, yelling. The exhibition was full of Pakistan-made imitations of Western goods: bathrooms in chocolate and strawberry, TVs with stereos attached; fans, air-conditioners, heaters; and an arcade full of space-invaders. The lawyer got agitated.

These were Western things, of no use to the masses. The masses didn't have water, what would they do with strawberry bathrooms? The masses wanted Islam, not space-invaders or . . . or elections. Are elections a Western thing? I asked. Don't they have them in India too? No, they're a Western thing, the lawyer said. How could they be required under Islam? There need only be one party—the party of the righteous.

This energetic lawyer would have pleased and then disappointed Third World intellectuals and revolutionaries from an earlier era, people like Fanon and Guevara. This talk of liberation—at last the acknowledgement of the virute of the toiling masses, the struggle against neo-colonialism, its bourgeois stooges, and American interference—the entire recognizable rhetoric of freedom and struggle, ends in the lawyer's mind with the country on its knees, at prayer. Having started to look for itself it finds itself . . . in the eighth century.

Islam and the masses. My numerous meetings with scholars, revisionists, liberals who wanted the Koran 'creatively' interpreted to make it compatible with modern science. The many medieval monologues of mullahs I'd listened to. So much talk, theory and Byzantine analysis.

I strode into a room in my uncle's house. Half-hidden by a curtain, on a verandah, was an aged woman servant wearing my cousin's old clothes, praying. I stopped and watched her. In the morning as I lay in bed, she swept the floor of my room with some twigs bound together. She was at least sixty. Now, on the shabby prayer mat, she was tiny and around her the universe was endless, immense, but God was above her. I felt she was acknowledging that which was larger than her, humbling herself before the infinite, knowing and feeling her own insignificance. It was a truthful moment, not empty ritual. I wished I could do it.

I went with the lawyer to the Mosque in Lahore, the largest in the world. I took off my shoes, padded across the immense courtyard with the other man—women were not allowed—and got on my knees. I banged my forehead on the marble floor. Beside me a man in a similar posture gave a world-consuming yawn. I waited but could not lose myself in prayer. I could only travesty the woman's prayer, to whom it had a world of meaning.

Perhaps she did want a society in which her particular moral and religious beliefs were mirrored, and no others, instead of some plural, liberal mélange; a society in which her own cast of mind, her customs, way of life and obedience to God were established with full legal and constituted authority. But it wasn't as if anyone had asked her.

In Pakistan, England just wouldn't go away. Despite the Lahore lawyer, despite everything, England was very much on the minds of Pakistanis. Relics of the Raj were everywhere: buildings, mon-

uments, Oxford accents, libraries full of English books, and newspapers. Many Pakistanis had relatives in England; thousands of
Pakistani families depended on money sent from England. Visiting
a village, a man told me through an interpreter, that when his
three grandchildren visited from Bradford, he had to hire an
interpreter to speak to them. It was happening all the time—the
closeness of the two societies, and the distance.

Although Pakistanis still wanted to escape to England, the old
men in their clubs and the young eating their hamburgers took
great pleasure in England's decline and decay. The great master
was fallen. Now it was seen as strikebound, drug-ridden, riot-
torn, inefficient, disunited, a society which had moved too suddenly from puritanism to hedonism and now loathed itself. And
the Karachi wits liked to ask me when I thought the Americans
would decide the British were ready for self-government.

Yet people like Rahman still clung to what they called British
ideals, maintaining that it is a society's ideals, its conception of
human progress, that define the level of its civilization. They
regretted, under the Islamization, the repudiation of the values
which they said were the only positive aspect of Britain's legacy
to the sub-continent. These were: the idea of secular institutions
based on reason, not revelation or scripture; the idea that there
were no final solutions to human problems; and the idea that the
health and vigour of a society was bound up with its ability to
tolerate and express a plurality of views on all issues, and that
these views would be welcomed.

But England as it is today, the ubiquity of racism and the
suffering of Pakistanis because of it, was another, stranger subject.
When I talked about it, the response was unexpected. Those
who'd been to England often told of being insulted, or beaten
up, or harassed at the airport. But even these people had attitudes
similar to those who hadn't been there.

It was that the English misunderstood the Pakistanis because they saw only the poor people, those from the villages, the illiterates, the peasants, the Pakistanis who didn't know how to use toilets, how to eat with knives and forks because they were poor. If the British could only see *them*, the rich, the educated, the sophisticated, they wouldn't be so hostile. They'd know what civilized people the Pakistanis really were. And then they'd like them.

The implication was that the poor who'd emigrated to the West to escape the strangulation of the rich in Pakistan deserved the racism they received in Britain because they really were contemptible. The Pakistani middle class shared the disdain of the British for the *émigré* working class and peasantry of Pakistan.

It was interesting to see that the British working class (and not only the working class, of course) used the same vocabulary of contempt about Pakistanis—the charges of ignorance, laziness, fecklessness, uncleanliness—that their own, British middle class used about them. And they weren't able to see the similarity.

Racism goes hand-in-hand with class inequality. Among other things, racism is a kind of snobbery, a desire to see oneself as superior culturally and economically, and a desire to actively experience and enjoy that superiority by hostility or violence. And when that superiority of class and culture is unsure or not acknowledged by the Other—as it would be acknowledged by the servant and master in class-stable Pakistan—but is in doubt, as with the British working class and Pakistanis in England, then it has to be demonstrated physically. Everyone knows where they stand then—the class inequality is displayed, just as any other snob demonstrates superiority by exhibiting wealth or learning or ancestry.

So some of the middle class of Pakistan, who also used the familiar vocabulary of contempt about their own poor (and, incidentally, about the British poor), couldn't understand when I explained that British racists weren't discriminating in their racial discrimination: they loathed all Pakistanis and kicked whoever was nearest. To the English all Pakistanis were the same; racists didn't ask whether you had a chauffeur, TV and private education before they set fire to your house. But for some Pakistanis, it was their own poor who had brought this upon them.

THREE: ENGLAND

It has been an arduous journey. Since Enoch Powell in the 1960s, there have been racist marches through South London approved by the Labour Home Secretary; attacks by busloads of racists on Southall, which the Asians violently and successfully repelled; and the complicated affair of young Asians burned to death and Asian shops razed to the ground by young blacks in Handsworth, Birmingham. The insults, the beatings, the murders continue. Although there has been white anger and various race relations legislation, Pakistanis are discriminated against in all areas.

Powell's awful prophecy was fulfilled: the hate he worked to create and the party of which he was a member, brought about his prediction. The River Tiber has indeed over-flowed with much blood—Pakistani blood. And seventeen years later Powell has once more called for repatriation, giving succour to those who hate.

The fight back is under way. The defence committees, vigilante groups, study groups, trade union and women's groups are flourishing. People have changed, become united, through struggle and self-defence. My white friends, like Bog Brush, didn't enjoy fighting Pakistanis. They had a reputation for premature sobbing and cowardice. You didn't get your money's worth fighting a Paki. That's quite different now.

The fierce truculent pride of the Black Panthers is here now, as is the separatism, the violence, the bitterness and pathetic elevation of an imaginary homeland. This is directly spawned by racism.

Our cities are full of Asian shops. Where one would want black united with black, there are class differences as with all groups. Those Pakistanis who have worked hard to establish businesses, now vote Tory and give money to the Conservative Party. Their interests are the same as those of middle-class business people everywhere, though they are subject to more jealousy and violence. They have wanted to elevate themselves out of the maelstrom and by gaining economic power and the opportunity and dignity it brings, they have made themselves safe—safer. They have taken advantage of England.

But what is the Conservative view of them? Roger Scruton in his book *The Meaning Of Conservatism* sets out the case against mutual respect and understanding.

Firstly he deplores all race relations legislation and tries to justify certain kinds of racism by making it seem a harmless preference for certain kinds of people. He calls this preference a 'natural offshoot' of allegiance. Secondly, and more tellingly he says that 'illiberal sentiments . . . arise inevitably from social consciousness: they involve natural prejudice, and a desire for the company of one's kind. That is hardly sufficient ground to condemn them as "racist".'

The crucial Conservative idea here is Scruton's notion of 'the company of one's kind'. What is the company of one's kind? Who exactly is of one's kind and what kind of people are they? Are they only those of the same 'nation', of the same colour, race and background? I suspect that that is what Scruton intends. But what a feeble, bloodless, narrow conception of human relationships and the possibilities of love and communication that he can only see 'one's kind' in this exclusive and complacent way!

One does seek the company of one's kind, of those in the same street, in the same club, in the same office. But the idea that these are the only people one can get along with or identify with, that one's humanity is such a heldback thing that it can't extend beyond this, leads to the denigration of those unlike oneself. It leads to the idea that others have less humanity than oneself or one's own group or 'kind'; and to the idea of Enemy, of the alien, of the Other. As Baldwin says: 'this inevitably leads to murder', and of course it has often done so in England recently.

Scruton quotes approvingly those who call this view 'death camp chic'. He would argue, I suppose, that loyalty and allegiance to one's kind doesn't necessarily lead to loathing of those not of one's kind. But Scruton himself talks of the 'alien wedge' and says that 'immigration cannot be an object of merely passive contemplation on the part of the present citizenship'.

The evil of racism is that it is a violation not only of another's dignity, but also of one's own person or soul; the failure of connection with others is a failure to understand or feel what it is one's own humanity consists in, what it is to be alive, and what it is to see both oneself and others as being ends not means, and as having souls. However much anodyne talk there is of 'one's kind', a society that is racist is a society that cannot accept itself, that hates part of itself so deeply that it cannot see, does not want to see—because of its spiritual and political nullity and inanition—how much people have in common with each other. And the whole society and every element in it, is reduced and degraded because of it. This is why racism isn't a minor or subproblem: it reflects on the whole and weighs the entire society in the balance.

Therefore, in the end, one's feeling for others, one's understanding of their humanity cannot be anything to do with their being of 'one's kind' in the narrow way Scruton specifies. It can't be to do with others having any personal qualities at all. For paradoxically, as Simone Weil says: 'So far from its being his person, what is sacred in a human being is the impersonal in him.

Everything which is impersonal in man is sacred, and nothing else.'

What of Labour?

The Pakistani working class is as unprotected politically as it has ever been. Despite various paternalistic efforts and an attempt at a kind of 'Raj decency', racism is the Trojan Horse within the labour movement. The Labour Party has failed to show that it is serious about combating racism and serious in representing the black working class. There are few black councillors, few black parliamentary candidates, few blacks on the General Management Committees of constituency Labour Parties, no blacks on the NEC and so on, right through the Labour and trade union movement.

In my own ward and management committee, I have seen racist attitudes that would shame some Tories. People have stood up at Labour Party meetings I have attended and delivered racist diatribes. I have seen blacks discouraged from joining the Labour Party, and when they have joined, actively discouraged from canvassing in case they discouraged white racists from voting Labour.

The Labour Party wishes to be egalitarian and liberal on the race issue but knows that vast numbers of its voters are neither. The party is afraid—in some parts consciously and in other parts unconsciously—that blacks and black issues are a vote loser. If the Labour Party occasionally wishes blacks to serve it, it does not desire to serve blacks. Hence it acknowledges that thousands of its supporters are racist. It refuses to confront that.

Others in the party believe that racism is a sub-issue which has to be subordinate to the class issues of the time: housing, unemployment, education, maintenance of the social services and so on. They believe that winning elections and representing the mass of the working class in Parliament is more important than giving office or power to blacks. This is the choice it has made. This is the kind of party it is, and insofar as this is true, the Labour

Party is a truly representative party, representing inequality and racism.

Coming back to England was harder than going. I had culture shock in reverse. Images of plenty yelled at me. England seemed to be overflowing with . . . things. Things from all over the world. Things and information. Information though, which couldn't bite through the profound insularity and indifference.

In Pakistan people were keen to know: not only about Asia and the Middle East, but about Europe and the United States. They sought out information about the whole world. They needed it. They ordered books from Europe, listened to international radio and chewed up visiting academics like pieces of orange.

In Britain today, among the middle class, thinking and argument are almost entirely taboo. The other taboo, replacing death in its unacceptability, is money. As our society has become more divided, the acknowledgement of that division—which is a financial division, a matter of economic power—is out of the question. So money is not discussed. It is taken for granted that you have it: that you have means of obtaining it: that you are reasonably well off and gain status and influence over others because of it.

Accompanying this financial silence, and shoring up both the social division and the taboo, is the prohibition on thought. The discussion of a serious subject to a conclusion using logic, evidence and counter-evidence is an unacceptable social embarrassment. It just isn't done to argue: it is thought to be the same as rowing. One has opinions in England, but they are formed in private and clung to in public despite everything, despite their often being quite wrong.

There is real defensiveness and insecurity, a Victorian fear of revealing so much as a genital of an idea, the nipple of a notion or the sex of a syllogism. Where sexual exhibitionism and the discussion of positions and emissions is fashionable, indeed orthodox, thinking and argument are avoided.

In Pakistan it was essential to have knowledge because political discussion was serious. It mattered what you thought. People put chairs in a circle, sat down, and *talked*. What was said to each other was necessary. Intellectual dignity was maintained, earned anxiety was expressed; you weren't alone; ideas and feelings were shared. These things had to be said, even in low voices, because absolute silence was intolerable, absolute silence was the acceptance of isolation and division. It was a relief to argue, to exercise intelligence in a country where intelligence was in itself a weapon and a threat.

I will never forget the hospitality, warmth and generosity of the people of Pakistan; the flowers on the lawn of the Sind Club, the sprawling open houses, full of air and people and the smell of spices; the unbelievable brightness of the light shining through a dust haze; the woman walking perfectly straight-backed along a street with an iron balanced on her head; the open-air typists outside the law courts; butterflies as big as clock faces; the man who slept with a chicken in his bed; my uncle's library, bought in the 1940s in Cambridge, where he was taught by Russell— though when I opened the books after being given the library, they were rotten with worms, the pitted pages falling apart just as I stood there. And the way the men shake hands. This is worth going into.

First you offer them your hand and they grasp it. The clasped hands are slapped then with their spare hand as an affirmation of initial contact. This is, as it were, the soup. Now they pull you to them for the main course, the full embrace, the steak. As you look over their shoulder, your bodies thrust together, your heat intermingled, they crack you on the back at least three times with their open palm. These are not negligible taps, but good healthy whacks, demonstrating equality and openness. Depending on the nature of the friendship, these whacks could go on a considerable time and may debilitate the sick or weak. But they must be reciprocated. This done, they will let you move away from them, but still holding your right hand. You are considered fully, with affection overbrimming, as they regard all of you, as they seem to take in your entire being from top to toe, from inside to out. At last, after complete contact has been made, all possibility of concealment or inhibition banished, they carefully let go of your hand as if it were a delicate object. *That is a greeting.*

And there was the photograph of my father in my uncle's room, in which he must have been about the same age as me. A picture in a house that contained fragments of my past: a house full of stories, of Bombay, Delhi, China; of feuds, wrestling matches, adulteries, windows broken with hands, card games, impossible loves, and magic spells. Stories to help me see my place in the world and give me a sense of the past which could go into making a life in the present and the future. This was surely part of the way I could understand myself. This knowledge, garnered in my mid-twenties, would help me form an image of myself: I'd take it back to England where I needed it to protect myself. And it would be with me in London and the suburbs, making me stronger.

When I considered staying in Pakistan to regain more of my past and complete myself with it, I had to think that that was impossible. Didn't I already miss too much of England? And wasn't I too impatient with the illiberalism and lack of possibility of Pakistan?

So there was always going to be the necessary return to England. I came home . . . to my country.

This is difficult to say. 'My country' isn't a notion that comes easily. It is still difficult to answer the question, where do you come from? I have never wanted to identify with England. When Enoch Powell spoke for England I turned away in final disgust. I would rather walk naked down the street than stand up for the National Anthem. The pain of that period of my life, in the mid-1960s, is with me still. And when I originally wrote this piece I put it in the third person: Hanif saw this, Hanif felt that, because of the difficulty of directly addressing myself to what I felt then, of not wanting to think about it again. And perhaps that is why I took to writing in the first place, to make strong feelings into weak feelings.

But despite all this, some kind of identification with England remains.

It is strange to go away to the land of your ancestors, to find out how much you have in common with people there, yet at the same time to realize how British you are, the extent to which, as Orwell says: 'the suet puddings and the red pillar boxes have entered into your soul'. It isn't *that* you wanted to find out. But it is part of what you do find out. And you find out what little choice you have in the matter of your background and where you belong. You look forward to getting back; you think often of England and what it means to you—and you think often of what it means to be British.

Two days after my return I took my washing to a laundrette and gave it to the attendant only to be told she didn't touch the clothes of foreigners: she didn't want me anywhere near her blasted laundrette. More seriously: I read in the paper that a Pakistani family in the East End had been fire-bombed. A child was killed. This, of course, happens frequently. It is the pig's head through the window, the spit in the face, the children with the initials of racist organizations tattooed into their skin with razor blades, as well as the more polite forms of hatred.

I was in a rage. I thought: who wants to be British anyway?

Or as a black American writer said: who wants to be integrated into a burning house anyway?

And indeed I know Pakistanis and Indians born and brought up here who consider their position to be the result of a diaspora: they are in exile, awaiting return to a better place, where they belong, where they are welcome. And there this 'belonging' will be total. This will be home, and peace.

It is not difficult to see how much illusion and falsity there is in this view. How much disappointment and unhappiness might be involved in going 'home' only to see the extent to which you have been formed by England and the depth of attachment you feel to the place, despite everything.

It isn't surprising that some people believe in this idea of 'home'. The alternative to believing it is more conflict here; it is more self-hatred; it is the continual struggle against racism; it is the continual adjustment to life in Britain. And blacks in Britain know they have made more than enough adjustments.

So what is it to be British?

In his 1941 essay 'England Your England' Orwell says: 'the gentleness of the English civilisation is perhaps its most marked characteristic'. He calls the country 'a family with the wrong members in control' and talks of the 'soundness and homogeneity of England'.

Elsewhere he considers the Indian character. He explains the 'maniacal suspiciousness' which, agreeing, he claims, with E. M. Forster in *A Passage To India*, he calls 'the besetting Indian vice . . .' But he has the grace to acknowledge in his essay 'Not Counting Niggers' 'that the overwhelming bulk of the British proletariat [lives] . . . in Asia and Africa'.

But this is niggardly. The main object of his praise is British 'tolerance' and he writes of 'their gentle manners'. He also says that this aspect of England 'is continuous, it stretches into the future and the past, there is something in it that persists'.

But does it persist? If this version of England was true then, in the 1930s and 1940s, it is under pressure now. From the point of view of thousands of black people it just does not apply. It is completely without basis.

Obviously tolerance in a stable, confident wartime society with a massive Empire is quite different to tolerance in a disintegrating uncertain society during an economic depression. But surely this would be the test; this would be just the time for this much-advertised tolerance in the British soul to manifest itself as more than vanity and self-congratulation. But it has not. Under real continuous strain it has failed.

Tolerant, gentle British whites have no idea how little of this tolerance is experienced by blacks here. No idea of the violence, hostility and contempt directed against black people every day by state and individual alike in this land once described by Orwell as being not one of 'rubber truncheons' or 'Jew-baiters' but of 'flower-lovers' with 'mild knobbly faces'. But in parts of England the flower-lovers are all gone, the rubber truncheons and Jew-baiters are at large, and if any real contemporary content is to be given to Orwell's blind social patriotism, then clichés about 'tolerance' must be seriously examined for depth and weight of substantial content.

In the meantime it must be made clear that blacks don't require 'tolerance' in this particular condescending way. It isn't this particular paternal tyranny that is wanted, since it is major adjustments to British society that have to be made.

I stress that it is the British who have to make these adjustments.

It is the British, the white British, who have to learn that being British isn't what it was. Now it is a more complex thing, involving new elements. So there must be a fresh way of seeing Britain and the choices it faces: and a new way of being British after all this time. Much thought, discussion and self-examination must go into seeing the necessity for this, what this 'new way of being British' involves and how difficult it might be to attain.

The failure to grasp this opportunity for a revitalized and broader self-definition in the face of a real failure to be human, will be more insularity, schism, bitterness and catastrophe.

The two countries, Britain and Pakistan, have been part of each other for years, usually to the advantage of Britain. They cannot now be wrenched apart, even if that were desirable. Their futures will be intermixed. What that intermix means, its moral quality, whether it is violently resisted by ignorant whites and characterized by inequality and injustice, or understood, accepted and humanized, is for all of us to decide.

This decision is not one about a small group of irrelevant people who can be contemptuously described as 'minorities'. It is about the direction of British society. About its values and how humane it can be when experiencing real difficulty and possible breakdown. It is about the respect it accords individuals, the power it give to groups, and what it really means when it describes itself as 'democratic'. The future is in our hands.

My Beautiful Laundrette

CAST

JOHNNY	Daniel Day Lewis
GENGHIS	Richard Graham
SALIM	Derrick Branche
OMAR	Gordon Warnecke
PAPA	Roshan Seth
NASSER	Saeed Jaffrey
RACHEL	Shirley Anne Field
BILQUIS	Charu Bala Choksi
CHERRY	Souad Faress
TANIA	Rita Wolf
ZAKI	Gurdial Sira
MOOSE	Stephen Marcus
GANG MEMBER ONE	Dawn Archibald
GANG MEMBER TWO	Jonathan Moore

Photography	Oliver Stapleton
Film Editor	Mick Audsley
Designer	Hugo Luczyc Wyhowski
Sound Recordist	Albert Bailey
Music	Ludus Tonalis
Casting	Debbie McWilliams
Costume Design	Lindy Hemming
Make-up	Elaine Carew
Screenplay	Hanif Kureishi
Producers	Sarah Radclyffe and Tim Bevan
Director	Stephen Frears

1. EXT. OUTSIDE A LARGE DETACHED HOUSE. DAY.
CHERRY *and* SALIM *get out of their car. Behind them, the* FOUR JAMAICANS *get out of their car.*

CHERRY *and* SALIM *walk towards the house. It is a large falling-down place, in South London. It's quiet at the moment—early morning—but the ground floor windows are boarded up.*

On the boarded-up windows is painted: 'Your greed will be the death of us all' and 'We will defeat the running wogs of capitalism' and 'Opium is the opium of the unemployed'.

CHERRY *and* SALIM *look up at the house. The* FOUR JAMAICANS *stand behind them, at a respectful distance.*

CHERRY: I don't even remember buying this house at the auction. What are we going to do with it?

SALIM: Tomorrow we start to renovate it.

CHERRY: How many people are living here?

SALIM: There are no people living here. There are only squatters. And they're going to be renovated—right now.

(And SALIM *pushes* CHERRY *forward, giving her the key.* CHERRY *goes to the front door of the house.* SALIM, *with* TWO JAMAICANS, *goes round the side of the house.* TWO JAMAICANS *go round the other side.)*

2. INT. A ROOM IN THE SQUAT. DAY.
GENGHIS *and* JOHNNY *are living in a room in the squat. It is freezing cold, with broken windows.* GENGHIS *is asleep on a mattress, wrapped up. He has the flu.* JOHNNY *is lying frozen in a deck chair, with blankets over him. He has just woken up.*

3. EXT. OUTSIDE THE HOUSE. DAY.
CHERRY *tries to unlock the front door of the place. But the door has been barred. She looks in through the letter box. A barricade has been erected in the hall.*

4.   EXT. THE SIDE OF THE HOUSE. DAY.
The JAMAICANS *break into the house through side windows. They
climb in.* SALIM *also climbs into the house.*

5.   INT. INSIDE THE HOUSE. DAY.
The JAMAICANS *and* SALIM *are in the house now.*

The JAMAICANS *are kicking open the doors of the squatted rooms.
The* SQUATTERS *are unprepared, asleep or half-awake, in disarray.*

The JAMAICANS *are going from room to room, yelling for everyone
to leave now or get thrown out of the windows with their
belongings.*

Some SQUATTERS *complain but they are shoved out of their rooms
into the hall; or down the stairs.* SALIM *is eager about all of this.*

6.   INT. GENGHIS AND JOHNNY'S ROOM. DAY.
JOHNNY *looks up the corridor to see what's happening. He goes
back into the room quickly and starts stuffing his things into a black
plastic bag. He is shaking* GENGHIS *at the same time.*
GENGHIS: I'm ill.
JOHNNY: We're moving house.
GENGHIS: No, we've got to fight.
JOHNNY: Too early in the morning.

> (*He rips the blankets off* GENGHIS, *who lies there fully
> dressed, coughing and shivering. A* JAMAICAN *bursts into
> the room.*)

All right, all right.

> (*The* JAMAICAN *watches a moment as* GENGHIS, *too weak
> to resist, but cursing violently, takes the clothes* JOHNNY
> *shoves at him and follows* JOHNNY *to the window.* JOHNNY
> *opens the broken window.*)

7.   EXT. OUTSIDE THE HOUSE. DAY.
A wide shot of the house.

The SQUATTERS *are leaving through windows and the re-opened front door and gathering in the front garden, arranging their wretched belongings. Some of them are junkies. They look dishevelled and disheartened.*

From an upper room in the house come crashing a guitar, a TV and some records. This is followed by the enquiring head of a JAMAICAN, *looking to see these have hit no one.*

One SQUATTER, *in the front garden, is resisting and a* JAMAICAN *is holding him. The* SQUATTER *screams at* CHERRY: *you pig, you scum, you filthy rich shit, etc.*

As SALIM *goes to join* CHERRY, *she goes to the screaming* SQUATTER *and gives him a hard backhander across the face.*

8.   EXT. THE BACK OF THE HOUSE. DAY.

JOHNNY *and* GENGHIS *stumble down through the back garden of the house and over the wall at the end,* JOHNNY *pulling and helping the exhausted* GENGHIS.

At no time do they see CHERRY *or* SALIM.

9.   INT. BATHROOM. DAY.

OMAR *has been soaking Papa's clothes in the bath. He pulls them dripping from the bath and puts them in an old steel bucket, wringing them out. He picks up the bucket.*

10.   EXT. BALCONY. DAY.

OMAR *is hanging out Papa's dripping pyjamas on the washing line on the balcony, pulling them out of the bucket.*

The balcony overlooks several busy railway lines, commuter routes into Charing Cross and London Bridge, from the suburbs.

OMAR *turns and looks through the glass of the balcony door into the main room of the flat.* PAPA *is lying in bed. He pours himself some vodka. Water from the pyjamas drips down Omar's trousers and into his shoes.*

When he turns away, a train, huge, close, fast, crashes towards

*the camera and bangs and rattles its way past, a few feet from the
exposed overhanging balcony.* OMAR *is unperturbed.*

11. INT. PAPA'S ROOM. DAY.
The flat OMAR *and his father,* PAPA, *share in South London. It's a
small, damp and dirty place which hasn't been decorated for
years.*

   PAPA *is as thin as a medieval Christ: an unkempt alcoholic. His
hair is long; his toenails uncut; he is unshaven and scratches his
arse shamelessly. Yet he is not without dignity.*

   His bed is in the living room. PAPA *never leaves the bed and
watches TV most of the time.*

   *By the bed is a photograph of Papa's dead wife, Mary. And on
the bed is an address book and the telephone.*

   PAPA *empties the last of a bottle of vodka into a filthy glass. He
rolls the empty bottle under the bed.*

   OMAR *is now pushing an old-fashioned and ineffective carpet
sweeper across the floor.* PAPA *looks at* OMAR's *face. He indicates
that* OMAR *should move his face closer, which* OMAR *reluctantly
does. To amuse himself,* PAPA *squashes* OMAR's *nose and pulls his
cheeks, shaking the boy's unamused face from side to side.*
PAPA: I'm fixing you with a job. With your uncle. Work now, till
   you go back to college. If your face gets any longer here you'll
   overbalance. Or I'll commit suicide.

12. INT. KITCHEN. DAY.
OMAR *is in the kitchen of the flat, stirring a big saucepan of dall.
He can see through the open door his* FATHER *speaking on the
phone to* NASSER. PAPA *speaks in Urdu. 'How are you?' he says.
'And Bilquis? And Tania and the other girls?'*
PAPA: *(Into phone)* Can't you give Omar some work in your garage
   for a few weeks, yaar? The bugger's your nephew after all.
NASSER: *(VO on phone)* Why do you want to punish me?

13. INT. PAPA'S ROOM. DAY.

PAPA *is speaking to* NASSER *on the phone. He watches* OMAR *slowly stirring dall in the kitchen.* OMAR *is, of course, listening.*

PAPA: He's on dole like everyone else in England. What's he doing home? Just roaming and moaning.

NASSER: *(VO on phone)* Haven't you trained him up to look after you, like I have with my girls?

PAPA: He brushes the dust from one place to another. He squeezes shirts and heats soup. But that hardly stretches him. Though his food stretches me. It's only for a few months, yaar. I'll send him to college in the autumn.

NASSER: *(VO)* He failed once. He had this chronic laziness that runs in our family except for me.

PAPA: If his arse gets lazy—kick it. I'll send a certificate giving permission. And one thing more. Try and fix him with a nice girl. I'm not sure if his penis is in full working order.

14. INT. FLAT. DAY.

Later. OMAR *puts a full bottle of vodka on the table next to Papa's bed.*

PAPA: Go to your uncle's garage.

(*And* PAPA *pours himself a vodka.* OMAR *quickly thrusts a bottle of tomato juice towards* PAPA, *which* PAPA *ignores. Before* PAPA *can take a swig of the straight vodka,* OMAR *grabs the glass and adds tomato juice.* PAPA *takes it.*)
If Nasser wants to kick you—let him. I've given permission in two languages. (*To the photograph.*) The bloody's doing me a lot of good. Eh, bloody Mary?

15. EXT. STREET. DAY.

OMAR *walks along a South London street, towards* NASSER'*s garage. It's a rough area, beautiful in its own falling-down way.*

A youngish white BUSKER *is lying stoned in the doorway of a boarded-up shop, his guitar next to him.* OMAR *looks at him.*

Walking towards OMAR *from an amusement arcade across the street are* JOHNNY *and* GENGHIS *and* MOOSE. GENGHIS *is a well-built white man carrying a pile of right-wing newspapers, badges etc.* MOOSE *is a big white man,* GENGHIS's *lieutenant.*

JOHNNY *is an attractive man in his early twenties, quick and funny.*

OMAR *doesn't see* JOHNNY *but* JOHNNY *sees him and is startled. To avoid* OMAR, *in the middle of the road,* JOHNNY *takes* GENGHIS's *arm a moment.*

GENGHIS *stops suddenly.* MOOSE *charges into the back of him.* GENGHIS *drops the newspapers.* GENGHIS *remonstrates with* MOOSE. JOHNNY *watches* OMAR *go. The traffic stops while* MOOSE *picks up the newspapers.* GENGHIS *starts to sneeze.* MOOSE *gives him a handkerchief.*

They walk across the road, laughing at the waiting traffic.

They know the collapsed BUSKER. *He could even be a member of the gang.* JOHNNY *still watches* OMAR's *disappearing back.*

GENGHIS *and* MOOSE *prepare the newspapers.*

JOHNNY: *(Indicating* OMAR*)* That kid. We were like that.

GENGHIS: *(Sneezing over* MOOSE's *face)* You don't believe in nothing.

16.   INT. UNDERGROUND GARAGE. DAY.
Uncle Nasser's garage. It's a small private place where wealthy businessmen keep their cars during the day. It's almost full and contains about fifty cars—all Volvos, Rolls-Royces, Mercedes, Rovers, etc.

At the end of the garage is a small glassed-in office.

OMAR *is walking down the ramp and into the garage.*

17.   INT. GARAGE OFFICE. DAY.
The glassed-in office contains a desk, a filing cabinet, a typewriter, phone etc. With NASSER *is* SALIM.

SALIM *is a Pakistani in his late thirties, well-dressed in an ex-*

pensive, smooth and slightly vulgar way. He moves restlessly about the office. Then he notices OMAR *wandering about the garage. He watches him.*

Meanwhile, NASSER *is speaking on the phone in the background.*

NASSER: *(Into phone)* We've got one parking space, yes. It's £25 a week. And from this afternoon we provide a special on the premises 'clean-the-car' service. New thing.

(From Salim's POV in the office, through the glass, we see OMAR *trying the door of one of the cars.* SALIM *goes quickly out of the office.)*

18.   INT. GARAGE. DAY.

SALIM *stands outside the office and shouts at* OMAR. *The sudden sharp voice in the echoing garage.*

SALIM: Hey! Is that your car? Why are you feeling it up then? *(OMAR looks at him.)* Come here. Here, I said.

19.   INT. GARAGE OFFICE. DAY.

NASSER *puts down the phone.*

20.   INT. GARAGE OFFICE. DAY.

NASSER *is embracing* OMAR *vigorously, squashing him to him and bashing him lovingly on the back.*

NASSER: *(Introducing him to* SALIM*)* This one who nearly beat you up is Salim. You'll see a lot of him.

SALIM: *(Shaking hands with* OMAR*)* I've heard many great things about your father.

NASSER: *(To* OMAR*)* I must see him. Oh God, how have I got time to do anything?

SALIM: You're too busy keeping this damn country in the black. Someone's got to do it.

NASSER: *(To* OMAR*)* Your papa, he got thrown out of that clerk's job I fixed him with? He was pissed?

(OMAR nods. NASSER looks regretfully at the boy.)

Can you wash a car?

(OMAR *looks uncertain.*)

SALIM: Have you washed a car before?

(OMAR *nods.*)

Your uncle can't pay you much. But you'll be able to afford
a decent shirt and you'll be with your own people. Not in a
dole queue. Mrs. Thatcher will be pleased with me.

21.   INT. GARAGE. DAY.

SALIM *and* OMAR *walk across the garage towards a big car.* OMAR
carries a full bucket of water and a cloth. He listens to SALIM.

SALIM: It's easy to wash a car. You just wet a rag and rub. You
know how to rub, don't you?

(*The bucket is overfull.* OMAR *carelessly hangs it against
his leg. Water slops out.* SALIM *dances away irritably.* OMAR
walks on. SALIM *points to a car.* RACHEL *swings down the
ramp and into the garage, gloriously.*)

Hi, baby.

RACHEL: My love.

(*And she goes into the garage office. We see her talking
and laughing with* NASSER.)

SALIM: *(Indicating car)* And you do this one first. Carefully, as if
you were restoring a Renaissance painting. It's my car.

(OMAR *looks up and watches as* RACHEL *and* NASSER *go
out through the back of the garage office into the room at
the back.*)

22.   INT. ROOM AT BACK OF GARAGE OFFICE. DAY.

RACHEL *and* NASSER, *half-undressed, are drinking, laughing and
screwing on a bulging sofa in the wrecked room behind the office,
no bigger than a large cupboard.* RACHEL *is bouncing up and down
on his huge stomach in her red corset and outrageous worn-for-a-
joke underwear.*

NASSER: Rachel, fill my glass, darling.

(RACHEL *does so, then she begins to move on him.*)

RACHEL: Fill mine.

NASSER: What am I, Rachel, your trampoline?

RACHEL: Yes, oh, je vous aime beaucoup, trampoline.

NASSER: Speak my language, dammit.

RACHEL: I do nothing else. Nasser, d'you think we'll ever part?

NASSER: Not at the moment.

(Slapping her arse) Keep moving, I love you. You move . . .
Christ . . . like a liner . . .

RACHEL: And can't we go away somewhere?

NASSER: Yes, I'm taking you.

RACHEL: Where?

NASSER: Kempton Park, Saturday.

RACHEL: Great. We'll take the boy.

NASSER: No, I've got big plans for him.

RACHEL: You're going to make him work?

23.   INT. GARAGE OFFICE. DAY.

OMAR *has come into the garage office with his car-washing bucket
and sponge.* SALIM *has gone home.* OMAR *is listening at the door
to his uncle* NASSER *and* RACHEL *screwing. He hears:*

NASSER: Work? That boy? You'll think the word was invented
for him!

24.   INT. COCKTAIL BAR/CLUB. EVENING.

RACHEL *and* NASSER *have taken* OMAR *to Anwar's club/bar.* OMAR
watches Anwar's son TARIQ *behind the bar.* TARIQ *is rather contemptuous of* OMAR *and listens to their conversation.*

OMAR *eats peanuts and olives off the bar.* TARIQ *removes the
bowl.*

NASSER: By the way, Rachel is my old friend. *(To her.)* Eh?

OMAR: *(To* NASSER*)* How's Auntie Bilquis?

NASSER: *(Glancing at amused* RACHEL*)* She's at home with the
kids.

OMAR: Papa sends his love. Uncle, if I picked Papa up—

NASSER: *(Indicating the club)* Have you been to a high-class place like this before? I suppose you stay in that black-hole flat all the time.

OMAR: If I picked Papa up, uncle—

NASSER: *(To RACHEL)* He's one of those underprivileged types.

OMAR: And squeezed him, squeezed Papa out, like that, uncle, I often imagine. I'd get—

NASSER: Two fat slaps.

OMAR: Two bottles of pure vodka. And a kind of flap of skin. *(To RACHEL.)* Like a French letter.

NASSER: What are you talking, madman? I love my brother. And I love you.

OMAR: I don't understand how you can . . . love me.

NASSER: Because you're such a prick?

OMAR: You can't be sure that I am.

RACHEL: Nasser.

NASSER: She's right. Don't deliberately egg me on to laugh at you when I've brought you here to tell you one essential thing. Move closer.

(OMAR attempts to drag the stool he is sitting on near to NASSER. He crashes off it. RACHEL helps him up, laughing. TARIQ also laughs. NASSER is solicitous.)

In this damn country which we hate and love, you can get anything you want. It's all spread out and available. That's why I believe in England. You just have to know how to squeeze the tits of the system.

RACHEL: *(To OMAR)* He's saying he wants to help you.

OMAR: What are you going to do with me?

NASSER: What am I going to do with you? Make you into something damn good. Your father can't now, can he?

(RACHEL nods at NASSER and he takes out his wallet. He

gives OMAR *money.* OMAR *doesn't want to take it.* NASSER
*shoves it down Omar's jumper, then cuddles his confused
nephew.)*

Damn fool, you're just like a son to me. *(Looking at* RACHEL.*)*
To both of us.

25.   INT. GARAGE. DAY.

OMAR *is vigorously washing down a car, the last to be cleaned in
the garage. The other cars are gleaming.* NASSER *comes quickly out
of the office and watches* OMAR *squeezing a cloth over a bucket.*

NASSER: You like this work? *(*OMAR *shrugs.)* Come on, for Christ's
   sake, take a look at these accounts for me.
   *(*OMAR *follows him into the garage office.)*

26.   INT. GARAGE OFFICE. NIGHT.

OMAR *is sitting at the office desk in his shirt-sleeves. The desk is
covered with papers. He's been sitting there some time and it is
late. Most of the cars in the garage have gone.*

   NASSER *drives into the garage, wearing evening clothes.* RACHEL,
looking divine, is with him. OMAR *goes out to them.*

27.   INT. GARAGE. NIGHT.

NASSER: *(From the car)* Kiss Rachel. *(*OMAR *kisses her.)*

OMAR: I'll finish the paperwork tonight, Uncle.

NASSER: *(To* RACHEL*)* He's such a good worker I'm going to
   promote him.

RACHEL: What to?

NASSER: *(To* OMAR*)* Come to my house next week and I'll tell
   you.

RACHEL: It's far. How will he get there?

NASSER: I'll give him a car, dammit. *(He points to an old convertible parked in the garage. It has always looked out of place.)*
   The keys are in the office. Anything he wants. *(He moves the*

car off. To OMAR.) Oh yes, I've got a real challenge lined up
for you.

(RACHEL *blows him a kiss as they drive off.*)

28.   INT. PAPA'S FLAT. EVENING.

PAPA *is lying on the bed drinking.* OMAR, *in new clothes, tie undone,
comes into the room and puts a plate of steaming food next to*
PAPA. *Stew and potatoes.* OMAR *turns away and looking in the
mirror snips at the hair in his nostrils with a large pair of scissors.*

PAPA: You must be getting married. Why else would you be
   dressed like an undertaker on holiday?

OMAR: Going to uncle's house, Papa. He's given me a car.

PAPA: What? The brakes must be faulty. Tell me one thing because there's something I don't understand, though it must
   be my fault. How is it that scrubbing cars can make a son of
   mine look so ecstatic?

OMAR: It gets me out of the house.

PAPA: Don't get too involved with that crook. You've got to study.
   We are under siege by the white man. For us education is
   power.

   (OMAR *shakes his head at his father.*)

   Don't let me down.

29.   EXT. COUNTRY LANE. EVENING.

OMAR, *in the old convertible, speeds along a country lane in Kent.
The car has its roof down, although it's raining. Loud music playing
on the radio.*

   *He turns into the drive of a large detached house. The house is
brightly lit. There are seven or eight cars in the drive.* OMAR *sits
there a moment, music blaring.*

30.   INT. LIVING ROOM IN NASSER'S HOUSE. EVENING.

A large living room furnished in the modern style. A shy OMAR *has
been led in by* BILQUIS, *Nasser's wife. She is a shy, middle-aged*

Pakistani woman. She speaks and understands English, but is un-
certain in the language. But she is warm and friendly.

OMAR *has already been introduced to most of the women in the*
room.

There are five women there: a selection of wives; plus Bilquis's
three daughters. The eldest, TANIA, *is in her early twenties.*

CHERRY, *Salim's Anglo-Indian wife is there.*

Some of the women are wearing saris or salwar kamiz, though
not necessarily only the Pakistani women.

TANIA *wears jeans and T-shirt. She watches* OMAR *all through*
this and OMAR, *when he can, glances at her. She is attracted to him.*

BILQUIS: *(To* OMAR*)* And this is Salim's wife, Cherry. And of
course you remember our three naughty daughters.

CHERRY: *(Ebulliently to* BILQUIS*)* He has his family's cheekbones,
Bilquis. *(To* OMAR.*)* I know all your gorgeous family in
Karachi.

OMAR: *(This is a faux pas)* You've been there?

CHERRY: You stupid, what a stupid, it's my home. Could anyone
in their right mind call this silly little island off Europe their
home? Every day in Karachi, every day your other uncles and
cousins are at our house for bridge, booze and VCR.

BILQUIS: Cherry, my little nephew knows nothing of that life there.

CHERRY: Oh God, I'm so sick of hearing about these in-betweens.
People should make up their minds where they are.

TANIA: Uncle's next door. *(Leading him away. Quietly.)* Can you
see me later? I'm so bored with these people.

*(*CHERRY *stares at* TANIA, *not approving of this whispering*
and cousin-closeness. TANIA *glares back defiantly at her.*
BILQUIS *looks warmly at* OMAR.*)*

31.   INT. CORRIDOR OF NASSER'S HOUSE. DAY.

TANIA *takes* OMAR *by the hand down the corridor to Nasser's room.*
She opens the door and leads him in.

32.   INT. NASSER'S ROOM. EVENING.

Nasser's room is further down the corridor. It's his bedroom but where he receives guests. And he has a VCR in the room, a fridge, small bar, etc. Behind his bed a window which overlooks the garden.

OMAR *goes into the smoke-filled room, led by* TANIA. *She goes.*

NASSER *is lying on his bed in the middle of the room like a fat king. His cronies are gathered round the bed.* ZAKI, SALIM, *an* ENGLISHMAN *and an American called* DICK O'DONNELL.

They're shouting and hooting and boozing and listening to NASSER*'s story, which he tells with great energy.* OMAR *stands inside the door shyly, and takes in the scene.*

NASSER: There'd been some tappings on the window. But who would stay in a hotel without tappings? My brother Hussein, the boy's papa, in his usual way hadn't turned up and I was asleep. I presumed he was screwing some barmaid somewhere. Then when these tappings went on I got out of bed and opened the door to the balcony. And there he was, standing outside. With some woman! They were completely without clothes! And blue with cold! They looked like two bars of soap. This I refer to as my brother's blue period.

DICK O'DONNELL: What happened to the woman?

NASSER: He married her.

(When NASSER *notices the boy, conversation ceases with a wave of his hand. And* NASSER *unembarrassedly calls him over to be fondled and patted.)* Come along, come along. Your father's a good man.

DICK O'DONNELL: This is the famous Hussein's son?

NASSER: The exact bastard. My blue brother was also a famous journalist in Bombay and great drinker. He was to the bottle what Louis Armstrong is to the trumpet.

SALIM: But you are to the bookie what Mother Theresa is to the children.

ZAKI: *(To* NASSER*)* Your brother was the clever one. You used to carry his typewriter.

(TANIA *appears at the window behind the bed, where no one sees her but* OMAR *and then* ZAKI. *Later in the scene, laughing and to distract the serious-faced* OMAR, *she bares her breasts.* ZAKI *sees this and cannot believe his swimming-in-drink eyes.)*

DICK O'DONNELL: Isn't he coming tonight?

SALIM: *(To* NASSER*)* Whatever happened to him?

OMAR: Papa's lying down.

SALIM: I meant his career.

NASSER: That's lying down too. What chance would the Englishman give a leftist communist Pakistani on newspapers?

OMAR: Socialist. Socialist.

NASSER: What chance would the Englishman give a leftist communist socialist?

ZAKI: What chance has the racist Englishman given us that we haven't torn from him with our hands? Let's face up to it.

(And ZAKI *has seen the breasts of* TANIA. *He goes white and panics.)*

NASSER: Zaki, have another stiff drink for that good point!

ZAKI: Nasser, please God, I am on the verge already!

ENGLISHMAN: Maybe Omar's father didn't make chances for himself. Look at you, Salim, five times richer and more powerful than me.

SALIM: Five times? Ten, at least.

ENGLISHMAN: In my country! The only prejudice in England is against the useless.

SALIM: It's rather tilted in favour of the useless I would think. The only positive discrimination they have here.

(The PAKISTANIS *in the room laugh at this. The* ENGLISH-MAN *looks annoyed.* DICK O'DONNELL *smiles sympathetically at the* ENGLISHMAN.)

DICK O'DONNELL: *(To* NASSER*)* Can I make this nice boy a drink?

NASSER: Make him a man first.

SALIM: *(To* ZAKI*)* Give him a drink. I like him. He's our future.

33. INT. THE VERANDAH. NIGHT.

OMAR *shuts the door of Nasser's room and walks down the hall, to a games room at the end. This is a verandah overlooking the garden. There's a table-tennis table, various kids' toys, an exercise cycle, some cane chairs and on the walls numerous photographs of India.*

TANIA *turns as he enters and goes eagerly to him, touching him warmly.*

TANIA: It's been years. And you're looking good now. I bet we understand each other, eh?

(He can't easily respond to her enthusiasm. Unoffended, she swings way from him. He looks at photographs of his Papa and Bhutto on the wall.)

Are they being cruel to you in their typical men's way?

(He shrugs.) You don't mind?

OMAR: I think I should harden myself.

TANIA: *(Patting seat next to her)* Wow, what are you into?

OMAR: Your father's done well.

(He sits. She kisses him on the lips. They hold each other.)

TANIA: Has he? He adores you. I expect he wants you to take over the businesses. He wouldn't think of asking me. But he is too vicious to people in his work. He doesn't want you to work in that shitty laundrette, does he?

OMAR: What's wrong with it?

TANIA: And he has a mistress, doesn't he?

*(*OMAR *looks up and sees* AUNTIE BILQUIS *standing at the door.* TANIA *doesn't see her.)*

Rachel. Yes, I can tell from your face. Does he love her? Yes. Families, I hate families.

BILQUIS: Please Tania, can you come and help.

(BILQUIS *goes.* TANIA *follows her.*)

34. INT. HALL OF NASSER'S HOUSE. DAY.

OMAR *is standing in the hall of Nasser's house as the guests leave their respective rooms and go out into the drive.* OMAR *stands there.* NASSER *shouts to him from his bed.*

NASSER: Take my advice. There's money in muck.

(TANIA *signals and shakes her head.*)

What is it the gora Englishman always needs? Clean clothes!

35. EXT. NASSER'S DRIVE. NIGHT.

OMAR *has come out of the house and into the drive. A strange sight:* SALIM *staggering about drunkenly. The* ENGLISHMAN, ZAKI *and* CHERRY *try to get him into the car.* SALIM *screams at* ZAKI.

SALIM: Don't you owe me money? Why not? You usually owe me money! Here, take this! Borrow it! (*And he starts to scatter money about.*) Pick it up!

(ZAKI *starts picking it up. He is afraid.*)

CHERRY: (*To* OMAR) Drive us back, will you. Pick up your own car tomorrow. Salim is not feeling well.

(*As* ZAKI *bends over,* SALIM, *who is laughing, goes to kick him.* BILQUIS *stands at the window watching all this.*)

36. INT. SALIM'S CAR, DRIVING INTO SOUTH LONDON. NIGHT.

OMAR *driving* SALIM'*s car enthusiastically into London.* CHERRY *and* SALIM *are in the back. The car comes to a stop at traffic lights.*

On the adjacent pavement outside a chip shop a group of LADS *are kicking cans about. The* LADS *include* MOOSE *and* GENGHIS.

A lively street of the illuminated shops, amusement arcades and late-night shops of South London.

MOOSE *notices that Pakistanis are in the car. And he indicates to the others.*

The LADS *gather round the car and bang on it and shout. From inside the car this noise is terrifying.* CHERRY *starts to scream.*

SALIM: Drive, you bloody fool, drive!

> (*But* MOOSE *climbs on the bonnet of the car and squashes his arse grotesquely against the windscreen. Faces squash aagainst the other windows.*
>
> *Looking out of the side window* OMAR *sees* JOHNNY *standing to one side of the car, not really part of the car-climbing and banging.*
>
> *Impulsively, unafraid,* OMAR *gets out of the car.*)

37.   EXT. STREET. NIGHT.

OMAR *walks past* GENGHIS *and* MOOSE *and the others to the embarrassed* JOHNNY. CHERRY *is yelling after him from inside the open-doored car.*

The LADS *are alert and ready for violence but are confused by* OMAR's *obvious friendship with* JOHNNY.

OMAR *sticks out his hand and* JOHNNY *takes it.*

OMAR: It's me.

JOHNNY: I know who it is.

OMAR: How are yer? Working? What you doing now then?

JOHNNY: Oh, this kinda thing.

CHERRY: (*Yelling from the car*) Come on, come on!

> (*The* LADS *laugh at her.* SALIM *is hastily giving* MOOSE *cigarettes.*)

JOHNNY: What are you now, chauffeur?

OMAR: No. I'm on to something.

JOHNNY: What?

OMAR: I'll let you know. Still living in the same place?

JOHNNY: Na, don't get on with me mum and dad. You?

OMAR: She died last year, my mother. Jumped on to the railway line.

JOHNNY: Yeah. I heard. All the trains stopped.

OMAR: I'm still there. Got the number?

JOHNNY: *(Indicates the* LADS*)* Like me friends?

*(*CHERRY *starts honking the car horn. The* LADS *cheer.)*

OMAR: Ring us then.

JOHNNY: I will. *(Indicates car.)* Leave 'em there. We can do something. Now. Just us.

OMAR: Can't.

*(*OMAR *touches* JOHNNY's *arm and runs back to the car.)*

38. INT. CAR. NIGHT.

They continue to drive. CHERRY *is screaming at* OMAR.

CHERRY: What the hell were you doing?

*(*SALIM *slaps her.)*

SALIM: He saved our bloody arses! *(To* OMAR, *grabbing him round the neck and pressing his face close to his.)* I'm going to see you're all right!

39. INT. PAPA'S ROOM. NIGHT.

OMAR *has got home. He creeps into the flat. He goes carefully along the hall, fingertips on familiar wall.*

He goes into Papa's room. No sign of PAPA. PAPA *is on the balcony. Just a shadow.*

40. EXT. BALCONY. NIGHT.

PAPA *is swaying on the balcony like a little tree. Papa's pyjama bottoms have fallen down. And he's just about maintaining himself vertically. His hair has fallen across his terrible face. A train bangs towards him, rushing out of the darkness. And* PAPA *sways precariously towards it.*

OMAR: *(Screams above the noise)* What are you doing?

PAPA: I want to pee.

OMAR: Can't you wait for me to take you!

PAPA: My prick will drop off before you show up these days.

OMAR: *(Pulling up Papa's bottoms)* You know who I met? Johnny.
   Johnny.

PAPA: The boy who came here one day dressed as a fascist with
   a quarter inch of hair?

OMAR: He was a friend once. For years.

PAPA: There were days when he didn't deserve your admiration
   so much.

OMAR: Christ, I've known him since I was five.

PAPA: He went too far. They hate us in England. And all you do
   is kiss their arses and think of yourself as a little Britisher!

41.   INT. PAPA'S ROOM. NIGHT.

They are inside the room now, and OMAR shuts the doors.

OMAR: I'm being promoted. To uncle's laundrette.

   *(PAPA pulls a pair of socks from his pyjama pockets and
   thrusts them at OMAR.)*

PAPA: Illustrate your washing methods!

   (OMAR throws the socks across the room.)

42.   EXT. SOUTH LONDON STREET. DAY.

*NASSER and OMAR get out of Nasser's car and walk over the road
to the laundrette. It's called 'Churchills'. It's broad and spacious
and in bad condition. It's situated in an area of run-down second-
hand shops, betting shops, grocers with their windows boarded-up,
etc.*

NASSER: It's nothing but a toilet and a youth club now. A finger
   up my damn arse.

43.   INT. LAUNDRETTE. DAY.

*We are inside the laundrette. Some of the benches in the laundrette
are church pews.*

OMAR: Where did you get those?

NASSER: Church.

(Three or four rough-looking KIDS, *boys and girls, one of whom isn't wearing shoes, sitting on the pews. A character by the telephone. The thunderous sound of running-shoes in a spin-drier. The* KID *coolly opens the spin-drier and takes out his shoes.)*

Punkey, that's how machines get buggered!

(The KID *puts on his shoes. He offers his hot-dog to another* KID, *who declines it. So the* KID *flings it into a spin-drier.*

NASSER *moves to throttle him. He gets the* KID *by the throat. The other* KIDS *get up.* OMAR *pulls his eager* UNCLE *away. The* TELEPHONE CHARACTER *looks suspiciously at everyone. Then makes his call.)*

TELEPHONE CHARACTER: Hi, baby, it's number one here, baby. How's your foot now?

44.   INT. BACK ROOM OF LAUNDRETTE. DAY.

NASSER *stands at the desk going through bills and papers.*

NASSER: *(To* OMAR*)* Get started. There's the broom. Move it!

OMAR: I don't only want to sweep up.

NASSER: What are you now, Labour Party?

OMAR: I want to be manager of this place. I think I can do it. *(Pause.)* Please let me.

*(*NASSER *thinks.)*

NASSER: I'm just thinking how to tell your father that four punks drowned you in a washing machine. On the other hand, some water on the brain might clear your thoughts. Okay. Pay me a basic rent. Above that—you keep.

(He goes quickly, eager to get out. The TELEPHONE CHAR-ACTER *is shouting into the phone.)*

TELEPHONE CHARACTER: *(Into phone)* Was it my fault? But you're everything to me! More than everything. I prefer you to Janice!

(The TELEPHONE CHARACTER *indicates to* NASSER *that a washing machine has overflowed all over the floor, with soap suds.* NASSER *gets out.* OMAR *looks on.)*

45.   INT. BACK ROOM OF LAUNDRETTE. DAY.
OMAR *sitting gloomily in the back room. The door to the main area open.* KIDS *push each other about. Straight customers are intimidated.*

From Omar's POV through the laundrette windows, we see SALIM *getting out of his car.* SALIM *walks in through the laundrette, quickly. Comes into the back room, slamming the door behind him.*
SALIM: Get up! *(*OMAR *gets up.* SALIM *rams the back of a chair under the door handle.)* I've had trouble here.
OMAR: Salim, please. I don't know how to make this place work. I'm afraid I've made a fool of myself.
SALIM: You'll never make a penny out of this. Your uncle's given you a dead duck. That's why I've decided to help you financially. *(He gives him a piece of paper with an address on it. He also gives him money.)* Go to this house near the airport. Pick up some video cassettes and bring them to my flat. That's all.

46.   INT. SALIM'S FLAT. EVENING.
The flat is large and beautiful. Some Sindi music playing. SALIM *comes out of the bathroom wearing only a towel round his waist. And a plastic shower cap. He is smoking a fat joint.*

CHERRY *goes into another room.*

OMAR *stands there with the cassettes in his arms.* SALIM *indicates them.*
SALIM: Put them. Relax. No problems? *(*SALIM *gives him the joint and* OMAR *takes a hit on it.* SALIM *points at the walls. Some erotic and some very good paintings.)* One of the best collections of recent Indian painting. I patronize many painters. I won't be a minute. Watch something if you like.

(SALIM *goes back into the bedroom.* OMAR *puts one of the cassettes he has brought into the VCR. But there's nothing on the tape. Just a screenful of static.*

Meanwhile, OMAR *makes a call, taking the number off a piece of paper.*)

OMAR: *(Into phone)* Can I speak to Johnny? D'you know where he's staying? Are you sure? Just wanted to help him. Please, if you see him, tell him to ring Omo.

47. INT. SALIM'S FLAT. EVENING.

Dressed now, and ready to go out, SALIM *comes quickly into the room. He picks up the video cassettes and realizes one is being played.* SALIM *screams savagely at* OMAR.

SALIM: Is that tape playing? *(OMAR nods.)* What the hell are you doing? *(He pulls the tape out of the VCR and examines it.)*

OMAR: Just watching something, Salim.

SALIM: Not these! Who gave you permission to touch these?

(OMAR *grabs the tape from* SALIM's *hand.*)

OMAR: It's just a tape!

SALIM: Not to me

OMAR: What are you doing? What business, Salim?

(SALIM *pushes* OMAR *hard and* OMAR *crashes backwards across the room. As he gets up quickly to react* SALIM *is at him, shoving him back down, viciously. He puts his foot on* OMAR's *nose.*

CHERRY *watches him coolly, leaning against a door jamb.*)

SALIM: Nasser tells me you're ambitious to do something. But twice you failed your exams. You've done nothing with the laundrette and now you bugger me up. You've got too much white blood. It's made you weak like those pale-faced adolescents that call us wog. You know what I do to them? I take out this. *(He takes out a pound note. He tears it to pieces.)*

I say: your English pound is worthless. It's worthless like you,
Omar, are worthless. Your whole great family—rich and powerful over there—is let down by you.

(OMAR *gets up slowly.*)

Now fuck off.

OMAR: I'll do something to you for this.

SALIM: I'd be truly happy to see you try.

48.   EXT. OUTSIDE LAUNDRETTE. EVENING.

OMAR, *depressed after his humiliation at* SALIM's, *drives slowly past
the laundrette. Music plays over this. It's raining and the laundrette
looks grim and hopeless.*

OMAR *sees* GENGHIS *and* MOOSE. *He drives up alongside them.*

OMAR: Seen Johnny?

GENGHIS: Get back to the jungle, wog boy.

(MOOSE *kicks the side of the car.*)

49.   INT. PAPA'S ROOM. EVENING.

OMAR *is cutting* PAPA's *long toenails with a large pair of scissors.*
OMAR's *face is badly bruised.* PAPA *jerks about, pouring himself a
drink. So* OMAR *has to keep grabbing at his feet. The skin on* PAPA's
legs is peeling through lack of vitamins.

PAPA: Those people are too tough for you. I'll tell Nasser you're
through with them. (PAPA *dials. We hear it ringing in Nasser's
house. He puts the receiver to one side to pick up his drink.
He looks at* OMAR *who wells with anger and humiliation.* TANIA
answers.)

TANIA: Hallo.

(OMAR *moves quickly and breaks the connection.*)

PAPA: *(Furious)* Why do that, you useless fool?

(OMAR *grabs* PAPA's *foot and starts on the toe job again.
The phone starts to ring.* PAPA *pulls away and* OMAR *jabs*

him with the scissors. And PAPA *bleeds.* OMAR *answers the phone.)*

OMAR: Hallo. *(Pause.)* Johnny.

PAPA: *(Shouts over)* I'll throw you out of this bloody flat, you're nothing but a bum liability!

(But OMAR *is smiling into the phone and talking to* JOHNNY, *a finger in one ear.)*

50. INT. THE LAUNDRETTE. DAY.

OMAR *is showing* JOHNNY *round the laundrette.*

JOHNNY: I'm dead impressed by all this.

OMAR: You were the one at school. The one they liked.

JOHNNY: *(Sarcastic)* All the Pakis liked me.

OMAR: I've been through it. With my parents and that. And with people like you. But now there's some things I want to do. Some pretty big things I've got in mind. I need to raise money to make this place good. I want you to help me do that. And I want you to work here with me.

JOHNNY: What kinda work is it?

OMAR: Variety. Variety of menial things.

JOHNNY: Cleaning windows kinda thing, yeah?

OMAR: Yeah. Sure. And clean out those bastards, will ya?

*(*OMAR *indicates the sitting* KIDS *playing about on the benches.)*

JOHNNY: Now?

OMAR: I'll want everything done now. That's the only attitude if you want to do anything big.

*(*JOHNNY *goes to the* KIDS *and stands above them. Slowly he removes his watch and puts it in his pocket. This is a strangely threatening gesture. The* KIDS *rise and walk out one by one. One* KID *resents this. He pushes* JOHNNY *suddenly.* JOHNNY *kicks him hard.)*

51.   EXT. OUTSIDE THE LAUNDRETTE. DAY.

Continuous. The kicked KID *shoots across the pavement and crashes into* SALIM *who is getting out of his car.* SALIM *pushes away the frantic arms and legs and goes quickly into the laundrette.*

52.   INT. LAUNDRETTE. DAY.

SALIM *drags the reluctant* OMAR *by the arm into the back room of the laundrette.* JOHNNY *watches them, then follows.*

53.   INT. BACK ROOM OF LAUNDRETTE. DAY.

SALIM *lets go of* OMAR *and grabs a chair to stuff under the door handle as before.* OMAR *suddenly snatches the chair from him and puts it down slowly. And* JOHNNY, *taking* OMAR's *lead, sticks his big boot in the door as* SALIM *attempts to slam it.*

SALIM: Christ, Omar, sorry what happened before. Too much to drink. Just go on one little errand for me, eh? *(He opens* OMAR's *fingers and presses a piece of paper into his hand.)* Like before. For me.

OMAR: For fifty quid as well.

SALIM: You little bastard.

> (OMAR *turns away.* JOHNNY *turns away too, mocking* SALIM, *parodying* OMAR.)
> All right.

54.   INT. HOTEL ROOM. DUSK.

OMAR *is standing in a hotel room. A modern high building with a view over London. He is with a middle-aged Pakistani who is wearing salwar kamiz. Suitcases on the floor.*

> *The* MAN *has a long white beard. Suddenly he peels it off and hands it to* OMAR. OMAR *is astonished. The* MAN *laughs uproariously.*

55.   INT. LAUNDRETTE. EVENING.

JOHNNY *is doing a service wash in the laundrette.* OMAR *comes in quickly, the beard in a plastic bag. He puts the beard on.*

JOHNNY: You fool.

(OMAR *pulls* JOHNNY *towards the back room.*)

OMAR: I've sussed Salim's game. This is going to finance our whole future.

56.   INT. BACK ROOM OF LAUNDRETTE. DAY.

JOHNNY *and* OMAR *sitting at the desk.* JOHNNY *is unpicking the back of the beard with a pair of scissors. The door to the laundrette is closed.*

JOHNNY *carefully pulls plastic bags out of the back of the beard. He looks enquiringly at* OMAR. OMAR *confidently indicates that he should open one of them.* JOHNNY *looks doubtfully at him.* OMAR *pulls the chair closer.* JOHNNY *snips a corner off the bag. He opens it and tastes the powder on his finger. He nods at* OMAR. JOHNNY *quickly starts stuffing the bags back in the beard.*

OMAR *gets up.*

OMAR: Take them out. You know where to sell this stuff. Yes? Don't you?

JOHNNY: I wouldn't be working for you now if I wanted to go on being a bad boy.

OMAR: This means more. Real work. Expansion.

(JOHNNY *reluctantly removes the rest of the packets from the back of the beard.*)

We'll re-sell it fast. Tonight.

JOHNNY: Salim'll kill us.

OMAR: Why should he find out it's us? Better get this back to him. Come on. I couldn't be doing any of this without you.

57.   INT. OUTSIDE SALIM'S FLAT. NIGHT.

OMAR, *wearing the beard, is standing outside* SALIM'S *flat, having rung the bell.* CHERRY *answers the door. At first she doesn't recognize him. Then he laughs. And she pulls him in.*

58.　INT. SALIM'S FLAT. NIGHT.

There are ten people sitting in SALIM's *flat. Well-off Pakistani friends who have come round for dinner. They are chatting and drinking. At the other end of the room the table has been laid for dinner.*

　SALIM *is fixing drinks, and talking to his friends over his shoulder.*

SALIM: We were all there, yaar, to see Ravi Shankar. But you all just wanted to talk about my paintings. My collection. That's why I said, why don't you all come round. I will turn my place into an art gallery for the evening . . . *(The friends are giggling at* OMAR, *who is wearing the beard.* SALIM, *disturbed, turns suddenly.* SALIM *is appalled by* OMAR *in the beard.)* Let's have a little private chat, eh?

59.　INT. SALIM'S BEDROOM. EVENING.

SALIM *snatches the beard from* OMAR's *chin. He goes into the bathroom with it.* OMAR *moves towards the bathroom and watches* SALIM *frantically examine the back of the beard. When* SALIM *sees, in the mirror,* OMAR *watching him, he kicks the door shut.*

60.　INT. SALIM'S BEDROOM. NIGHT.

SALIM *comes back into the bedroom from the bathroom. He throws down the beard.*

SALIM: You can go.

OMAR: But you haven't paid me.

SALIM: I'm not in the mood. Nothing happened to you on the way here? *(*OMAR *shakes his head.)* Well, something may happen to you on the way back. *(*SALIM *is unsure at the moment what's happened.* OMAR *watches him steadily. His nerve is holding out.)* Get the hell out.

61.   EXT. OUTSIDE SALIM'S FLAT. NIGHT.

As OMAR *runs down the steps of the flats to* JOHNNY *waiting in the revving car,* SALIM *stands at the window of his flat, watching them. Music over. We go with the music into:*

62.   INT. CLUB/BAR. NIGHT.

OMAR *has taken* JOHNNY *to the club he visited with* NASSER *and* RACHEL.

The club is more lively in the evening, with West Indian, English and Pakistani customers. All affluent. In fact, a couple of the JA-MAICANS *from the opening scene are there.*

OMAR *and* JOHNNY *are sitting at a table.* TARIQ, *the young son of the club's owner, stands beside them. He puts two menus down.*

TARIQ: *(To* OMAR*)* Of course a table is always here for you. Your Uncle Nasser—a great man. And Salim, of course. No one touches him. No one. You want to eat?

OMAR: Tariq, later. Bring us champagne first. *(*TARIQ *goes. To* JOHNNY*)* Okay?

JOHNNY: I'm selling the stuff tonight. The bloke's coming here in an hour. He's testing it now.

OMAR: Good. *(Smiles at a girl.)* She's nice.

JOHNNY: Yes.

63.   INT. CLUB/BAR. NIGHT.

OMAR *is sitting alone at the table, drinking.* TARIQ *clears the table and goes.* JOHNNY *comes out of the toilet with the white* DEALER. *The* DEALER *goes.* JOHNNY *goes and sits beside* OMAR.

JOHNNY: We're laughing.

64.   INT. NASSER'S ROOM. EVENING.

NASSER *is lying on his bed wearing salwar kamiz. One of the young* DAUGHTERS *is pressing his legs and he groans with delight.* OMAR *is sitting across the room from him, well-dressed and relaxed. He eats Indian sweets. The other* DAUGHTER *comes in with more sweets, which she places by* OMAR.

OMAR: Tell me about the beach at Bombay, Uncle. Juhu beach.

(But NASSER *is in a bad mood.* TANIA *comes into the room. She is wearing salwar kamiz for the first time in the film. And she looks stunning. She has dressed up for* OMAR).

(Playing to TANIA) Or the house in Lahore. When Auntie Nina put the garden hose in the window of my father's bedroom because he wouldn't get up. And Papa's bed started to float.

*(*TANIA *stands behind* OMAR *and touches him gently on the shoulder. She is laughing at the story.)*

TANIA: Papa.

(But he ignores her.)

OMAR: *(To* TANIA) You look beautiful.

(She squeezes his arm.)

NASSER: *(Sitting up suddenly)* What about my damn laundrette? Damn these stories about a place you've never been. What are you doing, boy!

OMAR: What am I doing?

65.   INT. LAUNDRETTE. DAY.

OMAR *and* JOHNNY *in the laundrette.* JOHNNY, *with an axe, is smashing one of the broken-down benches off the wall while* OMAR *stands there surveying the laundrette, pencil and pad in hand. Splinters, bits of wood fly about as* JOHNNY, *athletically and enthusiastically singing at the top of his voice, demolishes existing structures.*

OMAR: *(Voice over)* It'll be going into profit any day now. Partly because I've hired a bloke of outstanding competence and strength of body and mind to look after it with me.

66.   INT. NASSER'S ROOM. EVENING.

NASSER: *(To young* DAUGHTER) Jasmine, fiddle with my toes. *(To* OMAR) What bloke?

67.   INT. LAUNDRETTE. DAY.

JOHNNY *is up a ladder vigorously painting a wall and singing loudly. The washing machines are covered with white sheets. Pots and paints and brushes lie about.*

OMAR *watches* JOHNNY.

OMAR: *(Voice over)* He's called Johnny.

NASSER: *(Voice over)* How will you pay him?

68.   INT. NASSER'S ROOM. EVENING.

SALIM *and* ZAKI *come into the room.* SALIM *carries a bottle of whisky.* ZAKI *looks nervously at* TANIA *who flutters her eyelashes at him.*

SALIM *and* ZAKI *shake hands with* NASSER *and sit down in chairs round the bed.*

ZAKI: *(To* NASSER*)* How are you, you old bastard?

NASSER: *(Pointing at drinks)* Tania.

(TANIA *fixes drinks for everyone.* SALIM *looks suspiciously at* OMAR *through this. But* OMAR *coolly ignores him.)*

Zaki, how's things now then?

ZAKI: Oh good, good, everything. But . . .

(*He begins to explain about his declining laundrette business and how bad his heart is, in Urdu.* NASSER *waves at* OMAR.)

NASSER: Speak in English, Zaki, so this boy can understand.

ZAKI: He doesn't understand his own language?

NASSER: *(With affectionate mock anger)* Not only that. I've given him that pain-in-the-arse laundrette to run.

SALIM: I know.

NASSER: But this is the point. He's hired someone else to do the work!

ZAKI: Typically English, if I can say that.

SALIM: *(Harshly)* Don't fuck your uncle's business, you little fool.

TANIA: I don't think you should talk to him like that, Uncle.

SALIM: Why, what is he, royalty?

(SALIM AND NASSER *exchange amused looks.*)

ZAKI: *(To* NASSER*)* She is a hot girl.

TANIA: I don't like it.

OMAR: *(To* SALIM*)* In my small opinion, much good can come of
fucking.

(TANIA *laughs.* ZAKI *is shocked.* SALIM *stares at* OMAR.)

NASSER: *(To* OMAR*)* Your mouth is getting very big lately.

OMAR: Well. *(And he gets up quickly, to walk out.)*

NASSER: All right, all right, let's all take it easy.

SALIM: Who is it sitting in the drive? It's bothering me.

(*To* TANIA.) Some friend of yours?

(She shakes her head.)

NASSER: Zaki, go and check it for me please.

OMAR: It's only Johnny. My friend. He works for me.

NASSER: No one works without my permission.

(To TANIA). Bring him here now.

(She goes. OMAR *gets up and follows her.)*

69.   EXT. NASSER'S FRONT DRIVE. EVENING.

JOHNNY *is standing by the car, music coming from the car radio.*
TANIA *and* OMAR *walk over to him.* TANIA *takes* OMAR's *arm.*

TANIA: I know why you put up with them. Because there's so
much you want. You're greedy like my father. *(Nodding towards* JOHNNY.*)* Why did you leave him out here?

OMAR: He's lower class. He won't come in without being asked.
Unless he's doing a burglary.

(They get to JOHNNY, OMAR *not minding if he overhears
the last remark.)*

TANIA: Come in, Johnny. My father's waiting for you.

(She turns and walks away. OMAR *and* JOHNNY *walk towards the house.* BILQUIS *is standing in the window of the
front room, looking at them.* OMAR *smiles and waves at
her.)*

JOHNNY: How's Salim today?

OMAR: Wearing too much perfume as usual. (OMAR *stops* JOHNNY *a moment and brushes his face.*) An eyelash.

(TANIA, *waiting at the door, watches this piece of affection and wonders.*)

70. INT. NASSER'S ROOM. EVENING.

NASSER, SALIM, JOHNNY, ZAKI *and* OMAR *are laughing together at one of Nasser's stories.* JOHNNY *has been introduced and they are getting along well.* TANIA *hands* SALIM *another drink and checks that everyone else has drinks.*

NASSER: . . . So I said, in my street I am the law! You see, I make wealth, I create money.

(*There is a slight pause.* NASSER *indicates to* TANIA *that she should leave the room. She does so, irritably.* SALIM *tries to take her hand as she goes but she pulls away from him. She has gone now.*)

(*To* OMAR) You like Tania?

OMAR: Oh yes.

NASSER: I'll see what I can do.

(ZAKI *laughs and slaps* OMAR *on the knee.* OMAR *is uncomprehending.*)

To business now. I went to see the laundrette. You boys will make a beautiful job of it, I know. You need nothing more from there. (*To* JOHNNY). But in exchange I want you to do something. You look like a tough chap. I've got some bastard tenants in one of my houses I can't get rid of.

JOHNNY: No, I don't do nothing rough no more.

NASSER: I'm not looking for a mass murderer, you bloody fool.

JOHNNY: What's it involve, please?

NASSER: I tell you. Unscrewing. (*To* SALIM.) We're on your favourite subject.

SALIM: For Christ's sake!

JOHNNY: What is unscrewing?

ZAKI: You're getting into some family business, that's all.

SALIM: What the hell else is there for them in this country now?

NASSER: *(To* OMAR*)* Send him to my garage. And call Tania to bring us champagne. And we'll drink to Thatcher and your beautiful laundrette.

JOHNNY: Do they go together?

NASSER: Like dall and chipatis!

71.   EXT. OUTSIDE THE LAUNDRETTE. NIGHT.

JOHNNY *and* OMAR *have parked their car by the laundrette. They lean against the car, close together, talking.*

JOHNNY: The timber's coming tomorrow morning. I'm getting it cheap.

(They walk slowly towards the laundrette.)

OMAR: I've had a vision. Of how this place could be. Why do people hate laundrettes? Because they're like toilets. This could be a Ritz among laundrettes.

JOHNNY: A laundrette as big as the Ritz. Yeah.

(JOHNNY *puts his arm round* OMAR. OMAR *turns to him and they kiss on the mouth. They kiss passionately and hold each other.*

On the other side of the laundrette, GENGHIS, MOOSE *and three other* LADS *are kicking the laundrette dustbins across the pavement. They can't see* OMAR *and* JOHNNY.

JOHNNY *detaches himself from* OMAR *and walks round the laundrette to the* LADS. OMAR *moves into a position from where he can see, but doesn't approach the* LADS.

MOOSE *sees* JOHNNY *and motions to* GENGHIS *who is engrossed with the kicking.* GENGHIS *faces* JOHNNY. JOHNNY *controls himself. He straightens the dustbin and starts banging the rubbish back in. He gestures to a couple of the* LADS *to help him. They move back, away from him.*

JOHNNY *grabs* MOOSE *by the hair and stuffs his head*

into a dustbin. MOOSE, *suitably disciplined, then helps*
JOHNNY *stuff the rubbish back in the bin, looking guiltily
at* GENGHIS.)

GENGHIS: Why are you working for them? For these people? You
were with us once. For England.

JOHNNY: It's work. I want to work. I'm fed up of hanging about.

GENGHIS: I'm angry. I don't like to see one of our men grovelling
to Pakis. They came here to work for us. That's why we
brought them over. OK?

(And GENGHIS *moves away. As he does so, he sees* OMAR.
The others see him at the same time. MOOSE *takes out a
knife.* GENGHIS *indicates for him to keep back. He wants
to concentrate on* JOHNNY.)

Don't cut yourself off from your own people. Because there's
no one else who really wants you. Everyone has to belong.

72.   EXT. SOUTH LONDON STREET. NIGHT.

*They are in a street of desolate semi-detached houses in bad condition,
ready for demolition.* JOHNNY *kisses* OMAR *and opens the car door.*

JOHNNY: I can't ask you in. And you'd better get back to your
father.

OMAR: I didn't think you'd ever mention my father.

JOHNNY: He helped me, didn't he? When I was in school.

OMAR: And what did you do but hurt him?

JOHNNY: I want to forget all of those things.

*(He gets out quickly and walks across the front of the car.
He turns the corner of the street.* OMAR *gets out of the car
and follows him.)*

73.   EXT. STREET. NIGHT.

OMAR *follows* JOHNNY, *making sure he isn't seen.*

JOHNNY *turns into a boarded-up derelict house.* OMAR *watches him
go round the side of the house and climb in through a broken door.*
OMAR *turns away.*

74.   INT. PAPA'S FLAT. NIGHT.

PAPA *is asleep in the room, dead drunk and snoring.* OMAR *has come in. He stands by Papa's bed and strokes his head.*

He picks up an almost empty bottle of vodka and drinks from it, finishing it. He goes to the balcony door with it.

75.   EXT. BALCONY. NIGHT.

OMAR *stands on the balcony, looking over the silent railway line. Then, suddenly, he shouts joyfully into the distance. And throws the empty bottle as far as he can.*

76.   EXT. OUTSIDE THE LAUNDRETTE. DAY.

OMAR *and* JOHNNY *are working hard and with great concentration, painting the outside of the laundrette, the doors, etc. Although it's not finished, it's beginning to reach its final state. The new windows have been installed; but the neon sign isn't yet up.*

KIDS *play football nearby. And various cynical* LOCALS *watch, a couple of* OLD MEN *who we see in the betting shop later. Also* MOOSE *and another* LAD *who are amused by all the effort. They lean against a wall opposite and drink from cans.*

Further up the street SALIM *is watching all this from his parked car.*

JOHNNY *is up a ladder. He gets down the ladder, nods goodbye to* OMAR *and puts his paint brush away.* SALIM *reverses his car.*

JOHNNY *walks away.* OMAR *looks nervously across at* MOOSE *who stares at him.*

77.   INT. GARAGE OFFICE. DAY.

NASSER *and* SALIM *in the glassed-in office of the garage.* NASSER *is going through various papers on his desk.* SALIM *watches him and is very persistent.*

SALIM: I passed by the laundrette. So you gave them money to do it up? (NASSER *shakes his head.*) Where did they get it from, I wonder?

NASSER: Government grant. (SALIM *looks dubiously at* NASSER.) Oh, Omo's like us, yaar. Doesn't he fit with us like a glove? He's pure bloody family. (*Looks knowingly at* SALIM). So, like you, God knows what he's doing for money. (NASSER *looks up and sees* JOHNNY *squashing his face against the glass of the door of the office. He starts to laugh.*)

SALIM: That other joker's a bad influence on Omo. I'm sure of it. There's some things between them I'm looking into.

(JOHNNY *comes in.*)

(*To* JOHNNY) So they let you out of prison. Too crowded, are they?

JOHNNY: Unscrew.

(SALIM *reacts.* NASSER *quickly leads* JOHNNY *out of the office, while speaking to* SALIM *through the open door.*)

NASSER: (*In Urdu*) Don't worry, I'm just putting this bastard to work.

SALIM: (*In Urdu*) The bastard, it's a job in itself.

NASSER: (*In Urdu*) I'll have my foot up his arse at all times.

SALIM: (*In Urdu*) That's exactly how they like it. And he'll steal your boot too.

(JOHNNY *looks amusedly at them both.*)

78.   INT. HOUSE. DAY.

This is one of Nasser's properties. A falling down four-storey place in South London, the rooms of which he rents out to itinerants and students.

Peeling walls, faded carpets, cat piss. JOHNNY *and* NASSER *are on the top landing of the house, standing by a door.* JOHNNY *is holding a tool kit, which he starts to unpack.*

NASSER: He's changed the lock so you can take off the whole door in case he changes it again. He's only a poet with no money.

JOHNNY: I'm not hurting nobody, OK?

79.   INT. TOP CORRIDOR OF HOUSE. DAY.

Later. NASSER *has gone.* JOHNNY *has got through the lock and the door is open. He is unscrewing the hinges and singing to himself.*

At the end of the hall a Pakistani in his fifties watches him. JOHNNY *lifts the door off the frame and leans it against the wall.*

POET: Now that door you've just taken off. Hang it back.

> *(With great grunting effort* JOHNNY *picks the door up. He tries hard to move past the* POET *with it. The* POET *shoves* JOHNNY *hard.* JOHNNY *almost balances himself again but not quite, does a kind of dance with the door before crashing over with it on top of him.*
>
> JOHNNY *struggles to his feet. The* POET *advances towards him and* JOHNNY *retreats.)*

I'm a poor man. This is my room. Let's leave it that way.

> *(And the* POET *shoves* JOHNNY *again.*
>
> JOHNNY, *not wanting to resist, falls against the wall.*
>
> *At the end of the hall, at the top of the stairs,* NASSER *appears. The* POET *turns to* NASSER *and moves towards him, abusing him in Punjabi.* NASSER *ignores him. As the* POET *goes for* NASSER, JOHNNY *grabs the* POET *from behind and twists his arm up behind him.)*

NASSER: Throw this bugger out!

> *(*JOHNNY *shoves the struggling* POET *along the corridor to the top of the stairs and then bundles him downstairs.)*

80.   INT. ROOM. DAY.

The room from which JOHNNY *removed the door. A large badly furnished bedsit with a cooker, fridge, double-bed, wardrobe, etc.*

NASSER *is giving* JOHNNY *money. Then* NASSER *opens the window and looks out down the street. The* POET *is walking away from the house.* NASSER *calls out after him in Punjabi. And he throws the poet's things out of the window. The* POET *scrabbles around down below, gathering his things.*

JOHNNY: Aren't you giving ammunition to your enemies doing this kind of . . . unscrewing? To people who say Pakis just come here to hustle other people's lives and jobs and houses.

NASSER: But we're professional businessmen. Not professional Pakistanis. There's no race question in the new enterprise culture. Do you like the room? Omar said you had nowhere to live. I won't charge.

JOHNNY: Why not?

NASSER: You can unscrew. That's confirmed beautifully. But can you unblock and can you keep this zoo here under control? Eh?

81. EXT. LAUNDRETTE. EVENING.

Music.

JOHNNY *is working on the outside of the laundrette. He's fixing up the neon sign, on his own, and having difficulty.* OMAR *stands down below, expensively dressed, not willing to assist. Across the street* MOOSE *and a couple of* LADS *are watching.*

OMAR: I wish Salim could see this.

JOHNNY: Why? He's on to us. Oh yeah, he's just biding his time. Then he'll get us.

(He indicates to MOOSE. MOOSE *comes over and helps him.*

The OLD MEN *are watching wisely as* JOHNNY *and* MOOSE *precariously sway on a board suspended across two ladders, while holding the neon sign saying 'POWDERS'.)*

OMAR: You taking the room in Nasser's place?

(A ball is kicked by the KIDS *which whistles past* JOHNNY's *ear.* MOOSE *reacts).*

Make sure you pay the rent. Otherwise you'll have to chuck yourself out of the window.

*(*GENGHIS *walks down the street towards the laundrette.* OMAR *turns and goes.*

MOOSE *goes into a panic, knowing* GENGHIS *will be furious at this act of collaboration.* JOHNNY *glances at* MOOSE.

GENGHIS *is coming. The ladders sway. And the* OLD
MEN *watch.* GENGHIS *stops.* MOOSE *looks at him.)*

82.   INT. LAUNDRETTE. DAY.
The day of the opening of the laundrette.
   *The laundrette is finished. And the place looks terrific: pot plants;
a TV on which videos are showing; a sound system; and the place
is brightly painted and clean.*
   OMAR *is splendidly dressed. He is walking round the place, drink
in hand, looking it over.*
   *Outside, local people look in curiously and press their faces
against the glass. Two old ladies are patiently waiting to be let in.
A queue of people with washing gradually forms.*
   In the open door of the back room JOHNNY *is changing into his
new clothes.*
JOHNNY: Let's open. The world's waiting.
OMAR: I've invited Nasser to the launch. And Papa's coming.
   They're not here yet. Papa hasn't been out for months. We
   can't move till he arrives.
JOHNNY: What time did they say they'd be here?
OMAR: An hour ago.
JOHNNY: They're not gonna come, then.
   (OMAR *looks hurt.* JOHNNY *indicates that* OMAR *should go
   to him. He goes to him.)*

83.   INT. BACK ROOM OF LAUNDRETTE. DAY.
*The back room has also been done up, in a bright high-tech style.
And a two-way mirror has been installed, through which they can
see into the laundrette.*
   OMAR *watches* JOHNNY, *sitting on the desk.*
JOHNNY: Shall I open the champagne then?
   (He opens the bottle.)
OMAR: Didn't I predict this? *(They look through the mirror and
   through the huge windows of the laundrette to the patient*

punters waiting outside.) This whole stinking area's on its knees begging for clean clothes. Jesus Christ.

(OMAR touches his own shoulders. JOHNNY massages him.)

JOHNNY: Let's open up.

OMAR: Not till Papa comes. Remember? He went out of his way with you. And with all my friends. *(Suddenly harsh.)* He did, didn't he!

JOHNNY: Omo. What are you on about, mate?

OMAR: About how years later he saw the same boys. And what were they doing?

JOHNNY: What?

OMAR: What were they doing on marches through Lewisham? It was bricks and bottles and Union Jacks. It was immigrants out. It was kill us. People we knew. And it was you. He saw you marching. You saw his face, watching you. Don't deny it. We were there when you went past. *(OMAR is being held by JOHNNY, in his arms.)* Papa hated himself and his job. He was afraid on the street for me. And he took it out on her. And she couldn't bear it. Oh, such failure, such emptiness. *(JOHNNY kisses OMAR then leaves him, sitting away from him slightly. OMAR touches him, asking him to hold him.)*

84.   INT. LAUNDRETTE. DAY.

NASSER *and* RACHEL *stride enthusiastically into the not yet open laundrette, carrying paper cups and a bottle of whisky. Modern music suitable for waltzing to is playing.*

NASSER: What a beautiful thing they've done with it! Isn't it? Oh, God and with music too!

RACHEL: It's like an incredible ship. I had no idea.

NASSER: He's a marvellous bloody boy, Rachel, I tell you.

RACHEL: You don't have to tell me.

NASSER: But I tell you everything five times.

RACHEL: At least.

NASSER: Am I a bad man to you then?

RACHEL: You are sometimes . . . careless.

NASSER: *(Moved)* Yes.

RACHEL: Dance with me. *(He goes to her.)* But we are learning.

NASSER: Where are those two buggers?

85.   INT. BACK ROOM OF LAUNDRETTE. DAY.

OMAR *and* JOHNNY *are holding each other.*

JOHNNY: Nothing I can say, to make it up to you. There's only things I can do to show that I am . . . with you.

(OMAR starts to unbutton JOHNNY's shirt.)

86.   INT. LAUNDRETTE. DAY.

NASSER *and* RACHEL *are waltzing across the laundrette. Outside, the old ladies are shifting about impatiently.*

NASSER: Of course, Johnny did all the physical work on this.

RACHEL: You're fond of him.

NASSER: I wish I could do something more to help the other deadbeat children like him. They hang about the road like pigeons, making a mess, doing nothing.

RACHEL: And you're tired of work.

NASSER: It's time I became a holy man.

RACHEL: A sadhu of South London.

NASSER: *(Surprised at her knowledge)* Yes. But first I must marry Omar off.

87.   INT. BACK ROOM OF LAUNDRETTE. DAY.

OMAR *and* JOHNNY *are making love vigorously, enjoying themselves thoroughly. Suddenly* OMAR *stops a moment, looks up, sees* NASSER *and* RACHEL *waltzing across the laundrette.* OMAR *jumps up.*

88.   INT. LAUNDRETTE. DAY.

NASSER *strides impatiently towards the door of the back room.*

89.   INT. BACK ROOM OF LAUNDRETTE. DAY.

OMAR *and* JOHNNY *are quickly getting dressed.* NASSER *bursts into the room.*

NASSER: What the hell are you doing? Sunbathing?

OMAR: Asleep, Uncle. We were shagged out. Where's Papa?

   (NASSER *just looks at* OMAR. RACHEL *appears at the door behind him.*)

90.   INT. LAUNDRETTE. DAY.

The laundrette is open now. The ladies and other locals are doing their washing. The machines are whirring, sheets are being folded, magazines read, music played, video games played, etc.

   SALIM *arrives with* ZAKI. *They talk as they come in.*

ZAKI: Laundrettes are impossible. I've got two laundrettes and two ulcers. Plus . . . piles!

   (GENGHIS, MOOSE *and the rest of the gang arrive.* MOOSE *goes into the laundrette, followed by* GENGHIS. GENGHIS *turns and forbids the rest of the* GANG *from entering. They wait restlessly outside.*

   JOHNNY *is talking to* RACHEL.)

RACHEL: What's your surname?

JOHNNY: Burfoot.

RACHEL: That's it. I know your mother.

   (*The* TELEPHONE CHARACTER *is on the phone, talking eagerly to his Angela.*

   Through the window, OMAR, *who is talking to* NASSER, *sees* TANIA. *She is crossing the road and carrying a bouquet of flowers.*)

OMAR: I thought Papa just might make it today, Uncle.

NASSER: He said he never visits laundrettes.

   (TANIA *comes in through the door.*)

JOHNNY: *(To* RACHEL*)* Oh good, it's Tania.

RACHEL: I've never met her. But she has a beautiful face.

(JOHNNY *leaves* RACHEL *and goes to* TANIA, *kissing her. He takes the flowers delightedly.*

   NASSER *is disturbed by the sudden unexpected appearance of his daughter, since he is with his mistress,* RACHEL.)

NASSER: *(To* OMAR*)* Who invited Tania, dammit?

   (GENGHIS *and* MOOSE *shout out as they play the video game.)*

OMAR: I did, Uncle.

   (They watch as TANIA *goes to* RACHEL *with* JOHNNY. JOHNNY *has no choice but to introduce* TANIA *and* RACHEL.)*

TANIA: *(Smiles at* RACHEL*)* At last. After so many years in my family's life.

RACHEL: Tania, I do feel I know you.

TANIA: But you don't.

NASSER: *(Watching this)* Bring Tania over here.

TANIA: *(To* RACHEL*)* I don't mind my father having a mistress.

RACHEL: Good. I am so grateful.

NASSER: *(To* OMAR*)* Then marry her. (OMAR *looks at him.)* What's wrong with her? If I say marry her then you damn well do it!

TANIA: *(To* RACHEL*)* I don't mind my father spending our money on you.

RACHEL: Why don't you mind?

NASSER: *(To* OMAR*)* Start being nice to Tania. Take the pressure off my fucking head.

TANIA: *(To* RACHEL*)* Or my father being with you instead of with our mother.

NASSER: *(To* OMAR*)* Your penis works, doesn't it?

TANIA: *(To* RACHEL*)* But I don't like women who live off men.

NASSER: *(Shoving* OMAR *forward)* Get going then!

TANIA: *(To* RACHEL*)* That's a pretty disgusting parasitical thing, isn't it?

OMAR: *(To* TANIA*)* Tania, come and look at the spin-driers. They are rather interesting.

RACHEL: But tell me, who do you live off? And you must understand, we are of different generations, and different classes. Everything is waiting for you. The only thing that has ever waited for me is your father.

(Then, with great dignity, NASSER *goes to* RACHEL.*)*

NASSER: We'd better get going. See you boys.

(He shakes hands warmly with OMAR *and* JOHNNY. *And goes out with* RACHEL, *ignoring* TANIA.*

Ouside in the street, RACHEL *and* NASSER *begin to argue bitterly. They are watched by the rest of the gang.* RACHEL *and* NASSER *finally walk away from each other, in different directions, sadly.)*

91.   INT. LAUNDRETTE. DAY.

The laundrette is full now, mostly with real punters doing their washing and enjoying being there.

GENGHIS *and* MOOSE *are still drinking.* GENGHIS *talks across the laundrette to* JOHNNY. JOHNNY *is doing a service wash, folding clothes.*

OMAR *is saying goodbye to* TANIA *at the door.*

SALIM *has hung back and is waiting for* OMAR, ZAKI *says goodbye to him and goes, tentatively past the volatile breast-baring* TANIA.

TANIA: *(To* OMAR*)* I want to leave home. I need to break away. You'll have to help me financially.

*(*OMAR *nods enthusiastically.)*

GENGHIS: *(To* JOHNNY*)* Why don't you come out with us no more?

OMAR: *(To* TANIA*)* I'm drunk.

JOHNNY: *(To* GENGHIS*)* I'm busy here full-time, Genghis.

OMAR: *(To* TANIA*)* Will you marry me, Tania?

TANIA: *(To* OMAR*)* If you can get me some money.

GENGHIS: *(To* JOHNNY*)* Don't the Paki give you time off?

MOOSE: *(To* JOHNNY*)* I bet you ain't got the guts to ask him for time off.

SALIM: *(To* JOHNNY, *indicating* OMAR*)* Omo's getting married.

> (TANIA *goes.* SALIM *goes to* OMAR. *He puts his arm round him and takes him outside.* OMAR *is reluctant to go at first, but* SALIM *is firm and strong and pulls him out.* JOHNNY *watches.)*

GENGHIS: *(To* JOHNNY*)* You out with us tonight then?

92.   EXT. STREET OUTSIDE LAUNDRETTE. DAY.

It is starting to get dark. OMAR *and* SALIM *stand beside Salim's smart car.*

   Eager and curious customers are still arriving. SALIM *nods approvingly at them.*

   Above them the huge pink flashing neon sign saying 'POWDERS'.

   Some kids are playing football in the street opposite the laundrette.

   JOHNNY *rushes to the door of the laundrette. He shouts at the kids.*

JOHNNY: You mind these windows!

> (SALIM, *being watched by* JOHNNY, *starts to lead* OMAR *up the street, away from the laundrette.)*

SALIM: *(To* OMAR*)* I'm afraid you owe me a lot of money. The beard? Remember? Eh? Good. It's all coming back. I think I'd better have that money back, don't you?

OMAR: I haven't got money like that now.

SALIM: Because it's all in the laundrette?

> (GENGHIS *and* MOOSE *have come out of the laundrette and walked up the street away from it, parallel with* OMAR *and* SALIM. GENGHIS *stares contemptuously at* SALIM *and* MOOSE *spits on the pavement.* SALIM *ignores them.)*

I'd better have a decent down payment then, of about half. (OMAR *nods.*) By the time Nasser has his annual party, say. Or I'll instruct him to get rid of the laundrette. You see, if anyone does anything wrong with me, I always destroy them. (JOHNNY *comes out of the laundrette and runs up behind* GENGHIS *and* MOOSE, *jumping on* MOOSE's *back. They turn the corner, away from* SALIM *and* OMAR. OMAR *watches them go anxiously, not understanding what* JOHNNY *could be doing with them.*)

OMAR: Took you a while to get on to us.

SALIM: Wanted to see what you'd do. How's your Papa? (OMAR *shrugs.*) So many books written and read. Politicians sought him out. Bhutto was his close friend. But we're nothing in England without money.

93.   INT. BETTING SHOP. DAY.

There are only five or six people in the betting shop, all of them men.

And the men are mostly old, in slippers and filthy suits; with bandaged legs and stained shirts and unshaven milk-bottle-white faces and National Health glasses. NASSER *looks confident and powerful beside them. He knows them. There's a good sense of camaraderie amongst them.*

When OMAR *goes into the betting shop* NASSER *is sitting on a stool, a pile of betting slips in front of him, staring at one of the newspaper pages pinned to the wall. An* OLD MAN *is sitting next to* NASSER, *giving him advice.*

OMAR *goes to* NASSER.

OMAR: (*Anxiously*) Uncle. (NASSER *ignores him.*) Uncle.

NASSER: (*Scribbling on betting slip*) Even royalty can't reach me in the afternoons.

OMAR: I've got to talk. About Salim.

NASSER: Is he squeezing your balls?

OMAR: Yes. I want your help, Uncle.

NASSER: *(Getting up)* You do it all now. It's up to you, boy.

(NASSER goes to the betting counter and hands over his betting slips. He also hands over a thick pile of money.

Over the shop PA we can hear that the race is beginning. It starts.

NASSER listens as if hypnotized, staring wildly at the others in the shop, for sympathy, clenching his fists, stamping his feet and shouting loudly as his horse, 'Elvis', is among the front runners.

OMAR has never seen NASSER like this before.)

(To horse) Come on, Elvis, my son. *(To* OMAR.*)* You'll just have to run the whole family yourself now. *(To horse.)* Go on, boy! *(To* OMAR.*)* You take control. *(To horse and others in shop.)* Yes, yes, yes, he's going to take it, the little bastard black beauty! *(To* OMAR.*)* It's all yours. Salim too. *(To horse.)* Do it, do it, do it, baby! No, no, no, no.

(NASSER is rigid with self-loathing and disappointment as 'Elvis' loses the race. The betting slip falls from his hand. And he hangs his head in despair.)

OMAR: Where's Rachel?

NASSER: You can't talk to her. She's busy pulling her hair out. If only your damn father were sober. I'd talk to him about her. He's the only one who knows anything. *(Facetious.)* I'd ask him about Salim if I were you.

(OMAR stares at NASSER in fury and disgust. He storms out of the betting shop, just as the next race—a dog race—is about to start.)

94.   INT. LAUNDRETTE. EVENING.

The laundrette is fully functional now, busy and packed with customers.

Music is playing—a soprano aria from Madame Butterfly.

Customers are reading magazines. They are talking, watching TV with the sound turned down and one white man is singing along with the Puccini which he knows word for word.

The TELEPHONE CHARACTER *is yelling into the bright new yellow phone.*

TELEPHONE CHARACTER: *(Into phone)* 'Course I'll look after it! I'll come round every other night. At least. Honest. I want children!

(OMAR *walks around the laundrette, watching over it, proud and stern. He helps people if the doors of the renovated machines are stiff.*

And he hands people baskets to move their washing about in.

Shots of people putting money into the machines.

But JOHNNY *isn't there.* OMAR *doesn't know where he is and looks outside anxiously for him. He is worried and upset about Salim's demand for money.*

Finally OMAR *goes out into the street and asks a kid if he's seen* JOHNNY.)

95.   INT. TOP HALL OF THE HOUSE JOHNNY'S MOVED INTO. NIGHT.

A party is going on in one of the rooms on this floor. The noise is tremendous and people are falling about the hall.

A PAKISTANI STUDENT, *a man in his late twenties with an intelligent face, is bent over someone who has collapsed across the doorway between room and hall.*

PAKISTANI STUDENT: *(As* OMAR *goes past)* There's only one word for your uncle. (OMAR *walks on fastidiously, ignoring them, to Johnny's door. The* STUDENT *yells.)* Collaborator with the white man!

(OMAR *knocks on Johnny's door.*)

96.   INT. JOHNNY'S ROOM. NIGHT.

OMAR *goes into Johnny's room.* JOHNNY *is lying on the bed, drinking, wearing only a pair of boxer shorts.*

OMAR *stands at the open door.*

JOHNNY *runs to the door and screams up the hall to the* PAKISTANI STUDENT.

JOHNNY: Didn't I tell you, didn't I tell you 'bout that noise last night? *(Pause.)* Well, didn't I?

(The PAKISTANI STUDENT *stares contemptuously at him. The drunks lie where they are.* JOHNNY *slams the door of his room. And* OMAR *starts on him.)*

OMAR: Where did you go? You just disappeared!

JOHNNY: Drinking, I went. With me old mates. It's not illegal.

OMAR: 'Course it is. Laundrettes are a big commitment. Why aren't you at work?

JOHNNY: It'll be closing time soon. You'll be locking the place up, and coming to bed.

OMAR: No, it never closes. And one of us has got to be there. That way we begin to make money.

JOHNNY: You're getting greedy.

OMAR: I want big money. I'm not gonna be beat down by this country. When we were at school, you and your lot kicked me all round the place. And what are you doing now? Washing my floor. That's how I like it. Now get to work. Get to work I said. Or you're fired!

*(*OMAR *grabs him and pulls him up.* JOHNNY *doesn't resist.* OMAR *throws his shirt and shoes at him.* JOHNNY *dresses.)*

JOHNNY: *(Touching him)* What about you?

OMAR: I don't wanna see you for a little while. I got some big thinking to do.

*(*JOHNNY *looks regretfully at him.)*

JOHNNY: But today, it's been the best day!

OMAR: Yeah. Almost the best day.

97.   INT. TOP HALL. NIGHT.
JOHNNY, *dressed now, walks past the party room. The* PAKISTANI
STUDENT *is now playing a tabla in the hall.* JOHNNY *ignores him,
though the* STUDENT *looks ironically at him.*

98.   INT. BOTTOM ENTRANCE HALL OF THE HOUSE. NIGHT.
JOHNNY *stops by a wall box in the hall. He pulls a bunch of keys
out of his pocket and unlocks the wall box.*
   He reaches in and pulls a switch.

99.   EXT. OUTSIDE THE HOUSE. NIGHT.
JOHNNY *walks away from the house. He has plunged the party
room into darkness. In the room people are screaming.*
   The PAKISTANI STUDENT *yells out of the window at* JOHNNY.
PAKISTANI STUDENT: You are not human! You are cold people,
   you English, the big icebergs of Europe!
   (OMAR *stands at the next window along, looking out. This
   room is lighted.*
      JOHNNY *chuckles to himself as he walks jauntily away.)*

100.   INT. LAUNDRETTE. NIGHT.
Nina Simone's smooth 'Walk On By' playing in the laundrette.
   And there are still plenty of people around.
   The TELEPHONE CHARACTER *has turned to the wall, head down,
to concentrate on his conversation.*
   A MAN *is asleep on a bench.* JOHNNY *walks past him, notices
he's asleep and suddenly pokes him. The* MAN *jumps awake.*
JOHNNY *points at the man's washing.*
   A young black COUPLE *are dancing, holding each other sleepily
as they wait for their washing.*
   A BUM *comes in through the door, slowly, with difficulty in
walking. He's wearing a large black overcoat with the collar turned
up.* JOHNNY *watches him.*
JOHNNY: Hey!

(The BUM *doesn't respond.* JOHNNY *goes to him and takes his arm, about to chuck him out. Then the* BUM *turns to* JOHNNY.*)*

PAPA: I recognize you at least. Let me sit.

*(*JOHNNY *leads* PAPA *up the laundrette.*

The TELEPHONE CHARACTER *throws down the receiver and walks out.)*

JOHNNY: *(Deferential now)* We were expecting you today.

PAPA: I've come.

JOHNNY: The invitation was for two o'clock, Mr Ali.

PAPA: *(Looking at his watch)* It's only ten past now. I thought I'd come to the wrong place. That I was suddenly in a ladies' hairdressing salon in Pinner, where one might get a pink rinse. Do you do a pink rinse, Johnny? Or are you still a fascist?

JOHNNY: You used to give me a lot of good advice, sir. When I was little.

PAPA: When you were little. What's it made of you? Are you a politician? Journalist? A trade unionist? No, you are an underpants cleaner. *(Self-mocking.)* Oh dear, the working class are such a great disappointment to me.

JOHNNY: I haven't made much of myself.

PAPA: You'd better get on and do something.

JOHNNY: Yes. Here, we can do something.

PAPA: Help me. I want my son out of this underpants cleaning condition. I want him reading in college. You tell him: you go to college. He must have knowledge. We all must, now. In order to see clearly what's being done and to whom in this country. Right?

JOHNNY: I don't know. It depends on what he wants.

PAPA: No. *(Strongly.)* You must use your influence. *(*PAPA *gets up and walks out slowly.* JOHNNY *watches him go, sadly.* PAPA *turns.)* Not a bad dump you got here.   .

101.   EXT. OUTSIDE THE LAUNDRETTE. NIGHT.
PAPA *walks away from the laundrette.*

102.   EXT. THE DRIVE OF NASSER'S HOUSE. DAY.
JOHNNY *has come by bus to Nasser's house. And* OMAR *opens the front door to him.* JOHNNY *is about to step into the house.* OMAR *takes him out into the drive.*

JOHNNY: What you make me come all this way for?

OMAR: Gotta talk.

JOHNNY: You bloody arse. *(At the side of the house a strange sight.* TANIA *is climbing a tree.* BILQUIS *is at the bottom of the tree yelling instructions to her in Urdu.* JOHNNY *and* OMAR *watch.)* What's going on?

OMAR: It's heavy, man. Bilquis is making magical potions from leaves and bird beaks and stuff. She's putting them on Rachel. *(*JOHNNY *watches* TANIA *groping for leaves in amazement.)*

JOHNNY: Is it working?

OMAR: Rachel rang me. She's got the vicar round. He's performing an exorcism right now. The furniture's shaking. Her trousers are walking by themselves.

103.   INT. NASSER'S ROOM. DAY.
OMAR *and* JOHNNY *and* NASSER *are sitting at a table in Nasser's room, playing cards.* NASSER *is sulky. He puts his cards down.*

NASSER: I'm out.
   (He gets up and goes and lies down on the bed, his arm over his face.
      OMAR *and* JOHNNY *continue playing. They put their cards down.* JOHNNY *wins. He collects the money.)*

OMAR: Salim's gotta have money. Soon. A lot of money. He threatened me. *(They get up and walk out of the room, talking in low voices.* NASSER *lies there on the bed, not listening but brooding.)* I didn't wanna tell you before. I thought I could raise the money on the profits from the laundrette. But it's impossible in the time.

104.   INT. HALL OUTSIDE NASSER'S ROOM. DAY.

They walk down the hall to the verandah.

JOHNNY: This city's chock-full of money. When I used to want money—

OMAR: You'd steal it.

JOHNNY: Yeah. Decide now if you want it to be like that again.

105.   INT. VERANDAH. DAY.

They reach the verandah. Outside, in the garden, the two younger DAUGHTERS *are playing.*

At the other end of the verandah BILQUIS *and* TANIA *are sitting on the sofa, a table in front of them.* BILQUIS *is mixing various ingredients in a big bowl—vegetables, bits of bird, leaves, some dog urine, the squeezed eyeball of a newt, half a goldfish, etc. We see her slicing the goldfish.*

At the same time she is dictating a letter to TANIA, *which* TANIA *takes down on a blue airletter.* TANIA *looks pretty fed-up.*

OMAR *and* JOHNNY *sit down and watch them.*

OMAR: She's illiterate. Tania's writing to her sister for her. Bilquis is thinking of going back, after she's hospitalized Rachel. (BILQUIS *looks up at them, her eyes dark and her face humourless.*) Nasser's embarked on a marathon sulk. He's going for the world record.

(*Pause.* JOHNNY *changes the subject back when* TANIA— *suspecting them of laughing at her—gives them a sharp look.*)

JOHNNY: We'll just have to do a job to get the money.

OMAR: I don't want you going back to all that.

JOHNNY: Just to get us through, Omo. It's for both of us. If we're going to go on. You want that, don't you?

OMAR: Yes. I want you.

(*Suddenly* NASSER *appears at the door and starts abusing* BILQUIS *in loud Urdu, telling her that the magic business is stupid, etc. But* BILQUIS *has a rougher, louder tongue. She says, among other things, in Urdu, that* NASSER *is a big fat black man who should get out of her sight for ever.*

TANIA *is very distressed by this, hands over face. Suddenly she gets up. The magic potion bowl is knocked over, the evil ingredients spilling over Bilquis' feet.* BILQUIS *screams.* JOHNNY *starts laughing.* BILQUIS *picks up the rest of the bowl and throws the remainder of the potion over* NASSER.)

106.   EXT. OUTSIDE A SMART HOUSE. NIGHT.
A semi-detached house. A hedge around the front of the house.
   JOHNNY *is forcing the front window. He knows what he's doing. He climbs in. He indicates to* OMAR *that he should follow. And* OMAR *follows.*

107.   INT. FRONT ROOM OF THE HOUSE. NIGHT.
They're removing the video and TV and going out the front door with them. Their car is parked outside.
   Suddenly a tiny KID *of about eight is standing behind them at the bottom of the stairs. He is an* INDIAN KID. OMAR *looks at him, the* KID *opens his mouth to yell.* OMAR *grabs the* KID *and slams his hand over his mouth. While he holds the* KID, JOHNNY *goes out with the stereo. Then the compact disc player.*
   OMAR *leaves the stunned* KID *and makes a run for it.*

108.   INT. BACK ROOM OF LAUNDRETTE. NIGHT.
There are televisions, stereos, radios, videos, etc. stacked up in the back room. OMAR *stands there looking at them.*
   JOHNNY *comes in struggling with a video.* OMAR *smiles at him.* JOHNNY *doesn't respond.*

109. INT. HALL. DAY.

The top hall of the house JOHNNY *lives in.* JOHNNY, *wearing jeans and T-shirt, barefoot, only recently having woken up, is banging on the door of the Pakistani student's room.*

OMAR *is standing beside him, smartly dressed and carrying a briefcase. He's spent the night with* JOHNNY. *And now he's going to the laundrette.*

JOHNNY: *(To door)* Rent day! Rent up, man!

*(*OMAR *watches him.* JOHNNY *looks unhappy.)*

OMAR: I said it would bring you down, stealing again. It's no good for you. You need a brand new life.

(The PAKISTANI STUDENT *opens the door.* OMAR *moves away. To* JOHNNY.*)* Party tonight. Then we'll be in the clear.

PAKISTANI STUDENT: Unblock the toilet, yes, Johnny?

JOHNNY: *(Looking into the room)* Tonight. You're not doing nothing political in there, are you, man? I've gotta take a look.

*(*OMAR, *laughing, moves away.* JOHNNY *shoves the door hard and the* PAKISTANI STUDENT *relents.)*

110. INT. PAKISTANI STUDENT'S ROOM. DAY.

JOHNNY *goes into the room. A young* PAKISTANI WOMAN *is sitting on the bed with a* CHILD.

A younger PAKISTANI BOY *of about fourteen is standing behind her. And across the room a* PAKISTANI GIRL *of seventeen.*

PAKISTANI STUDENT: My family, escaping persecution.

*(*JOHNNY *looks at him).* Are you a good man or are you a bad man?

111. EXT. COUNTRY LANE AND DRIVE OF NASSER'S HOUSE. EVENING.

OMAR *and* JOHNNY *are sitting in the back of a mini-cab.*

JOHNNY *is as dressed up as is* OMAR, *but in fashionable street clothes rather than an expensive dark suit.* JOHNNY *will be out of keeping sartorially with the rest of the party.*

The young ASIAN DRIVER *moves the car towards Nasser's house.*

The house is a blaze of light and noise. And the drive is full of cars and PAKISTANIS *and* INDIANS *getting noisily out of them. Looking at the house, the lights, the extravagance,* JOHNNY *laughs sarcastically.*

OMAR, *paying the driver, looks irritably at* JOHNNY.

JOHNNY: What does he reckon he is, your uncle? Some kinda big Gatsby geezer? (OMAR *gives him a cutting look.*) Maybe this just isn't my world. You're right. Still getting married?

(They both get out of the car. OMAR *walks towards the house.* JOHNNY *stands there a moment, not wanting to face it all.*

When OMAR *has almost reached the front door and* TANIA *has come out to hug him,* JOHNNY *moves towards the house.*

TANIA *hugs* JOHNNY.

OMAR *looks into the house and sees* SALIM *and* CHERRY *in the crowd in the front room. He waves at* SALIM *but* SALIM *ignores him.* CHERRY *is starting to look pregnant.*

BILQUIS *is standing at the end of the hall. She greets* OMAR *in Urdu. And he replies in rudimentary Urdu.*

JOHNNY *feels rather odd since he's the only white person in sight.)*

112.   INT/EXT. THE VERANDAH, PATIO AND GARDEN. EVENING.
The house, patio and garden are full of well-off, well-dressed, well-pissed, middle-class PAKISTANIS *and* INDIANS.

The American, DICK, *and the* ENGLISHMAN *are talking together.*

DICK: England needs more young men like Omar and Johnny, from what I can see.

ENGLISHMAN: (*Slightly camp*) The more boys like that the better.

(We see OMAR *on the verandah talking confidently to various people. Occasionally he glances at* SALIM *who is engrossed in conversation with* ZAKI *and Zaki's* WIFE. *A snatch of their conversation.)*

SALIM: Now Cherry is pregnant I will be buying a house. I am going to have many children . . .

*(*BILQUIS *is there. She is alone but there is a fierceness and cheerfulness about her that we haven't noticed before.*

JOHNNY *doesn't know who to talk to.* CHERRY *goes up to him.)*

CHERRY: Please, can you take charge of the music for us?

*(*JOHNNY *looks at her. Then he shakes his head.*

NASSER, *in drunken, ebullient mood, takes* OMAR *across the room to* ZAKI, *who is with* SALIM.*)*

ZAKI: *(Shaking hands with* OMAR*)* Omar, my boy.

*(*SALIM *moves away.)*

NASSER: *(To* OMAR, *of* ZAKI*)* Help him. *(To* ZAKI.*)* Now tell him, please.

ZAKI: Oh God, Omo, I've got these two damn laundrettes in your area. I need big advice on them.

(We hear Omar's voice as we look at the party.)

OMAR: I won't advise you. If the laundrettes are a trouble to you I'll pay you rent for them plus a percentage of the profits.

NASSER: How about it, Zaki? He'll run them with Johnny.

(We see TANIA *talking to two interested* PAKISTANI MEN *in their middle twenties who see her as marriageable and laugh at everything she says. But* TANIA *is looking at* JOHNNY *who is on his own, drinking. He also dances, bending his knees and doing an inconspicuous handjive. He smiles at* TANIA.

TANIA *goes across to* JOHNNY. *He whispers something in her ear. She leads* JOHNNY *by the hand out into the garden.*

BILQUIS *looks in fury at* NASSER, *blaming him for this. He turns away from her.*

ZAKI *is happily explaining to his wife about the deal with* OMAR.)

113.   EXT. GARDEN. EVENING.

TANIA *leads* JOHNNY *across the garden, towards the little garden house at the end. A bicycle is leaning against it. She takes off her shoes. And they hold each other and dance.*

114.   INT. THE HOUSE. EVENING.

SALIM *is on his own a moment.* OMAR *moves towards him.* SALIM *walks out and across the garden.*

115.   EXT. GARDEN. EVENING.

OMAR *follows* SALIM *across the lawn.*

OMAR: I've got it. (SALIM *turns to him.*) The instalment. It's hefty, Salim. More than you wanted.

(OMAR *fumbles for the money in his jacket pocket. At the end of the garden* JOHNNY *and* TANIA *are playing around with a bicycle.* OMAR, *shaking, drops some of the money.* SALIM *raises his hand in smiling rejection.*)

SALIM: Don't ever offer me money. It was an educational test I put on you. To make you see you did a wrong thing.

(TANIA *and* JOHNNY *are now riding the bicycle on the lawn.*) Don't in future bite the family hand when you can eat out of it. If you need money just ask me. Years ago your uncles lifted me up. And I will do the same for you.

(*Through this* OMAR *has become increasingly concerned as* TANIA, *with* JOHNNY *on the back of the bicycle, is riding at Salim's back.* OMAR *shouts out.*)

OMAR: Tania!

(*And he tries to pull* SALIM *out of the way. But* TANIA

crashes into SALIM, *knocking him flying flat on his face.*
NASSER *comes rushing down the lawn.*

TANIA *and* JOHNNY *lie laughing on their backs.*

SALIM *gets up quickly, furiously, and goes to punch*
JOHNNY. OMAR *and* NASSER *grab an arm of* SALIM's *each.*
JOHNNY *laughs in* SALIM's *face.)*

(To SALIM*)* All right, all right, he's no one.

*(*SALIM *calms down quickly and just raises a warning finger
at* JOHNNY. *The confrontation is mainly diverted by* NASSER
going for TANIA.*)*

NASSER: *(To* TANIA*)* You little bitch! *(He grabs at* TANIA *to hit
her.* JOHNNY *pulls her away.)* What the hell d'you think you're
doing?

SALIM: *(To* NASSER*)* Can't you control your bloody people?
(And he abuses NASSER *in Urdu.* NASSER *curses and scowls
in English.)* Why should you be able to? You've gambled
most of your money down the toilet! *(*SALIM *turns and
walks away.)*

TANIA: *(Pointing after him)* That smooth suppository owns us!
Everything! Our education, your businesses, Rachel's stock-
ings. It's his!

NASSER: *(To* OMAR*)* Aren't you two getting married?

OMAR: Yes, yes, any day now.

TANIA: I'd rather drink my own urine.

OMAR: I hear it can be quite tasty, with a slice of lemon.

NASSER: Get out of my sight, Tania!

TANIA: I'm going further than that.

*(*NASSER *turns and storms away. As he walks up the lawn
we see that* BILQUIS *has been standing a quarter of the way
down the lawn, witnessing all this.*

NASSER *stops for a moment beside her, not looking at her.
He walks on.)*

OMAR: *(To* JOHNNY*)* Let's get out of here.

TANIA: *(To* JOHNNY*)* Take me.

(OMAR *shakes his head and takes* JOHNNY's *hand.)*

OMAR: Salim'll give us a lift.

JOHNNY: What?

OMAR: I need him for something I've got in mind.

116.   INT. SALIM'S CAR. NIGHT.

SALIM *is driving* JOHNNY *and* OMAR *along a country lane, fast, away from Nasser's house.*

JOHNNY *is sitting in the back, looking out of the window.*

OMAR *is sarcastic for* JOHNNY's *unheeding benefit and undetected by the humourless* SALIM.

OMAR: Well, thanks, Salim, you know. For saving the laundrette and everything. And for giving us a lift. Our car's bust.

SALIM: *(Accelerating)* Got to get to a little liaison. *(To* JOHNNY.*)* He doesn't have to thank me. Eh, Johnny? What's your problem with me, Johnny?

JOHNNY: *(Eventually, and tough)* Salim, we know what you sell, man. Know the kids you sell it to. It's shit, man. Shit.

SALIM: Haven't you noticed? People are shit. I give them what they want. I don't criticize. I supply. The laws of business apply.

JOHNNY: Christ, what a view of people. Eh, Omo? You think that's a filthy shit thing, don't you, Omo?

(*Suddenly* SALIM *steps on the brakes. They skid to a stop on the edge of a steep drop away from the road.*)

SALIM: Get out!

(JOHNNY *opens the car door. He looks down the steep hill and across the windy Kent landscape. He leans back in his seat, closing the car door.*)

JOHNNY: I don't like the country. The snakes make me nervous.

(SALIM *laughs and drives off.*)

117. INT. SALIM'S CAR. NIGHT.

They've reached South London, near the laundrette.

OMAR's *been explaining to* SALIM *about his new scheme.*

OMAR: . . . So I was talking to Zaki about it. I want to take over his two laundrettes. He's got no idea.

SALIM: None.

OMAR: Do them up. With this money. *(He pats his pocket.)*

SALIM: Yeah. Is it enough?

OMAR: I thought maybe you could come in with me . . . financially.

SALIM: Yeah. I'm looking for some straight outlets. *(Pause.)* You're a smart bastard. *(Suddenly.)* Hey, hey, hey . . . *(And he sees, in the semi-darkness near the football ground, a group of roaming laughing* LADS. *They are walking into a narrow lane.* SALIM *slows the car down and enters the street behind them, following them now, watching them and explaining. To* JOHNNY.) These people. What a waste of life. They're filthy and ignorant. They're just nothing. But they abuse people. *(To* OMAR.) Our people. *(To* JOHNNY.) All over England, Asians, as you call us, are beaten, burnt to death. Always we are intimidated. What these scum need—*(and he slams the car into gear and starts to drive forward fast)*—is a taste of their own piss.

(He accelerates fast, and mounting the pavement, drives at the LADS *ahead of him.* MOOSE *turns and sees the car. They scatter and run. Another of the* LADS *is* GENGHIS. *Some of the others we will recognize as mates of his.*

GENGHIS *gets in close against a wall, picking up a lump of wood to smash through the car windscreen. But he doesn't have time to fling it and drops it as* SALIM *drives at him, turning away at the last minute.* GENGHIS *sees clearly who is in the front of the car.*

As SALIM *turns the car away from* GENGHIS, MOOSE *is suddenly standing stranded in the centre of the road.* SALIM *can't avoid him.* MOOSE *jumps aside but* SALIM *drives over his foot.* MOOSE *screams.*

SALIM *drives on.*)

118.   INT. JOHNNY'S ROOM. NIGHT.
OMAR *and* JOHNNY *have made love.* OMAR *appears to be asleep, lying across the bed.*

JOHNNY *gets up, walks across the room and picks up a bottle of whisky. He drinks.*

119.   INT. ANOTHER LAUNDRETTE. DAY.
This is a much smaller and less splendid laundrette than Omar's.

OMAR *is looking it over 'expertly'.* ZAKI *is awaiting Omar's verdict. This is Zaki's problem laundrette.*

SALIM *is also there, striding moodily about.*
OMAR: I think I can do something with this. Me and my partner.
ZAKI: Take it. I trust you and your family.
OMAR: Salim?
SALIM: I'd happily put money into it.
OMAR: All right. Wait a minute.

120.   EXT. OUTSIDE THIS SMALLER LAUNDRETTE. DAY.
JOHNNY *is morosely sitting in the car, examining himself in the car mirror. In the mirror, at the far end of the street, he sees a figure on crutches watching them. This is* MOOSE.

OMAR *comes out of the laundrette and talks to* JOHNNY *through the car window.*
OMAR: You wanna look at this place? Think we could do something with it?
JOHNNY: Can't tell without seeing it.
OMAR: Come on, then.
JOHNNY: Not if that scum Salim's there.

(OMAR *turns away angrily and walks back into the laundrette.*)

121.   EXT. OUTSIDE OMAR AND JOHNNY'S BEAUTIFUL LAUN-
DRETTE. DAY.

GENGHIS *is standing on the roof of the laundrette, a plank of wood
studded with nails in his hand.*

Across the street, in the alley and behind cars, the LADS *are
waiting and watching the laundrette.* MOOSE *is with them, hobbling.
Inside,* JOHNNY *washes the floor.* TANIA, *not seeing* GENGHIS *or
the* LADS, *walks down the street towards the laundrette.*

122.   INT. LAUNDRETTE. DAY.

JOHNNY *is washing the floor of the laundrette. A white* MAN *opens
a washing machine and starts picking prawns out of it, putting them
in a black plastic bag.* JOHNNY *watches in amazement.*

TANIA *comes into the laundrette to say goodbye to* JOHNNY. *She
is carrying a bag.*

TANIA: *(Excited)* I'm going.

JOHNNY: Where?

TANIA: London. Away.

> *(Some* KIDS *are playing football outside, dangerously near
> the laundrette windows.* JOHNNY *goes to the window and
> bangs on it. He spots a* LAD *and* MOOSE *watching the
> laundrette from across the street.* JOHNNY *waves at them.
> They ignore him.)*

> *(To him)* I'm going, to live my life. You can come.

JOHNNY: No good jobs like this in London.

TANIA: Omo just runs you around everywhere like a servant.

JOHNNY: Well. I'll stay here with my friend and fight it out.

TANIA: My family, Salim and all, they'll swallow you up like a
little kebab.

JOHNNY: I couldn't just leave him now. Don't ask me to. You
ever touched him? *(She shakes her head.)* I wouldn't trust
him, though.

TANIA: Better go. *(She kisses him and turns and goes. He stands at the door and watches her go.)*

123. EXT. OUTSIDE THE LAUNDRETTE. DAY.

From the roof GENGHIS *watches* TANIA *walk away from the laundrette.*

At the end of the street, Salim's car turns the corner. A LAD *standing on the corner signals to* GENGHIS. GENGHIS *nods at the* LADS *in the alley opposite and holds his piece of wood ready.*

124. INT. CLUB/BAR. DAY.

NASSER *and* RACHEL *are sitting at a table in the club/bar. They have been having an intense, terrible, sad conversation. Now they are staring at each other.* NASSER *holds her hand. She withdraws her hand.*

TARIQ *comes over to the table with two drinks. He puts them down. He wants to talk to* NASSER. NASSER *touches his arm, without looking up. And* TARIQ *goes.*

RACHEL: So . . . so . . . so that's it.

NASSER: Why? Why d'you have to leave me now? *(She shrugs.)* After all these days.

RACHEL: Years.

NASSER: Why say you're taking from my family?

RACHEL: Their love and money. Yes, apparently I am.

NASSER: No.

RACHEL: And it's not possible to enjoy being so hated.

NASSER: It'll stop.

RACHEL: Her work. *(She pulls up her jumper to reveal her blotched, marked stomach. If possible we should suspect for a moment that she is pregnant.)* And I am being cruel to her. It is impossible.

NASSER: Let me kiss you. *(She gets up.)* Oh, Christ. *(She turns to go.)* Oh, love. Don't go. Don't, Rachel. Don't go.

125.   EXT. OUTSIDE LAUNDRETTE. DAY.

SALIM *is sitting in his car outside the laundrette.* GENGHIS *stands above him on the roof, watching. Across the street the* LADS *wait in the alley, alert.*

  SALIM *gets out of his car.*

126.   EXT. OUTSIDE ANWAR'S CLUB. DAY.

RACHEL *walks away from the club.* NASSER *stands at the door and watches her go.*

127.   EXT. OUTSIDE PAPA'S HOUSE. DAY.

NASSER *gets out of his car and walks towards Papa's house. The door is broken and he pushes it, going into the hall, to the bottom of the stairs.*

128.   EXT. OUTSIDE THE LAUNDRETTE. DAY.

SALIM *walks into the laundrette.*

129.   INT. PAPA'S HOUSE. DAY.

NASSER *sadly climbs the filthy stairs of the house in which Papa's flat is.*

130.   INT. LAUNDRETTE. DAY.

SALIM *has come into the busy laundrette.* JOHNNY *is working.*

SALIM: I want to talk to Omo about business.

JOHNNY: I dunno where he is.

SALIM: Is it worth waiting?

JOHNNY: In my experience it's always worth waiting for Omo.

   (The TELEPHONE CHARACTER *is yelling into the receiver.)*

TELEPHONE CHARACTER: No, no, I promise I'll look after it. I want a child, don't I? Right, I'm coming round now! *(He slams the receiver down. Then he starts to dial again.)*

131.   INT. PAPA'S HOUSE. DAY.

NASSER *has reached the top of the stairs and the door to Papa's flat. He opens the door with his key. He walks along the hall to Papa's room. He stops at the open door to Papa's room.* PAPA *is lying in bed completely still.* NASSER *looks at him, worried.*

132.   EXT. OUTSIDE THE LAUNDRETTE. DAY.
The LADS *are waiting in the alley opposite.* GENGHIS *gives them a signal from the roof.*

  The LADS *run across the street and start to smash up Salim's car with big sticks, laying into the headlights, the windscreen, the roof, etc.*

133.   INT. LAUNDRETTE. DAY.
We are looking at the TELEPHONE CHARACTER. *He is holding the receiver in one hand. His other hand over his mouth.* SALIM *sees him and then turns to see, out of the laundrette window, his car being demolished.*

134.   INT. PAPA'S ROOM. DAY.
NASSER *walks into Papa's room.* PAPA *hears him and looks up.* PAPA *struggles to get to the edge of the bed, and thrusts himself into the air.*

  NASSER *goes towards him and they embrace warmly, fervently. Then* NASSER *sits down on the bed next to his brother.*

135.   EXT. OUTSIDE THE LAUNDRETTE. DAY.
SALIM *runs out of the laundrette towards his car. He grabs one of the* LADS *and smashes the* LAD's *head on the side of the car.*

  GENGHIS *is standing above them, on the edge of the roof.*
GENGHIS: *(Yells)* Hey! Paki! Hey! Paki!

136.   INT. PAPA'S ROOM. DAY.
PAPA *and* NASSER *sit side by side on the bed.*
PAPA: This damn country has done us in. That's why I am like this. We should be there. Home.
NASSER: But that country has been sodomized by religion. It is

beginning to interfere with the making of money. Compared with everywhere, it is a little heaven here.

137.   EXT. OUTSIDE THE LAUNDRETTE. DAY.

SALIM *looks up at* GENGHIS *standing on the edge of the roof. Suddenly* GENGHIS *jumps down, on top of* SALIM, *pulling* SALIM *to the ground with him.*

GENGHIS *quickly gets to his feet. And as* SALIM *gets up,* GENGHIS *hits him across the face with the studded piece of wood, tearing* SALIM's *face.*

JOHNNY *is watching from inside the laundrette.*

138.   INT. PAPA'S ROOM. DAY.

PAPA *and* NASSER *are sitting on the bed.*

PAPA: Why are you unhappy?

NASSER: Rachel has left me. I don't know what I'm going to do.
   (*He gets up and goes to the door of the balcony.*)

139.   EXT. OUTSIDE THE LAUNDRETTE. DAY.

SALIM, *streaming blood, rushes at* GENGHIS. GENGHIS *smashes him in the stomach with the piece of wood.*

140.   EXT. SOUTH LONDON STREET. DAY.

OMAR *and* ZAKI *are walking along a South London street, away from Zaki's small laundrette.*

   Across the street is the club/bar. TARIQ *is just coming out. He waves at* OMAR.

ZAKI: So you're planning an armada of laundrettes?

OMAR: What do you think of the dry-cleaners?

ZAKI: They are the past. But then they are the present also. Mostly they are the past. But they are going to be the future too, don't you think?

141.   EXT. OUTSIDE THE LAUNDRETTE. DAY.

SALIM *is on the ground.* MOOSE *goes to him and whacks him with his crutch.* SALIM *lies still.* GENGHIS *kicks* SALIM *in the back. He is about to kick him again.*

JOHNNY *is standing at the door of the laundrette. He moves towards* GENGHIS.

JOHNNY: He'll die.

> (GENGHIS *kicks* SALIM *again.* JOHNNY *loses his temper, rushes at* GENGHIS *and pushes him up against the car.*)
> I said: leave it out!
> (*One of the* LADS *moves towards* JOHNNY. GENGHIS *shakes his head at the* LAD. SALIM *starts to pull himself up off the floor.* JOHNNY *holds* GENGHIS *like a lover. To* SALIM.)
> Get out of here!
> (GENGHIS *punches* JOHNNY *in the stomach.* GENGHIS *and* JOHNNY *start to fight.* GENGHIS *is strong but* JOHNNY *is quick.* JOHNNY *tries twice to stop the fight, pulling away from* GENGHIS.)
> All right, let's leave it out now, eh?
> (SALIM *crawls away.* GENGHIS *hits* JOHNNY *very hard and* JOHNNY *goes down.*)

142.   EXT. STREET. DAY.

ZAKI *and* OMAR *turn the corner, into the street where the fight is taking place.* ZAKI *sees* SALIM *staggering up the other side of the street.* ZAKI *goes to him.*

OMAR *runs towards the fight.* JOHNNY *is being badly beaten now. A* LAD *grabs* OMAR. OMAR *struggles.*

Suddenly the sound of police sirens. The fight scatters. As it does, GENGHIS *throws his lump of wood through the laundrette window, showering glass over the punters gathered round the window.*

OMAR *goes to* JOHNNY, *who is barely conscious.*

143.   EXT. BALCONY OF PAPA'S FLAT. DAY.

NASSER *is standing leaning over the balcony, looking across the
railway track.* PAPA *comes through the balcony door and stands
behind him, in his pyjamas.*

NASSER: You still look after me, eh? But I'm finished.

PAPA: Only Omo matters.

NASSER: I'll make sure he's fixed up with a good business future.

PAPA: And marriage?

NASSER: I'm working on that.

PAPA: Tania is a possibility?

    (NASSER *nods confidently, perhaps over-confidently.*)

144.   INT. BACK ROOM OF LAUNDRETTE. DAY.

OMAR *is bathing* JOHNNY'*s badly bashed up face at the sink in the
back room of the laundrette.*

OMAR: All right?

JOHNNY: What d'you mean all right? How can I be all right? I'm
    in the state I'm in. *(Pause.)* I'll be handsome. But where
    exactly am I?

OMAR: Where you should be. With me.

JOHNNY: No. Where does all this leave me?

OMAR: Are you crying?

JOHNNY: Where does it? Kiss me then.

OMAR: Don't cry. Your hand hurts too. That's why.

JOHNNY: Hey.

OMAR: What?

JOHNNY: I better go. I think I had, yeah.

OMAR: You were always going, at school. Always running about,
    you. Your hand is bad. I couldn't pin you down then.

JOHNNY: And now I'm going again. Give me my hand back.

OMAR: You're dirty. You're beautiful.

JOHNNY: I'm serious. Don't keep touching me.

OMAR: I'm going to give you a wash.

JOHNNY: You don't listen to anything.

OMAR: I'm filling this sink.

JOHNNY: Don't.

OMAR: Get over here! (OMAR *fills the sink.* JOHNNY *turns and goes out of the room.*) Johnny.

(*We follow* JOHNNY *out through the laundrette.*)

145. EXT. THE BALCONY. DAY.

PAPA *turns away from* NASSER.

A train is approaching, rushing towards NASSER. *Suddenly it is passing him and for a moment, if this is technically possible, he sees* TANIA *sitting reading in the train, her bag beside her. He cries out, but he is drowned out by the train.*

If it is not possible for him to see her, then we go into the train with her and perhaps from her POV in the train look at the balcony, the two figures, at the back view of the flat passing by.

146. INT. LAUNDRETTE. DAY.

JOHNNY *has got to the door of the laundrette.* OMAR *has rushed to the door of the back room.*

The shattered glass from the window is still all over the floor. A cold wind blows through the half-lit laundrette.

JOHNNY *stops at the door of the laundrette. He turns towards* OMAR.

147. INT. BACK ROOM OF LAUNDRETTE. DAY.

As the film finishes, as the credits roll, OMAR *and* JOHNNY *are washing and splashing each other in the sink in the back room of the laundrette, both stripped to the waist. Music over this.*

END

About
My Beautiful
Laundrette

I wrote the script of *My Beautiful Laundrette* in my uncle's house in Karachi, Pakistan, in February 1985, during the night. As I wrote, cocks crowed and the call to prayer reverberated through crackly speakers from a nearby mosque. It was impossible to sleep. One morning as I sat on the verandah having breakfast, I had a phone call from Howard Davies, a director with the Royal Shakespeare Company, with whom I'd worked twice before. He wanted to direct Brecht's *Mother Courage*, with Judi Dench in the lead role. He wanted me to adapt it.

That summer, back in England and at Howard's place in Stratford-upon-Avon, I sat in the orchard with two pads of paper in front of me: on one I rewrote *My Beautiful Laundrette* and on the other I adapted Brecht from a literal translation into language that could be spoken by RSC actors.

As *Laundrette* was the first film I'd written, and I was primarily a playwright, I wrote each scene of the film like a little scene for a play, with the action written like stage directions and with lots of dialogue. Then I'd cut most of the dialogue and add more stage directions, often set in cars, or with people running about, to keep the thing moving, since films required action.

I'd had a couple of lunches with Karin Bamborough of Channel

Four. She wanted me to write something for *Film on Four*. I was extremely keen. For me *Film on Four* had taken over from the BBC's *Play For Today* in presenting serious contemporary drama on TV to a wide audience. The work of TV writers like Alan Bennett (much of it directed by Stephen Frears), Dennis Potter, Harold Pinter, Alan Plater and David Mercer, influenced me greatly when I was young and living at home in the suburbs. On my way up to London the morning after a *Play For Today* I'd sit in the train listening to people discussing the previous night's drama and interrupt them with my own opinions.

The great advantage of TV drama was that people watched it; difficult, challenging things could be said about contemporary life. The theatre, despite the efforts of touring companies and so on, has failed to get its ideas beyond a small enthusiastic audience.

When I finished a draft of *My Beautiful Laundrette*, and *Mother Courage* had gone into rehearsal, Karin Bamborough, David Rose and I discussed directors for the film.

A couple of days later I went to see a friend, David Gothard, who was then running Riverside Studios. I often went for a walk by the river in the early evening, and then I'd sit in David's office. He always had the new books and the latest magazines; and whoever was appearing at Riverside would be around. Riverside stood for tolerance, scepticism and intelligence. The feeling there was that works of art, plays, books and so on, were important. This is a rare thing in England. For many writers, actors, dancers and artists, Riverside was what a university should be: a place to learn and talk and work and meet your contemporaries. There was no other place like it in London and David Gothard was the great encourager, getting work on and introducing people to one another.

He suggested I ask Stephen Frears to direct the film. I thought this an excellent idea, except that I admired Frears too much to have the nerve to ring him. David Gothard did this and I cycled to Stephen's house in Notting Hill, where he lived in a street known as 'director's row' because of the number of film directors living there.

He said he wanted to shoot my film in February. As it was November already I pointed out that February might be a little soon. Would there be time to prepare, to rewrite? But he had a theory: when you have a problem, he said, bring things forward; do them sooner rather than later. And anyway, February was a good month for him; he made his best films then; England looked especially unpleasant; and people worked faster in the cold.

The producers, Tim Bevan and Sarah Radclyffe, Stephen had worked with before, on promos for rock bands. So the film was set up and I started to rewrite. Stephen and I had long talks, each of us pacing up and down the same piece of carpet, in different directions.

The film started off as an epic. It was to be like *The Godfather*, opening in the past with the arrival of an immigrant family in England and showing their progress to the present. There were to be many scenes set in the 1950s; people would eat bread and dripping and get off boats a lot; there would be scenes of Johnny and Omar as children and large-scale set pieces of racist marches with scenes of mass violence.

We soon decided it was impossible to make a film of such scale. That film is still to be made. Instead I set the film in the present, though references to the past remain.

It was shot in six weeks in February and March of 1985 on a low budget and 16mm film. For this I was glad. There were no commercial pressures on us, no one had a lot of money invested in the film who could tell us what to do. And I was tired of seeing lavish films set in exotic locations; it seemed to me that anyone could make such films, providing they had an old book, a hot country, new technology and were capable of aiming the camera at an attractive landscape in the hot country in front of which stood a star in a perfectly clean costume delivering lines from the old book.

We decided the film was to have gangster and thriller elements, since the gangster film is the form that corresponds most closely to the city, with its gangs and violence. And the film was to be an amusement, despite its references to racism, unemployment and Thatcherism. Irony is the modern mode, a way of commenting on bleakness and cruelty without falling into dourness and didacticism. And ever since the first time I heard people in a theatre laugh during a play of mine, I've wanted it to happen again and again.

We found actors—Saeed Jaffrey, for whom I'd written the part; and Roshan Seth I'd seen in David Hare's play *Map Of The World*, commanding that huge stage at the National with complete authority. I skidded through the snow to see Shirley Ann Field and on arriving at her flat was so delighted by her charm and enthusiasm, and so ashamed of the smallness of her part, that there and then I added the material about the magic potions, the moving furniture and the walking trousers. It must have seemed that the rest of the film was quite peripheral and she would be playing the lead in a kind of 'Exorcist' movie with a gay Pakistani, a drug-dealer and a fluff-drying spin-drier in the background.

Soon we stood under railway bridges in Vauxhall at two in the morning in March; we knocked the back wall out of someone's flat and erected a platform outside to serve as the balcony of Papa's flat, which had so many railway lines dipping and criss-crossing beside and above it that inside it you shook like peas in maracas; in an old shop we built a laundrette of such authenticity that people came in off the street with their washing; and I stood on the set making up dialogue before the actors did it themselves, and added one or two new scenes.

When shooting was finished and we had about two-and-a-quarter hours of material strung together, we decided to have a showing for a group of 'wise ones'. They would be film directors, novelists and film writers who'd give us their opinions and thereby aid in editing the film. So I sat at the back of the small viewing cinema as they watched the film. We then cut forty-five minutes out.

The film played at the Edinburgh Film Festival and then went into the cinema.

The script printed here is the last draft before shooting. I haven't attempted to update it or cut out the scenes which were not used in the final version, since it may be of interest to people to compare script with film.

I must thank my friends Walter Donohue, David Gothard, Salman Rushdie, David Nokes and, of course, Sally Whitman, without whom.

Some Time with Stephen

Sammy and Rosie Get Laid

Some
Time with
Stephen

A DIARY

2 June 1986   I shove the first draft of *Sammy and Rosie Get Laid* through Stephen Frears's letterbox and run, not wanting him to see me. A few hours later he rings and says: 'This isn't an innocent act!' and refuses to read it. He says he's going to Seattle with Daniel Day Lewis for the weekend to attend a film festival and he'll read it on the plane.

I have many doubts about the script and in lots of ways it's rough, but I can't get any further with it at the moment. In fact, I can't even bear to look at it.

9 June 1986   Scared of ringing Frears and asking his opinion on the script, I ring Dan and ask about the Seattle trip. I also ask —and I am shaky here—if he managed to glance at the script himself, if he perhaps had a few moments in which to pass his eyes over it. He says firmly that he did read it. I ask if Frears liked it. He says Frears did like it. Finally I ring Frears and after much small talk about cricket he says: 'I know why you've rung and it's very good!' It begins then.

10 June 1986   I see the great Indian actor Shashi Kapoor on TV, on the balcony of the Indian dressing-room at the Test Match. I'd like him to play the lead in the film, the politician. I've had him in mind since Frears met him in India and said how interesting he was. We try to track him down, but by the time we get to him he's left the country.

12 JUNE 1986   Frears rings me to talk about his availability. He's not going to be around for a while, being preoccupied with *Prick Up Your Ears* and then a film he's shooting in India. I wonder if this is a subtle way of his saying he doesn't want to direct the film.

Meanwhile I send the script to Karin Bamborough at Channel 4. She and David Rose commissioned and paid for all of *My Beautiful Laundrette*. Then I ring Tim Bevan and tell him what's going on.

Bevan is a tall, hard-working man in his mid-twenties, in love with making films and doing deals. He and his partner Sarah Radclyffe are relative newcomers in films, but between them they've been involved in several recent British films: *My Beautiful Laundrette, Caravaggio, Personal Services, Elphida, Wish You Were Here* and *A World Apart*, with many more in the pipeline. Bevan has learned and developed very quickly. He's had to, moving rapidly from making pop promos to major features. His strength as a producer is his knowledge of all aspects of film-making and his ability to protect writers and directors from financial and technical problems. He's not a frustrated writer or director either. While he makes suggestions all along about the script, the direction, the actors, he ensures that everyone is working freely in their own area; his views are valuable and informed, but he never attempts to impose them.

He's keen to read the script and thinks that after the success of the *Laundrette* in the US it shouldn't be a problem raising some of the money there. But Frears won't give Bevan a script to read because Bevan's going to LA and Frears doesn't want him to try and raise money for it. Frears is still working out how best to get the film made. He doesn't want to be pushed into doing it any particular way.

It's a relief to me that other people are involved. Getting a film going is like pushing a huge rock up the side of a mountain and until now, writing the script, I've been doing this alone. Now other people can take the weight.

13 June 1986   I've known Stephen Frears since October 1984 when I sent him the first draft of *My Beautiful Laundrette*. It was made in February and March 1985 and released later that year. After its success in Britain and the US it is slowly opening around the world and Frears, Bevan, the actors and I are still promoting it in various places.

Frears is in his mid-forties and has made four feature films: *Gumshoe*, *The Hit*, *My Beautiful Laundrette* and *Prick Up Your Ears*. He's also produced and directed many films for television, where he served his apprenticeship and worked with many of the best British dramatic writers: Alan Bennett, David Hare, Stephen Poliakoff, Peter Prince, Christopher Hampton. Frears was part of the *Monty Python* generation at Cambridge, where he studied Law; many of his contemporaries went into film, TV, theatre and journalism. Later he worked at the Royal Court Theatre as an assistant to Lindsay Anderson.

Whatever Frears wears, he always looks as if he's slept in his clothes and his hair just stands straight up on the top and shoots out at the sides as if he's been electrocuted. His idea of dressing up is to put on a clean pair of plimsolls. The sartorial message is: I can't think about all that stuff, it means nothing to me, I'm a bohemian not a fashion slave. When we were shooting the *Laundrette* Daniel Day Lewis would go up to Stephen as if Stephen were a tramp, and press 20p in his hand, saying: 'Please accept this on behalf of the Salvation Army and buy yourself a cup of tea!'

I was drawn to him from the start because of his irreverence and seriousness, his directness and kindness. While he hates words like 'artist' and 'integrity', since they smack of self-regard, he is immensely skilled and talented; and though he talks a lot about how much money certain directors make, he never makes a film entirely for the money. He has great interest and respect for the young, for their music and films and political interests. As his own generation settles down into comfort and respectability, he is becoming more adventurous and disrespectful of British society, seeing it as part of his work to be sceptical, questioning, doubting and polemical.

Frear's nonconformity and singularity, his penchant for disruption and anarchy, suit and inform the area of film we inhabit, an area which has been especially exciting recently, that of low-budget films made quickly and sometimes quite roughly; films made, to a certain extent, outside the system of studios and big film companies, films that the people involved in can control themselves.

The freshness of these films has been due partly to the subject matter, the exploration of areas of British life not touched on before. Just as one of the excitements of British culture in the sixties was the discovery of the lower middle class and working class as a subject, one plus of the repressive eighties has been cultural interest in marginalized and excluded groups.

So I ring Frears and give an earful about why I think he should direct *Sammy and Rosie Get Laid*. I lay off the flattery for fear of making him extra suspicious, and get technical. I emphasize that it'll be a continuation of the work we've started with *Laundrette*—the mixture of realism and surrealism, seriousness and comedy, art and gratuitous sex.

Frears listens to all this patiently. Then he suddenly says we should make the film for television, on 16mm. I quickly say that I'm not convinced by that. He argues that the equipment is much lighter; you can make films faster. So he suggests we give it to the BBC. If they like it, he says they'll pay for it and our problems will be over. I counter by saying they've become too reactionary, terrified of ripe language and screwing, cowed by censors. If you want to show an arse on the BBC, they behave as if their entire licence fee were at stake.

All the same, he says finally, he sees it as a TV thing, done in the spirit of *Laundrette*.

I watch scenes on TV of South African police beating up protestors and wonder what the minds of the cops must be like. That's partly what I want to get at with *Sammy and Rosie*—it's my puzzling about the mind of a torturer, the character of a man capable of extreme violence and cruelty while he continues to live a life with others. Does he speak of love in the evenings?

Receive a letter from an aunt who lives in the north of England. After seeing *Laundrette* she frequently rings my father to abuse him. 'Your son is a complete bastard!' she screeches down the phone, as if it's my father's fault I write such things. 'Can't you control the little bastard!' she yells. 'Humiliating us in public! Suppose people find out I'm related to him!'

In her letter she says: 'I tried to phone you, but I believe you were in the USA boring the pants off the Americans with your pornography . . . Worst of all, the film was offensive to your father's distinguished family. Uncle was portrayed in a very bad light, drunk in bed with his brand of vodka, and uncut toenails . . . this was totally uncalled for and mischievous. It only brings to light your complete lack of loyalty, integrity and compassion . . . We didn't know you were a "poofter". We do hope you're aware of AIDS and its dangers, if not, then a medical leaflet can be sent to you. Why oh why do you have to promote the widely held view of the British that all evil stems from Pakistani immigrants? Thank goodness for top quality films like *Gandhi*.'

I think of something Thackeray wrote in *Vanity Fair*: 'If a man has committed wrong in life, I don't know any moralist more anxious to point his errors out to the world than his own relations.'

I decide to name the Asian lesbian in *Sammy and Rosie* after her.

Earlier this year I ran into Philip Roth at a party and told him about the hostility I'd received from this aunt and other Pakistanis complaining about their portrayal in *Laundrette* and other things I'd written. Roth said the same thing happened to him after *Portnoy's Complaint*. Indeed he writes about this in *The Ghost Writer*.

In that novel, Nathan, a young Jewish novelist 'looking for admiration and praise', writes a story about an old family feud. He shows it to his father. The father is shattered by the public betrayal. 'You didn't leave anything out,' he moans. Except the achievements, the hard work, the decency. He adds sadly: 'I wonder if you fully understand just how little love there is in this world for Jewish people.'

When Nathan protests that they are in Newark, not Germany, father seeks a second opinion, that of Judge Leopold Wapter. Wapter immediately applies the literary acid test which he believes every Jewish book must endure: will the story warm the heart of Joseph Goebbels? The result is . . . positive. So why, why, screams Wapter, in a story with a Jewish background, must there be adultery, incessant fighting within a family over money and warped human behaviour in general?

What Wapter's Complaint demands is 'positive images'. It requires useful lies and cheering fictions: the writer as public relations officer, as hired liar.

Like *Laundrette*, *Sammy and Rosie* is quite a personal story, autobiographical, not in its facts, but emotionally. The woman involved (I'll call her Sarah) asked to read the script. I said no, because the character will change as the film goes through several drafts; the actress playing the part will also change it, as will Frears when he starts to work on it. It's also difficult to write accurately about real people in fiction—however much you might want to—because the demands of the idea are usually such that you have to transform the original person to fit the constraints of the story. All the same, I'm nervous about what Sarah will think of it. I know that in certain passages I've been spiteful.

On the phone Frears talks about Art Malik for the part of Sammy. He's an attractive actor, but we both wonder if he's fly enough for the role.

20 JUNE 1986 Meeting at Channel 4 with Karin Bamborough and David Rose to discuss the film. Together they've been the architects of a remarkable number of low-budget independent films which are mostly (or partly) funded by TV money for theatrical release. This series of films has ensured a revival in British film-making (they're almost the only people making films in Britain today) and has given encouragement to women and black film-makers, first-time directors and writers, working on material that wouldn't be acceptable to the mainstream commercial world.

Their success has partly been due to their initiative in approaching writers from other forms—novelists, playwrights, short-story writers and journalists—to write films. They know that usually the best screenplays are not written by people who call themselves screenwriters, but by good writers, writers who excel in other forms. After all, the 'rules' of screenwriting can be learned in an hour. But the substance of a decent screenplay, character, story, mood, pace, can only come from a cultivated imagination. Although it's virtually impossible to make a good film without a good screenplay, screenwriting itself is such a bastardized, ignoble profession (director Joseph Mankiewicz said 'the screenwriter is the highest-paid secretary in the world') that writers who wish to survive, have to avoid it, turning only to the movies as a well-paid sideline, regrettably not regarding it as a serious medium.

Karin tells me that the characters in the first draft aren't strong enough yet. I'll have to do two or three more drafts. David Rose says he regrets it all being set in London since he feels too many C4 films have been set there. Can't I set it in Birmingham, he says.

21 JUNE 1986   The contract arrives from C4 offering a commission for *Sammy and Rosie*. They're offering a pathetic amount of money.

6 JULY 1986   My agent rings me in New York to say the idea now is to form a three-way company to make the film: Frears, Bevan and Sarah Radclyffe, and I. This way we'll be able to control everything about the film.

9 JULY 1986   I speak to Frears who is about to start filming *Prick Up Your Ears*. He says he wants to prepare *Sammy and Rosie* after he's finished his Indian film. This means we'll shoot it in the autumn of 1987. It's a long time to wait: I feel let down, life goes slack once more. But it'll force me to write something else in the meantime.

9 AUGUST 1986   Lunch at '192' in Notting Hill with Bevan and Radclyffe, and Frears. Shashi arrives with his secretary after everyone else. He has on a loose brown costume, with a dark red and chocolate scarf flung over his shoulder. He is so regal and dignified, stylish and exotic, that a shiver goes through the restaurant.

I mention that though this is the first time we've met, I saw him on the balcony at the Lord's Test. He says he wore the same clothes then and had trouble getting into the pavilion, so conventional and uptight are the MCC. So he told them he's just had lunch with Mrs Thatcher and if his national dress was good enough for the Prime Minister surely it would be acceptable to the MCC.

In the charm department he has real class and yet he is genuinely modest. I feel a little embarrassed at asking him to be in this film, small and fairly sordid as it is. But Shashi says he thinks the script is better than that for *Laundrette*. He adds that he's available at our convenience.

It's a sunny day and when Shashi leaves we stroll back to Frears's house, pleased with Shashi's enthusiasm. We talk a bit about the other parts: Claire Bloom as Alice, with Miranda Richardson or Judy Davis as Rosie perhaps.

Frears talks about the part of Anna, the American photographer, saying she isn't sympathetic enough: I've parodied her. He's right about this and I lack grip on the character. The process of writing is so much one of seeking ideas in one's unconscious, whatever they are, and then later justifying them, filling them out and finding what the hell they mean, if anything. The entire script will have to be subject to this scrutiny.

14 August 1986 At last I give the script to Sarah to read. Sarah and I met at university and lived together for six years. Since she moved out, we've continued to see a lot of each other.

When Sarah reads it she is angry and upset at the same time. I've said things that she feels are true, but which I've never said to her. The worry is, she adds, that people will think she is Rosie and she'll be petrified like that for ever, with her freedom possessed by the camera. She'll no longer be in reasonable control of the way people think of her. Won't they have this crude cinema idea?

All this makes me feel guilty and sneaky; it makes me think that writers are like spies, poking into failures and weaknesses for good stories. Necessarily, because that's how they see the world, writers constantly investigate the lives of the people they are involved with. They keep private records of these private relationships. And on the surface they appear to be participating normally in life. But a few years later, it's all written down, embellished, transformed, distorted, but still a recognizable bit of someone's lived life.

Bevan has sent the script to Art Malik and Miranda Richardson, who I ran into the other day at the Royal Court. I told her about the film and she seemed interested, but it seems she'll be doing the Spielberg film *Empire of the Sun* at the same time.

I SEPTEMBER 1986   To Paris with Frears, Bevan and Daniel Day Lewis. Everywhere you go here British films are showing: *Clockwise*, *Mona Lisa*, *Room with a View*, *Laundrette*. There seem to be more cinemas per square kilometre here than anywhere else I've been. I do interviews all day through an interpreter who is the daughter-in-law of Raymond Queneau.

Dan is something of a star now, and as an actor has moved on to another plane. He's here rehearsing for the movie of *The Unbearable Lightness of Being*. Dan dresses in black and doesn't shave. He carries a black bag hooped across his body and looks like an artist, a painter, as he strides across bridges and down boulevards.

We meet to chat in the bar of the George V Hotel where Frears is being interviewed. The journalist says admiringly to Frears: 'I've met a lot of men like you, only they're all Italian.'

Frears has thought a great deal about how to do *Sammy and Rosie* and has now decided that the best thing is to make it on 35mm for theatrical release, keeping the budget as low as possible. Bevan thinks we can raise most of the money for the film in America. Frears thinks this is a good idea since it'll save Channel 4 money: they'll be able to give the money to film-makers who can't get money elsewhere.

18 December 1986 Suddenly we're going into production at the beginning of January, shooting early in March, as Frears's Indian project has been delayed. So the script has to start looking ready. Try to get the story going earlier, Frears says. And the riots: we're too familiar with them from television. Something more has to be going on than people throwing bottles at policemen. I interpret this to mean that what happens between the characters during these scenes is of primary interest.

I meet Frances Barber in the production office. She's a very experienced theatre actor and I've known her work for years, as she's risen up through the fringe to join the RSC. She's done some film work (she was in *Prick Up Your Ears*), but not yet played a major role. The feeling is that she's ready, that she's at the stage Daniel was at just before *Laundrette*. She talks well about the script and can see the problems of playing against characters with charm I've tried to give Rafi, and the bright childishness of Sammy. Rosie mustn't seem moralistic or self-righteous.

Later Frears rings me, delighted to be in the middle of an interview with a young Pakistani actor, Ayub Khan Din, who is upstairs having a pee and is being considered for the part of Sammy. Art Milak, who we discussed first but were sceptical of, has anyway complained about the scenes in bed with Anna and about the scene where Sammy wanks, snorts coke and sucks on a milkshake at the same time. In the end he says the script isn't good enough. I think he prefers easier and more glamorous kinds of roles.

Ayub had a small part in *Laundrette* which was later cut from the film. I remember him coming to the cast screening, eager to see himself in his first film, and Frears having to take him to one side to explain that, well, unfortunately, he'd had to cut his big scene. Since then Ayub has grown and developed, though he's only twenty-five and the part was written for someone older.

Now the film is going ahead and other people are starting to get involved, I can feel my responsibility for it diminishing. This is a relief to me. I've done most of the hard work I have to do. Now I can enjoy the process of the film being shot and released. Any rewriting I do from now on will be nothing compared with the isolated and unhelped strain of working out the idea in the first place.

I remember sitting in a hotel room in Washington, overlooking the Dupont Circle, drinking beer after beer and trying to jump over the high wall which was the halfway point of the script. I got stuck for months with the film after the 'fuck' night—the climax, the section at the centre where three couples copulate simultaneously. (Originally I wanted to call the film *The Fuck*.) What would be the consequences of these three acts? What would they mean to all the characters and how would these acts change them? It wasn't until I decided to extend the waste ground material and the consequent eviction, until I introduced this new element, that I was able to continue. The problem was whether this material would be convincing. It wasn't based on anything I'd known, though for a long time I've been interested in anarchist ideas—a respectable English political tradition, from Winstanley, through William Godwin and onwards. If anything, it was based on some of the young people who'd attended theatre workshops I'd given. They had terrific energy, intelligence and inventiveness. But because of poverty, homelessness, unemployment and bad schooling, they were living in the interstices of the society: staying in squats, dealing drugs, and generally scavenging around. It seemed to me that this society had little to offer them, no idea how to use them or what to do with their potential.

Because of this block I frequently thought of abandoning the film. I wrote the same scene twenty-five or thirty times in the hope of a breakthrough. I'd set up this complicated story; I'd invented the characters and let things happen between them, but then it all stopped. This is where real life or direct autobiography fails you: the story has to be completed on its own terms.

Sarah Radclyffe has some reservations about the script. She doubts whether Sammy and Rosie would be ignorant of Rafi's involvement in the torture of his political enemies, especially if they'd been to visit him in his own country. Karin Bamborough said something similar and suggested I change it so the film opened with them all meeting for the first time. That would be a considerable rewrite. Also, there's no reason why they should have found out about the details of Rafi's crimes since he would have worked through hired hit-men and through people who wouldn't necessarily have been immediately identified with him. It would have taken years for this information to be discovered and collated.

This morning in our office it was like the Royal Court in exile. Frears, myself, and Debbie McWilliams (the casting director) all worked at the Court. Tunde Ikoli, a young writer and director who worked as Lindsay Anderson's assistant at the Court, was in the office. We see a number of interesting and experienced black actors. Things have certainly changed in that respect from four or five years ago. Many of these actors who have either worked at the National Theatre's Studio with Peter Gill (ex-Royal Court) or at the Court serve to remind us of the importance of the theatre, not only in itself, but as a seedbed for film and TV.

We talk about the audience there is for our kind of films. Aged between eighteen and forty, mostly middle class and well-educated, film- and theatre-literate, liberal progressive and leftish, this massive and sophisticated audience doesn't want to be patronized by teen films: they'll support a poor and rough cinema rich in ideas and imagination.

21 December 1986 Michael Barker from Orion Classics rings to say Orion are going to push for an Oscar nomination for me. He doesn't think I'll win—Woody Allen will win for *Hannah and Her Sisters*—but he thinks he can swing the nomination.

23 DECEMBER 1986   Hugo, the film's designer, rings to say they've found an excellent location for the caravan site. This is in Notting Hill. The flat concrete curve of the motorway hangs above a dusty stretch of waste ground which itself is skirted by a mainline railway line and a tube track. I know the area he means and it's excellent.

They're also looking for a house in the area to serve as Sammy's and Rosie's flat. There's been talk of building it in a studio, which would be easier, but Frears feels at the moment it should be done on location.

Bevan is trying to find an area where we can stage the riots. There are obviously problems with the police over this, and I'll have to prepare a doctored script to show them. When he goes to see them he refers to the riots as 'scuffles'!

I run into Claire Bloom in the street nearby and yesterday I met her husband, Philip Roth, in a health-food shop in Notting Hill. He asks how the film is going and tells me he prefers to keep away from films, not having liked any of the films made from his books. It reminds me of the second time I met Philip and Claire. Frears and I were outside the American Embassy walking through the crowd protesting against the bombing of Libya. Mostly the occasion was like a Methodist church fête. Then, there at the barrier nearest to the Embassy were Philip and Claire, very angry.

24 DECEMBER 1986   Frears and I talk about *Sammy and Rosie* in its style and rhythm, being far more leisurely than *Laundrette*. The relationships are more developed; it needs more room to breathe. It's less of a shocker; more of a grown-up film.

29 DECEMBER 1986   Frears slightly miffed by the realization of how much Thatcher would approve of us: we're a thrifty, enterprising, money-making small business. I say: But part of our purpose is to make popular films which are critical of British society. He says: Thatcher wouldn't care about that, she'd just praise our initiative for doing something decent despite the odds; the real difficulty of making films in Britain today made more difficult by this government.

4 JANUARY 1987 Long meeting with Frears last night at his house. The first time, really, we've sat down and discussed the script. His ideas are exactly the stimulation I've been waiting for to enable me to find a resolution to the film. After the 'fuck' night the film fragments, the intercutting is too quick, the scenes are too short. This is because I haven't worked out exactly what is going on, what I want to say. What Frears and I do, as we talk, as he puts his children to bed, is invent new elements to bind the story together: Rani and Vivia putting pressure on Rafi; Rani and Vivia putting pressure on Rosie with regard to Rafi living in her flat; some of the other women pursuing Rafi through the city, perhaps harrying him to his death; all the characters (and not just some of them, as it is now) meeting at the eviction scene and their relationships being resolved there.

Now I have to sit down and look at the whole thing again. It's not as if I can write bits and pieces. It'll be an entirely new draft. I suppose if you want to be a decent writer you have to have the ability to rip up what you've done and go back and start again, tear up your best lines and replace them with better lines and ideas, however hard this is and however long it takes.

5 JANUARY 1987 I get up at six in the morning, unable to sleep so paranoid am I about this thing ever getting rewritten. In this frozen deserted city I start to fiddle with the script, contra what I said yesterday. When I realize the futility of this fiddling I put a fresh sheet in the typewriter and start at page 1. I do no planning, give it no thought and just go at it, walking out on the tightrope.

The idea is not to inhibit myself, not be over-critical or self-conscious or self-censoring, otherwise I'll get blocked and the act of writing will be like trying to drive a car with the brakes on.

Today is the first day of pre-production and everyone officially starts work: the director, the casting director, the production manager, designer and so on. The young lighting cameraman, Oliver Stapleton, is going to shoot this film, as he did *Laundrette.* That film was his first feature, though since then he's done *Absolute Beginners* and *Prick Up Your Ears.* So it's all terrifically exciting. What a shame that it feels as if the script is disintegrating in my hands. The new ideas touch every other element in the film, altering them, giving them different significance. Little of what I've written seems secure now, except the characters; certainly not the story. As the whole thing goes into the mixer my fear is that it'll all fall apart.

7 JANUARY 1987   I write a scene this morning between Rani, Vivia and Rosie at the end of the party, which is crucial to the film. Rani and Vivia accuse Rosie of lacking political integrity. It's a dramatic scene and will wind the film up just when it needs it. I'm surprised that it's taken me so long to see how useful this kind of pressure on Rosie could be. It's partly because it's only since that conversation with Frears that I've seen the point of Rani and Vivia in the film. They were in the first draft—I dropped them in because unconsciously I knew they'd be of use. It's taken me till the fourth draft to find out for what exactly.

8 JANUARY 1987   I spend most of the day trying to write a final scene for the film, which at the moment is Rafi staggering around on the waste ground during the eviction, and Sammy standing on the motorway shouting down at Rosie without being heard. This isn't satisfactory. So I try going back to a previous ending, which has Rosie and Margy and Eva, her women friends, deciding to move into the flat with Rosie while Sammy goes off on his own to a house he's bought. But I don't believe in this ending.

Usually when I have a block I put the film or story in a drawer for thirty days, like putting a pie in the oven, and when I take it out it's cooked. But there isn't time for that now.

So I put the last few pages in the typewriter and rewrite them, trying to quieten my mind and allow fresh ideas to pop in as they will. So it occurs to me, or rather it writes itself, that Rafi should hang himself. As the words go down I know I'm on to something dramatic and powerful. I'm also doing something which will be depressing. I've no idea how this suicide will affect the rest of the film and no idea what it means or says. I can work that out later. It's a relief to have had a new idea, and a creative pleasure to solve a problem not be refining what one has already done, but to slam down a bizarre and striking fresh image!

10 JANUARY 1987 Bevan, Rebecca (the location manager), Jane (production manager) and I go to North Kensington to look at locations for the scenes at the beginning of the film with Rosie visiting the old man and finding him dead in the bath, waiting for the ambulance, and watching the boys' bonfire in the centre of the estate. To the thirtieth floor of a tower block (which won design awards in the sixties), with several young kids in the lift. The lift is an odd shape: very deep, with a low roof. Jane says this is so they can get bodies in coffins down from the thirtieth floor. We walk around other blocks in the area. They are filthy, derelict places, falling down, graffiti-sprayed, wind-blown, grim and humming with the smell of shit, implacable in the hatred of humanity they embody. The surrounding shops are barricaded with bars and wire mesh. I was brought up in London. It's my city. I'm no Britisher, but a Londoner. And it's filthier and more run down now than it's ever been.

I get home and speak to Frears on the phone. The double

imperative: that the rewritten script be handed in on Monday and yet, as he says, be more intricate. 'Deeper' is the word he uses. Christ. Have told no one yet about the new ending.

I have the sense today of the film starting to move away from me, of this little thing which I wrote in my bedroom in Fulham now becoming public property. On the crew list there are now already fifty names, at least a quarter of them from *Laundrette*.

12 JANUARY 1987 Frears comes over. I sit opposite him as he turns over the pages of the script. We talk about each page. Because the film is about the relations between men and women in contemporary Britain and has political content, we're beginning to realize how important it is that it says what we want it to say. That means working out what it is we believe!

As Frears gets nearer the end I get more nervous. I've typed up the scene where Rafi hangs himself and it's quite different from the innocuous and rather dissipated finales so far.

After reading it Frears says nothing for a while. He jumps up and walks round and round the flat. It's started to snow outside; it's very cold. Is he just trying to keep warm?

We talk until 1.30 about this end and worry whether it's too brutal both on the audience and as an act of aggression by Rafi against the rest of the characters he's become involved with. We talk about the possibility of Rafi dying of a heart attack! But this is too contingent. It's the power of the deliberate act that we like.

We discuss Chekhov's *Seagull*. I saw Rafi's suicide could be like Trepliov's at the end of that play: understated, with the action off-stage, one person discovering it and then returning to the room to tell everyone else. In this room there'd be: Rani, Vivia, Alice, Anna, Eva, Bridget, Rosie.

We decide to leave it for the moment. More importantly, we're going to New York soon to cast Anna the photographer. I'm still not clear what she's doing in the film. I've deliberately avoided rewriting her bits.

13 JANUARY 1987 Seven in the morning and freezing cold. Streets covered in snow. Behind me I can hear the tubes rattling along at the back of the house. Outside the careful traffic and people starting to go to work. I'm not in the mood for rewriting this thing. Still a few scenes to be revised, but I'm sick of it. It says on the piece of paper in front of me: fifth draft, but in reality it must be the eighth or ninth. If each draft is about 100 pages, that's 900 pages of writing!

When I first moved into this part of West London, in 1978, I felt vulnerable. It was like living on the street. People walked by on their way to work just yards from my head. In time I relaxed and would lie in bed and hear and feel London around me, stretching out for miles.

These West London streets by the railway line have gone wrong. In 1978 most of the five-storey houses with their crumbling pillars, peeling façades and busted windows were derelict, inhabited by itinerants, immigrants, drug-heads and people not ashamed of being seen drunk on the street. On the balcony opposite a man regularly practised the bagpipes at midnight. Now the street is crammed with people who work for a living. Young men wear striped shirts and striped ties; the women wear blue jumpers with white shirts, turned-up collars and noses, and pearls. They drive Renault 5s and late at night as you walk along the street, you can see them in their clean shameless basements having dinner parties and playing Trivial Pursuit on white tablecloths. Now the centre of the city is inhabited by the young rich and serviced by everyone else: now there is the re-establishment of firm class divisions; now the sixties and the ideals of that time seem like an impossible dream or naivety.

Though I was at school and not politically active in 1968, I was obsessively aware of the excitement and originality of those years. I had the records, the books, the clothes; I saw the sixties on TV and was formed by what I missed out on. I wasn't involved enough to become disillusioned. The attitudes that formed me are, briefly: that openness and choice in sexual behaviour is liberating and that numerous accretions of sexual guilt and inhibition are psychologically damaging; that the young are innately original and vigorous, though this special quality is to do with not being burdened with responsibility and the determinations of self-interest; that there should be a fluid, non-hierarchical society with free movement across classes and that these classes will eventually be dissolved; that ambition and competitiveness are stifling narrowers of personality; and that all authority should be viewed with suspicion and constantly questioned.

The past ten years of repression have been a continuous surprise for me. Somehow I haven't been able to take them seriously, since I imagine the desire for more freedom, more pleasure, more self-expression to be fundamental to life. So I continue to think, in that now old way, in terms of the 'straight' world and the rest, the more innocent and lively ones standing against the corrupt and stuffy. I still think of businessmen as semi-criminals; I'm suspicious of anyone in a suit; I like drugs, especially hash, and I can't understand why people bother to get married. Ha!

14 JANUARY 1987   Frears rings and says the scene where Alice tells Rafi to go, at the end of the film after he's been chased out of Sammy's and Rosie's flat by Vivia and Rani, is boring, boring, boring. There has to be a dramatic action rather than extended verbals as it is now. I say: well what fucking dramatic action? He says: no idea—you do the paperwork, I just do the pictures!

16 JANUARY 1987   Frances Barber seems enthusiastic about the rewrites but says she'd been disturbed by the new end. It reverses the film, she thinks, in that Rafi now seems to accept his guilt for torturing people. Frances says this seems inconsistent with his having argued so strongly for political expendiency in the restaurant scene. I say I don't want him committing suicide out of guilt. It's that he's come to the end. No one wants him. There's nowhere for him to go, neither at home nor in Britain.

Frears has a session with Frances and Ayub, which he videotapes. Ayub is very nervous, not surprisingly. We've cast Frances and probably Ayub will be offered the part tomorrow.

17 JANUARY 1987 We look at the tape of Frances and Ayub together. They look good together. Ayub waits downstairs in his agent's office, refusing to go home until we make our decision. He comes into the room looking dazed with tension. We offer him the job. He thanks us all and shakes hands with us.

Frears has decided that the film should be much more about young people than I'd imagined. Because of Ayub being five years younger than Frances we could as easily cast the people around them down in age as up. Frears says casting it young will make it more cheerful. I'm all for cheefulness, though worried that Rosie will seem oddly older than everyone else.

18 JANUARY 1987 Frears talks obout the problems of shooting the riots, especially after a friend said: Oh no, not a lot of black people rioting. So we talk about avoiding the TV news-footage approach: screaming mobs, bleeding policemen. What you don't get in news footage is detail. In *The Battle of Algiers*, for example, the director humanizes the violence. You see the faces of those to whom violence is being done. In the torture scene, you don't see the act, but only the faces of those around it, streaming tears.

In *Sammy and Rosie* you do see the circumstances from which the riot comes—the shooting of a black women by the police. And we see, in the circumstances, how justifiable the riot is. The difficulty arises from the fact that black people are so rarely represented on TV; if when they are shown, they're only throwing rocks at the police, you're in danger of reinforcing considerable prejudice. I suppose this depends partly on how you see the riot, or revolt. I know I supported it, but as Orwell says about Auden, it's easy to say that if you're elsewhere when the violence takes place.

After Frears said the Alice-Rafi parting scene at the end of the film isn't dramatic enough I shake my brains and come up with a Miss Havisham scene set in the cellar of the house. I have Alice furiously throwing open a suitcase in which she's packed the clothes she'd intended to take on her planned elopement with Rafi in the mid-fifties. I also have her showing Rafi the diaries she kept then, in which she poured out her heart to him—the physical and visual representation of what was formerly just dialogue.

To the opera on Friday with a vegetarian friend. A woman in a long sable coat sits next to us. My friends says: I wish I carried a can of spray paint in my bag and could shoot it over her coat. Thought it might be an idea to stick in the film. But where?

20 JANUARY 1987   Debbie McWilliams saw a pop group, the Fine Young Cannibals, on TV and asks the singer, Roland Gift, to come into the office. He shows up looking splendid, proud and vulnerable, with his manager. I ask the women in the office to get a look at him through the office window and let us know if they want to rip his clothes off with their teeth. As most of them seem to want this, Roland inches closer to the part of Danny.

On the way home from the movies the other night, at Piccadilly tube station a group of young Jewish kids gathers at the top of the escalator. Suddenly, around them, are a bunch of Arsenal football supporters who stand and chant 'Yiddo, yiddo!' at these kids. The kids look embarrassed rather than frightened, but they do move closer together, standing in a little huddle. It's a difficult moment. What do you do when it comes to it? Walk on, watch, or pile in? What are you made of? What would you give up? I can see a lot of other dithering people in the vicinity have this dilemma. But no one does anything. The chanting goes on. Then the youths disappear down the escalator, their voices echoing around the building. It's the first time I've seen this kind of anti-Semitism in London. Decide to put it in the film somewhere. The structure is secure enough now for anything odd or interesting that happens to have a place. All the bits and pieces will just have to get along with each other, like people at a party.

23 JANUARY 1987   Problems with Meera Syal, the actress we want to play Rani. Max Stafford-Clark, artistic director of the Royal Court, rings to say Meera has already committed herself to Caryl Churchill's play *Serious Money*. She also wants to play Rani in our film. At the moment the schedule can't be arranged so she can do both. We don't want to press her to choose, for fear she'll choose the Court. It's painful to her, especially as Asian actors get offered so little work.

Anyway, we'll deal with it later. In the meantime we're going to my favourite city, New York!

25 JANUARY 1987   *New York*. This city is snowbound and every time you look round, someone has skidded on to their back in the street. New York is cold in a way London never is: here your face freezes, here the fluid in your eyes seems to ice over.

The entrance of our hotel, on Central Park West, has a silver-lined overhang in which bright lights are embedded. This ensures that the hotel shines like a battery of torches in a blackout for hundreds of yards around; indeed, if you're driving through the park you can see it glowing through the trees. In this overhang there are heaters which warm the street and melt insubordinate snowflakes which may drift on to the hotel's red carpet or float on to the hat of the doorman. Everywhere you go in this city there are notices urging you to save energy while outside this hotel they are heating the street!

Frears is a prisoner in his hotel room, doing publicity for *Prick Up Your Ears*. Food and drink is brought up to him. Between interviews he looks out of the window at Central Park. His talk schedule is exhausting. There was a time when I thought that talking about yourself to someone who said little, listened intently, and made notes or recorded what you said was the ideal relationship. But after the first three hours your tongue is dry, your mouth will not work, your jaws ache, as after six hours of fellatio. The only respite is to question the journalists and hope they'll revive you by telling you about themselves.

A journalist asks me how I came upon the central idea of *Sammy and Rosie*. I start to think about it, but it is complicated; an idea usually has many sources.

One source was the great Japanese film *Tokyo Story* in which an old couple who live in the country go to visit their children in the city and are treated shabbily by them. I started off thinking of *Sammy and Rosie* as a contemporary remake of this desperately moving and truthful film. Sometimes I wish my own script had the simplicity, luminosity and straightforward humanity of Ozu's masterpiece, that I hadn't added so many characters, themes and gewgaws.

Another source was a play I once wrote and abandoned about an Asian politician living in London in the sixties and having an affair with a young woman. I retained the politician and dropped everything else.

There was also a story I was told about a member of my family who loved an Englishwoman, left her after promising to return to England to marry her, and never came back, though the word is she loves him still and continues to wait.

When Frears has finished his interviews for the day he says a journalist told him, when they were discussing British films, that he didn't think anything dramatic ever happened in Britain now. This jounalist's view of Britain sounds like Orson Welles in *The Third Man* talking about Switzerland, only capable of producing the cuckoo clock!

The journalist's remark hits a nerve. It relates to the British sense of inferiority about its film industry: not only the feeling that the British can't really make good films, but that contemporary British subjects and themes are really too small, too insignificant as subjects. So British films are often aimed at American audiences and attempt to deal with 'universal' or 'epic' themes as in *Gandhi, The Mission, The Killing Fields, Cry Freedom*.

The journalist's view isn't entirely surprising since a lot of English 'art' also dwells, gloats on and relives nostalgic scenarios of wealth and superiority. It's easy therefore for Americans to see Britain as just an old country, as a kind of museum, as a factory for producing versions of lost greatness. After all, many British films do reflect this: *Chariots of Fire, A Room with a View*, the Raj epics, and the serials *Brideshead Revisited* and *The Jewel in the Crown*. Even the recent past, the Beatles, punks, and numerous Royal Weddings, are converted into quaintness, into tourist mugs and postcards, into saleable myths. If imperialism is the highest form of capitalism, then tourism is its ghostly afterlife in this form of commercial nostalgia which is sold as 'art' or 'culture'.

But some British dignity remains, unlike in New York where a friend of mine rings a fashionable restaurant on a Saturday night and they tell him they don't have a table. My friend, who in the American manner is very persistent, says he is bringing a screenwriter with him—me. The person in the restaurant asks: We may be able to squeeze your party in, sir, but please tell me: what are the screenwriter's credits?!

26 JANUARY 1987   We troop off to the famous theatrical restaurant Sardi's for an awards dinner. Like executioners, photographers in black balaclavas crowd the entrance. Going in, I realize we've arrived too early. We sit down and they bring us our food while others are still arriving. The salmon tastes like wallpaper. Around the walls there are hideous caricatures of film stars and famous writers. Thankfully the ceremony is not televised or competitive: you know if you've won; they don't torment you with any opening of envelopes. Sissy Spacek and Lynn Redgrave, obviously experienced at the awards game, time it just right, so that when they arrive the whole room is in place and is forced to turn and look at them. Photographers shove through the crowd and climb across tables to get to them.

I see Norman Mailer come in. He is stocky like a boxer and healthy of face, though he looks frail when he walks. It will be a thrilling moment for me to have the great man rest his eyes on me when I receive my award for the *Laundrette* screenplay. When the playwright Beth Henley announces my name I eagerly look out for Mailer from the podium. I start into my speech but almost stop talking when I see Mailer's place is now vacant and across the restaurant he is rapidly mounting the stairs to watch the final of the Super Bowl on TV.

27 JANUARY 1987   Spend two mornings in the hotel room interviewing actresses for the part of Anna. About twenty come in and we have longish conversations with all of them: they're frank and lively and seem healthier and more confident than their British counterparts, somehow less beaten down by things. They are less educated too. The American film world isn't adjacent to the theatre or literary world as it can be in London. It's closer to rock 'n' roll, if anything.

An actress called Wendy Gazelle seems untypical of the group we see. She is less forthright, more sensitive and attractive in a less orthodox way. When Wendy reads, in that room overlooking the park through which people are skiing, it is heartbreaking. I'm so pleased she can invest the somewhat duff dialogue with feeling and meaning that I urge the others to choose her.

In the evening to the Café Luxembourg with Leon from Cinecom, the company that, along with Channel 4, is financing our film. Frears and I refer to Leon as 'the man that owns us,' which he doesn't seem to mind. He's thirty-four, friendly and intelligent, with long hair in a pigtail. Bevan, Frears and I are apprehensive about the pressure his company might put on us to massage or roll our film in a certain direction. We'll just have to wait and see.

28 JANUARY 1987 To a smart party on the Upper West Side, given by a New York agent for the German director Doris Dorrie. It's a large apartment in front of which is a courtyard and behind it a view of the river. Marcie, the publicist for *Laundrette* in New York, says: I wouldn't object to being the accountant of the people in this room! She points out: Isabella Rossellini, Alan Pakula, Matthew Modine, Michael Douglas and various others. Michael Douglas, polite and friendly, praises the British Royal Family to Frears and me for a considerable time, obviously thinking this'll please us. On the way back we pass a laundromat called *My Beautiful Laundrette* done up in neon: it offers Reverse Cycle Washing, Fluff Drying and Expert Folding. Two days later I go back and this laundrette has closed for good.

We wonder why the film has done well in the US. It's partly, I think, because of its theme of success at any price; and partly because the puritan and prurient theme of two outcast boys (outcast from society and having escaped the world of women) clinging together in passionate blood-brotherhood is a dream of American literature and film from *Huckleberry Finn* to the work of Walt Whitman and on to *Butch Cassidy and the Sundance Kid*.

29 JANUARY 1987 I ride the subway across New York to have lunch with Leon at the Russian Tea Room. In the subway car a couple with a kid kiss shamelessly. A legless black man in a wheelchair propels himself through the car, carrying a paper cup. Everyone gives him something. The streets are full of beggars now; every block someone asks you for money. Before going out I ensure I have a selection of loose change to give away, just as I would in Pakistan.

The young people in NY that you see on the street or subway are far less eccentric, original and fashionable than kids are in Britain. The kids in London, despite unemployment and poverty, have taste; they're adventurous and self-conscious. They're walking exhibitions: billboards of style, wearing jumble-sale and designer clothes together. In Britain fashion starts on the street. Here the kids are sartorial corpses. They all wear sports clothes. *There are even women wearing business suits and running shoes.*

The Russian Tea Room is a fashionable restaurant for movie people. It's plusher than Sardi's, apparently more 'cultured', and patronized by people who have money. It has semi-circular booths in red and gold: booths for two in the entrance, convenient for both seeing and being seen, and larger ones inside. It has a festive astmosphere. There are shining samovars, red and gold pompons on the lamp-shades and the staff wear red tunics. It's like a kind of Santa's grotto with waitresses. Powerful New York agents do business here, reserving several booths for their clients and associates and moving from booth to booth like door-to-door salesmen, dealing and negotiating.

Leon has this time brought with him some serious reinforcements to deal with the script 'difficulties', a beautiful and smart woman called Shelby who works with him.

Oh, how we eat! Oh, how I like life now! I have dark brown pancakes on which the waitress spreads sour cream. She forks a heap of orange caviar on to this and pours liquid butter over the lot. This is then folded. This is then placed in the mouth.

Shelby leans forward. As each caviar egg explodes on my tongue like a little sugar bomb, Shelby tells me she has just read all five drafts of the script. I am flattered. But more, she has compared and contrasted them all. More wine? She talks knowledgeably about them. She seems to know them better than I do. Scene 81 in draft 2, she says, is sharper than scene 79 in draft 4. Perhaps I could go back to that? Well. I look at her. She is telling me all this in a kindly tone. In the end, she implies, it is up to me, but . . . She expresses her reservations, which are quite substantial, at argued length.

I nod to everything, not wanting to induce indigestion. I am also experimenting with the Zen method of bending with the wind, so that when the cleansing storm stops, the tree of my spirit will gaily snap back to its usual upright position. But will this helpful puffing ever stop?

We talk about the end of the film and the hanging of Rafi. They suggest Rafi be murdered by the Ghost. I manage to say (though I object on principle to discussing such things at all) that this would be predictable. Leon says: How can a Ghost murdering a politician in an anarchist commune be predictable?

By now I am sucking and licking on light ice-cream with whipped cream and grenadine. Shelby is into her stride. Perhaps my lack of response means I am thinking about what she is saying? The script hasn't necessarily improved at all, it's become cruder, more obvious. Why have you developed the black women, Vivia and Rani? Well . . . I almost begin to fight back when she starts to fumble in her bag. She brings out a letter. There, read this please, she says. It's from someone who cares.

The letter, from a reader in the company, is addressed to me. Its tone implores me to see sense. 'The version I read in October was just about perfect and the fifth draft has been tinkered with entirely too much . . . The fifth draft seems a little preachy and one-dimensional. It's lost so much for the sake of clarity and it's not nearly as successful as a film . . . I hope you'll consider going back to the terrific screenplay you wrote in October.'

I leave the restaurant burping on caviar and heavy with ice-cream. All afternoon I wander the city. Two dozen wasps are free within my cranium. Perhaps all those people are right. I don't know. Can't tell. God knows. My judgement has gone, swept away by the wind of all this advice. Eventually I settle down in an Irish bar—a grimy piece of Dublin—and have a few beers. I toast myself. The toast: long may you remain waterproof and never respect anyone who gives you money!

30 JANUARY 1987   Motivated entirely by greed I stay in the hotel room all day writing a 1,000-word piece about Frears for an American film magazine. They promise me $1000. On finishing it, sending it round and listening to their reservations, I realize how rarely any kind of writing is simple and how few easy bucks there are to be made. Whatever you write you always have to go back and rethink and rewrite. And you have to be prepared to do that. You never get away with anything.

5 FEBRUARY 1987   *London.* Good to talk to Frears again. We both say that some of the people around us have made us gloomy by expressing doubts, by emphasizing the difficulty of what we want to do. We want to work confidently, with certainty, and with pleasure. Frears is an extraordinarily cheerful man who takes great pleasure in his work and in the company of others. There's no poisonous negativity in him. It's as if he knows how close dejection and discouragement always are, that they are the converse of everything you do, and how comforting it is to let them put their arms around you.

He says this is the hardest film he's made. He said the same about *Laundrette*, and I remember feeling glad that we were doing something risky and dangerous.

10 FEBRUARY 1987   Meeting at Channel 4 with David Rose and Karin Bamborough. Karin says I'll have to give Sammy more substance as he's such a jerk and constantly making glib, flip remarks. Stephen and Tim Bevan sit chuckling at me, knowing there's some autobiography in the character. We tell Karin that Ayub is such a delightfully complicated person and so intent on playing the Oepidal relationship that he'll give the character depth. I also explain that the end will be rewritten. At the moment Rafi just hangs himself. It seems an ignoble act whereas Frears and I want it to be a justified thing, chosen, dignified, something of a Roman act.

Shashi sends his measurements in and hasn't lost any weight. We feel he's too big for the part and should look fitter and trimmer. The plan has been for Shashi to arrive a few weeks before shooting and then Bevan will shunt him off to a health farm. But so far, no sign of Shashi. Some of us are wondering whether he'll turn up at all.

As we've been concentrating on casting the other parts it now seems that Claire Bloom may not be available. A real nuisance. Fortunately the problems with Meera have been worked out and she's going to be in the film.

12 FEBRUARY 1987   I go into the production offices off Ladbroke Grove to talk about casting. There is a row of offices with glass partitions. About twenty yards away I can see Bevan waving his arms. He dashes up the corridor to tell me there's been a call from the States to say I've been nominated for an Oscar. I call my agent and she says: Goody, that'll put a couple of noughts on your fee.

I think of a letter F. Scott Fitzgerald wrote from Hollywood in 1935 where he was working on the script of *Gone with the Wind*: 'It's nice work if you can get it and you can get it if you try about three years. The point is once you've got in—Screen

Credit 1st, a Hit 2nd, and the Academy Award 3rd—you can count on it for ever . . . and know there's one place you'll be fed without being asked to even wash the dishes.'

Later in the day Frears and I drive to West London to check out an actress for the part of Alice. Frears says what a strange cast it is: a mixture of inexperienced young people, a rock singer, a famous and glamorous movie star who's never worked in Britain, and a theatre actress without a great deal of film experience.

The irascible actress we've come to see, in her genteel West London sitting room, starts off by flapping the letter we've written her and saying how flattered she is to be offered the part of Anna. Surely though, at her age, early fifties, she shouldn't be expected to have two Ws tattooed on her buttocks.

I look at Frears. As he sits there in her high-backed leather chair with his ripped green-striped plimsolls resting on her cream carpet, I can't help thinking of him as a punk at heart. He is a little distracted, though perfectly polite. I know what he doesn't like to do is explain things. Art Malik has complained to me that Frears wouldn't explain Sammy's role in the movie to him. Frears said he didn't know that much about Sammy's role in the movie: it's all so much in Hanif's head, he says; let's hope we can pull it out some time near the day. Malik was horrified by Frears's flipness. But Frears wants people to work intuitively and spontaneously. He wants them to work things out for themselves and not be lazy; what they've worked out they'll bring to the film. He also expects other people to be as intelligent as he is.

Frears pulls himself together and hastily explains that the actress is being considered for the part of Alice, not Anna. She then looks at me as if I'm a very small boy and asks, severely, what the film is about. I explain that it concerns a number of relationships unfolding against a background of uprising and social deterioration. 'That's easy to say,' she says. 'Very easy. Now can you tell me what it's about?' I tell her I'm not one of those people who think plays or films ought to be 'about' anything. 'What are you trying to say then?' she asks, putting her head in her hands and making a frightening gurgling noise. At first I think she's choking; I consider hammering her on the back. But surely she's crying? When she looks up I can see she's laughing hysterically. 'Oh, poor England's changed,' she says. 'And I don't know where it's gone. A black boy attacked me in the street the other day. Before, you'd never even lock the door to your house.'

Frears is knocking back a fat slug of whiskey and looking in the other direction. The actress starts up on a rambling monologue about her career. She keeps you alert because you have no idea what she's going to say next. In some ways she is rather like Alice, delicate, decent and unable to understand why her world has changed.

16 FEBRUARY 1987   Roland Gift who is playing Danny comes over. He admits being nervous of Frears's method of working, of not rehearsing. I tell him of the dangers of over-preparation which kill spontaneity and creativity; also that he's in the film partly because of what he'll bring himself to the part, not because of his technical abilities as an actor. The idea is to avoid performances. British actors, because of their training, tend to be theatrical on film.

Roland talks about being brought up in Birmingham and being in a class at school in which there were only five white kids. And then moving to Hull and being the only black kid in the class. The racism was constant and casual. One day he was walking along and heard someone calling out, 'Nigger, nigger, nigger.' When he turned round he saw it was a woman calling her dog.

Later he worked as a nude model for architects. Architects? In a life-drawing class, he says, so the barbarians of the future would get a sense of beauty.

We talk about the character of Danny being underwritten.

Hanif Kureishi

Roland might fill it out by having a strong sense of what the character is. He thinks there's much of himself he can bring to the part.

Bevan has managed to get permission from the police to block off some streets in North Kensington to stage the riot scenes, or the 'scuffles' as he describes them. They don't even ask to see a script.

17 FEBRUARY 1987 To see Claire Bloom, Stephen and I. Chat for a while to Philip Roth. Roth fizzes and whirls with mischief and vibrant interest in the world. He is a wicked teller of tales! I tell him that on taking his advice and writing some fiction, a story I've written for the *London Review of Books* may not be accepted in the US because of the sex and four-letter words in it. He says he's had similar trouble: imagine the nuisance, he tells me, of having to find a suitable synonym for the perfectly adequate 'dog-shit' just so your story can be published in the prissy *New Yorker*. He also tells us with great glee that he's written a story called 'The Tormented Cunt', but had to change the title.

Claire looks younger than her fifty-six years and I did want Alice older than that, partly so that the scene I lifted from *A Sentimental Education*—the woman lets down her hair and it has gone white—is effective. Claire hunts through the script for a line she doesn't understand. It is: 'The proletarian and theocratic ideas you theoretically admire grind civilization into dust.' It seems to me that no clearer line has ever been written. Frears explains the line and adds that the line 'that country has been sodomized by religion' in *Laundrette* mystified him long after the film had been finished. Claire looks sceptical and says she doesn't think she can say something she doesn't understand.

On the way home Frears says Shashi has rung to ask if he can leave early on the first day of shooting to go to a cocktail party.

Frears says if this is how stars behave, it might all be difficult to deal with.

23 FEBRUARY 1987 I run into Roland. He says: Why does Danny have to have a girlfriend and a kid? I say because it makes the character seem more complex. I can see Roland wants Danny to be more romantic. I tell him the character's unreal enough and idealized as it is.

Talk to Karin Bamborough about the end of the movie. The idea of it ending with the hanging is still not necessarily the best. It'll send people away in a gloomy mood. Karin thinks there should be some image of reconciliation. I say, well, if one occurs to me I'll put it in. I'm not sure Sammy and Rosie should be reconciled at the end of the film, not sure they'd want that.

Stephen and I talk about the music we'll use in the film. Some kind of street music, plus some American soul, perhaps Otis Redding or Sam Cooke, music from the sixties which seems to me to have really lasted, something that everyone recognizes.

24 FEBRUARY 1987 Roland, Ayub and Wendy Gazelle (who has just flown in from New York) are in the production office today and on the walls are photographs of Meera and Suzette Llewellyn, who are playing Rani and Vivia respectively. Ayub and Wendy together look like Romeo and Juliet! Their all being so young will mean there's little bitterness in the film, so a story that involves the shooting of a black woman by the police, an exiled torturer and the eviction of dozens of people from their homes, while ending with a hanging, won't be as grim as this description sounds.

The actors are pretty nervous and complain to me that Frears and I haven't spent much time talking about the backgrounds to their characters. I urge them to work it out for themselves, maybe writing out a few pages of background detail. Despite their worries, when I sit down with them and they discuss various scenes with each other, they seem to know what they're about. The important thing is that they like each other and can relax. I know they've started to hang out together.

Stephen and I talk about the end of the film once more. It's still not worked out properly. Maybe there should be another scene, after the hanging, maybe with Sammy and Rosie in each other's arms, a scene that was cut from earlier in the script. I'm not against the idea; but maybe there's something more interesting I could write.

25 FEBRUARY 1987 To Milan for the opening of *Laundrette* in Italy. I do an interview through an interpreter and go to the bar with the publicist, the distributor and the journalist. They talk politics. The journalist, a fashionably dressed woman in her thirties, turns to me and says: Isn't it funny, all the Italians round the table are communists? It's a disconcerting remark, since I haven't heard anyone describe themselves as a communist for at least ten years, since I was a student. Indeed, I reflect, it's only with embarrassment and in low voices that the people I know in London will admit to being socialists. Generally we don't admit to believing in anything at all, though we sometimes disapprove of the worst abuses. It's as if in London it's considered vulgar or exhibitionist to hold too strongly to anything, hence the London contempt for Mrs Thatcher along with the failure to do anything about her. In some ways this British insouciance is a manifestation of British scepticism and dislike of extremes; in another way it's just feebleness.

To a massive Gothic church in Milan. The stained-glass windows tell, in sequence, like bright cartoons, biblical stories. And with strong sunlight behind each of them, they resemble the frames of a film.

26 FEBRUARY 1987 To Florence by train. The fast and comfortable Italian trains and the businessmen around me in their sharp clothes. The care they take: everything matches; not a garment is worn or shapeless. What surprises me is the affluence and attractiveness of northern Italy and that despite Thatcher's talk about the boom in British industry, compared with this place it's in desperate straits.

In Florence I do more interviews. This publicizing of films is an odd business. I have no Italian money and little grasp of what is going on. Norboto, the publicist, takes me from city to city. When I am thirsty he buys me a Coke; when I am hungry he fetches me a sandwich. He takes me to the hotel and in the morning he wakes me up. It reminds me of being a kid and being out with my father. You veer in these publicity tours between feeling you are important, a minor celebrity, someone to be listened to, and the predominant feeling that you're a kind of large parcel, a property at the disposal of a nervous distributor with which things can be done, films sold and money made. You hope in return that you'll get a decent view of the Grand Canal from the window of your Venice hotel.

27 FEBRUARY 1987 To Venice for the Carnival. I stand in the railway station and read the board: there are trains to Vienna, Trieste, Munich, Paris, Rome. That these places are merely a train ride away gives one a sense of being a part of Europe that isn't available in Britain. When I'm in the US and people talk of making a trip to Europe it still takes me a beat to realize they're also referring to Britain. I think of the legendary sign at Dover: Fog over Channel, Continent cut off.

Then out into the crumbling, drowning city of tourists which is packed with people in medieval costumes and gold masks. They dance all night in St Mark's Square and fall to the ground where they sleep beneath people's feet until morning. Looking at the bridges I wonder how they don't collapse under the weight of people. I walk with the distributor through this wild celebration to a cinema where *Laundrette* is opening. The cinema is virtually empty. A man is asleep and snoring loudly, the sound filling the place. To my horror the film is dubbed: strange Italian voices are coming from the mouths of Saeed Jaffrey and Roshan Seth. The Italian hairdresser on *Sammy and Rosie* said he grew up hearing Cary Grant, Frank Sinatra and Marlon Brando all with the same voice, dubbed by the same Italian actor.

I watch the audience watching the film. At the points where the audience usually laugh there is complete silence. The film is no longer a comedy.

I get up to speak. The snoring man opens his eyes briefly, looks at me and goes back to sleep. The audience puts questions to me through the interpreter. But though she has a good accent, what the interpreter says to me makes no sense. So I describe how the film came to be made and talk a little about the gay theme. She blushes when I say this. Then she stumbles and backs away from me and the microphone. I glare at her. She recovers and talks to the audience for a long time. But I know she isn't repeating what I said. So I turn to her and say the aim of the film is to induce world-wide sexual excitement. Now she won't go to the microphone at all. She is backing away, wide-eyed. The audience whistles and shouts and claps. I get out as soon as I can.

3 MARCH 1987   First day of shooting. I go to pick up Shashi who turned up late last night. 'I nearly didn't come at all,' he says, 'I've got big tax problems. Rajiv Gandhi himself had to sort them out.' Shashi has three Indian writers staying with him in his flat. They're working on a script Shashi will direct at the end of the year. He tells me that Indian film-writers often write ten films a year and earn £250,000. Some writers only work out the story and are no good at dialogue, while others just come in for the verbals.

Shashi looks splendid, if a little plump. He's less familiar with the script than I'd hoped—and in the car he asks me to remind him of the story—but he's serious and keen. Soon everyone is in love with him.

We shoot the scene of Rosie finding the old man dead in the bath. I turn up and find Frances in a long green coat with a furry black collar. On her head she has a black pillbox hat. Instead of a social worker she looks like an extra from *Doctor Zhivago*. I take it as a direct blow to the heart, as if it's a complete misunderstanding of everything I've been trying to do. Frances is very nervous and apprehensive, as it's the first day, and she clings to the coat as if it's a part of Rosie's soul. But Frears is enjoying himself. He can get along with actors. Where I'd have them by the throat with my foot in the back of their neck, he sits down and talks gently with them. Frances changes the coat. But it's not the last we'll see of that coat.

When Shashi comes on set—we're shooting the scene outside and inside the off-licence—the local Asians come out of their shops in amazement. One immediately gives him three boxes of crisps. Another gives him perfume and aftershave. For them Shashi is a massive star, like Robert Redford, and he has been around for considerably longer, making over 200 films since he first started, aged eight. When they believe it is him, the kids dress up in their best clothes—the Asian girls in smart shalwar kamiz and jewellery—to be photographed with him. Others ring their relatives who come in cars across London and wait patiently in the freezing cold for a break in filming so they can stand next to their idol.

Seeing the off-licence with wire-mesh across the counter, the dogs, the siege-like atmosphere—it is based on places I know in Brixton, where buying a bottle of wine can be like entering a battle zone—Shashi is taken aback, as Rafi would be. Shashi asks: 'Are there really places like this in London?'

Shashi decides to wear a moustache for the part. It makes him

look older and less handsome, less of a matinée idol; but also
formidable, imposing and sort of British in the right military,
authoritarian sort of way.

4 MARCH 1987   Sarah comes to the set where we're shooting a
scene between Sammy and Rosie set in a looted Asian grocer's
shop. Frances is still tense and unsure and she complains to Frears
about Sarah being there watching her as she is trying to create
the character of Rosie. Sarah leaves. She is amused by the clothes
Frances is wearing, as if a social worker would wear a mini-skirt
and three-inch-high heels to work. Before that, of course, the
hours in make-up, the hairdresser constantly standing by to adjust
any hair that might fall out of place. All seemingly absurd when
the attempt is to do something that is, in some ways, realistic.
But then the cinema has never stopped being a palace of dreams.
Even in the serious cinema there is some emphasis on the ideal.
Imagine casting a film with only ugly or even just ordinary-looking
actors. The cinema cannot replace the novel or autobiography as
the precise and serious medium of the age while it is still too
intent on charming its audience!

5 MARCH 1987   Much falsity in what I wrote in anger yesterday,
partly to do with my failure to let go of the script and let Frears
make the film he has to make. I think that despite the clothes
and the paraphernalia of glamour, the voice of the film collabo-
rators can transcend the trivial messages of escape that the cinema
must transmit if it is to reach a large audience.

Also, and today I have to repeat this to myself, the film-writer
always has to give way to the director, who is the controlling
intelligence of the film, the invisible tyrant behind everything. The
only way for a writer to influence a film is through his relationship
with the director. If this is good then the film will be a successful
collaboration; if not, the writer has had it. And most writers are
lucky if directors even allow them on the set.

Presumably, it is because of this contingency that serious writers don't venture into the cinema. You don't find many American writers—in a country with a film industry—thinking of film as a serious possibility.

Also contra what I said yesterday: I do think the constraints of playing to a wide audience can be useful. You have to ensure that your work is accessible. You can't indulge yourself; you have to be self-critical; you have to say: is this available? So, to take a literary analogy, you have popular Thackeray and Dickens, say, as opposed to some recent American writing, loaded with experiment, innovation and pretty sentences which is published by minor magazines for an audience of acolytes, friends and university libraries.

I wake up, pull the curtains and it is snowing! The snow is settling too. This morning we're shooting the aftermath of the riots, when Rafi decides to go out for a walk. He meets Danny and they go to visit Alice.

When I get to the set the snow doesn't seem to matter. Burnt-out cars are scattered about; there are mobs throwing rubber bricks and police with batons charging them. Padded stuntmen dive over cars and policemen kick them. Among it all, in the awful cold, wanders Shashi, bearing a bunch of flowers. The kids in the mob are locals, not extras. These kids refuse to sit in the caravan with the actors in police uniform in case their friends think they're fraternizing with the police.

The charges and fighting look terrifying and we haven't shot the main riot yet. That's tonight. Frears says: If we can get through that we'll be OK, we'll survive!

6 MARCH 1987   Night shoot. A row of derelict houses and shops with asbestos over their windows with gas-fired jets in little window boxes in front of them to give the impression of the neighbourhood in flames. In front of this are exploding cars, fire-engines, ambulances and a divided mob of 200 extras plus police with riot shields. There are four cameras. It's massive, for a British film, and brilliantly organized. I think of the script: it just says something like: in the background the riot continues!

The rioting itself is frightening, thrilling and cathartic. It's not difficult to see how compelling and exciting taking part in a riot can be and how far out of yourself such compulsion can take you. On some takes the kids playing rioters continue to attack the extras in uniform after we've cut. Some of the extras playing police threaten to go home if this doesn't stop!

Late at night from the mob emerges a strange sight. Nearby is a hostel for the blind, and about fifteen bewildered blind people with dogs emerge from the mob and walk across the riot area as cars explode around them and Molotov cocktails are flung into shops. At the far end of the set they release their dogs into a park.

I see rushes of yesterday's material. It looks pretty effective. I can see how thrilling it must be to film large-scale set-pieces. It's far easier and often more effective than the hard stuff: subtle acting and the delineation of complicated relationships.

Each day Frears asks me to give him a detailed report of the rushes: what was that scene like? he asks. And the other one? He refuses to watch rushes. The discovery that he can avoid this has liberated him from the inevitable discouragement of staring daily at his own work and its limitations.

10 MARCH 1987 More rushes and some of the riot material cut together. At last it comes alive! I talk to Oliver (the lighting cameraman) about the way he's shot it. He's eschewed the pinks and blues of *Laundrette*, going for a more monochrome look, though at times the screen positively glows! Originally I was sceptical of this, liking the heightened and cheap quality of *Laundrette*. But Oliver felt that the more real *Sammy and Rosie* looks the better as the oddness of the story and strangeness of the juxtapositions are sufficient unreality. He has given the film a European quality, sensuous and warm. I haven't seen a film like it made in Britain.

It's a hard film to make and much to do in six weeks. Everyone looks exhausted already, not surprisingly. They start work at eight in the morning and usually knock off around eleven at night. With night shoots we've been starting at six in the evening and finishing at seven in the morning, though people aren't getting to bed till nine.

The worries about Ayub: he's stiff at the moment and the humour of the part is beyond him. He's better in close-up, being handsome. In mid-shot he wilts and looks as if he doesn't quite know what to do with his body. His pleasantness of character comes through, playing against the unpleasantness of Sammy. But it's going to be difficult for him in the first big part he's played. Wendy looks effective in the rushes, powerful and vulnerable. American actors are trained for the screen. Where you sometimes feel Ayub is delivering his performance to the back of the stalls, Wendy understands the intimacy of the cinema.

On the way to today's shoot, in an East End loft, a battleship passes along the river. The taxi I'm in stops. 'Why have you stopped?' I ask. 'I can't go on,' the driver says, gazing at the ship. 'My eyes have misted over. Doesn't it do you in?' I refrain from telling him the battleship is French. When I turn up I find they've managed to work the battleship into the scene. Let's hope people think it's a symbol.

In the script most of the scenes between Anna and Sammy take place in Anna's bed. But Frears opens them up, using the whole space, even creating a new scene by moving into the loft's tiny bathroom which has a spectacular view over London. Because of these scenes I write new dialogue for Anna about an exhibition she's having, called 'Images of a Decaying Europe'.

13 MARCH 1987   Today Frears rails at the actors for lacking flair, for thinking too much about their costumes, for being too passive and not helping him enough. He's been cheerful all through it, but now the strain is starting to tell. It's partly because the scene we're shooting—outside Sammy's and Rosie's flat, with Rosie returning with Danny on a motorbike, the Ghost walking past, Vivia watching Rafi from the window and Rosie's two friends also watching Rafi—is very complicated. The cold—working fifteen hours a day in snow flurries—is getting people down. Frears also blames me for this scene going badly: 'You should never set a scene as complicated as this outside,' he says. 'Haven't you learned that yet? I can't control it out here!' In fact, this is the only scene in the film we will have to reshoot.

16 MARCH 1987   To Frears's last night to discuss the waste-ground eviction scene at the end of the film. It has to be choreographed precisely and it hasn't been yet. What I've written isn't clear. So we work out, almost shot by shot, the final relationships between the characters. The problem with the end of the film, with the eviction as opposed to the already shot riot scene, is the danger of it being sentimental. Ambiguities and ironies have to be excavated just as Rafi and Sammy and Anna bumbling around during the riots made all the difference to a scene which could easily be one-dimensional.

Have the idea that in order to reflect on what has gone on in the film it might be a good notion to have, during the closing credits, some of Anna's photographs shown to us.

17 MARCH 1987   Shooting the waste-ground material on the large piece of unused ground under the motorway. Bit of a shock to turn up at the location and find Frances Barber in a black and white corset. I look at her wondering if she has forgotten to put the rest of her clothes on. Her breasts, well, they are jammed into an odd shape: it looks as though she has two Cornish pasties attached to her chest. I tell Stephen she looks like a gangster's moll from a western. He takes it as a compliment. 'That's exactly what I intended,' he says. 'John Ford would be proud of me.'

Between takes, the corset debate continues between us, as in a snowstorm Shashi sits in a filthy flea-ridden armchair in front of a smoking fire, surrounded by young people in grey costumes banging tins. Frears argues that the corset is an inspired idea; it liberates Rosie from do-goodery; she looks bizarre, anarchistic and interesting, not earnest or condescending. What he then describes as the 'simplistic politics of the film' he says are transcended by imaginativeness. At the end of the argument he calls me a prude and for the rest of the afternoon he refers to me as Mrs Grundy.

The corset depresses me because after everyone's work on the film it is still easy to hit a wrong note. I feel uneasy in complaining because I think Frears's judgement is less conservative than my own; I could be wrong. Maybe, too, I'm being sentimental about the woman the character is based on, a more dignified and sensitive person than the one signified by the corset.

19 MARCH 1987   We shoot the eviction and exodus from the waste ground. With the trailers and caravans whirling in the mud and dust, the bulldozers crashing through shops, lifting cars and tossing them about, the straggly kids waving flags and playing music as the police and heavies invade and evict them, it is like a western! Frears runs among it all, yelling instructions through a megaphone.

It is tough on Shashi. India's premier actor, a god to millions, is impersonating a torturer having a nightmare while bouncing on a bed in the back of a caravan which is being wildly driven around a stony waste ground in a snowstorm. Books scatter over his head. When he emerges, shaken and stirred, dizzy and fed up, he threatens to go back to Bombay. The next morning, when we tell him as a joke that we have to reshoot his scene in the back of the caravan, he goes white.

It is obvious that he has a difficult part. The character of Rafi is complex and contradictory and he has to play against many different kinds of character. Shashi is not used to making films in English and the part is physically demanding. But with his modesty, generosity and unEnglish liking for women, he is the most adored person on the film.

So a glorious day—mostly to do with the pleasure of working with other people, especially the 'straggly kids' who jam all day and some of the night by the fire. Most of them are alternative comedians and buskers from the London Underground. Few of them have a regular place to live, and when Debbie wants to inform them of a day's shooting, she has to send her assistants round the tube stations of central London to find them.

Coming out of my hutch for this film has made me realize how hard it is sometimes to bear the isolation that all writers have to put up with.

20 MARCH 1987   To Kew where we're shooting the suburban material—in Alice's house and the street she lives in. We film the scene where Alice comes to the door and sees Rafi for the first time for thirty years. We do several takes and find it works best when Claire and Shashi do least, when they contain their reaction and we have to strain to imagine their feelings.

Here, where it is quiet and sedate, leafy and affluent, we have more complaints from residents than at any other location, though there are no charging bulldozers and we burn nothing down, though severely tempted.

Being brought up in the suburbs myself, this location reminds me of slow childhood Sundays on which you weren't allowed to yell in the street and your friends were kept in for the holy day. Sundays in the suburbs were a funeral and it's still beyond me why the celebration of God's love for the world has to be such a miserable business.

I know now that England is primarily a suburban country and English values are suburban values. The best of that is kindness and mild-temperedness, politeness and privacy, and some rather resentful tolerance. The suburbs are also a mix of people. In my small street lived a civil servant, an interior decorator, secretaries, a local journalist, an architect, a van driver, a milkman, and so on, all living together in comfortable houses with gardens, in relative harmony.

At worst there is narrowness of outlook and fear of the different. There is cruelty by privacy and indifference. There is great lower-middle-class snobbery, contempt for the working class and envy of the middle class. And there is a refusal to admit to humanity beyond the family, beyond the household walls and garden fence. Each family as an autonomous, self-sufficient unit faces a hostile world of other self-contained families. This neurotic and materialistic privacy, the keystone of British suburban life, ensures that the 'collective' or even the 'public' will mean little to these people. It's interesting that the Labour leader, Neil Kinnock, has repudiated the now discredited notion of the collective in favour of left-wing individualism. He has said: 'They have got to be told that socialism is the answer for them because socialism looks after the individual.'

My love and fascination for inner London endures. Here there is fluidity and possibilities are unlimited. Here it is possible to avoid your enemies; here everything is available. In the suburbs everything changes slowly. Heraclitus said: 'You can't step in the same river twice.' In the inner-city you can barely step in the same street twice, so rapid is human and environmental change.

I sit in the first sunshine of the year in this English garden in Kew reading the papers. There is much written today about the verdict in the Blakelock case, where a policeman was hacked to death during an uprising on the Broadwater Farm Estate in North London. A man was sentenced to life imprisonment for the killing. The uprising followed the death of a much respected middle-aged black woman, Cynthia Jarrett, who died of a heart attack during a police raid on her home on the estate. The Police Commissioner, Sir Kenneth Newman, claimed that 'anarchists and Trotskyists' planned the uprising in advance, though there is no evidence for this. There is confusion and inconsistency in the police account of the incident, to say the least. The police also broke numerous rules and acted illegally in their treatment of two young 'suspects'. A fifteen-year-old boy was held three days without access to his parents or a solicitor. A sixteen-year-old, with a mental age of seven, was interrogated without his mother or solicitor.

It's all depressing, as was the incident around which I based the opening of the film: the shooting of a black woman, Cherry Groce, who was permanently paralysed after being shot during a police raid in which her son was being sought.

But what are we doing using this material in the film? Today, when confronted once more by the racism, violence, alienation and waste of the Broadwater Farm Estate uprising, our little film has to be justified over again. After all, real life has become part of a film, reduced perhaps, maybe trivialzed. We will make money from it; careers will be furthered; film festivals attended. But aren't we stealing other people's lives, their hard experience, for our own purposes? The relation we bear to those people's lives is tangential, to say the least. Perhaps because of that we seriously misunderstand their lives.

I can't work out today if the question about the relation between the real people, the real events, and the portrayal is an aesthetic or moral one. In other words, if the acting is good, if the film is well made, if it seems authentic, does that make it all right, is the stealing justified? Will the issue be settled if experience is successfully distilled into art?

Or is the quality of the work irrelevant to the social issue, which is that of middle-class people (albeit dissenting middle-class people) who own and control and have access to the media and to money, using minority and working-class material to entertain other middle-class people? Frequently during the making of the film I feel that this is the case, that what we're doing is a kind of social voyeurism.

At the same time I can justify our work by saying it is the duty of contemporary films to show contemporary life. This portrayal of our world as it is valuable in itself, and part of the climate of opposition and dissent.

In one part of me I do believe there is some anger in the film; and it does deal with things not often touched on in British films. In another part of me, when I look at the film world, run by the usual white middle-class public-school types, with a few parvenu thugs thrown in, I can see that the film is just a commercial product.

Frears and I talk this over. He says the film is optimistic about the young people portrayed in it: their vivacity, lack of conformity and rebelliousness are celebrated in it.

20 MARCH 1987   In the evening to rushes—uncut takes of the waste-ground material. It looks good and people are pleased with their work. Leon from Cinecom is there, as is his boss. Leon sleeps through the rushes and his boss says: For rushes they're not bad, but it's not family entertainment.

After, we drive through London and go to a pub. It's a shock that London and other people's lives are continuing while we're making a film. Film-making is an absorbing and complete world; the relationships are so intense and generous, the collaboration so total, that the rest of the world is blanked out.

24 MARCH 1987   In the studio at Twickenham at last and off the street. Here we're shooting all the material in Sammy's and Rosie's flat. It is easier to watch the performances in this calmer and more controlled place, even if the atmosphere is slightly flat.

It seems to me that Shashi is going to turn out to be very good, portraying a complex and dangerous character, a murderer and a man eager to be loved, a populist and an élitist. Frears is carefully and patiently teasing out the power and subtlety in Shashi by getting him to act simply and underplay everything. You can see the performance developing take by take. After eight or nine takes Shashi is settled, a little tired and bored, more casual and relaxed. Now he is able to throw the scene away. And this is when he is at his best, though he himself prefers the first few takes when he considers himself to be really 'acting'. Sometimes he can't see why Frears wants to do so many retakes.

Ayub improving too. He is inexperienced as an actor (it is of course difficult for Asian actors to gain experience), but Oliver is doing a wonderful job in making him look like a matinée idol. The balance of the script has gone against Sammy. It is Rafi and Rosie that I've developed as there is more scope for conflict with them. Sammy doesn't believe in a great deal, so it's hard to have him disagree much with anyone. His confusion isn't particularly interesting. Rosie is a more complex character and harder to write, especially as she isn't a character I've written before.

25 MARCH 1987   I turn up on the set and find that Frears has Rosie going out to meet her lover not only in that ridiculous coat, but wearing only her underwear. He seems to think that someone would go to see their lover, via a riot, wearing only a thermal vest and a pair of tights. I certainly wouldn't. I hope I'll be able to watch the film in the future without suffering at this moment.

Thank God I'm leaving London in a couple of days for the

Oscar ceremonies. I've been on the set every day, though I'm not sure it's been as essential as it was on *Laundrette*. There hasn't been much rewriting this time.

28 MARCH 1987   *Los Angeles*. I wind down the window of the cab as we hit the freeway and accelerate. Air rushes in, gloriously warm to me after an English winter of freezing balls. I pull three layers of clothes over my head. LA is blazingly green and bright: how easy it is to forget (one's senses accustomed to dullness) that this industry town is also subtropical; its serious and conservative business takes place among the palm trees, exotic birds and pre-ternaturally singing flowers. Everything is as resplendent as if I'd taken LSD. Walking into the hotel, the Château Marmont, a small, friendly European place on a hill, the grass appears to have been sprayed with gloss and the air pumped full of perfume. It is eucalyptus.

The phone calls begin as soon as I open the windows of my room: from agents, press people, producers, recommending the numerous totally beautiful human beings I should impress in the next few days. I say to my agent: But most of these people do not interest me. She says: Dear, all that is important is that you interest them—whatever you do, don't discourage them. As long as they're saying your name as they eat all round this city you've got nothing to worry about.

As we talk I eat some fruit. Swollen nature in my hands: strawberries long as courgettes, thick as cucumbers. Here the most natural things look unnatural, which is fitting in a mythical city in a hotel in which Bogart proposed to Bacall, where John Belushi died, where Dorothy Parker had an apartment and Lillian Hellman and Norman Mailer would come to tea and no one wanted to be the first to leave, and in which, when I get into bed to read—Robert Stone's *Children of Light*—I find myself staring

into a novel about a burned-out screenwriter living at the Château
Marmont drinking and drugging himself while a screenplay he
wrote is being shot in another country.

29 MARCH 1987   At breakfast the waiters are discussing films
they've seen recently. Then they start to worry about the Oscars.
They can't believe that *Betty Blue* is the French entry in the Best
Foreign Picture Category. What about *Vagabonde*? At another
table a young man is hungrily explaining the plot of a film he's
written to an older man. 'This film could change lives,' he says,
not eating. The other man eats croissants as big as boomerangs.
'It's about an alien disguised as a policeman. But it's a good alien,
right? It's about the renewal of the human spirit.'

Later, with some friends, I drive through this baking city to
Venice Beach. I'm being shown the city. How attractive it is too,
and not vulgar. I notice how few black people there are. What
little poverty. I'd have thought this city was bereft of unhappiness
if I hadn't stayed downtown on my last visit here. That time the
manager of the hotel said, when I checked in: Whatever you do,
sir, don't go out after dark.

Venice Beach—so called because of the rotting bits of Venetian
architecture still left over from a time when a minor Venice was
being contemplated here. It is in its wild spirit something like the
Venice, Italy, I saw a few weeks ago, though less stylish and more
eccentric, which you'd expect in a country without an aristocratic
culture. Herds of people cruise the boardwalk. A man is juggling
a chainsaw and a ball, hurling the humming saw into the air and
catching it. A dog in sunglasses watches. A man with pierced
nipples, with rings hanging from them, also watches. All along
the beach there are masseurs, rolfers, shiatsu experts, astrologers,
yoga masters and tattoo freaks. Further along, at Muscle Beach,
in an enclosed area, men and women work out, twitching, shaking,

vibrating, tensing and generally exhibiting their bodies to the crowds.

Back at the hotel the phone rings constantly. People tell me: The greatest day of your life is approaching. I try to think of the one day in my life in which I had more happiness than any other.

Later, to a cocktail party given by Orion, the distributors of *Laundrette* in the US. It is as interesting as a convention of carpet salesmen. I sit next to a woman whose husband is an executive in the company. In her early twenties, she tells me how she hates it all, how you just have to keep smiling if you want your husband to be promoted and how desperate she is to go home and get some drugs up her nose. Everyone leaves early. Drive the LA streets at eleven and they're deserted. It's like Canterbury. Everyone goes to bed early because they work so hard.

30 MARCH 1987   After lunch in Santa Monica near the beach, to the Bel-Air hotel with its lush gardens, its white Moorish architecture and its private suites and cottages in the grounds with their own patios. Here, you go somewhere, get out of your car and someone parks it. When you leave the restaurant, bar or hotel, the car is waiting outside. If you've got the dough, there's always someone around to save you doing something yourself. I'm beginning to see how addictive such a luxurious place as this could become. Once you'd really got the taste for it, how could you be detoxicated? To which clinic could you go to dry out from the juices of wealth and pleasure that had saturated you in this city?

It's interesting how few notable American film directors actually live in Los Angeles: Coppola, Pakula, Pollack, Scorsese, Demmie, all live in other cities. The directors and writers who do live here are British, often successful in British television, now flailing around in the vacuum of Los Angeles, rich but rootless and confused, attempting the impossible task of finding decent work, exiled from a country that doesn't have a film industry.

31 MARCH 1987 The day of the Oscars. People leave work after lunch in order to get home and watch it on TV at five o'clock. All over the city Oscar parties are beginning in lounges and beside pools. For weeks since the nominations, there has been speculation about possible winners. Turn on the TV and grave pundits are weighing the merits of Bob Hoskins and Paul Newman; open a paper and predictions are being made. Here the Oscars are unavoidable, as competitive and popular as a Cup Final, as dignified and socially important as a Royal Wedding.

A last swim on my back in the hotel pool, watching the sky through the trees before the extensive pleasures of the bathroom where I sip champagne and receive phone calls and gifts. Slipping on my elastic bow-tie I suspect this will be the best time of the day. Outside in the lane the limo is already waiting. By now I have definitely had enough of people saying: It's enough to be nominated, it's an honour in itself. By now that isn't enough: by now I want to win; by now, I know I will win!

When your four-seater black stretch limo pulls up outside the venue all you see on either side of you are other limos, a shimmering sea of shining black metal. When you slide out, you see the high grandstands lining the long walk to the entrance. In these packed grandstands screaming people wave placards with the names of their favourite films written on them. '*Platoon, Platoon, Platoon!*' someone is yelling. Another person bellows: '*Room with a View, Room with a View!*' One man holds a placard which says: 'Read the Bible.'

Inside there are scores of young people, the women in long dresses, the men in tuxedos, who have small signs around their neck saying: 'The 59th Academy Awards'. They are the seat-fillers. Their role is essential, so that when the cameras sweep across the auditorium there isn't an empty seat in the place, whereas in fact the sensible people are in the bar watching it all, like everyone else, on TV, only going in to sit down for their bit. In the bar with friends we look out for stars and discuss them: doesn't Elizabeth Taylor look tiny and doesn't her head look big—perhaps she's had all the fat in her body sucked out by the modish vacuum method; doesn't Bette Davis look shrivelled and fragile; doesn't Sigourney Weaver look terrific and what was wrong with Jane Fonda and doesn't Dustin Hoffman always look the same?

When it comes to your section and Shirley MacLaine starts to read out the names of the nominees, you silently run over your speech, remove a speck of dried semen from your collar and squeeze the arms of your seat, ready to propel yourself into the sight of a billion people. You wonder where in the sitting room you'll put your Oscar, or maybe you should hide it somewhere in case it's stolen? What does it weigh anyway? You'll soon find out.

When they make a mistake and don't read out your name you vow never to attend any such ridiculous ceremony of self-congratulation, exhibitionism and vulgarity again.

I April 1987   The next day by the pool drinking iced tea, several young producers come by. My impression is that they come to have a look at you, to check you out, to see if there's anything in you for them. One drives me around the city in his Jag. He asks me if I want to fly to San Francisco for lunch. I ask if there isn't anywhere a little nearer we can go. He swears eternal love and a contract.

An idea for a story: of someone who inadvertently writes a successful film and lives off its reputation for years, so afraid of ending the shower of financial seductions and blandishments that he never writes anything again.

2 APRIL 1987   I return to find Frears in heaven on the set, sitting with his plimsolls up and gossiping, waiting for a shot to be set up. To ruin his day I tell him about the directors I've met in Hollywood and how much they earn and the kind of luxury in which they live. Frears goes into agonies of frustration and jealousy, especially when I mention money. He keeps saying: 'What am I doing here, fuck all this art, just give me the money!' This makes Shashi laugh and laugh. But there is another element of neurosis in all this American craziness which is more serious, especially for a film-maker. Since the 1950s the United States is the place where the action is, where things happen, and because the US has the central role in the world which England had in the nineteenth century, America is always present for players in the culture game. Like a mountain that you have to climb or turn away from in disgust, it is an existential challenge involving complicated choices and threats and fear. Do you make an attempt on this height or do you withdraw into your corner? How much of yourself are you prepared to put into this enterprise? Unfortunately for British film-makers, America has been something of a Bermuda Triangle into which many careers have crashed without trace.

They are shooting the party scenes and some kissing between Rani and Vivia; also between Rani and another woman, Margy. I remember Meera (who plays Rani) as a student coming to see me in 1981 at Riverside Studios where we were rehearsing a play for the Royal Court. She asked me if I thought she would ever become an actress. She desperately wanted to go into the theatre, and she wanted to write too. There was some resistance from her parents who, like the parents of many Asian girls, were mostly concerned with her having an arranged marriage. But her enthusiasm and ambition were so obvious, I just told her to stick at it. I wonder what her parents would say if they could see her having a grape removed from between her teeth by the tongue of another actress!

Perhaps these kisses, like the ones between Johnny and Omar in *Laundrette*—

Each kiss a heart-quake,—for a kiss's strength
I think it must be reckon'd by its length.

—are subversive in some way. It's as if they poke social convention and say: There are these other ways to live; there are people who are different, but aren't guilt-ridden. When I went to see *She's Gotta Have It* recently, and it was mostly a young black audience, when the two women kissed the audience screamed with disapproval and repulsion.

We also shoot the scene where Rafi arrives at Sammy's and Rosie's flat and finds Rosie's friends putting a condom on a carrot. Later in the scene Rani and Vivia stand in the centre of the room and kiss, rather ostentatiously. Shashi is agitated by all this and yells for his agent, a taxi, and a first-class flight to Bombay.

God knows what this film will look like when it's all stuck together. I suppose it's a film of juxtapositions and contrasts, of different scenes banging hard together. One danger is that the film lacks narrative force and focus; it may be too diffuse.

3 APRIL 1987 Frears and I rejig the scene where Rafi comes home from the party and finds Vivia and Rani in bed. Originally they chase him around the room with lumps of wood and attempt to beat him to a pulp. He barricades himself in the study and climbs out of the window and down the drainpipe. When it comes to shooting it, it doesn't seem as believable or funny as when I wrote it.

So at lunch-time we rework it. Rafi comes in, finds Vivia and Rani in bed, and is outraged. Abusing them in Punjabi, a row breaks out. So Shashi and Meera work out a couple of pages of

abuse to scream at each other. Meera will also throw things at
him. It's terrifying when we come to shoot it, with Meera hammering a piece of wood with nails in it into the door behind which
Shashi is cowering! As the scene is all Punjabi abuse we talk about
putting sub-titles on it.

7 APRIL 1987   We shoot Sammy and Rosie crying and rocking
together on the floor at the end of the film, with the women slowly
leaving the flat behind them. I get to the studio at eight in the
morning and leave at nine in the evening. This seems to me to
be an ideal solution to living: erect this saving girder of necessity
around you: you don't have to think or decide how to live!

Frears saw a good deal of the film on Saturday, as it's being
edited as we shoot it. He says: Christ, it's a weepie, a complete
heartbreaker! We'll have to put hundreds of violins on the sound-
track!

8 APRIL 1987   I look at a good chunk of the film on the tiny screen
of an editing machine at Twickenham Studios. It makes me laugh,
partly, I think in relief that it isn't completely terrible. It's less
rough than *Laundrette*, more glamorous, more conventional, with
Hollywood colours. I look at the scene where Rafi catches Rani
and Vivia in bed; they attack him and he climbs out of the window
and down the drainpipe. We were thinking of cutting him climbing out of the window, it seemed unconvincing. Yet looking at it
in context, I think it'll work.

Frears comes into the cutting room while I'm watching and
talks to Mick, the editor. It's very impressive the way Frears can
hold every shot of the film in his head at once, even though he's
barely seen any of it. He can remember every take of every shot.
So when he's talking to Mick about scenes he shot weeks ago,
he'll say: Wasn't take 5 better than take 3? Or: Didn't the actress
have her hand over her face on take 11 on the mid-shot and not
on take 2?

We talk about the kind of harmless threat of disorder that films like *Laundrette* or *Prick Up Your Ears* represent, which partly explains their success. The pattern is one of there being a fairly rigid social order which is set up in detail in the film. Set against this order there is an individual or two, preferably in love, who violate this conventional structure. Their rebellion, their form of transgressional sex, is liberating, exciting. Audiences identify with it. Films as diverse as, say, *Billy Liar, Room with a View, Midnight Cowboy, Guess Who's Coming to Dinner?*, have this pattern, following an alienated individual or couple, unable to find a place for themselves in the society as it is. Usually there's some kind of individual reconciliation at the end of the film; or the individual is destroyed. But there is rarely any sense that the society could or should be changed. The pattern is, of course, a seductive one because we can see ourselves in the alienated, but authentic, individual standing up against stuffiness, ignorance and hatred of love. In all this we are not helped to think in any wider sense of the way societies repress legitimate ideals, groups of people, and possible forms of life.

In some films of the middle and late sixties, when the rigid social order was eschewed entirely as no longer relevant, and only 'liberated' individuals were portrayed, the films have little power or interest, lacking the kind of conflict and tension that the classic pattern necessarily produces.

9 APRIL 1987 Filming in the cellar of a pub in Kew. Cramped and dusty; the lights keep going out. Claire, whose performance until now has been, rightly, contained, starts to reveal her power in this cellar scene with Shashi. Furiously jerking things out of the suitcase she packed thirty years ago, and shoving the whole lot on the floor, she reveals such a combination of wild anger, vulnerability and pain, that when the camera cut, there was complete silence. Even Shashi looked shaken. It was especially difficult

for her as the Ghost was in the scene as well, standing at her
elbow.

10 APRIL 1987   We spend the day in a South Kensington restaurant filming the confrontation scene between Rosie, Rafi and
Sammy when they go out to dinner. This is the pivotal scene of
the movie. It starts off simply. The three of them are at the table;
the violinists play a little Mozart in the background, the drag
queen sits behind them. But the violinists have extraordinary
faces: English features, pale shoulders (ready to be painted by
Ingres), Pre-Raphaelite hair, and after twelve solid hours of fiddling, very worn fingers.

As the day progresses Shashi and Frances become more heated
in their argument. The playing of the violinists becomes more
frenzied. The drag queen does a very exasperated flounce. Shashi
eats a finger made from sausage meat and spits out the nail, putting
it politely on the side of the plate.

I can see Frears's imagination racing as he uses these few elements to their fullest and most absurd effect. He becomes increasingly inventive, his control and experience allowing him to
play. I am a little afraid the scene will be drowned in effects, but
I did write the scene in a similar spirit—putting the people in
the restaurant and experimenting until something came of it.

Of course, the conditions of Frears's creativity are different
from mine. Alone in a room I can take my time and rewrite as
often as I like. I can leave the scene and rewrite it in two weeks'
time. For Frears in that small restaurant crowded with seventy
people there is no way of going back on the scene. It has to be
done there and then and it has to work. It takes a lot of nerve to
play with a scene under those conditions, especially as the medium
is so ridiculously expensive.

I notice how comfortable Frances is in her part now. She has
discovered who she is playing; and that is something you find

out only in the course of filming. But unlike the theatre, there's never another opportunity to integrate later discoveries into earlier scenes.

If the conditions in which film directors usually work make it difficult for them to be original, a film actor's life is certainly no bed of roses. You are picked up at seven or earlier in the morning; you may shoot your first scene at ten or eleven, if you're lucky. Or you may be hanging around until three or four before you begin work. Wendy came in early for several days, thinking they were going to shoot her 'fuck night' scene with Ayub that day, then nothing was done, though she didn't know that until early evening. But if your scene is going to be shot, however bored and cold and confused by the entire thing you are, you have to drag your concentration to the sticking place, you have to pull out your performance immediately. You may have to play a very emotional scene and you have to play it now! But whatever you're doing, it's very expensive, so the faster you do it the more you will be appreciated. As there's little time for exploration and experiment you will probably have to give a performance much like one you've given before because at least you can be sure it will work.

When that acting job's finished there might possibly be another one. Should you turn it down and hope something better will turn up? Perhaps it won't; but perhaps it will. If it does, the director may be duff or the script no good or the part too small. Whatever happens, most of the work actors get doesn't stretch them and 80 per cent of the directors they work with will have little talent. Of the good 20 per cent, 5 per cent will be tyrants who think of actors as puppets.

Despite these difficulties, all the British actors I know have one thing in common: they are well-trained, skilled and dedicated people who want to do good work and give of their best within a profession that only rarely gives them the opportunity to reach their potential. No wonder so many actors become neurotic or dull through lack of interest in anything but their careers.

11 APRIL 1987   In a tiny studio off the Harrow Road we film the interior scenes set in Danny's caravan. Outside the caravan, a row of gas jets reproduce the waste ground fires. The props man and the assistant art director wearily dance behind the gas jets to reproduce the celebration of the 'fuck' night as Frances and Roland roll around naked. Frears sinks down in a chair next to me. 'I've become completely paranoid,' he says. 'I've had it. Is this any good or not?' 'I don't know,' I say. 'What's it about anyway?' he says. 'Fuck knows,' I reply. He needs support and for no one to speak in too loud a voice. Anything above a whisper is interpreted as hatred. 'We should have had more time,' he says, after a while. 'About two more weeks would have done it. But it would have cost £300,000 and we didn't have it.'

I leave early and go to a book publishing party. On the way I see the police have stopped a black man and woman and are questioning them. It's odd going to the party: the world going on as normal. Later, I see someone I recognize coming towards me, black hair sticking up, face white, a week's growth on his face. I try and work out who it is. At last I know: Stephen Frears.

Later, I run into a friend who drags me away from the restaurant and tells me to sit in her car. She says there's something I have to see that I've never seen before. Well, she drives me to an Arts Centre in West London. I take one look at the scene and try to leave. It looks as if she's brought me to an Asian wedding. Women and kids of all ages are sitting on rows of chairs around the walls, not talking. The men, mostly Sikhs, stand together at the bar, talking. The women have gone to a lot of trouble tonight, really dressing up for this one in much jewellery, in shalwar kamizes threaded with silver and gold. By ten o'clock the hall is packed with Asian families, with babies and children and old men and women. I've no idea what to expect. The stage is full of rock 'n' roll gear.

The band comes on: eight men in red and white costumes. They look like assistants in a fast-food joint. One of them announces the singers: 'Welcome the greatest Bhangra singers in the world!' Two men bounce on stage in spangled T-shirts and tight white pants.

The music starts. The music is extraordinary. After years of colonialism and immigration and Asian life in Britain; after years of black American and reggae music in Britain comes this weird fusion. A cocktail of blues and r 'n' b shaken with Indian film songs in Hindi, cut with heavy guitar solos and electric violin runs and African drumming, a result of all the music in the world being available in an affluent Asian area, Southall, near Heathrow Airport—it is Bhangra music! Detroit and Delhi, in London!

For a few seconds no one moves. The dance floor is a forbidden zone with everyone perched like tense runners around it. Then no one can hold themselves back. Men fly on to the floor. They dance together, thrusting their arms into the air and jerking their hips and thighs, tight-buttocked. Sometimes the men climb on each others' shoulders or wrap their legs around the others' waists to be swept in dizzy circles inches from the floor. Women and girls dance with each other; women dance with tiny babies. An old Indian colonel with a fine moustache and military importance weaves amongst it all, taking photographs.

And they all know each other, these people. They were at school together and now they live in the same streets and do business with each other and marry amongst themselves. This gig, such a celebration, is unlike any other I've been to for years: it's not to do with boys and girls trying to pick each other up; it's not aggressive. Makes you aware of the violence and hostility you expect of public occasions in Britain.

Now we've almost finished filming, in the morning I sit down and try to write something new.

I've enjoyed being out of the house every day and the intense involvement of film-making. The cliché of film-making which talks of the set as being a family is inaccurate, though the set is hierarchical and strictly stratified in the family way. But unlike with a family the relationships are finite, everyone knows what they're doing and there's a strong sense of purpose. The particular pleasure of a film set is in being with a group of people who work well and happily together.

Now, back at the desk, I immediately feel that writing is something of a dingy business. Why this unhealthy attempt to catch life, to trap it, rearrange it, pass it on, when it should be lived and forgotten? Why this re-creation in isolation of something that had blood and real life in it? The writer's pretence and self-flattery that what is written is even realer than the real when it's nothing of the kind.

16 APRIL 1987   To Frears's house. He's being photographed with his kids to coincide with the opening of *Prick Up Your Ears*. David Byrne comes by in a green and black tartan jacket, jeans, with a little pigtail. He has a luminous round face, and bright clear skin. It's the first time I've met him, though his band, the Talking Heads, are heroes of mine. We walk round the corner to the Gate Diner where the waiter inadvertently sits us under a poster for *Stop Making Sense*. Various people in the street recognize him and a woman comes over to our table and gives him a note with her phone number on it, thanking him for his contribution to music and films.

Byrne is shy and clever and unpretentious. The disconcerting thing about him is that he listens to what you say and thinks it over before replying seriously. The only other person I've met who has done this is Peter Brook. A most unusual experience.

Byrne was given the script of *Sammy and Rosie* in New York by the great David Gothard, and wants to do some music for it. Byrne has picked up some African music in Paris, composed by street musicians, which Frears thinks is superb. Byrne talks about using similar rhythms in the music he might do for *Sammy and Rosie*. We'll show Byrne a cut of the movie as soon as possible and he can put music over the parts that interest him. The problem is time, as Byrne is composing the music for the new Bertolucci film, *The Last Emperor*, as well as writing the songs for the new Talking Heads record.

In the street waiting for a cab with Byrne I see the cops have stopped another car with black people in it. The black people are being very patient. What the hell is going on in this city?

18 APRIL 1987 Big day. First rough assembly of the film. I meet the editor, Mick Audsley, who is pulling the film on a trolley in its numerous silver cans through the streets. It's 110 minutes long, he says. As it's a rough-cut the film is a little like a home movie, with the sound coming and going; and of course there's no music.

We watch it in a small viewing theatre off Tottenham Court Road. The first forty minutes are encouraging and absorbing and we laugh a lot. Shashi is excellent: both menacing and comic, though his performance seems to lack subtlety. I am elated all the same. Then it begins to fall apart. My mind wanders. I can't follow the story. Entire scenes, which seemed good in themselves at the time of shooting, pass without registering. They bear no relation to each other. It is the centre of the film I'm referring to: the party, the 'fuck' night, the morning after, the breakfasts. Towards the end the film picks up again and is rather moving.

Each of us, cameraman, editor, director, me, can see the faults of the thing from our own point of view. I can see the character of Danny fading out; can see that the character of Anna is not sufficiently rounded; that the riots are not developed in any significant way.

But there are pluses: Shashi of course. And Frances, who portrays a strong, complex person very clearly. Roland too, especially as I'd worried that he might have been a little wooden.

What I don't get is any sense of the freshness of the thing, of how surprising and interesting it may be to others.

After, I stagger from the viewing theatre, pleased on the one hand that it's up on the screen at last. On the other, I feel disappointed that after all the work, the effort, the thought, it's all over so quickly and just a movie.

Frears is pleased. These things are usually hell, he says, but this wasn't, entirely. Some of it, he says, is the best work he's done; it's a subtle and demanding film. Part of the problem with it, he thinks, is that maybe it's too funny at the beginning and not serious enough. He suggests it could be slowed down a bit. I say I don't want to lose any of the humour especially as the end of the film is so miserable. It's a question, over the next few weeks, of reconciling the two things.

30 April 1987   Mick Audsley has been furiously cutting the film for the last two weeks. When we all walk into the preview theatre—including Karin Bamborough and David Rose from Channel 4—to see how the film's progressed, Mick's as nervous as a playwright on a first night. I reassure him. But it's his film now; this is his draft; it's his work we're judging. 'I've taken some stuff out,' he says nervously. 'And moved other things around.'

There are about twelve people in the room. Frears's film *Prick Up Your Ears* is successful in the States and Bevan's *Personal Services* is number three in the British film charts, so they're both pretty cheerful.

For the first forty minutes I can't understand what's happened to the film. It's more shaped now, but less bizarre somehow, less unpredictable. I suppress my own laughter in order to register every gurgle and snort of pleasure around me. But there is nothing: complete silence.

The film begins to improve around the 'fuck' night and takes off when the Ghetto-lites dance and mime to Otis Redding's 'My Girl' and we cut between the avid fuckers. It's unashamedly erotic, a turn-on, running right up against the mean monogamous spirit of our age. There must be more jiggling tongues in this film than in any other ever made.

I cringe throughout at the ridiculousness of the dialogue, which seems nothing like the way people actually talk. A lot of this will go, I expect, or we can play some very loud David Byrne music over it, though I am attached to some of the ideas contained in the more strident speeches.

At the end I feel drained and disappointed. I look around for a chair in the corner into which I can quickly disappear. I feel like putting a jacket over my head.

Then you have to ask people what they think. David Rose is a little enigmatic. He says the film is like a dream, so heightened and unreal it is. It bears no relation to the real world. I say: We want to create a self-sustaining, internally coherent world. He says, yes, you've done that, but you can't be surprised when what you've done seems like an intrusion to those it is about.

Frears says it's a different film from the one we watched two weeks ago. Now we have to fuse the seriousness of this version with the frivolity of the first version.

A journalist who came to see me the other day asked why I always write about such low types, about people without values or morality, as it seems all the characters are, except for Alice. It's a shock when he says this. I write about the world around me, the people I know, and myself. Perhaps I've been hanging out with the wrong crowd. Reminds me of a story about Proust, who when correcting the proofs of *Remembrance of Things Past*, was suddenly disgusted by the horrible people he'd brought to life, corrupt and unpleasant and lustful all of them and not a figure of integrity anywhere in it.

4 MAY 1987   A very confused time for us in trying to work out what kind of film we want to release. We talk frequently about the shape of it, of pressing it experimentally all over to locate the bones beneath the rolling fat. But you have to press in far to touch hardness. There's barely any story to the thing. If there is a story, it belongs to Shashi. Frears is talking of 'taking things out'. He says, 'Less means better' and adds ominously, 'There's far too much in it.' It's painful, this necessary process of cutting. I think, for consolation, of Jessica Mitford's: 'In writing you must always kill your dearest darlings!'

7 MAY 1987   Frears in good form in the cutting room. He hasn't been so cheerful for days. He's cutting swathes out of the movie. It's funnier and more delicate, he says. He adds: Your talent will seem considerably greater after I've done with it!

He's put his finger on something which will inevitably bother film-writers. If the movie is successful you can never be sure to what extent this is due to you, or whether the acting, editing and direction have concealed weaknesses and otherwise lifted an ordinary script which, if it were to be shown in its entirety or as written, wouldn't work at all.

11 MAY 1987   Frears rings and says it's vital I come in later today and see the film. You'll have to brace yourself, he adds, ringing off.

The first shock is in the first minute: the shooting. Mick has obviously worried a great deal about this. He has removed the moment when the black woman gets shot, when you see her covered in blood and falling to the ground. Even Frears is surprised that this has come out, but he's pleased with it. What such a powerful and upsetting moment does, they both argue, is overwhelm the opening. Frears also says that its removal improves the subtlety of the story-telling—we find out later what has happened. I do like the shooting, not for aesthetic reasons, but for didactic ones: it says, this is what happens to some black people in Britain—they get shot up by the police.

Halfway through this cut I can see it's going to work. The shape is better, it's quicker, less portentous. Danny's long speech has gone, as have various other bits of dialogue. A scene between Anna and Sammy has gone, which means that Anna's part in the film is diminished. Alice's speech on going down the stairs, before the cellar scene, has gone, which I missed. I'll try and get them to put it back.

I argue to Frears that in some ways the film has been depoliticized, or that private emotions now have primacy over public acts or moral positions. In one sense, with a film this is inevitable: it is the characters and their lives one is interested in. Frears argues that, on the contrary, the film is more political. Ideas are being banged together harder now: the audience is being provoked. But I can see that my remark has bothered him.

I can't deny it's a better film: less grim, less confused and lumpy, funnier and maybe tearjerking at the end. Frears has put the music from *Jules et Jim* over the scene where Sammy tells us what he likes about London, which brings that section to life, thank God, especially as three or four people have moaned about it being redundant. Next week Frears will shoot a couple more sections for that particular homage to Woody Allen and maybe reprise the music at the end.

After the viewing we talk about there being another scene at the very end of the film, a scene between Sammy and Rosie under a tree, maybe at Hammersmith, by the river. Of course, there's the danger of sentimentalizing this, of saying that despite everything—the shooting, the revolts, the politics of Rafi—this odd couple end up being happy together, the implication being that this is all that matters. This is, of course, the pattern of classical narration: an original set-up is disrupted but is restored at the end. Thus the audience doesn't leave the cinema thinking that life is completely hopeless. I say to Frears that at least at the end of *Jules et Jim* Jeanne Moreau drives herself and her lover off a bridge. He says, sensibly: Well, let's shoot the scene and if it doesn't work we can dump it.

17 MAY 1987   Frears and I talk about the odd way in which *Sammy and Rosie* has developed. The oddness is in not being able to say in advance what kind of film it is since the process seems to have been to shoot a lot of material and then decide later, after chucking bits of it away, what the film will be like. It's like a structured improvisation. Frears says: Shouldn't we be more in control at the beginning? Surely, if we had more idea of what we're doing we could spend more time on the bits we're going to use? But, with some exceptions, it's difficult to tell what's going to be in the final film, partly because I'm no good at plots, at working out precisely what the story is.

21 MAY 1987   Frears and I were both moaning to each other about the Tory Election broadcast that went out yesterday. Its hideous nationalism and neo-fascism, its talk of 'imported foreign ideologies like socialism' and its base appeals to xenophobia. Seeing the film once again Frears has taken the socialist Holst's theme from 'Jupiter' in *The Planets*, later used for the patriotic hymn 'I Vow to Thee My Country' (which was, incidentally, played at the Royal Wedding) from the Tory broadcast, and played it over the eviction scene, giving it a ritualistic quality.

Later there is intense discussion of the film between David and Karin, Mick, Bevan, Frears and I. I find these discussions quite painful. But Frears invites them. He listens carefully to everything people have to say and then he goes back to the film. So secure is he in what he is doing that he isn't threatened by criticism; he can absorb it and use it to improve his work.

An Election has been called. I do some leafleting for the Labour Party. I cover estates which I walk past every day, but haven't been inside since the last Election. In the meantime, the buildings have been 'refurbished'. From the outside the blocks and low-rise houses look modern: rainproof, wind resistant, nature-blocking. I wonder if they have really changed since the last time around. My trips to New York and Los Angeles now seem utterly unimportant when there are parts of my own city, my own streets, for Chrissakes, five minutes walk from me, that are unknown to me!

I walk off the main road and across the grass to the entrance of the first block. The door is open; the glass in the door is smashed. A woman in filthy clothes, in rags I suppose, stands in the entrance waving her arms around. She is in another place: stoned. I go on through and into the silver steel cage of the lift. Inside I hold my nose. At the top of the block the windows are smashed and the wind blows sharply across the landing. Broken bottles, cans and general detritus are whisked about.

Someone has a sign on their door: 'Don't burgle me I have nothin'.' Many of the doors have been smashed in and are held together with old bits of wood. The stench of piss and shit fills the place.

An old distressed woman in a nightdress comes out of her flat and complains that a party has been going on downstairs for two days. One man comes to the door with a barely controlled Alsatian. Come and take back this fucking leaflet, he screams at me; come and get it, mate!

There are at least two dogs on each floor, and you can hear their barking echo through the building.

It is difficult to explain to the people who live here why they should vote Labour; it is difficult to explain to them why they should vote for anyone at all.

23 MAY 1987   Last day of shooting. Bits and pieces. Colin McCabe at the ICA, Sammy and Rosie by the river (for the last shot of the film) and Aloo Baloo at the Finborough pub in Earls Court for the 'Sammy and Rosie in London' part of the film. It is a strange day because these are all things Sarah and I have done together; they are places we go. So you live them and then go back a few weeks later with some mates, a camera, and some actors, and put it all in a film. Sarah has yet to see the film and that's good, I think, as it is improving all the time. But she rang me last night, angry at being excluded, thinking this was deliberate, or just more evidence of my general indifference. Whatever it is, she has started to call the film 'Hanif Gets Paid, Sarah Gets Exploited'.

5 JUNE 1987   Frears and Stanley Myers are working away on the music. Charlie Gillett, the great rock DJ and music expert, is suggesting various bands and styles of music to go over different parts of the film. David Byrne, from whom we've heard not a word for ages, has finally said he's too busy to do anything.

Sarah finally comes to see the film. She sits in front of Frances Barber. After, she tells me she likes it. She confidently says she can see it as an entire object, just a good film, something quite apart from herself.

10 JUNE 1987   My agent Sheila goes to see the uncompleted *Sammy and Rosie* and rings this morning. Some of it's wonderful, she says. But it's heartless and anti-women. Why anti-women? I ask. Because all the women in the film are shown as manipulative. And Rosie doesn't care for Sammy at all. When he sleeps with someone else it doesn't appear to bother her. I thought, she says, that this was because you were going to show Rosie as a lesbian. I ask her why she should think this. Because most of her friends are lesbian. Plus, she adds, you make Sammy into such a weak, physically unattractive and horrible character it's difficult to see how she could take much interest in him. Is he what you and Stephen think women like?

Sheila doesn't like the end of the film, with Sammy and Rosie sitting crying on the floor. It makes them seem callous, especially with all the women trailing out of the flat and not doing or saying anything. In addition she dislikes the 'Sammy and Rosie in London' sequence, one of my favourites in the film, which she compares to a cheap advertisement. That just has to go, she says, it's so ridiculous. Anyway, couldn't at least fifteen minutes of the film be cut? Like what? Well, Alice's speech to Rafi on walking down the stairs, just before the cellar scene. One doesn't listen to all this, she says. Well, I feel like saying, we could chop fifteen minutes out. But that would make the film just over an hour long. We'd have to release it as a short.

For a while after this conversation I am perforated by doubt and think Sheila might be right; our judgement has gone and the entire thing is some terrible, arrogant mistake.

There's going to be at least another eighteen months of this, of exposure, of being judged. This is a 'profession of opinion' as Valéry calls it, where to make a film or to write a book is to stand up so that people can fire bullets at you.

I go off to the dubbing theatre where the actor playing the property developer is yelling into the mike about communist, lesbian moaning minnies. This will be put through a megaphone and added to the eviction scene. Frears is in as good cheer as ever. When I tell him about Sheila's attack on the film he says we will get attacked this time around. People will want to engage with the issues the film raises; they'll want to argue with the movie and they'll get angry. It won't be an easy ride as with *Laundrette* or *Prick*, with people just being grateful these kinds of films are being made at all.

As we walk through Soho, Frears and Mick are talking once more about the shooting of the black woman at the beginning of the film. They're now thinking of putting it back. It's a hard decision to make: do you forfeit an important and powerful scene because it throws out the balance of the film?

I spend the evening leafleting the estates again, as it's the day before the Election. The feeling in the committee room, where people are squatting on the floor addressing envelopes, is that it'll be close. No one actually thinks we'll put an end to Thatcherism this time, but at least Thatcher won't have put an end to socialism.

I'd seen Kinnock at a Labour rally held in a sports hall in Leicester on Friday. There are at least 2000 people there and it is strictly an all-ticket affair: they are very nervous of hecklers, as the meeting is being televised. There is a squad of large women bouncers who, when a heckler starts up, grab the dissident by the hair and shove her or him out of the hall at high speed. They are also nervous of anything too radical: I've been instructed not to use the word 'comrade' in my speech, though it is Kinnock's first word.

The Labour organization has wound up the crowd expertly and they are delirious, kicking out a tremendous din with their heels against the back of the wooden benches. When I introduce Kinnock, he and Glenys come through the hall surrounded by a brass band, pushing through photographers and fans like a couple of movie stars.

Kinnock speaks brilliantly, contrasting levity and passion, blasting off with a string of anti-Tory jokes. I know that various sympathetic writers and comedians have been sending lines and gags round to his house and he's been working them into the speeches he always insists on writing himself. The impression is of someone who is half stand-up comic and half revivalist preacher. What is so clear is his humanity and goodness, his real concern for the many inequalities of our society. At the end of the meeting the crowd sings 'We Shall Overcome' and 'The Red Flag' and we cheer and cheer. For these two hours I can't see how we can fail to win the Election.

15 JUNE 1987 Everyone reeling from the shock of the Election defeat and from the knowledge that we were completely wrong about the extent of the Labour failure. We lost in Fulham by 6000 votes, though we'd won the seat at a recent by-election. Someone tells me that the people on the estate I leafleted voted 3 to 1 for the Tories. What this Tory victory means is the death of the dream of the sixties, which was that our society would become more adjusted to the needs of all the people who live in it; that it would become more compassionate, more liberal, more tolerant, less intent on excluding various groups from the domain of the human; that the Health Service, education, and the spectrum of social services would be more valued and that through them our society would become fairer, less unequal, less harshly competitive; and that the lives of the marginalized and excluded would not continue to be wasted. But for the third time running, the British people have shown that this is precisely what they don't want.

We invite a bunch of friends to a showing of *Sammy and Rosie*, mainly to look at two significant changes: one is the putting back of the shooting of the black woman; the other the inclusion of Roland's long speech about domestic colonialism.

Well, as we stand around in the preview theatre, some people argue that we don't need the shooting as it's too obvious. Others say you need its power and clarity. I can see that Frears has made up his mind in favour of it at last. I can also see that he is glad to have put back Roland's speech as it anchors the first half of the film and gives Danny's character more substance. The hardest scene to decide about is the very end, with Sammy and Rosie walking by the river. Frears says he hates unhappy endings, so he'd added it to lighten the tone. But someone else says it gives the movie two endings; and, worse than that, it's an attempt to have it both ways—to cheer up what is a sad and rather despairing film.

Despite these bits and pieces, I feel it now has shape and thrust and pace, due to the incredible amount of work Frears and Mick Audsley have done in the editing.

Sarah also comes to this screening, and we leave together, walking down Charing Cross Road. She has said little so far and when I ask about the film this time around, her reaction is more ambiguous. She says: 'Yes, this time it wasn't so easy. Rosie seemed too hard and uncaring; surely I am not hard and uncaring? Perhaps I am like that and haven't been able to see that side of myself? Perhaps that is your objective view of me. Oh, it's difficult for me because I have had the sensation recently, when I'm at work or with a friend—it just comes over me—that I'm turning into the character you've written and Stephen has directed and the actress has portrayed. What have you done?'

19 June 1987   Frears exceedingly cheerful and enjoying finishing the film, putting the frills on, playing around with it. He never stops working on it or worrying about it. He talks about using some of Thatcher's speeches: over the beginning, he says, just after the credits, the St Francis speech would do nicely. And somewhere else. Where? I ask. You'll have to wait and see, he replies.

Stanley Myers, who is in charge of the music, gives me a tape of music which has been put together by Charlie Gillett. It's terrific stuff: bits of African rhythms, reggae, and some salsa and rap stuff.

8 JULY 1987   To see the almost finished *Sammy and Rosie*. It's been dubbed now; the sound is good and the music is on. Frears has put back the scene between Anna and Sammy where she pushes him half out of her studio and interrogates him about his other girlfriends. I thought this scene had gone for good, but Frears continues to experiment. He'd said it would be a surprise where he'd use the Thatcher material. It is. It's right at the front, before the credits, over a shot of the waste ground after the eviction. It works as a kind of prologue and hums with threat and anticipation, though with its mention of the 'inner city' it also seems to be presenting an issue film. But anger and despair following the Election have gone straight into the film, giving it a hard political edge. Frears's struggle over the last few weeks has been to reconcile those two difficult things: the love of Sammy and Rosie for each other, and the numerous issues that surround them. At last he's given the story a clarity and definition I couldn't find for it in the script.

I sit through the film in a kind of haze, unable to enjoy or understand it. I can see how complete it is now, but I have no idea of what it will mean for other people, what an audience seeing it freshly will make of it. Only then will the circle be complete. We'll just have to wait and see.

After the screening someone says how surprised they are that such a film got made at all, that somehow the police didn't come round to your house and say: This kind of thing isn't allowed! Of course it won't be when the new Obscenity Bill goes through.

Later that night I go out for a drink with a friend in Notting Hill. We go to a pub. It's a dingy place, with a dwarf barmaid. It's mostly black men there, playing pool. And some white girls,

not talking much, looking tired and unhealthy. On the walls are
warnings against the selling of drugs on the premises. Loud music,
a DJ, a little dancing. A fight breaks out in the next bar. Immediately the pub is invaded by police. They drag the fighters
outside and throw them into a van. People gather round. It's a
hot night. And soon the air is full of police sirens. Six police vans
show up. The cops jump out and grab anyone standing near by.
They are very truculent and jumpy, though no one is especially
aggressive towards them. We leave and drive along the All Saints
Road, an area known for its drug dealers. Twice we're stopped
and questioned: Where are we going, why are we in the area,
what are our names? Black people in cars are pulled out and
searched. Eventually we park the car and walk around. The area
is swamped with police. They're in couples, stationed every
twenty-five yards from each other. There's barely anyone else in
the street.

14 JULY 1987   A showing of *Sammy and Rosie* at nine in the
morning. Frears and Audsley have been working all weekend,
juggling with bits and pieces. It seems complete, except for some
music which has been put on over the cellar scene and seems to
dissipate the power of Claire's performance at that point. Otherwise the film works powerfully, with a lot of soul and kick. We
talk about how much has gone back in and Frears says how foolish
it seems in retrospect to have taken out so much and then put it
back. But of course that process of testing was essential, a way
of finding out what was necessary to the film and what not.

We stand outside the cutting room in Wardour Street and
Frears says: Well, that's it then, that's finished, we've made the
best film we can. I won't see it again, he adds, or maybe I'll run
it again in five years or something. Let's just hope people like it.

Sammy and Rosie Get Laid

CAST

RAFI	Shashi Kapoor
ALICE	Claire Bloom
SAMMY	Ayub Khan Din
ROSIE	Frances Barber
DANNY	Roland Gift
ANNA	Wendy Gazelle
VIVIA	Suzette Llewellyn
RANI	Meera Syal
CABBIE/GHOST	Badl Uzzaman

Producers	Tim Bevan and Sarah Radclyffe
Director	Stephen Frears
Screenplay	Hanif Kureishi
Lighting cameraman	Oliver Stapleton
Production designer	Hugo Luczyc Wyhowski
Editor	Mick Audsley
Music	Stanley Myers

1.   INT. TUBE STATION. DAY.

A young black man, DANNY, *stands in the open doors of a tube train. The doors are shutting. He holds them apart for an old woman to get through, yells up at the train guard, slips out himself, and runs up the platform. The tube platform is filled with music from a large straggly band of kids who play in a tunnel off the platform.*

2.   EXT. STREET. DAY.

A South London street. It is a residential area, foul, rundown. The police are tying off the street with white tape. A number of people have gathered to look on—some to protest. A mixture of black and white. But people are taken by surprise. Outside a house in the street are two police vans. The police are running about. The police are armed.

3.   EXT. YARD. DAY.

The yard of a poor house in the South London street. A high wall surrounds the yard. A dog runs round and round the yard, barking, chasing its tail. We hold on this wretched dog for as long as possible or bearable—maybe intercutting it with incidents from scene 2.

4.   INT. KITCHEN. DAY.

The kitchen looks out on the yard. A middle-aged black woman is cooking in the kitchen. A frying pan full of bacon and tomatoes. Also a full chip pan bubbling away. The woman talks and laughs with her son, a young black man sitting at the kitchen table playing the trumpet.

5.   EXT. YARD. DAY.

And now the police, armed, jump over the wall into the yard. The dog goes berserk.
Cut to: Now the police are breaking into the front of the house.
Cut to: At the tied-off section of the street we see DANNY. *He presses against the tape, looking anxiously towards the house.*
Cut to: In the kitchen, the kid sees the police coming over the wall.

He stands up and sits down. Then runs to the door of the kitchen. This door leads to a hall.

Cut to: DANNY, *at the tape, takes out a pair of scissors or a knife and cuts through the tape. People surge forward now, past the police.*

Cut to: The woman's hall is full of police. They are trying to grab the boy. The woman runs screaming into the hall. She carries the chip pan. She hurls it at the police, spraying them with boiling fat. A young hysterical cop at the end of the hall, frightened and confused, blasts two bullets into the woman's body. She falls to the ground.

Cut to: Outside, DANNY *has got to the house now. He hears the shots. There is chaos.*

TITLES

6.   INT. ANNA'S STUDIO. DAY.
We see a woman's naked back. She has a 'W' tattooed on each buttock. Behind it the sound of a man and woman in bed together. The woman is on top of the man. They are not copulating but playing. Numerous official papers are spread everywhere. SAMMY *then tries to write something down but* ANNA *bites him. She is American.* SAMMY, *in his late twenties, wears an open black shirt. We are in Anna's photographic studio. It is a huge room, in a converted warehouse, rather like a New York loft. Video and photographic equipment. Also many Indian things: fabrics, carvings, carpets, pictures of plump gurus, etc. On the table next to them is a cat. Through the open window trees are visible and the sound of kids playing is heard. A dog barks in the distance. The sound of an aeroplane.*

7.   INT. AEROPLANE. DAY.
Cross-fade on to each buttock of the swaying arse two seats in the plane. One seat is empty. In the other sits RAFI, *a suave old man with an angelic face. He is always exquisitely dressed in English*

suits. RAFI *takes a large sherbet out of a paper bag and pops it into his mouth, sucking contentedly, with white sherbet on the end of his nose. The captain addresses the aircraft: 'We are approaching London, Heathrow, and will be landing shortly . . . the temperature in London is . . .'*

8.   INT. ANNA'S STUDIO. DAY.

SAMMY *and* ANNA *are in bed.* ANNA *laughs as* SAMMY *tries to get up, against her wishes.*

SAMMY: As your accountant, Anna, I think we should look for some offshore investments for you. *(Pause.)* Now I've gotta go, baby. Meet someone at the airport.

ANNA: You'll get pimples on your tongue for telling lies, you couch potato. You mean your wife's got the dinner on and you gotta get home.

SAMMY: My wife. It's funny, Anna, the more Rosie hears about you, the more she's knocked out by you.

ANNA: *(Pulling his outstretched tongue)* That's another one—right there.

SAMMY: She's especially intrigued and totally knocked out by you having a 'W' tattooed on each buttock. Rosie wants to know if it's some kind of New York code.

ANNA: You know what it is, you couch potato. It's just so that if I bend over it spells 'wow'!

9.   INT. COUNCIL FLAT. DAY.

ROSIE, *beautiful and well dressed, about thirty, a social worker, walks through an old man's filthy falling-down council flat. There are many photographs of his children and grandchildren.* ROSIE *looks for him.*

ROSIE: Mr Weaver, Mr Weaver! It's Rosie Hobbs!
   (She sits down in the middle of the room for a moment and we hold on her face. We hear SAMMY'S *voice.)*

SAMMY: *(Voice over)* There's two things my main squeeze Rosie doesn't believe in. Getting the dinner on and sexual fidelity. She says jealousy is wickeder than adultery.

(Cut to: now ROSIE *pushes open the door of the old man's bathroom.)*

(Voice over) Rosie doesn't want to possess anyone. If she could see us now doing your accounts she'd feel so unpossessive she'd open a bottle of champagne.

10.   EXT. HEATHROW AIRPORT. DAY.

Surrounded by suitcases RAFI *stands, waiting for his son* SAMMY *outside the airport terminal. He is getting very impatient. Finally he waves at the nearest cab and picks up his suitcases.*

11.   INT. ANNA'S STUDIO. DAY.

SAMMY *lies there, greedily cracking another beer. Meanwhile* ANNA *has got up and is adjusting photographic screens around the bed.*

SAMMY: I haven't seen my old man for five years. When he was young and poor he lived in England. Then he went home to get powerful. He dumped me with my mother when they split up. He never wanted me. He left me here. I think I must have been the result of a premature ejaculation.

12.   EXT. AIRPORT. DAY.

We see RAFI *getting into the cab. The cab drives away. The* CABBIE *is an Asian man in a brown suit. One eye is bandaged and part of his skull has been smashed in.* RAFI *doesn't notice this but it's important we see and remember the* CABBIE'S *face.*

SAMMY: *(Voice over)* Rosie and I visited him there. He's a great patriarch and a little king, surrounded by servants.

(Cut to: In the studio ANNA *is ready to photograph* SAMMY.*)*

ANNA: You worship him, don't you? Does he have any kids from his other wife?

SAMMY: Not really. Only daughters.

(*They laugh.*)
Give me a comb, will ya, Anna?

13.   INT. COUNCIL FLAT. DAY.

SAMMY: (*Voice over*) Anna, he's got to see me at my best tonight—plenty of dough, decent flat, Rosie not looking too tired.
(ROSIE *has pushed the bathroom door. She goes into the bathroom. The walls are peeling. Water drips from the walls. The old man is dead in the bath, his thin body under the water. His head is jaundice yellow. The water steams. She stares at him and pulls out the plug, accidentally touching his leg.*)

14.   INT./EXT. CAB. DAY.

It is dusk now. RAFI *in the cab is well into London, heading towards the grimmer stretches of South London.*

RAFI: (*To* CABBIE) For me England is hot buttered toast on a fork in front of an open fire. And cunty fingers.
(*The cab stops in the traffic.* RAFI *pulls down the window and sticks his old grey head out. The cab accelerates. Above* RAFI, *and around him, he sees criss-crossed motorways, flyovers, huge direction indicators, and a swirl of fast-moving traffic, dreamlike, noisy, strange. We see it through his eyes as if for the first time. This isn't the England he remembers.*)

15.   EXT. BALCONY OF TOWER BLOCK. DAY.

ROSIE *stands on the balcony of the tower block where the old man lives. It is on one of those estates that look as if they have been transplanted from the outskirts of Warsaw. She is waiting for the ambulance. She looks out over London, towards the concrete sledge of the motorway in the distance. Then she looks down. A group of youngish kids knock on the door of the flat opposite. They push*

*the owner aside and stream into the flat, wearing masks and scarves
tied around their faces. Down on the ground, in the centre of the
courtyard, there is a huge bonfire burning. Black and white kids
stoke it, throwing things on. The ambulance, its siren going, lights
flashing, screams into the courtyard.*

16.   INT. SAMMY'S AND ROSIE'S BATHROOM. DAY.

ROSIE *is now washing her hair in their 'Victorian' bathroom. She
plunges her hair into the water. She pulls her head out. We hold
on her face and see her hair full of water. This could be shot,
perhaps using a mirror, so that we can see through into the large,
long, living room. There are several of* ROSIE'*s women friends gathered here, plus one white and one black boy, both deaf and dumb,
who dance to music. Then one of the women,* RANI, *appears behind*
ROSIE, *banging the door shut.*

RANI: Rosie, there's trouble outside. I think there will be fires
    tonight.
    (ROSIE *turns and looks at her. Then they look into the
    bathroom mirror. They do not see themselves but instead
    a derelict shed in a green wood. It is pouring with rain. In
    the shed a young man is painting a portrait of* ROSIE.)
ROSIE: That's my lover, Walter. I'm seeing him later.
RANI: What will Sammy say about that?
ROSIE: Though a forest fire will have broken out in his heart,
    lungs and liver, his tongue will try to say: What an interesting
    life you have, Rosie.
RANI: How damaging for him.

17.   EXT. STREETS. DUSK.

Now RAFI'*s cab enters the South London street where* SAMMY *and*
ROSIE *live.*

RAFI: *(To* CABBIE) My son Sammy is a very successful accountant.
CABBIE: And he lives here?
    (*Halfway up, the street is blocked by police cars, police*

*vans, and an ambulance. This is the street from scene 2.
The cab stops. It cannot go any further. We see puzzled*
RAFI *taking in the chaotic scene. Now* RAFI, *with his suitcases, walks past the police cars and ambulance. The ex-
teriors at night have a heightened, unreal feel. As* RAFI
*passes by the terraced house from scene 3, two ambulance
men carry out a body on a stretcher. A crowd of black
people and some whites have gathered outside, many truculent, others weeping.* DANNY *stands apart from it all. His
young black girlfriend and their kid are there now, with
him.* RAFI *walks past, taking it all in. We hold fully and
carefully on the faces.* RAFI *walks past some larger houses.
The* CABBIE *watches him. On the steps of these houses*
ROSIE *and* VIVIA *are standing, anxiously watching the ambulance incident.* RAFI *pushes his way through the crowd,*
DANNY *watching him.* ROSIE *spots* RAFI *in the crowd and
rushes down into the midst of it all to get him, pushing
her way through.)*

ROSIE: Rafi! Rafi!

(She finds him and embraces him. DANNY *is watching.)*

What's wrong? Didn't Sammy pick you up?

RAFI: The only thing that boy's picking up at the moment is a
sexually transmitted disease!

18.   INT. SAMMY'S AND ROSIE'S FLAT. EVENING.

*A spacious flat, plenty of books stacked up, a jungle of plants, some
decent prints, music playing. The flat is wild and untidy, not yuppie.
Charts and maps on the walls, pictures of flowers, old Buddhas, lots
of junk furniture, home-made sculpture, bidets full of books, velvet
curtains on the walls, huge wrecked armchairs, layers of Turkish
carpets, hookahs, brass pots, high-tech accoutrements . . . a hammock
strung across the window, red silk billowing down from the ceiling.
Four of Rosie's friends are drinking wine:* EVA, RANI, BRIDGET *and*

MARGY. EVA *is a Jewish intellectual.* BRIDGET *has her head shaved at the sides, the rest of her hair is long.* MARGY *is very committed politically.* BRIDGET *and* EVA *massage each other.*

MARGY: *(Ironic)* Sammy may be an accountant, but he's a radical accountant . . .

RANI: *(To* BRIDGET*)* Won't you massage me? Don't I need support too? Where's Rosie and Vivia gone?

BRIDGET: *(Part of a continuing conversation)* I've always been on the pill. Better cancer than pregnant. I've never even seen a rubber. I'm not that generation. Margy?
(Meanwhile the white boy is rubbing himself off on the carpet. RANI *pulls him up and he stares panting at the women. They ignore him.)*

MARGY: I always carry half a dozen with me. In case I meet a tall dark, hard stranger.
(She pulls a packet of rubbers out of her pocket.)

19.   INT. STAIRS. EVENING.
ROSIE *and* VIVIA *struggle up the stairs with Rafi's suitcase. This area of the flats is also spacious and open.* RAFI *climbs up the broad stone steps in front of them, with immaculate dignity as usual.*
RAFI: Is this world war typical of your streets?

ROSIE: *(To* RAFI*)* The police shot a woman by mistake. They were looking for her son. It's easy enough to mistake a fifty-year-old office cleaner for a twenty-year-old jazz trumpeter.
(When RAFI *and* VIVIA *come into the room they see and hear:)*

MARGY: You hold the condom there and pull down.
*(*MARGY *pulls the condom down over a large knobbly carrot. The women have gathered round to look and laugh.)*

EVA: Carrots are certainly more attractive than ding-dongs. And more prolific in vitamins, I'd imagine.
(Now RAFI *stands there slightly bewildered. He also sees*

the deaf and dumb boys, one of whom tries to dance with him. RANI *watches* RAFI *carefully. She recognizes him.)*

ROSIE: Rafi, these are my friends.

RAFI: *(Under his breath)* Good God, are they really?

*(*MARGY *is hastily rolling the condom off the carrot.)*

BRIDGET: *(To* VIVIA*)* Everything all right outside?

VIVIA: Not at all. Let's go, Margy. Eva. Everyone.

*(*MARGY *bites into the carrot. They get up.* ROSIE *takes* RAFI's *arm and leads him away from the women to show him the flat.* VIVIA, *who is in the early stages of seducing* RANI, *looks expectantly at her.)*

RANI: *(To* VIVIA*)* I'll see you later. I'll stay for a while.

VIVIA: Will you ring me?

RANI: Yes, yes.

(They take each other's hands and kiss goodbye, a longish tonguey kiss, which RAFI *sees and is rather thrown by.* RANI *looks up defiantly at him.* VIVIA, *laughing at this, leads the women out.* RANI *joins* ROSIE, *who is showing* RAFI *the flat. The deaf and dumb boys peer through the foliage at* RAFI.)

ROSIE: How d'you like our place, Rafi?

RANI: Aren't they just in clover?

RAFI: Well, 50 per cent clover, 50 per cent synthetic materials.

RANI: Have you entirely retired from politics, Mr Rahman?

RAFI: Oh yes, yes.

RANI: Asians in Britain have followed your political career with absolute fascination. I'd love to interview you for a paper I'm involved with.

*(*RAFI *shakes his head and puts his arms around* ROSIE.)

RAFI: I'm here as a purely private person.

RANI: Mr Rahman, someone like you could never be a purely private person.

20.   INT. FRONT DOOR OF FLAT. EVENING.

ROSIE *is saying goodbye to* RANI *and kissing her.* RAFI, *not seen by them, is walking towards the kitchen. When he hears* RANI *and* ROSIE *talking about him he stops in a place where he can overhear them.* RANI *has the deaf and dumb boys with her.*

ROSIE: Why are you so interested in Rafi?

RANI: How much d'you know about him?

ROSIE: Only that he was something in the government over there. He's always claiming to be a friend of Mao Tse-tung.

RANI: Not that that'll get him into any nightclubs. I'll dig out some stuff about him. I think it'll interest you.

21.   INT. LIVING ROOM. EVENING.

RAFI *sits at the table. Everyone has gone now.* RAFI *steadily eats his main course, having finished the avocado.* ROSIE *shouts through to him.*

ROSIE: I expect Sammy's got stuck with a client. He's got a lot of freelance work—actors, disc jockeys, photographers. The cream of the scum use Sammy.

22.   EXT. MOTORWAY. DUSK.

We are on the motorway through London. A high shot of sunset over London town. We close in to see SAMMY *in his car, shirt open to the waist, driving frantically at high speed, loud music playing in the car. A straggly band of kids, about twelve or fifteen of them, strangely dressed, some carrying musical instruments, have just crossed the motorway. Now they are climbing the rim of it and down, throwing a long rope over the side. One plays the trumpet, another a drum, one more the violin, etc. They are white and black, men and women.*

RAFI: *(Voice over)* My boy is very well respected?

ROSIE: *(Voice over)* For an accountant.

23. INT. LIVING ROOM. EVENING.

Now ROSIE *is sitting down for her food. She takes a long gulp of wine.* RAFI *watches her censoriously.*

RAFI: *(Eating)* I hear the food in the West is a tribute to chemistry rather than nature.

ROSIE: *(Drinking quickly)* What do you want to do in London, Rafi?

RAFI: I want to see you both, because I love you. Plus there's an old friend I have here, Alice. And before I die I must know my beloved London again: for me it is the centre of civilization—tolerant, intelligent and completely out of control now, I hear.

ROSIE: That depends on which newspaper you read.

24. EXT. STREET. EVENING.

Having necessarily dumped his car nearby, SAMMY *is running along the street towards the house. But he can't get through the crowd. The ambulance has gone. There are several police vans instead. Black and white kids have gathered in the street. The atmosphere is very heavy.* DANNY *stands there. A white kid of about thirteen on a bicycle rides after* SAMMY.

KID: Hey, dude. Dude. Wanna buy some black hash? Coke?

     (SAMMY *is now with the* KID. *As the* KID *sells him some stuff:)*

SAMMY: What the fuck's going on here, man?

KID: Shooting. Bad murder, man. Big trouble.

25. INT. SAMMY'S AND ROSIE'S LIVING ROOM. EVENING.

ROSIE *and* RAFI *talk at the table.*

RAFI: There has been a strong hand on this country, yes?

ROSIE: The working class have not been completely beaten down by it but—

RAFI: Exactly. In my country the English not-working class we

call them. In my factory people really work. That is how
wealth is created.

(He helps himself to food. She grinds pepper over it.)

Luckily black is my favourite colour.

ROSIE: Rafi, you are still wicked.

RAFI: And you are still my favourite daughter-in-law. Look. To
prove it I'll give you something. *(Pulls a rather wretched cap
out of a brown bag.)* Put it on!

(She puts it on.)

Who do you think gave it to me! Mao Tse-tung, that's who!

*(A sound behind them. Through the foliage they turn to
see* SAMMY *at the door, looking exhausted, terrible.)*

SAMMY: Hallo, Dad. Rosie. Sorry I'm late. I was just looking into
one or two important avenues. *(To* ROSIE*)* What have you
got on your head?

ROSIE: The Chinese revolution.

(Cut to: The meal is over and ROSIE *and* SAMMY *are now
clearing the table.* SAMMY *has a beer in each hand, sandwich
in gob.)*

RAFI: Of course Auntie Rani's dog bites everyone, including her
husband, the children—

ROSIE: *(Coldly)* I'm going out soon, Samir.

RAFI: —and the servants . . .

SAMMY: *(To* ROSIE*)* Where? Tonight? Tonight?

RAFI: But she won't have the dog destroyed. I'd put a bullet
through his balls myself. Wouldn't you, Sammy?

SAMMY: *(To* ROSIE*)* Don't go anywhere tonight. Something's happening out there. It'll be bloody, you know.

ROSIE: When black people were attacked before and defended
themselves, you didn't used to stay in and have your supper.

SAMMY: My father's here, Rosie.

ROSIE: One of my cases died today. An old man. You wonder
what your own life means. I hate my job, picking up the

smashed pieces of people's lives. Everyone despises you for
it: the people whose lives you're poking into, and the others
who think you're pretending to be a fucking saint.

(RAFI *watches them. He gets up.*)

RAFI: I will recover. Am I in your own room?

SAMMY: *(Perfunctory)* We're putting you in Rosie's study.

(RAFI *goes.*)

ROSIE: Don't hurt him.

SAMMY: He did abandon me years ago. He's a stranger to me.

ROSIE: I think he wants to know you again.

26.   INT. ROSIE'S STUDY. EVENING.

*A huge dark wood desk. A large framed photo of Virginia Woolf
and a photograph of Rodin's* The Kiss. *Many books. A bed has
been installed for* RAFI. *He unpacks his numerous medicines: oint-
ments, pills, suppositories.*

SAMMY: *(Voice over)* Stay with us tonight, Rosie.

ROSIE: *(Voice over)* I've arranged to see Walter.

(*Cut back to living room.*)

SAMMY: Your boyfriend. Lover.

ROSIE: I said I would. But I am honest with you at least. *(Pause.)*
Sammy. Freedom plus commitment. Those were our words.
They were to be the two pillars of our love and life together.
(*Cut back to the study:* RAFI *unwraps a suppository. As he
does so he pulls aside the curtain and looks out the window.
He sees aggressive people running about. And in the distance a car burns—the flames strangely shooting straight
up in the air. Nearer, a group of kids, black and white,
some of them masked, are kicking down a wall, gathering
the bricks up and running off with them.*)
(Voice over) Didn't we agree? I'll tell you what I want. I don't
want deadness or order. *(Cut to living room.)*
(Putting her coat on) Sometimes I want a little passion.

SAMMY: Don't let me stand in your way.

ROSIE: *(Kindly)* I can't always mother you, baby.

27.   EXT. STREET. EVENING.

ROSIE *runs up the street past the kids kicking the wall down. She runs towards the burning car. Firemen are trying to reach it, but the kids, joyfully, are succeeding in keeping them back. One kid has a ghetto-blaster with him.* ANNA *is there photographing everything, posing people by the car.* ROSIE *watches her, laughing at her charming cheek.*

28.   INT. ROSIE'S STUDY. EVENING.

SAMMY *tucks* RAFI *up in bed. He pulls the curtains on the wild street.*

SAMMY: We thought we'd give you a room with a view. And here's some cotton-wool for your earholes.

(*Outside someone screams and there's an explosion. A petrol bomb.*)

I expect it's a wild street party.

RAFI: Where's Rosie?

SAMMY: Just popped out for some fresh air.

RAFI: How's married life? Good? Bad?

SAMMY: Married life? It's a scream.

RAFI: *(Taking* SAMMY's *hand)* Son, I am in great danger. I am here in London partly because my life is threatened there.

SAMMY: Who from? *(Pause.)* Can't you tell me?

RAFI: Does it matter? Let's just say that from now on I am in your hands.

29.   EXT. STREET. NIGHT.

ROSIE *runs into a shopping street. Chaos. A black man, accompanied by a white man and large crowd of assorted others, black and white, men and women, is about to smash a sledgehammer into the window of a hi-fi shop. The glass shatters. A cheer goes up. The crowd rushes*

*into the shop. A young black man falls into the glass, getting up
with his hands and face streaming blood. A TV crew films it all.
The others grab electrical goods and flee with their loot through
noise and chaos.* DANNY *stands there looking at* ROSIE, *with some
of the straggly kids.* ROSIE *runs on. A little old white woman, with
a shopping basket on wheels, rushes into the electrical shop and
loots a transistor radio. She rushes out as fast as she can.*

30.   INT. ROSIE'S STUDY. NIGHT.
RAFI *lies in bed in the half-lit room. He's asleep, having a nightmare.
He cries out, then awakes. He lies there being stared at by Virginia
Woolf, which becomes more horrible the more she looks at him.
The noise from outside rises around him. It could be in his head
or for real: he doesn't know. He sits up. On the edge of the bed
he pulls cotton-wool out of his ears. He covers his face with his
hands.*

31.   INT. LIVING ROOM. NIGHT.
SAMMY *is swigging a beer. An unnaturally large half-eaten hamburger and milkshake are on the table next to an open porn magazine.* SAMMY's *trousers are round his ankles. He's listening to a
CD of something loud and noble—Shostakovich, for example. With
half a straw stuck up his nose he leans over a line of coke he's laid
out on the glass-topped table. Now* RAFI *is at the door. He yells
but cannot be heard above the music and* SAMMY *sits with his back
to him, having snorted the coke, bitten into the giant hamburger
and eagerly turned over a page of the magazine. Disturbed,* SAMMY
*turns to see, over the back of the sofa, his father gesticulating at
him. Determinedly* RAFI *goes to the door of the flat, picking up his
overcoat as he goes.* SAMMY *stands up, trousers round his ankles,
and falls over, the rest of his coke flying everywhere. He could try
to snort it out of the carpet.*
Cut to: SAMMY *stands at the top of the stairs pulling up his trousers
as* RAFI *runs downstairs.*

SAMMY: *(Yelling after him)* Haven't you got jet-lag, Dad?

RAFI: I have seen wars, you know!

SAMMY: Don't go out there, Dad!

32. EXT. STREET. NIGHT.

RAFI *is now in the street and heading full-tilt towards the riot area.*
SAMMY *comes out of the house, hamburger and shake in hand, and down the street after him. There is much running about in the street. The street is covered with debris.* RAFI *stops by the car that* ROSIE *saw in flames. It is burnt out now but little flames unnaturally flicker all over it.*

RAFI: My God, I can't understand it, why ever do you live here?

SAMMY: It's cosmopolitan, Pop. And cheap. Come on. Let's go, eh? Please.

RAFI: No, I want to see this.

> (RAFI *pulls away from him. A young black man comes out of his house and runs down the street pursued by his father trying to stop him going out. His mother stands at the door. Father and son struggle.)*

SAMMY: Leonardo da Vinci would have lived in the inner city.

RAFI: You know that for certain, do you?

SAMMY: Yes, because the city is a mass of fascination.

> (Now we see RANI, VIVIA, (EVA, MARGY, BRIDGET, *taking care of each other, watching the riot.* RANI *screams abuse at the violence of the police in dealing with people.* MARGY *is disgusted with the violence of the entire thing and by the sympathy of the other women for the rioters.)*

MARGY: But it's just men, rotten men, being men!

> (EVA *is sympathetic to the rioters and carries an iron bar threateningly. Suddenly a brick comes from somewhere and smashes* VIVIA *in the side of the head. She goes down. The women gather round her. They pick her up and rush her away as a phalanx of police with riot shields makes towards*

them. EVA *throws her iron bar at the police. As* SAMMY
and RAFI *flee, we see injured people lying in the rubble,
some attended by friends and ambulance people. A young
white man squats under a hedge crying.)*

SAMMY: Rosie says—

RAFI: What does the great Rosie say?

SAMMY: Rosie says these revolts are an affirmation of the human
spirit. A kind of justice is being done.
(Pause. The situation becomes more dangerous. But SAMMY
is excited.)
Let's get the hell out of here!
*(*RAFI *stumbles. Now* ANNA *runs towards them, taking pictures. A bunch of white and black kids run past* RAFI.*)*
(To ANNA*)* What are you doing here, Anna? This isn't your
part of town!

RAFI: These are fools and madmen!

SAMMY: *(As she photographs)* Anna, cut it out! This is my father!

ANNA: *(Shaking his hand)* Pleased to meet you, sir. Welcome to
England. I hope you enjoy your stay! *(Kisses* SAMMY.*)* I'll give
you a ring.
(She goes. Cut to: Later. SAMMY *is now hurrying* RAFI *back.
Suddenly they turn a corner and stop beside a car. The
windows have been smashed, the radio and speakers ripped
out, etc. In the distance we see the backs of a line of police,
as they charge the screaming mob.* SAMMY *is more concerned about the car and he kicks it wildly.)*

SAMMY: For fuck's fucking fuck sake, fuck it!

RAFI: Boy, didn't they teach you more than one word at the school
I paid through the arse for you to attend?

SAMMY: But this is my fucking car!

RAFI: Surely an affirmation of the human spirit?
(Cut to: SAMMY *and* RAFI *walk through gloomy reverber-*

ating alleys back to the house. RAFI *has his arm around*
SAMMY *now.)*

I don't want anything any more. The things I own are a burden
to me. So I've given the factory to your cousins.

SAMMY: What, those idiots?

RAFI: They are going into air-conditioners. I think making heaters
in one of the world's hottest countries was not good business
sense.

*(Cut to: The steps of the house. On the steps an injured
white kid is with his black girlfriend.)*

The money I've managed to get out of the country, and it's
a lot of money—

SAMMY: Which total prick have you thrown that at, Pop?

RAFI: One of my main purposes in coming here is to transfer that
money to your account, son.

*(Cut to: Now they are in the comparative silence of the
stone hallway.)*

You can have the money provided you buy yourself a house
in a part of England that hasn't been twinned with Beirut!
Is there anywhere like that left? I would also like some grandchildren. Please. There is money for them too.

SAMMY: How much?

33.   INT. OFFICE. MORNING.

The office of an organization rather like Amnesty. VIVIA *and* RANI
sitting across the desk from a young Japanese woman.

JAPANESE WOMAN: Rafi Rahman.

RANI: Yes, I rang you yesterday to ask for information.

(The JAPANESE WOMAN *rises, smiles.)*

JAPANESE WOMAN: I remember. Let me get the file to show you
what we've got.

(She goes. VIVIA *and* RANI *hold hands nervously.)*

VIVIA: *(To* RANI*)* Suppose we find out some stuff about Rafi that you wouldn't want to hear while you were eating your breakfast? What do we do then—just tell Rosie and let her get on with it?

RANI: Wouldn't it be worse to conceal something we knew?

VIVIA: I know, I know, but we'll be putting her in a difficult position.

(The JAPANESE WOMAN *returns with a thick file and puts it down on the desk.* RANI *and* VIVIA *lean forward to look at it.)*

JAPANESE WOMAN: That's volume one.

34.   INT. LIVING ROOM. MORNING.

RAFI *eats breakfast in his silk pyjamas. In front of him is his chequebook. He has written the cheque and it lies on the table. Now he writes a postcard. It is a few days later. He looks across the flat, fascinated by the sight of* ROSIE *who, in a T-shirt and shorts, is doing muscle-bursting vigorous weight-training and body-building exercises to the sound of Mozart's Requiem.*

Cut to: A little later. ROSIE *is dressed for work now.*

RAFI, *walking about the flat, drops the postcard and bends over stiffly to retrieve it.* ROSIE *picks it up for him.*

ROSIE: Writing home already? But you've only been here a few days, Rafi. And you've hardly been out.

RAFI: Sweetie, read it. It's to my fondest relatives.

ROSIE: *(Reads:)* 'Streets on fire—wish you were here!'

RAFI: *(Pats her arse as she laughs.)* Rosie, one thing more. What about the sound of little footsteps, eh? Isn't it about time?

ROSIE: *(Having to control herself)* Rafi . . .

RAFI: Eh? I know you're a kind of feminist, but you're not a lesbian too, are you?

ROSIE: I'm thinking about having a child.

RAFI: *(Taking her hand)* It would give me so much happiness.

ROSIE: And that's exactly what I want, Rafi.

RAFI: You've cheered me up. I may even have the nerve to go out today.

(Cut to: A little later. ROSIE is leaving for work. VIVIA has called round. She stands at the door with ROSIE. VIVIA gives ROSIE a brown envelope.)

VIVIA: This is from Rani.

ROSIE: Great. Thanks. *(Calls to RAFI:)* See you later, Rafi.

(Cut to: On the stairs down ROSIE opens the envelope. VIVIA looks over ROSIE's shoulder. RANI has sent ROSIE material about RAFI: press cuttings from the Subcontinent and Britain: we can see his picture; photocopies of articles, Amnesty reports, etc.)

VIVIA: Does Sammy know about all of it?

ROSIE: He's always tried to cut his father out of his mind. *(Pause.)* Poor Sammy.

35.   EXT. STREET. MORNING.

RAFI is out for a walk. In his natty hat he passes through an alley with high walls and emerges into a run-down housing estate. One of those estates that looks a little like Soweto—no shops, no nothing. RAFI walks across the open area between graffiti-sprayed tower blocks. Kids roam around, some with scarves over their faces. Others wear crash helmets.

Cut to: RAFI has left the estate and turned the corner into another street, a main street. Here shops have been looted, burned out, the wrecked hulks of cars litter the place, paving stones discarded, etc. Plenty of onlookers, journalists, disconsolate shopkeepers, a film crew, street cleaners, etc. RAFI looks on. Now a white kid runs across the street carrying a hi-fi deck in his arms. He's followed by three cops. They all run incredibly fast. The kid drops the deck. The police grab him. A fight breaks out. Other people, both black and white, men and women, appear suddenly and pile in. DANNY stands watching on the edge of this. Someone is thrown against DANNY *and he crashes back into the doorway. More police charge down the street.* DANNY *gets up and prepares to flee. As others run,* RAFI *can't get out of the way quickly enough, and gets knocked down. He falls to the ground.* DANNY *is tearing past him.* DANNY *stops though, picks* RAFI *up, and his natty hat, and pulls him away. Cut to: Breathless,* DANNY *and* RAFI *have made it to an alleyway.* RAFI'*s hands and knees are cut and grazed. He pulls up his trouser leg to examine the bloodied skin.* DANNY *takes* RAFI'*s handkerchief, spits into it, and rubs* RAFI'*s knee. There is noise all around them.* RAFI *is concerned about the state of his suit.*

DANNY: Where d'you live? Take you back home?

RAFI: Riot or no riot—

DANNY: Revolt. It's a revolt.

RAFI: Yes. Good. This society may be on its last legs but I am expected in Cockfosters. Please point me north and say a prayer in my favour.

(*A* TORY MP *and the* PROPERTY DEVELOPER *walk past the end of the alley at this moment.* RAFI *and* DANNY *hear this.*)

TORY MP: You're a wealthy, intelligent businessman.

(DANNY *spits.*)

You've got to invest in this area—for your sake and ours. You can do whatever you like.

PROPERTY DEVELOPER: I want that open space under the motor-way—then we can talk.

(*When they've gone* DANNY *pulls* RAFI.)

DANNY: Come on. I'll take you.

RAFI: Where?

DANNY: Come on.

36.   INT. TUBE TRAIN. DAY.

DANNY *and* RAFI *sit down,* DANNY *whipping away a newspaper from the seat before* RAFI *sits down. Opposite them sits a huge*

white man in a tracksuit. He is doing various finger-strengthening
exercises. RAFI *watches him warily. Next to the* FINGER MAN *sits*
a woman, middle-aged, off-white, with a wretched dog that eats a
sandwich off the floor. The woman has a cigarette in her mouth.
And as she scratches her ear the fag jumps from left to right in her
mouth.

RAFI: Do we have to change trains?

(*Suddenly the* FINGER MAN *rises up on the arm-rests of the*
seat. And there he suspends himself like a fat bat. This is
obviously some kind of tube-train calisthenic.)

FINGER MAN: (*To* DANNY) Time me, man!

(RAFI *practically has a heart attack as* DANNY *grabs his arm*
and pulls his sleeve up to look at Rafi's watch. Mean-
while:)

DANNY: (*To* RAFI) Danny, my name is. But people who like me
call me Victoria. People who don't like me call me jerk-off.
(*Pause.*) I know these tube lines. Sometimes I ride the tubes
all day. It's my office, the Victoria Line. It's where I do my
paperwork. Paperwork overwhelms me.

(*He glances over at the* FINGER MAN *whose face is about*
to explode. He collapses back in his seat.

Cut to: DANNY *and* RAFI *now walk together down a long*
tube tunnel.)

As an expert, I suggest the tunnel that connects the Piccadilly
with the Victoria Line at Green Park—a superb sensation
you get here of endless walking in both directions. The acous-
tics are excellent.

RAFI: I'm going to meet a woman—Alice—who I haven't seen
for over twenty years. I stayed in her house when I left university. In those days before you were born there was a colour
bar in England. They gave me shelter, she and her husband.
Then I went back home to marry. But I . . . I loved her
terribly.

(In the tunnel the straggly band of musicians are playing. We last saw them crossing the motorway. They play the theme song of the movie—there are trumpeters, saxophonists, a hurdy-gurdy player, bassoon groovers, etc. Rappers. The dog from scene 2 is with them. As DANNY and RAFI walk past, everyone in the band says simultaneously, 'Wotcha, Danny boy.' DANNY nods regally. Also, a couple of girls and boys are dancing to the music. If we could film them from the front for a moment, we could easily see for a second, the whole tube tunnel dancing, like in a Cliff Richard film.)

DANNY: Why didn't you get it on with her?

RAFI: My father wanted me to marry someone else. And Alice's husband was watching me like a hawk. When I die and go to heaven, I will marry her there.

DANNY: You don't know what she's like now.

(The Asian CABBIE, in the brown suit, with the bandage over one eye, walks towards them and on past them quickly.)

37.   EXT. STREET. DAY.

A leafy North London suburb, tree-lined, sedate, quiet. RAFI and DANNY walk towards Alice's house—a detached four-bedroom place with a front and back garden. RAFI has bought a large bunch of flowers, a box of chocs and a bottle of champagne which DANNY carries. Whites in the street stop and stare at RAFI and DANNY. RAFI smiles politely at them.

RAFI: Why are they looking at us like that?

DANNY: They think we're gonna rob their houses.

RAFI: God, things have changed so little! Poor Alice—she was born and brought up in India, you know.

DANNY: She's black then?

RAFI: No, extremely white. But her family were in India for gen-

erations. I think I probably threw anti-colonial stones at her
father's house in Bombay. *(They arrive at the house.)* This is
it.

(RAFI *tries to get rid of* DANNY.)

OK then, Victoria. Be seeing you. Thanks.

(RAFI *pats him patronizingly on the shoulder and goes up
the front path and rings the bell. He turns and sees* DANNY
standing halfway up the path.)

DANNY: You won't make it alone out here in the country.

RAFI: This isn't the country, you damn fool. It's just respectable.

(DANNY *sees that* ALICE *has opened the door. He indicates
to* RAFI. RAFI *turns, sees* ALICE, *and goes towards her. It
is* DANNY *who is moved.* ALICE *and* RAFI *go into the house.*
DANNY *stands there a moment, then goes round the side
of the house.*

Cut to: Now DANNY *is in the back garden. An old white
man and a mentally defective boy are doing Alice's
gardening.*

Cut to: In Alice's living room RAFI *and* ALICE *sit on the
sofa drinking tea. As they put their cups to their old lips
we see their faces are streaming with tears although they
talk normally. Alice's house is full of Indian memorabilia
from the twenties and thirties. The walls are crumbling,
everything is falling apart, it is a much stranger and darker
place than it seems at first.)*

I'll never forget the kindness you showed me.

ALICE: But you did forget, Rafi. You forgot all about me.

(Cut to: In the garden DANNY *is walking about. He finds
an old gardening hat on a bench which looks as if it's made
from crushed budgie.)*

Sometimes when you were in the government there, I'd see
you on the TV, talking about some crisis or other. You were
impressive, though I did come to associate you exclusively

with aeroplane hijackings. *(Pause.)* I thought you would come and see me before, you know.

(ALICE *has got up to put on a record, something romantic from the forties. When she sits beside him once more, they move into each other's arms.* RAFI *looks up to see* DANNY, *with the hat on, gazing through the window.* RAFI *becomes agitated, as you would. With his spare stroking hand he indicates that* DANNY *should disappear immediately. Just as* ALICE *looks up,* DANNY's *face moves away.)*

Shall I make some more Earl Grey tea? Don't be distressed, Rafi. For me, you are still a charming and delightful man. What about a piece of Jamaica rum cake?

RAFI: Alice, there's someone I think you should meet.

(Cut to: The garden. DANNY *stands there.* ALICE *and* RAFI *outside.* ALICE *looks at* DANNY.)*

(To ALICE) This is my map-reader and guide, Victoria. We owe this visit to his ingenuity and kindness.

(She greets him graciously.)

38.   EXT. SOUTH LONDON STREET. DUSK

A police car careers up the street. RAFI *and* DANNY *are crossing the road on their way home.* DANNY *pulls* RAFI *out of the way of the screaming police car.*

RAFI: *(To* DANNY) You nearly gave me a fucking heart attack when I saw you outside Alice's window. *(Pause.)* What are you doing now? Haven't you got anywhere to go?

DANNY: Yeah. I'm going with you.

39.   INT. SAMMY'S AND ROSIE'S LIVING ROOM. DUSK.

RAFI *and* DANNY *enter the flat.* DANNY *looks around.*

Cut to: We see DANNY *standing alone in the flat. He is clenching and unclenching his fists, obviously distressed about something, unable to get it out of his mind.* RAFI *comes up behind him.*

RAFI: Victoria, what's wrong?

DANNY: For a long time, right, I've been for non-violence. Never gone for burning things down. I can see the attraction but not the achievement. OK. After all, you guys ended colonialism non-violently. You'd sit down all over the place, right? We have a kind of domestic colonialism to deal with here, because they don't allow us to run our own communities. But if full-scale civil war breaks out we can only lose. And what's going to happen to all that beauty?

RAFI: If I lived here . . . I would be on your side. All over the world the colonized people are fighting back. It's the necessity of the age. It gives me hope.

DANNY: But how should we fight? That's what I want to know.

40.   EXT. SOUTH LONDON STREET. DUSK.

SAMMY *waiting in the street.* ROSIE *walks through the crowd towards him.* SAMMY *stands drinking from a can of beer. Scenes of patched-up desolation around them. People are reconstructing their shops. Gangs roam about, watching. A heavy police presence. A* TORY MP *and the* PROPERTY DEVELOPER *stand in the street talking with their advisers.* ROSIE *goes to* SAMMY *and they kiss and greet each other warmly.*

ROSIE: Good day at the office, dear? I had only one suicide today.

(Cut to: Later. They are walking through the shopping area.)

SAMMY: How's that dreary untalented prick?

ROSIE: Cut it out. Walter's got an exhibition.

SAMMY: Christ, a Renaissance man. Rosie, I think we should have a kid, you know. My seed's pretty rich at the moment——I've examined it. I'm well hot to trot in that respect.

ROSIE: But you wouldn't be a responsible father. The unfair sex has so far to go. *(Pause.)* Aren't you interested in politics any more? You were always out improving society, Sammy.

SAMMY: I find more and more that the worst thing about being on the left is the other people you've got on your side.

(She kisses him, holding him, laughing.)

41.   INT. ASIAN SHOP. DUSK.

Now SAMMY *and* ROSIE *are in a wretched dark Asian shop on the front line. The Asian* SHOPKEEPER *is familiar to them. The shop was looted during the revolt. A white woman customer in the shop has a Siamese cat on her shoulder, on a lead.*

SAMMY: *(To* ROSIE*)* I can't see my old man staying too long, can you? *(To* SHOPKEEPER*)* Any noodles, Ajeeb?

ROSIE: You kissed your father on the nose and said he could stay forever.

SAMMY: You have to do that. It's a well-known lie.

SHOPKEEPER: The noodles are looking right at you.

SAMMY: So they are. Any Indian sweets?

*(*SHOPKEEPER *shakes his head.)*

You're joking. You're not joking? Ajeeb, it's a terrible disgrace.

SHOPKEEPER: Samir, I tell you, the trash took everything in the looting. They're jealous of us. But why? In this country aren't we all in the same position?

ROSIE: *(To* SAMMY*)* Your father announced how long he wants to stay with us. *(Pause.)* One or two years, he said.

SAMMY: What?

42.   INT. SAMMY'S AND ROSIE'S FLAT. EVENING.

DANNY *has Sammy's huge TV in his arms and is staggering around under the weight of it. The TV is on and* RAFI *watches it with his feet in a bowl of water as* DANNY *perilously manoeuvres it into position for* RAFI. *This is to prevent* RAFI *from having to move.* RAFI *is watching footage of the riots on TV. He is wearing pyjamas and eating sherbets from a paper bag.*

43. INT. THE STAIRS UP TO THE FLAT. EVENING.

SAMMY *and* ROSIE *walk up drinking, stop at the landing for an altercation and finally reach the door to their flat. They are getting on really well, despite everything.*

ROSIE: And did you see him filing his fingernails and—

SAMMY: Putting powder between his toes!

ROSIE: Or cutting the hair in his ears! D'you know he handed me his washing and said, 'Be sure not to use too hot an iron on the silk shirts!'

(ROSIE *and* SAMMY *crack up, leaning against the wall, laughing and slapping each other exaggeratedly.* SAMMY *stops abruptly.)*

SAMMY: Stop badmouthing my father, you silly bitch!

ROSIE: Oh fuck off.

SAMMY: I better tell you, Rosie. He's pretty keen to unload some dough on us. It's a lotta dough I'm on about here, darling. So we better get fucking respectful right now!

(*Cut to: Seconds later. They walk up,* SAMMY *behind, his hand up her skirt playfully.)*

ROSIE: We went to that factory where Rafi made his money, remember? I know Dante based the Inferno on it. You don't have to be radical to see that to accept one penny from him is to get into bed with all kinds of evil.

(*At the top of the stairs* ROSIE *fumbles for her keys but* SAMMY *leans lazily on the bell.)*

SAMMY: I don't think they come any more against inherited wealth than me, Rosie. But didn't Engels have a factory?

(*She nods.)*

Right, let's take the money.

ROSIE: Sammy, I think you should know, your father was probably guilty of some other things too.

SAMMY: What things, beside paternalism, greed, general dissipation, mistreatment of my mother and vicious exploitation?

ROSIE: Well, he—

(DANNY *opens the door. He's holding a bottle of whisky and a glass.* DANNY *indicates for them to come into the flat. He pours a drink, which he gives to* ROSIE. SAMMY, *convinced they're being burgled, drops some of his shopping in fear. Through the open door* ROSIE *sees* RAFI *sitting there with his tired feet in the bowl.* ROSIE *smiles at* DANNY. DANNY *is now picking up* SAMMY's *dropped shopping.* SAMMY *walks into the room and stares at* RAFI.)

RAFI: What's the matter, boy?

SAMMY: What the hell's going on?

(*Cut to:* DANNY *and* ROSIE, *bending down to pick up the shopping, look at each other with great interest.*)

ROSIE: (*To* DANNY) Live nearby?

DANNY: Not far. You?

ROSIE: Right here.

DANNY: What a thing.

44.   INT. LIVING ROOM. EVENING.

Later. The washing-up bowl has been removed. DANNY *and* RAFI *sit there watching TV.* SAMMY *walks uncomfortably around the room, drinking, trying to get rid of them.*

SAMMY: (*To* RAFI) I've gotta finish some accounts right now. And Rosie's got to get on with her writing.

RAFI: And what is Rosie writing?

(*By mistake* SAMMY *stands in front of the TV.* DANNY *stares affrontedly at him.*)

SAMMY: Oh sorry. (*To* RAFI) Yeah, she's doing a major article.

RAFI: On body-building?

SAMMY: Yeah. Kind of. It's on the ins and outs, the types, qualities and varieties of . . . It's a kind of historical sociopolitical investigation. Into kissing.

RAFI: Kissing? Speak up, son. Did you say kissing?

SAMMY: Yeah. 'The Intelligent Woman's Guide to Kissing in History.'

RAFI: Oh my God!

(DANNY *and* RAFI *catch each other's eye and laugh. Meanwhile* SAMMY *picks up the cheque his father wrote in the morning. He is impressed. He goes to his father and kisses him tenderly.*)

SAMMY: Thanks a double-bundle for this, Pop.

RAFI: (*To* SAMMY) I want to give you and my grandchildren everything I possess. Everything that is me. (*To* DANNY) And you, have you got any money? (*To* SAMMY, *indicating* DANNY.) Give him some damn dough.

(ROSIE *walks into the room, having showered and changed. She looks stunning.*)

Rosie, what is all this I hear?

ROSIE: About what, Rafi?

RAFI: Kissing. 'The Intelligent Woman's Approach'?

ROSIE: Snogging as a socio-economic, political-psychological-physical event sunk in a profound complex of determinations? Don't tell me that for you a kiss is just a kiss?

RAFI: Just a kiss.

(*She goes to* SAMMY *and kisses him on the mouth.*)

ROSIE: My husband. Our married mouths. That is one thing. It's meaning is clear. Now this—

(*She goes to* DANNY *and kisses him on the mouth. A long kiss. He almost falls off the chair.* SAMMY *and* RAFI *watch wide-eyed.*)

Now that's a different kind of kiss, with a different social and political meaning.

(*She takes a step towards* RAFI. *He cowers. She kisses him lightly on the mouth.*)

So as you all can see, there's so much to say on the subject of snogging you don't know where to begin.

(RAFI *laughs loudly in pleasure at her charm.*)

(*To* RAFI) Let's go out to dinner, eh? And how have you been today?

RAFI: Pretty well, in myself, despite the fact that several large people walked up and down on my head. Victoria saved me. Presumably this form of social exercise is an English custom now—a sort of Trooping of the Colour?

ROSIE: Yes, but less exciting for the working class.

(ROSIE *sees* SAMMY *glance again at the cheque before folding it and sliding it in his pocket.*)

SAMMY: Well, Victoria, won't your mother be wanting to know where you are?

(DANNY *gets up. He starts to walk towards the door.*)

RAFI: (*Quickly to* SAMMY *indicating* DANNY) Help him out. Please do what I say for once.

(SAMMY *reluctantly gives* DANNY *a fiver.* RAFI *nods at* SAMMY *again and he gives him, painfully, another fiver.* RAFI *nods once more.* ROSIE *is laughing, egging* RAFI *on.*)

(*To* ROSIE) But this is capitalism, Rosie. Redistribution once capitalism has created wealth, eh?

(DANNY *turns to go.* ROSIE *holds out her hands to him. He goes to her, shakes her head, dropping the money in her lap. They look at each other.*)

SAMMY: Now, let's celebrate!

45.   EXT. THE STEPS OF THE HOUSE. EVENING.

The three of them stand on the steps looking out on the street. RAFI *has his arm round* SAMMY'S *shoulder.* SAMMY—*more or less unconsciously—pulls away from his father and takes* ROSIE'S *arm.* RAFI *is offended by this. They all walk down.*

46.   INT. RESTAURANT. EVENING.

ROSIE, SAMMY *and* RAFI *are eating in a smart expensive London restaurant. This is affluent, attractive London for a change. A*

*string quartet of beautiful punks plays Mozart at the far end of
the restaurant.* SAMMY *leaves the table a moment, excusing
himself.*

RAFI: He hardly speaks to me, Rosie. Why doesn't he look after
me and spoil his only father? Has he no feeling for me at all?

ROSIE: Why doesn't he carve miniatures?

RAFI: Perhaps he should. But why doesn't he?

ROSIE: Rafi, he doesn't know how to love you.

RAFI: Perhaps being ignorant of feelings helps him in his career.

ROSIE: He isn't completely ignorant of feelings. You did reject
him.

RAFI: It was his ugly mother I rejected. I was made to marry her.
So I sent her to London and married again. You are very
loyal to Samir.

(SAMMY *rejoins them.*)

(*To* SAMMY) She is a decent woman. (*Pause. To* SAMMY) So
you got the nice cheque I gave you?

SAMMY: (*Nervous*) In my pocket, Daddio.

ROSIE: (*To* SAMMY) Let me have a look at it.

SAMMY: You know what a cheque looks like, don't you?

(*She nods.*)

Well, it's just one of those.

ROSIE: I want to know if you're going to return it to your father
as you said you would.

SAMMY: Why should I? Rosie, we're all set up now.

RAFI: (*To* ROSIE) Yes. Your principles annoy me and will pull
down my son.

(*There is a pause.* ROSIE *is furious with both of them.*)

Cheers to you all.

(ROSIE *admires a drag queen in the restaurant.*)

ROSIE: That woman is a real star.

RAFI: Now you're talking like a damn dyke.

ROSIE: (*To* RAFI) More wine? (*Pause.*) By the way—

RAFI: Yes—

ROSIE: Didn't a journalist who once described you as balding have his teeth smashed in?

RAFI: *(Careful)* If his face had a mishap it improved his appearance. *(To* SAMMY*)* Besides, his wife stole underwear from Marks and Spencer's and lowered the reputation of my country.

ROSIE: *(To* RAFI*)* When you were in the government there, people—opposition people sometimes—were tortured and murdered, weren't they?

SAMMY: Rosie, let's enjoy our meal.

ROSIE: I want him to answer. It's important.

RAFI: *(To* ROSIE*)* Sometimes. A little bit. It happens in the world. It is necessary at times, everyone will admit that.

*(*RAFI*, finishing his meal, jabs his fork into a piece of meat on his plate. As he raises it to his mouth we can see that it is a dead and bloody finger with a long fingernail. We are aware of the people at the next table, very straight yuppies in striped shirts and pearls, close enough to hear* ROSIE. RAFI *places the indigestible fingernail on the side of his plate, delicately.)*

ROSIE: Didn't they have to drink the urine of their gaolers?

*(*SAMMY *splutters into his drink.)*

Didn't you hang mullahs—religious people—upside down on skewers and weren't red chillis stuck up their arses?

(The yuppies call over the waiters.)

RAFI: If they were, it was a waste of food. Let's have more wine. Waiter!

SAMMY: *(To* ROSIE*)* I think Rosie wants to say that charm is no substitute for virtue.

RAFI: *(Exploding)* Our government awoke the down-trodden and expelled Western imperialists! I nationalized the banks! I forged links with the Palestinians! Remember that! *(Irony.)* Comrade. Khrushchev and I—

ROSIE: I just want to know—

(The MANAGER *hurries towards them.)*

RAFI: You know nothing but self-righteousness!

ROSIE: What does it feel like to kill, to torture, to maim, and what did you do in the evenings?

MANAGER: Please, could you keep the noise down?

SAMMY: Yes, I'm terribly sorry.

RAFI: I was imprisoned myself, you know! For ninety days, ill with malaria, I didn't see sunshine! In the next cell lunatics screamed. Their voices were even more irritating than yours!

ROSIE: You have increased the amount of evil in the universe.

RAFI: *(Furious)* You've never suffered! Never had to make hard political decisions!

ROSIE: Yes, every day in my work!

RAFI: You are only concerned with homosexuals and women! A luxury that rich oppressors can afford! We were concerned with poverty, imperialism, feudalism! Real issues that burn people!

ROSIE: We're only asking what it is like to destroy another life.

(The MANAGER *stands there beside them, angry himself.)*

MANAGER: Please—

ROSIE: *(To him)* All right, we're going!

RAFI: *(Pulling her towards him)* A man who hasn't killed is a virgin and doesn't understand the importance of love! The man who sacrifices others to benefit the whole is in a terrible position. But he is essential! Even you know that. I come from a land ground into dust by 200 years of imperialism. We are still dominated by the West and you reproach us for using the methods you taught us. I helped people for their own good and damaged others for the same reason—just like you in your feeble profession!

47.   EXT. SOUTH KENSINGTON. NIGHT.

They walk through South Kensington, from the restaurant to the car.

RAFI: *(Threatening)* Be careful what you say to me in the future, little girl. Remember who I am and have respect.

ROSIE: Who are you, Rafi? Who?

SAMMY: Rosie, he's my father.

48.   EXT. SOUTH KENSINGTON. NIGHT.

They have reached the car now. ROSIE *goes to the driver's side.*

RAFI: *(To* SAMMY*)* You'll be able to buy a new car for yourself now, eh? Rosie's car is good, but small.

49.   EXT./INT. OVER THE RIVER. NIGHT.

ROSIE *and* RAFI *in the front of the car,* SAMMY *in the back. They look at the Thames.*

RAFI: The river is ravishing tonight. But it must always be depressing to go back to that ghetto.

SAMMY: We try to entertain ourselves. And Rosie suggested the other day that we have a little party for you, Dad.

(ROSIE *swerves the car dangerously.*)

Yes, just a few friends, ours and yours. Would you like that?

RAFI: That would be delightful. I must say, you have both been very kind to me—most of the time.

50.   INT. LIVING ROOM. NIGHT.

RAFI *stands on his head in a yoga position in his pyjamas.* SAMMY, *only a towel around his waist, carries two bee*

He watches RAFI *and walks across the room.*

RAFI: Nothing matters as long as you and I respect each other.

SAMMY: I know that.

RAFI: God bless you.

51.   INT. SAMMY'S AND ROSIE'S BEDROOM. NIGHT.

Continuous. ROSIE *doing stretching exercises in the bedroom, wearing a pair of blue silk pyjamas.* SAMMY *comes in.*

ROSIE: It was Rani and Vivia that got the information about your father.

SAMMY: There's all kinds of rumours about him! Some people say he gave hundreds of pounds to beggars in the street. Others say their relatives were bumped off! No one knows a thing for sure, Rosie, least of all you!

ROSIE: Sammy, you've got to face up to it and—

SAMMY: *(Cutting in)* Despite everything, Rosie, just admit it, he's a cheerful bastard with great spirit and—

ROSIE: *(Cutting in)* Sammy, listen to me—

SAMMY: Great generosity and optimism! He did miracles for that country. He was a freedom fighter.

ROSIE: *(Cutting in)* No, no, no!

ROSIE: We're just soft middle-class people who know nothing and have everything!

ROSIE: Just shut up and let me read this. Will you let me?

SAMMY: What is it?

ROSIE: You'll see.

> *(Finally he nods and gets into bed.* ROSIE *picks up the brown envelope and reads from a testimonial given by a victim.)*
>
> *(Reads:)* 'I will tell the truth of what prison was like there. On the first day they began to hit me on the back of my neck. Then they tied a wire around my testicles. A thin tube was pushed into my penis while someone forced a gun up into my arse, ripping the walls of my rectum until I was bleeding badly. I wanted to kill myself. Another man sat on my chest and stuck two fingers into each of my nostrils, tearing upwards until I thought I was going to choke. There were people I would willingly have betrayed. But I couldn't speak.'

(Sammy gets out of bed and goes to the door. He opens it and looks across the flat. RAFI *sits at the table, reading a newspaper, listening to Wagner and drinking a glass of milk. He raises his glass to* SAMMY.)

(Reads, as SAMMY *looks at* RAFI:) 'Two soldiers would ask me a question and then push my head into a toilet overflowing with human excrement. Later they taped adhesive over the end of my penis so I didn't pee for five days. The pain got worse and worse. I began to . . .'

*(*SAMMY *slams the door.)*

SAMMY: All right, all right!

(He tears the paper from her hands.

Cut to: Later that night. The living room. SAMMY *can't sleep. He listens to his father's contented snores at the door of his room. He goes to the window and looks out on the street. The man in the brown suit with the smashed head, the* CABBIE, *lights a cigarette under a street lamp.* SAMMY *turns and* ROSIE *is at the door to their room.)*

What am I going to do? We did say we'd have a little do, get some people round to meet him. We can't let a bit of torture interfere with a party. But who will we invite?

ROSIE: We'll just have to round up the usual social deviants, communists, lesbians and blacks, with a sprinkling of the mentally sub-normal—

SAMMY: Yeah—

ROSIE: To start the dancing. And Victoria, yes?

SAMMY: I do love you more than anyone else I've known.

ROSIE: Me too, stupid. But we're both looking for a way out. Aren't we, eh?

52.   INT. LIVING ROOM. EVENING.

SAMMY *is getting the flat ready for the little party. Furniture has been pushed back.* SAMMY *is putting out food.* RAFI *stands there moving things away. He takes the key to the drawer out of the fruit bowl.* RAFI *opens the drawer, revealing a number of nasty-looking weapons: lumps of woods with nails in them, big spanners, etc.*

SAMMY: We're gonna need more booze, Pop. You wouldn't mind popping out, would you?

(SAMMY *notices the table drawer is open.*)

RAFI: I can feel that you've turned against me in the last few days, even though your ignorance about me is profound. But there's something you must hear me say. *(Indicates the weapons.)* Look at this.

SAMMY: They're for self-protection. We're always getting burgled. Those depraved deprived are right out of control.

RAFI: Yes, London has become a cesspit. You'd better come home, Samir.

SAMMY: I am home, Pop. This is the bosom.

RAFI: What a sullen young man you are. I mean, home to your own country where you will be valued, where you will be rich and powerful. What can you possibly like about this city now?

SAMMY: Well . . .

(Now we see a number of London scenes that SAMMY *and* ROSIE *like:* SAMMY *and* ROSIE *are walking along the towpath towards Hammersmith Bridge.)*

(Voice over) On Saturdays we like to walk along the towpath at Hammersmith and kiss and argue.

(Next we see SAMMY *and* ROSIE *in 'Any Amount of Books'.)*

(Voice over) Then we go to the bookshop and buy novels written by women.

(Next, SAMMY *and* ROSIE *outside the Albert Hall.)*

(Voice over) Or we trot past the Albert Hall and up through Hyde Park. On Saturday nights things really hot up.

(Cut to: outside the Royal Court Theatre in Sloane Square.)

(Voice over) If we can get cheap seats we go to a play at the

Royal Court. But if there's nothing on that hasn't been well
reviewed by the *Guardian*—
*(Now we are in the small amused audience of a cabaret
above a pub. This is the Finborough in Earl's Court. A
man wearing a huge fat man's outfit, head disappeared into
the neck, is dancing to an old French tune. (This is* ALOO
BALOO.*)* SAMMY *and* ROSIE *sit in the audience laughing
and drinking.)*
(Voice over) We go to an Alternative Cabaret in Earl's Court
in the hope of seeing our government abused. Or if we're
really desperate for entertainment—
(We are now in the seminar room at the ICA. COLIN
MCCABE *is talking to an enthralled audience about Derrida.
A member of the audience has her hand up.)*
(Voice over) We go to a seminar on semiotics at the ICA
which Rosie especially enjoys.
*(*ROSIE *also has her hand up. But* MCCABE *points to someone
else.* ROSIE *looks at* SAMMY, *disgusted with* MCCABE'*s indifference to her.)*

AUDIENCE MEMBER: What, would you say, is the relation between
a bag of crisps and the self-enclosed unity of the linguistic
sign?
*(*COLIN MCCABE *starts to laugh.)*
SAMMY: *(Voice over)* We love our city and we belong to it. Neither
of us are English, we're Londoners you see.

53.   INT. SAMMY'S AND ROSIE'S BEDROOM. EVENING.
Minutes later. In the bedroom ROSIE *is now getting changed
for the party.* SAMMY, *agitated and upset by* RAFI, *watches her
sexually.*
ROSIE: Did you give him the money back?
SAMMY: *(Wanting her)* Before I do anything, I need something to
relax me.

ROSIE: *(Deliberately misunderstanding)* OK. Here's a couple of Valium.

54.   EXT. STREET. EVENING.

RAFI, *now out to buy booze, strolls across the street in his natty hat.*

55.   INT. ROSIE'S AND SAMMY'S LIVING ROOM/BEDROOM. EVENING.

ROSIE *continues to dress. During this* SAMMY *combs her hair and puts her shoes on. Through the open door of the bedroom we can see that* RANI *and* VIVIA *have arrived. They have their arms around each other. They sit and snog on the sofa opposite the bedroom. They've brought the deaf and dumb boys with them.*

SAMMY: *(To* ROSIE*)* Why d'you think we don't want to screw now?

ROSIE: The usual reasons. Boredom. Indifference. Repulsion. *(Cut to:)*

VIVIA: Are they rowing?

RANI: Just talking each other to death.

VIVIA: No, listen, they're talking about sex.

RANI: Yes, but it's only heterosexual sex. You know, that stuff when the woman spends the whole time trying to come, but can't. And the man spends the whole time trying to stop himself coming, but can't.

(Cut to:)

SAMMY: *(To* ROSIE*)* I wonder if it matters, us lying there night after night as if the Berlin Wall had been built down the middle of the bed.

ROSIE: Don't ask me about sex. I know more about carrots. But I expect it's an acquired taste that one could do without.

SAMMY: You? Not you.

(Cut to:)

RANI: *(To* VIVIA*)* I'm always suspicious of those relationships where the couple have read about Simone de Beauvoir and Jean-Paul Sartre at too early an age. I want my partner to be on the rack or nowhere at all.

VIVIA: Kiss me, darling.

(Cut to:)

ROSIE: I've just started to enjoy screwing.

SAMMY: Christ, how can things become so strange between a common couple?

(Cut to:)

RANI: *(To* VIVIA*)* Rosie calls this household 'the hedgehogs'.

*(*VIVIA *looks at her.)*

Because there are so many pricks around.

*(*SAMMY *and* ROSIE *come out of their bedroom,* SAMMY *overhearing the last bit. They have their arms around each other.)*

SAMMY: Yeah but not all pricks are men.

56.   INT/EXT. OFF-LICENCE. EVENING.

RAFI *is in an off-licence across the street. The counter of the off-licence is separated from the shop by chicken wire, with a small gap for the money. Two Alsatians run up and down barking behind the counter. A huge white man, the* FINGER MAN *that we met in the tube, sits in the shop, a baseball bat beside him.* RAFI *buys booze and is pretty disturbed by the shop. The* FINGER MAN *fingers his bat, craning to watch* RAFI *as* RAFI *shops.*

Cut to: outside the off-licence we see DANNY *looking through the window at him.* DANNY *is with his girlfriend, the kid and the dog.* DANNY *indicates to his girlfriend to come and have a look. They peer through the glass at him. This makes* RAFI *rather uncomfortable.*

Cut to: RAFI *coming out of the off-licence.* DANNY *takes the booze from him.*

RAFI: Come on. You'd better come to a party.

57. INT. SAMMY'S AND ROSIE'S FLAT. EVENING.

Now some guests have arrived. SAMMY *and* ROSIE *are together,* RANI *and* VIVIA *with them.* RAFI, *now elegantly dressed, goes to* SAMMY *and* ROSIE.

RAFI: Now you are together, tell me quickly: have you decided to buy a house in Hatfield with the money I've given you?

(ROSIE, *irritated by him, just looks across the room and sees that* DANNY *has arrived, among other guests.* DANNY *has the kid and the dog with him,* OMAR *and* JOHNNY *are there too,* JOHNNY *and* DANNY *talking. And then* ALICE *arrives.* RAFI *goes to her.*

Cut to: Later on. The party swings. DANNY *stands by a sofa on which sit* RAFI *and* ANNA. *Bits of conversation as we move across the room.* RANI *and* BRIDGET *dance together, cheek to cheek.* VIVIA *watches jealously.*)

RANI: I said to her, it's love this time, I want to be with you.

BRIDGET: I couldn't imagine being with anyone for more than two weeks.

(ROSIE *watches* DANNY. SAMMY *watches* ROSIE. ANNA *watches* SAMMY. OMAR *and an* ASIAN ACCOUNTANT *watch* RAFI.)

OMAR: Sammy's our accountant. He never said his father was Rafi Rahman. He kept that quiet.

ASIAN ACCOUNTANT: I was in Dacca when their army came in. How d'you think my father was killed—falling out of bed?

(RAFI, *slightly drunk now—jacket off—has pulled up his polo-necked shirt and is showing* ANNA *his scars.*)

RAFI: I'll show you my life!

(ANNA *peers interestedly at them.* RAFI's *stomach, chest and back are criss-crossed with long scars.*)

(*Indicating*) The geography of suffering. Open-heart surgery, gall-bladder, appendix, lung removal. It's a miracle I am alive. Touch them.

ANNA: Are you sure?

RAFI: Treat yourself—the Kennedy children used to stay in my house.

ANNA: I like men who try to impress me. They make me laugh.
(RAFI *looks up nervously and sees the white deaf and dumb boy staring at him. Cut to:*)

JOHNNY: (*To* OMAR) If you had to sleep with anyone in this room who would you choose?

OMAR: (*Pause, looks around.*) Er . . . You.
(*Cut to:* ALICE *is talking to* VIVIA. *She also glances at* RAFI *and* ANNA, *a little disconcerted.*)

ALICE: Although I was curious about—

VIVIA: Other bodies—
(RANI *goes to* VIVIA *and kisses her warmly, looking at* ALICE.)

ALICE: Other men—and one is curious. And although I loved someone else—I loved RAFI—I was faithful to my husband. For no other reason than that we believed in not lying to each other. Loyalty and honesty were the important things for us. Not attraction. Not something called pleasure.
(*Cut to: Now* ROSIE *is with* DANNY.)

ROSIE: You look cool. (*Pause.*) Is it your kid? What's he called?

DANNY: Rosie, I missed you.

ROSIE: You don't know me.

DANNY: If I knew you it would have been worse.
(*Cut to:*)

ALICE: (*To* VIVIA) In that old world of certainty and stability you didn't take it for granted that a marriage would smash up in ten years. It was your entire life you gave to someone else.
(*Cut to:*)

ANNA: (*To* RAFI) I do Gestalt therapy, an hour of Indian yoga, followed by Buddhist chanting. Do you chant?

RAFI: Chant what, my dear?

ANNA: Mantras, to calm yourself.

RAFI: I am calm. It is agitation I seek. You young international people mystify me. For you the world and culture is a kind of department store. You go in and take something you like from each floor. But you're attached to nothing. Your lives are incoherent, shallow.

ANNA: I am for self-development above all. The individual reaching her fullest potential through a wide range of challenging experience.

RAFI: Ah yes. The kind of thing I used to call bourgeois indulgence in the days when I believed in reason and the struggle. My ideal evening then was a dialogue by Plato followed by women wrestling in mud.

(Cut to:)

ALICE: *(To VIVIA)* We didn't have exaggerated expectations of what sex and love could offer so we didn't throw each other over at the first unhappiness.

VIVIA: You didn't have your own lives. You lived through men. The penis was your life-line.

(ROSIE and DANNY go off together, watched by RAFI and ALICE.)

(To ALICE) Let's keep in touch anyway. Can we exchange phone numbers?

(Cut to: ROSIE's study. ROSIE shows DANNY her books, drawings, etc. Now they hold each other. Their faces move closer together. Incredible sensuality, their hands in each other's mouths.)

DANNY: Why don't we get out of this lonely place? And go to a lonelier one?

(Cut to: SAMMY is with RAFI now. ANNA is photographing him. RAFI holds up his jumper, having a wonderful time.)

RAFI: *(To SAMMY)* And where is Lady Chatterley?

SAMMY: Piss off. *(To ANNA)* What are you doing, please?

RAFI: I think I'm becoming a very free and liberated person.

(Cut to: SAMMY *stands disconsolately outside Rosie's study.*
ANNA, *from the end of the hall, photographs him.* VIVIA
and RANI *stand behind* ANNA *with their arms around each
other.)*

SAMMY: Let's go, Anna!

(We see VIVIA *and* RANI *slip away.)*

58.   INT. ROSIE'S STUDY. NIGHT.

Seconds later, RAFI *is in his room, under the picture of Virginia
Woolf. He's taking a couple of pills with a glass of whisky. He
looks up—and the room is dark—and sees* VIVIA *and* RANI *standing
there. They are not threatening him directly, but he is frightened.*

RANI: We wanted to talk to you, Mr Rahman.

VIVIA: Yes, if you don't mind.

RANI: About politics and things.

VIVIA: About some things that happened to some people.

RAFI: If I were you two girls, I'd—

VIVIA: Yeah?

(Suddenly the door opens and ROSIE *is standing there. The
atmosphere is broken.* ROSIE *clocks the situation immediately and ensures that* RAFI *gets out.)*

ROSIE: Rafi, Alice is looking for you.

*(*RAFI *goes.)*

ROSIE: *(To* RANI *and* VIVIA*)* Please, not now.

RANI: But you do know who you have living in your flat?

ROSIE: I don't hate him.

RANI: Typically of your class and background. Your politics are
just surface.

ROSIE: What do you want to do?

RANI: We want to drive him out of the country. *(To* VIVIA*)* This
is liberalism gone mad!

*(*VIVIA *and* RANI *look pityingly at* ROSIE. *A hand appears
on* ROSIE'*s head. She looks up to see* DANNY *there.)*

ROSIE: *(To* DANNY*)* Ready?

DANNY: *(To* ROSIE*)* For anything.

59.   INT./EXT. CAR OUTSIDE ALICE'S HOUSE. NIGHT.

ALICE *is in the front of* SAMMY's *new car, next to him.* ANNA *and* RAFI *sit in the back, the electric windows going up and down. The suburbs are silent.*

SAMMY: Anna, how d'you like me new car?

RAFI: *(To* ANNA*)* I bought it for him.

ANNA: And what does he have to do for you in return?

RAFI: Only care for me a little.

   *(*ANNA *kisses* RAFI *goodbye, affectionately. He slides his hand up her skirt.)*

ANNA: You're quite an entertainment.

   (Cut to: ALICE *walks towards her house, through the beams of the headlights.* SAMMY *and* RAFI *stand beside the car,* ANNA *inside. The car door is open and the music spills out into the street.* ANNA *can sing along with it.)*

RAFI: I'm staying here tonight because I want to be with Alice.

SAMMY: Now? At night?

RAFI: At all hours.

SAMMY: And on all-fours?

RAFI: The English waste their women. There's a good ten years' wear in Alice. You don't know what a good woman she is. In fact you don't know anything about women full stop.

SAMMY: What d'you mean, for God's sake?

RAFI: Where is your wife, for instance?

60.   EXT. RAILWAY BRIDGE. NIGHT.

ROSIE, DANNY, *the kid and the dog are crossing the railway bridge towards the waste ground. The kid and the dog run on, leaving* ROSIE *and* DANNY. *They stop and look over the bridge;* ROSIE, *never having seen the waste ground before, is startled and amazed. She watches the kids play chess on a huge iron-sculpted chess set. The players sit above the game like tennis umpires and order eager minions to move their pieces for them.* DANNY *is behind her, with his face in her hair. She tells him about herself.*

ROSIE: My father has a small furniture store and used to be the Mayor of Bromley! My mother was having an affair with the official chauffeur. I haven't spoken to Dad for five years. He's crude, vicious, racist and ignorant. I'd happily die without seeing his face again. I changed my name and became myself. *(She turns. They kiss a little.)*

DANNY: Are you going to come in for some hot chocolate? *(She nods. He takes her hand.)* Come on then, follow me up the yellow brick road.

61.   INT./EXT. STREET. NIGHT.

SAMMY *stops the car outside* ANNA's *studio. She is still sitting in the back seat of the car, her arms around him, her hands over him. Her studio is in a working-class area of London now being taken over by the rich and the smooth.*

ANNA: Wouldn't you like to be with me tonight?

SAMMY: I'm trying to get on to a whole new regime.

ANNA: What for?

SAMMY: My prick keeps leading me into trouble. I'm like a little man being pulled around by a big dog. *(She touches him. He groans. He goes to get out of the car.)* Desire is pretty addictive though.

62.   EXT. UNDER THE MOTORWAY. NIGHT.

Here, on a large area of waste ground, is Danny's caravan. This is where he lives. There are many other caravans and shacks for the straggly kids. Some of them—maybe Danny's—are decorated with flashing Christmas lights. The traffic thunders overhead. ROSIE, DANNY *waving a stick, the kid and the dog, walk towards the caravan. Kids in their teens and twenties, black and white, girls and boys, stand around open fires or sit in old car seats, dragged out into the open. Next to one fire, on a crate, is a huge TV which the kids watch. On TV a headless man reads the news. On another part of the waste ground, the straggly kids are playing a variety of instruments, the stranger and more home-made the better, of course. Nearby, two cars are half buried in mud, as if they plunged over the rim of the motorway and nose-dived into the ground. A huge red Indian totem pole sticks up into the sky. A swing hangs down from under the motorway. A kid swings in it.*

ROSIE: My father would smash me across the room. Then he'd put on his mayor's chain and open church bazaars. Since then I've had difficulty in coming to terms with men's minds. Their bodies are all right.

DANNY: The neighbourhood's busy tonight.

(DANNY and ROSIE walk up the steps into Danny's caravan.)

63.   INT. ANNA'S STUDIO. NIGHT.

The light is strange and gloomy in the studio tonight. A lot of clothes—lace, silk, velvet, leather—lying about from a photography session. SAMMY is very anxious, drinking, pacing about. She watches him, while putting various things in a bag: rugs, candles, cushions.

ANNA: You've got some bad anxiety, man. There are two types of people—or combinations of both at different times. Toxic and nourishing types. T and N. You're more T than N right now. It'll take more that that to stop me loving you. You better come with me.

64.   EXT. FIRE ESCAPE. NIGHT.

ANNA is leading SAMMY up a fire escape at the back of the building. He stops. She pulls him on. She carries a bag.

65.   INT. CARAVAN. NIGHT.

In the large caravan, full of plants, pictures of Gandhi, Tolstoy, Martin Luther King. DANNY lies naked on the bed, reading a pa-

perback. He looks desperately attractive. ROSIE *walks towards the bed and sees him. She stands and watches him, swigging from a bottle of cider, dancing a little. He throws the book aside. She is fully dressed. The dog stretches out on the floor.*

ROSIE: Danny, God, you are gorgeous. Your legs. Head. Chest. You excite me. You're really doing it to me. Can you . . . would you do something? Just turn over.

(Unselfconsciously he turns over on to his stomach. ROSIE *moves down towards him. And she touches him, moving her lips lightly over him.*

Cut to: Outside, the band plays for the lovers and fires can be seen from the caravan windows. And of course inside the music can be heard.)

66.   INT. ALICE'S BEDROOM. NIGHT.

ALICE, *who has several Jane Austen novels beside her bed, is untying her hair in the crumbling eerie bedroom. Also, in this room, some Indian memorabilia. She wears a dressing-gown.* ALICE *looks at* RAFI.

RAFI: I like you in that dressing-gown. *(Pause.)* I'd like you out of it too. *(Pause.)* Do your kids come to see you?

ALICE: Once or twice a year.

RAFI: Is that more or less times than they go to the dentist?

ALICE: One works in the City. The other is in property.

RAFI: Rich?

ALICE: Of course, Rafi.

RAFI: The natural bonds are severed, though. And love is sought everywhere but at home. What is wrong with the home?

ALICE: Generally the people who live there. *(Pause.)* It's years since I've done this. And for you?

RAFI: *(Removing his trousers)* When I can . . . I like to.

ALICE: Like most women my life has been based on denial, on the acknowledgement of limits.

RAFI: Christ, Alice, let's just enjoy ourselves, eh?

(RAFI, *cheerfully naked, is about to hang his clothes in the wardrobe. He catches sight of his own squat, hairy, wrinkled body in the wardrobe mirror. He jumps with shock. She laughs.*)

ALICE: Never look in a mirror you don't know.

(*But he continues looking in the mirror. Standing behind him for a moment, he sees the* CABBIE *with the caved-in head.* RAFI *turns away and collects himself.*)

RAFI: Perhaps you're right. Right that we must contain and limit ourselves and learn to be content. The West has become very decadent, sex-mad and diseased since I came back. In my country you know what I did?

ALICE: Was it terrible?

RAFI: I shut all the night-clubs and casinos. The women have gone back in their place. There is restriction. There is order. There is identity through religion and a strict way of life.

ALICE: It is tyrannical no doubt.

RAFI: While here there is moral vertigo and constant change.

67.   INT. CARAVAN. NIGHT.

ROSIE *and* DANNY *lie on the bed in the caravan.* ROSIE *is half undressed now. Music from around the caravan. Their tongues dance over the other's face.*

ROSIE: In my kissing research I've learned that some people have hard tongues. Others, tongues that are too soft. You feel like sticking a fork in them. Others kiss so much like vacuum cleaners you fear for your fillings. But this is a kiss.

DANNY: I can't stop touching you.

ROSIE: Would you rather be writing a letter?

DANNY: I'm telling you something, Rosie.

ROSIE: I'm biting your neck. I love necks. Necks are mine.

(*And they wrestle a little.*)

DANNY: The woman who brought me up—because my mum was out at work all day—lived right near you. That's why I've watched you so often in the street.

ROSIE: Why didn't you say anything?

DANNY: I felt, well, that's quite a woman. But I thought: Victoria, you're well outclassed here. Until I realized that you're down-wardly mobile!

ROSIE: What about the woman who brought you up?

DANNY: Paulette. The police just went into her house and shot her up. That was the start of the rebellion. Nobody knows the shit black people have to go through in this country.
(We pull back to see, at the partition between the bed and the rest of the caravan, the kid standing there looking on.)

68.   INT. ALICE'S BEDROOM. NIGHT.

An old record plays on the gramophone in the room. ALICE and RAFI are in bed. She kisses him. She is releasing her hair, which until now has been tied at the top of her head. He pulls away from her and her hair tumbles free, all of it perfectly white, which shocks RAFI. Now she reaches down to pull up her nightdress.

ALICE: Women like Vivia are unnatural and odious, of course, but there's something I've noticed about men that she would understand. One is constantly having to forgive men. Always they're wanting their women to see into them, understand them, absolve them. Is there anything in that line you'd like me to help you with, Rafi dear?

69.   EXT. ROOF OF ANNA'S STUDIO. NIGHT.

Here, overlooking London, the motorway nearby, are SAMMY and ANNA. ANNA is dancing for SAMMY, energetic, balletic, fluid, soundless. SAMMY watches her. A helicopter passes over their heads, the thick beam of its light illuminating them, the hurricane wind of its propellers driving them into each other's arms.

ANNA: You must be thinking about Rosie right now.

(He nods.)

How completely odd and freakish for a husband to think about his wife when he is with his lover.

(Suddenly she grabs him and pushes him violently towards the side of the building, thrusting him half over the low wall which separates the roof from the long drop.)

SAMMY: What the fuck—

ANNA: How many lovers have you had in the past two years?

SAMMY: About . . . about . . .

ANNA: Yeah?

SAMMY: Twelve or so.

ANNA: For you pursuing women is like hang-gliding. They're a challenge, something to be overcome. It's fucking outta date, man! It's about time you learned how to love someone!

(She shoves him so we are looking straight down, with him.)

That's what fucking life is, baby!

(Cut to: He lies at her feet now, on the roof. ANNA has spread exotic rugs out and lit candles. There are also storm lanterns. He massages her right foot.)

That's it, that point's directly related to my Fallopian tubes . . . and there, that's my small intestine . . . yes, diaphragm . . .

SAMMY: What would you do if you discovered that someone close to you, a parent say, had done some stuff that was horrific and unforgivable? They had ways of justifying it, of course. But still it so disturbed you, you couldn't bear it?

ANNA: Your father? I don't know what I'd do, Sammy.

SAMMY: I don't know either, you know.

ANNA: Come here.

(She indicates to SAMMY and he goes to her. They hold each other and roll away across the roof.)

70.   INT./EXT. COLLAGE OF COPULATION IMAGES. NIGHT.

Now there is a collage of the three couples coupling. This is cut with the kids and the straggly band outside the caravan dancing in celebration of joyful love-making all over London. Some of the straggly kids play instruments or bang tins. Others are dressed in bizarre variations of straight gear—like morris dancers, pearly queens, traffic wardens, naval ratings, brain surgeons, witches, devils, etc. The cinema screen suddenly divides vertically (or would it be more appropriate horizontally?) and we see the three couples in energetic, tender and ecstatic climax, with DANNY *and* ROSIE *in the centre.*

71.   INT./EXT. WASTE GROUND. MORNING.

ROSIE *has woken up alone in the caravan. She goes out of the caravan. The straggly kids, with* DANNY *and his kid, are having breakfast outside. They eat at a long table set out in the open, the motorway above them. In the daylight* ROSIE *can see the kids have planted vegetables in the waste ground and a young black woman walks up and down with a watering can with a dildo-penis for a funnel. A number of sculptures have been built in the vegetable patch. In the background a shop has been set up in an old shack. Here customers buy vegetables, books, etc. On the long table* ROSIE *sees a printing press has been set up and the kids run off pages for books they're printing.* ROSIE *sits down next to* DANNY *and has breakfast. When she looks to the periphery of the site, beyond the barbed wire, she sees three white men standing in the open back of a lorry. One of them has a pair of binoculars. They watch the kids.*

ROSIE: *(To* DANNY*)* What's going on?

DANNY: They're chucking us off this site—either today, the next day or the day after that.

72.   INT. ANNA'S STUDIO. MORNING.

ANNA *is asleep.* SAMMY *goes to* ANNA *with a tray—on it are croissants, juice, eggs and coffee. He kisses her and she opens her eyes.*

SAMMY: Let's look at the photographs you took of that place I want to buy.

(*Cut to: A little later.* ANNA *and* SAMMY *sit on the bed.* ANNA *shows him photographs of a smart and inhabited house in Fulham. Wittily, she has photographed the ridiculous yuppie inhabitants showing the place off.*)

Which'll be Rosie's room?

ANNA: I'm having an exhibition in New York. I'm going to call it 'Images of a Decaying Europe'. So I should photograph that black guy at the party. D'you know where he is?

SAMMY: On top of my wife I expect.

73.   INT. ALICE'S LIVING ROOM. DAY.

ALICE *and* RAFI *are sitting at the table having breakfast. They've almost finished.* RAFI *is eager to leave.*

ALICE: What would you like to do today?

RAFI: (*Rising, wiping his mouth*) I think I'd better get moving, Alice. Sammy and Rosie will be expecting me.

ALICE: Why should they be expecting you? You really want to go, don't you? Is there anything you have to urgently do? I'd just like to know.

RAFI: Alice. I want to start writing my memoirs.

74.   INT. SAMMY'S AND ROSIE'S FLAT. DAY.

RAFI *has returned. The flat looks wrecked from the night before.*

RAFI: Sammy! Sammy!

(RAFI *goes into Rosie's study. Hearing a noise in the bedroom he opens the door and sees* RANI *and* VIVIA *in bed. He is very shocked and angry. He starts to abuse them in Punjabi. This is sub-titled.*)

What are you doing, you perverted half-sexed lesbians cursed by God?

RANI: Fuck off out of it, you old bastard!

RAFI: God save my eyes from the sights I'm seeing!

(He shuts the door and cowers behind it as RANI *and* VIVIA *throw stuff at him.)*

RANI: *(Raving at him)* Come here and let me bite your balls off with my teeth and swallow them! I'll rip off your prick with a tin opener! I'll sew live rats into the stomach of your camel, you murdering fascist!

(As she throws books at him:) Who the fuck do you think you are! *(Now she is opening the drawer and removing the weapons.)* That pigshit bastard, I'll crush his testicles right now!

(As she lunges with her piece of wood at him:)

Let me get at that withered sperm-factory with this and put the world out of its misery!

(And she bangs wildly on the door of the room. We see RAFI *climbing out of the window.)*

75.   EXT. OUTSIDE SAMMY'S AND ROSIE'S HOUSE. DAY.

RAFI *is climbing down the drainpipe. When he looks down he sees the* GHOST *looking up at him. Along the street* ROSIE *is getting off the back of Danny's motorbike.* RAFI *jumps the last few feet to the ground, damaging his arm as he falls. The* GHOST *walks away backwards, watching him.* RAFI *walks towards* ROSIE *and* DANNY. *He sees them warmly embrace. The police in the street look on in disgust.* RAFI *is furious, on Sammy's behalf, with* ROSIE *and* DANNY. DANNY *spots* RAFI *over* ROSIE'S *shoulder. He calls out to* RAFI *as* RAFI *tries to slide past unnoticed, concealing his damaged arm.*

DANNY: Hey Rafi, why don't you come by for a talk sometime? I'd like to see you.

RAFI: I don't know where you live, Victoria.

DANNY: Here, let me draw you a map.

*(*DANNY *goes over to his bike for pen and paper.* RAFI *and* ROSIE *are to one side.)*

ROSIE: *(Wickedly)* Up all night?

(RAFI *looks back at the house and sees* RANI *and* VIVIA *standing on the steps watching him.* BRIDGET *approaches* RANI *and* VIVIA, *and they talk briefly, indicating* RAFI.)

RAFI: *(To* ROSIE*)* What the hell are you doing kissing this street rat and bum Danny on the road!

ROSIE: I find that rat bums have an aphrodisiac effect on me, Rafi.

(DANNY *goes over with the map and gives it to* RAFI.)

DANNY: See you then.

RAFI: I was adored once, too.

(RAFI *walks away.* BRIDGET *comes down the steps of the house and follows him.* DANNY *and* ROSIE *embrace to say goodbye.*)

ROSIE: *(To* DANNY*)* You're fond of that old man, aren't you?

DANNY: It's easy for me to like him. But it's you that makes my bones vibrate.

ROSIE: Uh-huh. *(Pause.)* I'd better go. Or Sammy will be anxious.

76. INT. THE TUBE. DAY.

RAFI *is lost in the tube. He is standing in the ticket area of somewhere like Piccadilly with all the people swirling around him.* BRIDGET *is watching him. A group of young Jewish kids are being harangued by a group of young men. They yell: 'Yiddo, yiddo, yiddo!' at the kids.* RAFI *is confused and lost.* BRIDGET *is whispering to* EVA. *And* EVA *follows* RAFI *from now on, as he decides to go down a tube tunnel.*

77. INT. SAMMY'S AND ROSIE'S FLAT. DAY.

SAMMY, *in a good mood, has come home.* ROSIE, *alone in the flat, is sawing the legs off the bed, as it's too high. When she hears* SAMMY *she goes into the living room. He kisses her. But she is in a very bad mood.*

SAMMY: Where's Daddio?

ROSIE: He went off somewhere.

SAMMY: You didn't offend him, did you?

ROSIE: Offend him?

SAMMY: Yeah, you know, 'What's your favourite torturing method out of all the ones you know?'

ROSIE: He's been here long enough.

SAMMY: We can't just chuck the old fucker's arse out on to the street. What'll he do, become a busker?

ROSIE: Why, does he play a musical instrument? It's not as if he's poor, is it?

SAMMY: It is. We've got his money. And there are people who want to kill him. Listen, I've seen a house which would suit both of us bunny rabbits. So much room we could go for days without seeing each other. Or without seeing Pop.

ROSIE: Your father?

SAMMY: He could have the basement, or dungeon, as we could call it.

(She turns away from him, unable to share his ebullience.)

Let's try and love each other a little. Can't we try to touch each other or something?

ROSIE: How did you enjoy sleeping with Anna last night?

SAMMY: To be honest, I'd rather have stayed in and redecorated the kitchen. You? *(Pause.)* You're smiling inside at the thought of Danny. Did you like each other?

ROSIE: He excited me terribly.

SAMMY: And the traffic didn't get on top of you?

78.   EXT. OUTSIDE ALICE'S HOUSE. DAY.

RAFI *walks towards the house.*

79.   INT. ALICE'S BATHROOM. DAY.

ALICE *in the bathroom bandaging* RAFI's *damaged arm.*

RAFI: I can't live in that part of London. That's why I came back. Day after day those kids burn down their own streets. It's hard on tourists like me.

ALICE: *(Shocked, indicating arm)* Is that how this happened—in a mad riot?

(RAFI *nods and tries to kiss her. She turns away from him. Cut to: They walk down the stairs,* RAFI *in front.)*

I hate their ignorant anger and lack of respect for this great land. Being British has to mean an identification with other, similar people. If we're to survive, words like 'unity' and 'civilization' must be understood.

RAFI: I like rebels and defiance.

ALICE: You funny little fraud, you shot your rioters dead in the street! The things we enjoy—Chopin, Constable, claret —are a middle-class creation. The proletarian and theocratic ideas you theoretically admire grind civilization into dust!

(At the bottom of the stairs, in the hall, RAFI *tries to hold her. She evades him.)*

RAFI: Please.

ALICE: What is it, Rafi?

RAFI: Sammy and Rosie have no human feeling for me. It would be terribly painful to have me living here?

ALICE: You couldn't leave quickly enough this morning. There was barely a heartbeat between your eyes opening and the tube doors shutting!

RAFI: I know, I know. Alice, take pity on me. I've got a lot of personal problems.

ALICE: *(Taking his hand)* Come. Let me show you something now.

80.   INT. CELLAR. DAY.

ALICE *takes* RAFI *through a door in the hall and down the perilous stairs into the gloomy cellar of the house. The place is stuffed full of old furniture, boxes, files, more Indian memorabilia—mosquito nets, hockey sticks, old guns. As* RAFI *follows* ALICE *through all this, picking his way to the far end, he sees that the* GHOST *is in the cellar with him, walking immaterially through objects. To turn away from this frightening sight, he turns to look at a framed picture. This is of Alice in India as a baby, with her ayah—the Indian servant who would have brought her up.*

ALICE: That's me as a baby, with the ayah that brought me up for the first eight years of my life.

*(*ALICE *is taking down an armful of large dusty notebooks from the shelves at the end of the cellar. Accompanied by the* GHOST RAFI *goes to her as she opens the notebooks.)*

RAFI: What is this, Alice?

(As she flips slowly through them we can see there is an entry for each day through the years 1954, 1955, 1956. Each entry begins 'Dear Rafi . . .' or 'My Darling Rafi . . .' or 'Dearest Rafi . . .')

ALICE: Every day for years as I waited for you, I poured out my heart to you. I told you everything! Look, pages and pages of it! I really waited like a fool for you to come back and take me away, as you said you would. Look at this.

(She goes to an old suitcase, covered in dust. With difficulty she opens it. The GHOST *watches* RAFI.*)*

It's thirty years since I closed this case.

(Slowly she pulls out and holds up the rotting garments.)

These are the clothes I packed to take with me. The books. The shoes. Perfume . . .

RAFI: Alice . . .

ALICE: I waited for you, for years! Every day I thought of you! Until I began to heal up. What I wanted was a true marriage.

But you wanted power. Now you must be content with having introduced flogging for minor offences, nuclear capability and partridge-shooting into your country.

RAFI: *(To the* GHOST*)* How bitterness can dry up a woman!

81. EXT. OUTSIDE ALICE'S HOUSE. DAY.

RAFI *leaves* ALICE*'s house. From the door she watches him go.*

82. INT. SAMMY'S AND ROSIE'S BATHROOM. DAY.

SAMMY *and* ROSIE *in the bath together.* SAMMY *shampoos* ROSIE*'s hair.*

ROSIE: Soap?

SAMMY: No, I already washed today. *(Pause.)* Where can the old man have got to?

ROSIE: Sammy, this is all false, isn't it? I think we should try not living together. I think we should try being apart now.

83. EXT. SOUTH LONDON STREET. DAY.

RAFI, *with his bandaged arm and disintegrating map (that Danny drew for him), walks through the desolate tunnels and grim streets of South London. Now it is raining.* RAFI *stops under a railway bridge where other wretched rejects are sheltering—the poor, the senile, the insane, the disabled. Some of them sleep in cardboard boxes, others in sleeping bags.* RAFI *trips over someone. He turns to them. During all this, the Indian in the filthy brown suit, with a scarf over his head, the* GHOST, *is watching him. Further away,* EVA *watches* RAFI *with* MARGY.

RAFI: *(To man)* Will you pull off my shoe?

(The man, who is black, tries to pull RAFI*'s shoe off.*

Cut to: Now RAFI *walks on. The brown-suited man follows him, carrying* RAFI*'s discarded shoe.*

Cut to: Now RAFI *is walking in another part of South London in the pouring rain. Soaked through, bandage dangling, he is approaching the waste ground. In the street*

two bulldozers are being driven to the site. Around the
perimeter of the waste ground several big cars are parked.
White men, in suits, look at the site, talk about it, and
point to things. The Indian in the brown suit, the CABBIE,
looks on. RAFI *walks past the nose-dived cars, ankle deep*
in mud. One of the kids—the one whose mother was shot
at the beginning of the film—points out Danny's caravan
to him. Music blares out over the waste ground. RAFI *goes*
to Danny's caravan and bangs on the door.

84.   INT. DANNY'S CARAVAN. DAY.

RAFI *stumbles into the caravan.* DANNY *sits writing at an old type-*
writer. A young black woman stands on a chair playing keyboards.
The keyboard is slung over her shoulder like a guitar. They look
up at RAFI. DANNY *goes to* RAFI *and holds him up.*

RAFI: I thought I'd take you up on your offer of tea. Is it real or
    tea-bags?
    (Cut to: Now DANNY *is making tea. The woman plays the*
    keyboards. A white rabbit runs around the caravan. RAFI
    looks around the place and at the pictures.)
    You really live here all the time? Like you it's the middle
    class I hate.

DANNY: This land's been bought by the property people. The
    government's encouraging fat white men with bad haircuts
    to put money into the area.

RAFI: When we first met, you and I, in the street, you were very
    kind to me. I'll never forget it.

DANNY: Yeah, an old woman I loved got shot up by the police.
    Friends of ours were pulling whites out of cars and beating
    them in revenge. I didn't know if I should be doing it.
    (DANNY gives RAFI *his tea.* RAFI *looks behind him out of*
    the window into the pouring rain. The leaves of the

drenched bushes frame RAFI's *view of the brown-suited man who stares through the window.)*

85.   INT. SAMMY'S AND ROSIE'S LIVING ROOM. EVENING.

ROSIE *is helping* SAMMY *learn to stand on his head. Now he is up.* ROSIE *holds him up straight.*

ROSIE: If you had to choose between sleeping with George Eliot or Virginia Woolf, who would you choose?

SAMMY: On looks alone, I'd go for Virginia. Now you. De Gaulle or Churchill, including dinner, full intercourse and blow job.

ROSIE: *(Pause. Thinks, then:)* If we don't live together, if we live with other people, if we do entirely different things, I won't stop loving you.

SAMMY: That's not enough. We've got to be committed to each other.

ROSIE: It's not commitment you want. It's fatal hugging that you're into.

SAMMY: Rosie, where's the old man? D'you think he's gone back to Alice's for a second helping of trifle? *(Pause.)* Danny or me?

ROSIE: That's easy.

86.   EXT. THE WASTE GROUND. NIGHT.

A meeting is taking place. The kids and RAFI *sit around a huge bonfire discussing what they should do. Around the perimeter fence the bulldozers, the* PROPERTY DEVELOPER *and his cronies are discussing what to do. Some kids play music.*

DANNY: *(To the group)* They'll remove us tomorrow morning.

KID: *(To the group)* What do people think we should do?

KID TWO: Not go without a fight.

KID THREE: Go peacefully. We're anarchists, not terrorists.

KID FOUR: *(To RAFI)* You're a politician. What do you think?

(Sitting among the kids, the man in the brown suit watches.
The kids look at RAFI *respectfully.)*

RAFI: We must go. The power of the reactionary state rolls on.
But we must never, ever be defeated.

87. EXT./INT. THE WASTE GROUND/CARAVAN. NIGHT.

It is late. Everyone is asleep. The Asian in the brown suit, the
GHOST, *has walked across the silent waste ground to Danny's*
caravan.
Outside he removes his suit until he is naked.
Cut to: Inside the caravan RAFI *has got up from his bed to wash*
his face. He runs water into the bowl. He has his back to the door
of the caravan. As he washes suddenly the bowl is full of human
blood and hair and bone. A noise behind him. RAFI *turns and sees*
the GHOST *covered in blood and shit, with serious burns over his*
body. The body is criss-crossed with wires from the electric shock
treatment he received in detention. Over his head he wears a rubber
mask through which it is impossible to breathe. He makes a terrible
noise. RAFI *turns and stares. The* GHOST *removes his rubber mask.*
We can see now that the head is half caved in and one eye (with
the bandage removed) has been gouged out.

GHOST: I'm sure you recognize me, though I don't look my best.
   (RAFI nods. The GHOST sits on the bed. He pats the bed
   next to him. RAFI *has got to sit next to him. The* GHOST
   puts his arms around RAFI. *Then the* GHOST *takes the pads*
   connected to the wires which are stuck to his temples and
   puts the two of them over RAFI's *eyes.)*
   You said to Rosie that I was the price to be paid for the
   overall good of our sad country, yes?

RAFI: Forgive me.

GHOST: How could that be possible?

RAFI: Since, I have tried to love people. And it wasn't I who did
the mischief! I wasn't there, if it happened at all!

GHOST: You were not there, it is true, though you gave the order. You were in your big house, drinking illegally, slapping women's arses adulterously, sending your money out of the country and listening, so I heard, to the songs of Vera Lynn.

RAFI: The country needed a sense of direction, of identity. People like you, organizing into unions, discouraged and disrupted all progress.

GHOST: All of human life you desecrated, Rafi Rahman!
(*The* GHOST *raises his arms. Now the caravan is plunged into darkness.* RAFI *screams. Electricity buzzes.*)

88.   INT. ALICE'S LIVING ROOM. MORNING.
The following morning. ALICE *is on the phone.*

ALICE: (*To* VIVIA) I'm a little worried about him, Vivia. Do you know where he is? Oh good. Yes I'd like to see him. (*Writes on a pad.*) I'll be there.

89.   EXT. THE WASTE GROUND. MORNING.
Around the perimeter fence the bulldozers are in place. The property developer's men are arriving. They discuss how to do the job. Some of the kids are spreading cloth, wool, cotton, and large areas of brightly coloured material over the barbed wire. In their caravans and trucks other kids are packing up. The GHOST *in the brown suit leaves Danny's caravan.*

90.   INT. SAMMY'S AND ROSIE'S LIVING ROOM. MORNING.
SAMMY *is separating the books. Rosie's are left on the shelves—Sammy's go into boxes.* ROSIE *comes into the room. She is just about to go out.*

ROSIE: Sammy, what are you doing?

SAMMY: Getting ready to leave, now the decision has been made. (*Continues, not bitterly.*) That's mine. Mine. Yours, mine. (*Holds up* The Long Goodbye.) Mine?

ROSIE: No, I bought it. When we were at college.

SAMMY: I bought it for you.

ROSIE: Whose does that make it, officially? Oh, you take it. We read it to each other in Brighton. We made love on the train. *(Pause.)* I've got to go. They're being evicted today. Any news on Rafi?

SAMMY: I wondered why I was feeling so cheerful—I haven't thought about him today. I'll find him this morning.

91.   EXT. THE WASTE GROUND. DAY.

Now the exodus has begun. The caravans are starting to move; the fence has come down. The PROPERTY DEVELOPER *and his men are moving over the site with dogs. Police accompany them. The heavies smash down the shop to clear the way. The heavies hustle the straggly kids. Caravans get stuck in the mud. Some kids are trying to dig them out.* DANNY *is at the wheel of one of these trailers. The bulldozers start to move across the waste ground, clearing the debris, flattening the earth. The* PROPERTY DEVELOPER *stands in the back of an open-roofed car yelling instructions through a megaphone. The kid whose mother was shot (*MICHAEL*) is defiant, shouting at the heavies and the police who accompany them.*

Cut to: Inside Danny's caravan. RAFI *lies moaning on the bed. Frightened by the caravan's movement, he staggers to the door.*

Cut to: Opening the door of the slowly moving caravan, we see RAFI'S *view of the waste ground. We see the convoy moving slowly off, kids being pushed around, trying to organize themselves.*

Cut to: On the periphery, being held back by the police, is ROSIE, *and with her* VIVIA, RANI, EVA. *A woman in a long sable coat is watching the action—the property developer's wife.* RANI, *standing beside her for a moment, sprays a cross in green paint on her back.*

VIVIA: *(To* ROSIE*)* Your father-in-law has finally joined the proletariat.

ROSIE: What? Is he here?

RANI: Somewhere.

(ALICE *has arrived now. We see her getting out of her car and walking through the police to* ROSIE, RANI, VIVIA. *She watches the police brutally arresting young women. She is shocked by this. She takes* VIVIA's *arm. The other women try to move forward, along with a lot of the other spectators. They are obstructed by the heavies and police. The* PROPERTY DEVELOPER *in his jeep rides past yelling through his megaphone.*)

PROPERTY DEVELOPER: Here we go, here we go, here we go! Fuck off, you lesbian communists!

(*Then he recognizes* ALICE *and she him. He stops.*)

Alice, what brings you here?

ALICE: (*Indicating everything*) Is this you, Norman?

PROPERTY DEVELOPER: Yes, I'm proud to say—making London a cleaner and safer place.

ALICE: I'm after someone. Can I get through a minute?

(*He waves* ALICE *through.*)

PROPERTY DEVELOPER: How's Jeffrey?

ALICE: Probably I see my son less than you!

(*As* ALICE *goes through on to the site,* ROSIE, VIVIA, EVA, RANI, *etc., accompany her. The* GHOST, *walking away in the opposite direction, slips in the mud and, unnoticed by anyone but the kid whose mother was shot, goes under the wheels and is broken. By now* ANNA *has arrived on site. We see her moving around quickly, photographing where she can without getting hurt.* ALICE *has reached* RAFI, *who is staggering around in the mud.*

Cut to: Wider shot of the convoy moving away. ALICE *is taking care of* RAFI. *He is in a terrible state.* ROSIE *joins them.*)

ROSIE: (*To* ALICE) Come on, let's get him out of here. Take him to my place.

(RANI *watches this and* ROSIE *sees her.*

Cut to: The convoy is leaving the waste ground and heading for the road. The kids remain defiant, cheerful and rebellious, like the PLO leaving Beirut. Some of them sit on the top of the moving caravans, playing music as they go.

Cut to: ALICE *walks away with* RAFI, *supporting him as they go.* RAFI *is raving.)*

RAFI: I'm not leaving! Take me back! We must not allow those fascist bastards to drive us away! We must fight, fight! *(To* ALICE) You've never fought for anything in your damn life! *(She gets* RAFI *in the car. He collapses in the back. She is very upset by what has happened to him.)*

92.   EXT. MOTORWAY. DAY.

SAMMY, *who is driving to Alice's, heads along the motorway. He stops the car, gets out. On the waste ground, looking up, we can see* SAMMY *standing on the rim of the motorway, watching it all. He calls and shouts down to* ROSIE. *He shouts with all his might.*

SAMMY: Rosie! Rosie! Rosie! Rosie!

(But of course she doesn't hear him. ANNA *notices* SAMMY, *though. She looks up and waves.* DANNY *shouts to* ROSIE *from the truck.)*

DANNY: Looks like I'm on my way out!

(A final shot, later: The convoy having left, the bulldozers doing their work, the waste ground having been cleared, we see ROSIE, VIVIA *and* RANI *walking across the waste ground.* VIVIA *carries the black anarchist flag which fell from the top of one of the caravans.)*

93.   INT. SAMMY'S AND ROSIE'S FLAT. DAY.

It is later that day. The women—taking RAFI *with them, have gone to Rosie's flat to discuss the morning's events.* RAFI *is in the study. The women,* RANI, VIVIA, ALICE, ANNA, ROSIE, BRIDGET, *eat and talk.*

RANI: The way Danny's lot were treated shows just how illiberal and heartless this country has become—

ALICE: But they were there illegally—

ANNA: Surely they'd been there for so long, though—

(We get the flavour of their intense and good-natured conversation. As it continues, we move across to see RAFI watching them from his room a moment, before shutting the door of the study. Now we are in the room with him. The conversation from the living room can continue over, muffled.)

ALICE: It doesn't affect the law. The law is to protect the weak from the strong, the arranged from the arbitrary—

RANI: But they are the powerless just trying to find a place in this rotten society for themselves!

(RAFI moves slowly. He is tired and distressed, but there is great dignity in his actions. He takes the sheets from the bed and starts, almost experimentally, to tie them together securely. The voices outside get louder.)

ALICE: *(Out of shot)* Their place can only be found on society's terms, not on their own whim—

(Cut to: SAMMY has come into the flat. He stands there a while, looking at everyone.)

ROSIE: *(To ALICE)* It's hardly whim, they have no given place in this society!

(SAMMY goes to ANNA and touches her lightly. She doesn't ignore him, but it's as if she doesn't notice him. He looks at ROSIE.

Cut to: Back in the study RAFI has proceeded quite far with the joining together of the sheets. He climbs the ladder and ties the sheet to the top rung. Finally we see him put the other end of the sheet around his neck. During this, he is breathing deeply. He seems very alert now and aware of everything.

Cut to: SAMMY *leans over* ROSIE.)

SAMMY: Where's my dad?

ROSIE: He's in his room. You OK?

(Now we hear RAFI *kill himself as he jumps from the ladder.)*

SAMMY: *(To* ROSIE*)* Sure.

*(*SAMMY *goes to Rafi's room. He sees his father hanging. He looks at him.* SAMMY *leaves the study and goes back into the living room. He watches the women talking for a moment.)*

(To ROSIE*)* Rosie, I think there's something you should come and look at.

(She looks up and goes to SAMMY. *They go into the study. We see* SAMMY *and* ROSIE *in the study looking at* RAFI.*)*

94.   INT. SAMMY'S AND ROSIE'S LIVING ROOM. DAY.

SAMMY *and* ROSIE *sit on the floor together, rocking each other, waiting for the ambulance. We can see the others leaving, solemnly, one by one,* ANNA *turning back to look at* SAMMY *as she goes. But he doesn't see her. It is just the two of them together.*

END

The Alchemy of Happiness

London Kills Me

The
Alchemy
of Happiness

One day in the summer of 1989 I was followed along the Portobello Road by a boy of about twenty-one. He was selling drugs, as were many people around here, but this kid was an unusual salesman. For a start, he didn't mumble fearfully or try to intimidate. And he didn't look strong enough to shove a person in an alley and rob them. He was open-faced, young and direct; and he explained unasked the virtues of the drugs he was selling—hash, acid, Ecstasy—holding them up as illustration. As I vacillated, he explained lyrically about the different moods, settings, and amounts appropriate for each drug.

We started to meet regularly. He liked to stand outside pubs, discussing people in the street. He'd think about which drug they'd prefer and wonder whether they'd purchase it from him, perhaps right now. Then he'd follow them.

He relished the game or challenge of selling, the particular use of words and the pleasures of conscious manipulation. He liked to con people too. On the whole he was proud of his craft. He reminded me of the salesman in Barry Levinson's *The Tin Man*. He was in a good position, that particular summer of love. He had a regular supply of drugs and there were plenty of customers. The kid knew there was a limitless market for what he had to

sell. After all, drug-taking was no longer the sub-cultural preserve
of those who knew its arcane language. Thirty years of a world-
wide, sophisticated and mass culture, introduced by the Beatles,
the Doors, Hendrix, Dylan and others, had spread the drug word,
making certain drugs both acceptable and accessible. There was
no combating it.

New drugs like Ecstasy were especially in demand. Unlike LSD,
for example, these were party drugs, weekend drugs, without
noticable after-effects. More usefully for the end of the 1980s,
they were compatible with both holding down a full-time job and
dancing in a field at four in the morning.

So most of the time the kid didn't much care if he made a sale
or not. He wasn't desperate—yet. He moved from squat to squat
and wasn't yet weary of being ejected, often violently, in the
middle of the night. Anyhow, if things didn't go well he'd leave
for Ibiza, Ecstasy Island, where many other young people were
headed.

He loved to talk about himself, dwelling in vivid and creative
detail on the fantastic adventures and tragedies of his life. Along
with his drug dealing, these horrific and charming stories were
his currency, his means of survival, enabling him to borrow money,
ask a favour or stack up an ally for the future. So he told them
to anyone who'd listen and to plenty of people who wouldn't.
Again, it was a while before these stories became repetitive and
self-pitying.

This kid's subject, his speciality let us say, or his vocation, was
illegal drugs. He'd discuss enthusiastically the marvels and possibilities of Ecstasy, the different varieties of the drug and the
shades of feeling each could induce. He looked forward to the
new drugs he believed were being produced by hip chemists in
San Francisco. This evangelical tone reminded me of the way LSD
was talked about in the 1960s. I kept thinking that had the kid

known about, say, the Victorian novel in the same detail, he'd
have been set up for life by some university.

But a penchant for getting high and dealing to strangers was
getting him banned from local pubs. He'd been stabbed, beaten
up and slashed across the face. Sometimes he was picked up by
the police, who 'disappeared' him into a police cell for two or
three days, without charging him or informing anyone he was
there. He'd been comforted and warned by social workers, probation officers and drug counsellors. Despite his glorious stories,
he led a hard and painful life, not helped by the fact he was foolish
as well as smart, indiscreet too, and without much foresight.

The intensity of this kid's life as he ran around the rich city,
stealing, begging, hustling, was the starting point for *London Kills
Me*. But his activities were bound up with the new music—Hip-
Hop, House, Acid Jazz—and the entrepreneurial bustle surrounding it; the band, record labels, shops, raves and warehouse
parties organized in the squats, pubs and flats of Notting Hill.
This reliable generational cycle of new music, fashion and attitude
amounted to a creative resurgence reminiscent of the mid-1960s,
and, of course, of the mid-1970s punk and New Wave, which
was DIY music of another kind.

Notting Hill seemed an appropriate setting for the London
branch of what had been a mostly provincial and northern music
movement. The North Kensington area has always had a large
immigrant community: Afro-Caribbean, Portuguese, Irish, Moroccan. Many Spanish people, escaping fascism, had settled there.
Its mixture of colours and classes was unique in London and it
had a lively focal point, the Portobello Road and its market. Of
the other previously 'happening' places in London, Chelsea had
become a tourist's bazaar; and Soho has been overrun by the
advertising industry. But like both these places, Notting Hill had
cultural history. George Orwell was living in the Portobello Road

in 1928 when he started to write the first pages of a play (one character of which was called Stone). Colin McInnes was part of the area's 1950s bohemia. In the late 1960s Nicholas Rogue's seminal *Performance* was set and filmed there. Not long afterwards David Hockney took a studio in Powis Terrace. And in the 1970s the Clash's first album featured a montage of the 1976 carnival riot on its cover.

In 1959, after seeing Shelagh Delaney's *A Taste of Honey*, Colin McInnes wrote: 'As one skips through contemporary novels, or scans the acreage of fish-and-chip dailies and the very square footage of the very predictable weeklies, as one blinks unbelievingly at "British" films, it is amazing—it really is—how very little one can learn about life in England here and now.'

A few years later his wish began to be granted. There developed a tradition, coming out of Brecht and stemming from the Royal Court and the drama corridor of the BBC, of plays, series and films which addressed themselves to particular issues—unemployment, or racism, or housing—usually seen through the inescapable British framework of class. This work was stimulated by the idea of drama having a use or purpose, to facilitate society's examination of itself and its values, creating argument and debate about the nature of life here and now. Many actors, writers, directors and designers were trained to see their work in this way.

Out of this came the brief resurgence of low-budget British films in the mid-1980s. The myriad tensions of life under Thatcher were irresistible to writers and film-makers. Here was the challange of a Conservatism that had, at last, admitted to being an ideology. Here were ideas—at a time when the Left had none. The cultural reply was not presented in the language of social realism; both victims and heroes of the class struggle were eschewed. These were popular films wishing to reach a large audience hungry for debate about the new age of money and what it meant.

One issue rarely discussed in this way has been drug use. It's an odd omission as, since the mid-1960s, in most towns and cities of a good deal of the world, young people have been using illegal drugs of various kinds. There hasn't been much fiction about this subject and the life that goes with it; and remarkably little hard information about drugs is provided to people, though cautionary and scary stories are propagated in the vain hope of frightening them.

Although drugs are fundamental to the story, *London Kills Me* was never primarily 'about' drug use. The film is concerned mainly with the lives of the characters. It was always, for me, a story about a boy searching for a pair of shoes in order to get a job as a waiter in a diner. Even so, when we were seeking out money for the movie—and it was not expensive—there was criticism from potential backers about the drug use in the film. They were worried that they might be accused of 'recommending' drugs.

The text published here is the film's fifth draft, the version we began with on the first day of shooting. Some scenes were filmed exactly as written but others developed as we rehearsed. Some just changed in front of the camera. A certain amount of the dialogue was made up by the actors.

Many films and more television plays are planned meticulously before they start shooting. There are shot-lists and story-boards for every second of the film. The director, cameraman, producer, art director and assistants work out the camera- and actor-moves on scale plans before shooting begins. Making the film itself is then a process of reproduction. It isn't the necessary requirements of planning that make this way of working seem objectionable. It is the expectation or hope of safety and security that is deadening, the desire to work without that moment of fear—when you really don't know how to go on—and therefore to create without utilizing the unexpected.

I've never written in a planned way and I tried, even as a first-time director, not to work like this. It would bore me to know in the morning what exactly I'd be doing in the afternoon. And Stephen Frears, whose advice I sought, said it was 'fatal' to work to a strict plan. Having worked with him twice as a writer, I didn't want to have any less enjoyment than he clearly had when shooting a film.

Much to my surprise, having written the film and then being in the powerful position of being able to direct it too, I felt less possessive about my dialogue and the shape of the script than I had when someone else was in charge. In the end, all I clung to was the story, to getting that, at least, in front of the camera.

The script of *London Kills Me* was only ninety pages long: a tight little film without much wastage. I couldn't see there'd be much to lose in the editing. I thought every scene was essential and in the best place. We wouldn't waste a lot of time shooting material we'd never use. Editing would be relatively simple. So I was pretty surprised when the first rough assembly of the film was over two and a half hours long. I found myself in the odd position of having written a film and then shot it—and still I didn't know what sort of movie I was supposed to be making, what the tone was to be. The editing, like writing, I realized, would also become a form of exploration and testing of the material. It was all, even this, an attempt to tell a story by other means.

Hanif Kureishi
London, April 1991

London
Kills
Me

CAST

CLINT	Justin Chadwick
MUFFDIVER	Steven Mackintosh
SYLVIE	Emer McCourt
DR BUBBA	Roshan Seth
HEADLEY	Fiona Shaw
LILY	Eleanor David
STONE	Alun Armstrong
TOM-TOM	Stevan Rimkus
BURNS	Tony Haygarthy
FAULKNER	Nick Dunning
BIKE	Naveen Andrews

Director of Photography	Ed Lachman
Production Designer	Stuart Walker
Stills Photographer	Jacques Prayer
Music Consultant	Charlie Gillett
Music Composers	Mark Springer and Sarah Farhandi
Editor	Jon Gregory
Associate Producer	David Gothard
Producer	Judy Hunt
Director	Hanif Kureishi

A Working Title Production

EXT. STREET. DAY.

As the credits roll we see CLINT *on the street:* CLINT *is white, fair-haired, pretty, thin, vain, with much charm and nerve. He suffers from eczema all over his body—skin broken and cracked—so he's perpetually scratching himself and twitching.*

He's carrying a large bottle of mineral water which he uncaps. He produces a toothbrush and toothpaste from the top pocket of his jacket and using the bottled water he cleans his teeth.

Then he produces a dirty old piece of soap from his pocket and once more using the water, he washes his face and hands.

Finally he wets his hair.

Cut to:

EXT. STREET. DAY.

CLINT *walking purposefully through the city.*

Cut to:

EXT. STREET. DAY.

Now CLINT's *checking his look in the reflecting glass of the diner. He thinks he looks fine: He's had a wash, and his clothes, at this point, are pretty good.*

Cut to:

EXT. GOLDBORNE ROAD. DAY.

CLINT *walking purposefully through the city. We see* HEADLEY, HEMINGWAY *and* TOM-TOM *on street.*

Cut to:

EXT. VERNON YARD. DAY.

CLINT *in a secluded doorway. He's smoking a spliff as he takes out a roll of money and hides it in different bits of his clothing, including his shoes and socks. He does this quickly, as if practised at it.*

Cut to:

EXT. STREET. DAY.

CLINT *on the phone in the street, a tower of ten pences on the box,
a wretched piece of paper in hand, with phone numbers on it.
A young girl comes by and puts her prostitute's calling card in the
glass booth. Very businesslike.* CLINT *tries to talk to her as she
walks away, as well as talking into the phone.
Cut to:*

EXT. STREETS. DAY.

CLINT *walking purposefully through the city.*

EXT. STREET. EVENING.

We see CLINT *on the bridge, walking. He stops to tie his shoe-
laces. Picks up something from the ground, pockets it. He's always
alert in this way.
* SYLVIE *has seen him and she watches him doing this, amused by
him. She goes to him. They haven't seen each other for a while.
They greet each other warmly.* MUFFDIVER *is hanging out in doorway, watching them.* MUFFDIVER *is a skinny little kid of nineteen,
a wiry dirty boy without* CLINT's *charisma. But he's tougher than*
CLINT, *more determined and more organized. He's a drug-dealer
and starting to move into the big time.*

SYLVIE: How you doing, Clint?

CLINT: Good, good. Not too bad. Looking for a job.

SYLVIE: Now?

CLINT: No. Come with me.

SYLVIE: Where, little Clint?

CLINT: Little rave.

EXT. MOROCCAN CAFÉ. DAY.

*They walk past the Moroccan Café where the Moroccans sip mint
tea. They walk past the Rasta Information Centre. The street is
busy and lively, colourful and mixed. Music comes from various
cafés and shops. There is music on the street constantly. They talk*

and laugh, arm in arm, though CLINT *never relaxes and glances around continually, both out of nervousness and interest.*

Across the street MUFFDIVER *is standing in a doorway.*

MUFFDIVER: *(to himself)* Tsa-Tsa, she's nice.

> *(He knows* CLINT *well.* CLINT *works for him. They're very old friends.* MUFFDIVER *goes across to them.)*
>
> Wha' 'appening?

CLINT: Going to a rave, later.

MUFFDIVER: *(Looking at* SYLVIE*)* Yeah? Something 'appening.

CLINT: Sylvie 'appening. Sylvie. Muffdiver.

SYLVIE: Pleased to meet you, Muffdiver. Always nice to make new friends.

> *(*MUFFDIVER *looks at* SYLVIE. *She is less interested in him than he in her. He stares at her, fascinated. Meanwhile* CLINT *calls out to* BURNS, *who is sipping tea at a table inside the Moroccan place.* CLINT *goes inside.)*

INT. MOROCCAN CAFÉ. DAY.

CLINT: Burns! Burns! Yo, man, rave.

EXT. MOROCCAN CAFÉ. DAY.

And BURNS, *a fat scotsman in his fifties, comes paddling into the frame, eating. As the four of them walk,* MUFFDIVER *nudges* SYLVIE *and she does a double-take as he pulls a string of handkerchiefs out of his mouth.*

MUFFDIVER: Squad.

> *(Two plainclothes policemen pass in front of them. Automatically they cool down, their faces becoming masks. When the men have gone,* CLINT *gives an Indian whoop.* SYLVIE *looks at him and laughs.)*

INT. HOUSE PARTY. NIGHT.

A party. The place jumping. A mixed, black and white, party. Music. Dope. Dancing. Everything you'd expect.

CLINT *and* MUFFDIVER *are accompanied by* BURNS. *We see them swing into the room and greet people. They're obviously well-known there.*

A couple of kids go to BURNS *and ask him questions. He's dealing. He turns away with them, putting his hand in his pocket.*

MUFFDIVER *experimentally puts his arm around* SYLVIE *and whispers in her ear. Then he kisses her cheek. She is surprised by his attention.*

CLINT *is surprised by* MUFFDIVER's *move, but as usual he's concerned with other things, always curious.*

Cut to:

INT. ANOTHER PART OF HOUSE. NIGHT.

Later. MUFFDIVER *leaning back against a wall, stoned, with a joint.* CLINT *and* SYLVIE *talking in another part of the room.* BURNS *dancing with a girl, enjoying himself.*

A young black MAN *goes to* MUFFDIVER. *They greet each other, their faces close.*

MUFFDIVER: Buyin'?

MAN: Na.

MUFFDIVER: Sellin'?

MAN: I hear you lookin' for Mr G. You ready for Mr G I reckon. But he want to know you properly organized and everything.

MUFFDIVER: Yeah, I appreciate.

MAN: OK, I'll fix it. *(Indicates* CLINT.*)* Who that geezer?

MUFFDIVER: That's Clint. Why, he in trouble again?

> *(The* MAN *winks and moves away.* MUFFDIVER *is alarmed as the* MAN *moves towards* CLINT. CLINT *gets up. The* MAN *takes* CLINT *away from* SYLVIE. *The* MAN *indicates to* MUFFDIVER *to keep out of it.* MUFFDIVER *sits with* SYLVIE.*)*

INT. BARE ROOM. NIGHT.

The man throws CLINT *into a bare dark room, maybe with just a mattress on the floor. Pots of paint etc. There are two other guys*

in the room now, one BLACK, *one* WHITE, *all young and threatening.*
CLINT *backs away, terrified, whimpering.*

MAN: You owe me some money, Mr Clint, man, from that time
you are recalling now, right?

(CLINT *is furious with himself for getting into this shit.
His hands are shaking as he empties his pockets. Then,
after a nod from the* MAN, *he removes a fiver from the
collar of his shirt. The* MAN *takes the money but is un-
impressed by it.*)

That all you carryin', boy? You strip.

WHITE MAN: Yeah.

CLINT: I got nothin'.

(CLINT *removes his clothes to his underpants. The* MAN
nods and the pants come off, too. The men laugh at CLINT's
*puny eczema-ridden body. They search his clothes. Sud-
denly one of them holds up money.*)

WHITE MAN: In the shoe!

BLACK MAN: In the shoe? Chew the shoe, chew the shoe, boy!

(*They all close in on* CLINT. *Suddenly one of the men hits
him across the legs with a pool cue. He cries out.*)

INT. HOUSE PARTY. NIGHT.

Quick cut to the loud music of the house. Here MUFFDIVER *is talking
to* SYLVIE. BURNS *is eating a plate of food.*

MUFFDIVER: I've seen you around the pub and in the street, Sylvie,
but I've never talked to you, though I've wanted to. For a
long time.

(*Pause. He's getting nowhere with her.*)

Shall I tell you something? Burns is quite fat. He had his
stomach sewn up, to stop him eating. But the bit that was
left has expanded. Or maybe the stitches burst, I can't remember what he told us. A person's stomach is only the size
of your fist, you know. But it's elastic.

(Pause.

He pulls a lighted cigarette out of her ear. She doesn't respond.

He pulls a lighted match from the other. She smiles.)

SYLVIE: Where's that boy?

MUFFDIVER: You're right about him. He needs us, his friends. That's why I'm getting us a place. Need somewhere yourself. *(She is interested in him.)*

Why don't you come with me? Come on. We'll go somewhere. How about it?

EXT. PARTY HOUSE. NIGHT.

MUFFDIVER *and* SYLVIE *walk down the steps of the house, or stand at the top of the steps.*

MUFFDIVER: What sort of music do you like? I like House and Hendrix. The three Hs are for me, eh? That was a dread party. Clint's idea. What a fool.

Cut to:

EXT. STEPS UNDER HOUSE. NIGHT.

We see CLINT, *naked and covered in mud, under the steps, shivering but then laughing as he hears his friend* MUFFDIVER's *pretentious rap to the aloof* SYLVIE.

EXT. PARTY HOUSE. NIGHT.

MUFFDIVER *is about to put his arm around* SYLVIE *when* CLINT *rises up.* SYLVIE *goes to him.*

SYLVIE: Clint, Clint, for God's sake, get up! Are you hurt? We didn't know where you'd gone.

CLINT: I like fresh air, innit. Sylvie, I tell you, I'm finished with this shit life. This eating shit fuckin' life. I'm really getting a job.

MUFFDIVER: When?

CLINT: Tomorrow. Meet me at ten fifteen outside the diner and

I'll show you how to conduct an interview with an employer.

SYLVIE: Don't be hasty, Clint. Things are not that bad.

MUFFDIVER: And you'll have to find some clothes first, man.

CLINT: It was smoky in there, so I flogged my clothes to a man with no trousers.

SYLVIE: Have a heart, Muffdiver.

MUFFDIVER: He brings these things on himself. Do they happen to me?

CLINT: You've got to know. It's my birthday. Now, at this moment in the whole history of the world I'm twenty years old.

SYLVIE: Say happy birthday, Muffdiver.

(She nudges MUFFDIVER *to congratulate* CLINT. *He murmurs a few words.)*

MUFFDIVER: Happy birthday, Clint.

*(*MUFFDIVER *makes a gesture towards* SYLVIE, *and she responds.* CLINT *sees they're together now. He feels excluded. He moves away, hurt.)*

CLINT: I'm just glad I spent it with friends.

(He walks away naked.)

MUFFDIVER: *(To* SYLVIE*)* They won't let him into the Subterrania like that. They've got a very strict door policy.

EXT. STREET. NIGHT.

A shopping street at three in the morning. CLINT *walks naked along the street.* BIKE, *a young Indian kid (on his bicycle) circles around him, eating a Chinese takeaway.*

CLINT: I'm gonna live an ordinary life from now on. I know it's possible.

(Two transvestites, FAULKNER *and another, pass* CLINT *and glance coolly at him.)*

FAULKNER: Hi Clint.

EXT. TRASH BAGS ON STREET. NIGHT.

Another part of Notting Hill. CLINT *is going through a pile of plastic rubbish bags bursting with puked Chinese dinners. But he's found a pair of trousers, and—hey presto—a filthy pair of work-man's boots. These are big boots.*

CLINT *turns and sees an extraordinary apparition. A large black tramp, in rags, wild hair, covered in filth, carrying an immense number of bags (some of which are tied to his body), moves closer and closer to* CLINT, *his eyes fixed on him.*

EXT. JEWELLER'S DOORWAY. DAWN.

Three or four young people are sleeping, wrapped in cardboard, blankets and papers, one of them cowering behind umbrellas. CLINT *has spent the night here. He wakes up. He flattens his hair with spit. Then he sneaks a pair of socks from the person behind the umbrella.* BUSY BEE *is awake, shaking out a jumper.* CLINT *watches him.*

BUSY BEE *notices* CLINT *and watches him warily.*

CLINT: I need to lend that jumper.

BUSY BEE: What's wrong with *The Times*?

(*And he throws* The Times *at him.*)

CLINT: You don't understand, Busy Bee. I got a job interview this morning. Big interview ting.

BUSY BEE: What drugs you gonna give me, Mr Clint Eastwood?

(CLINT *grabs the jumper and runs away with it.* BUSY BEE *chases him,* CLINT *laughing and running, pulling on the jumper.*)

INT. DINER. DAY.

We're in a busy hamburger diner at lunchtime. This is an upmarket place frequented mainly by well-off media types. The tables are full, the activity frantic. A young well-dressed young woman snaps her fingers and calls sharply to a waiter.

A young black waitress, MELANIE, *hurries over to her. The woman speaks to* MELANIE.

At another table two SMART WOMEN *are working—looking through*

a pile of papers and files, and discussing them. One of them drops
a piece of paper.

CLINT, *who we now see is observing all this, just standing there,*
nips over and picks up the papers. He holds on to the document,
gaining the WOMAN's *attention. His clothes are too big and dirty*
and he sticks out in the restaurant.

There is, behind the bar, throughout this film, an incredibly flashy
barman, mixing complicated cocktails in a particularly theatrical
way. The SMART WOMAN *smiles at* CLINT. *He whispers at her.*

CLINT: Need any washing done?

SMART WOMAN: What?

CLINT: Car cleaned? Washing by hand. Gardening by hand.
    (She glances at her friend and they both laugh.)
    Need any black hash? Proper ting.
    (They're interested, after a nodded consultation, but now
    HEMINGWAY, *the American manager in a suit and open-*
    necked shirt, comes out, looks for CLINT, *and seeing him,*
    takes his arm and examines his face with natural affection
    and interest.
    HEMINGWAY *is very cool, and sees everything about a per-*
    son immediately.)

HEMINGWAY: You Clint, yeah?
    *(*CLINT *struggles to cope, to appear straight and normal.)*

CLINT: Yeah. Mr Clint. How you doing? Do you think you can
    do like what your friend promised me?

HEMINGWAY: What promise did my friend make to you, exactly?

CLINT: Get me a job here. She say the manager a wally but you
    know the manager intimately close, she say.

HEMINGWAY: I am the manager, Mr Hemingway.

CLINT: All this is you? Cool photos. Sturdy chairs. Top people
    sitting.
    (He winks at the two SMART WOMEN.)*

HEMINGWAY: OK, OK. Underneath everything you might be a

good boy. Work experience? *(Pause.)* What work have you done?

(CLINT thinks for a while, looking at the waitress flying spectacularly about, the barman mixing drinks.)

CLINT: But I could pick up one of them plates.

(And he goes to the SMART WOMEN's table and starts removing their plates, piling them up on his arm.)

HEMINGWAY: All right, OK, you gotta start somewhere. It's decent work when you learn how to do it.

(He takes CLINT aside.)

Just don't mess me around, OK? Come back Tuesday morning. I feel someone's gonna walk out on me that day. Clean yourself up. And do one thing. Just one, right?

(We pan down CLINT's legs to his boots. We see, with HEMINGWAY, his disgusting boots.)

You understand, don't you, that I can't have footgear like that in my place. There is disease there. Film people come in here. So, no new shoes—no job. No job—back on the street. Back on the street—(and he shrugs.)*

(CLINT nods, glances at the window to make sure MUFF-DIVER is outside watching all this, which he is. When he sees CLINT looking at him he turns away, not acknowledging him. CLINT puts out his hand.)

CLINT: Put it there, Mr Hemingway. I wish all my problems were of that cool order. See you Tuesday.

(HEMINGWAY watches him go. As he goes, CLINT smiles at MELANIE, who smiles back at him. He stops for a moment to talk to her, but sees HEMINGWAY looking at him. He goes.)

EXT. STREET. DAY.

CLINT *strides cheerfully out of the restaurant.* MUFFDIVER *is waiting outside for him and runs to catch up with* CLINT *as he walks confidently away from the diner.*

CLINT: Start Tuesday. Everything's A-1 fixed up. There's just one
 thing I need—

MUFFDIVER: Clint, Clint—

CLINT: A pair of shoes. Good shoes. Great shoes.

MUFFDIVER: The job's out then. It's a dead-end, it—

CLINT: All these people got shoes. Look. Hush-puppies, DMs,
 sandals, brogues, loafers, high-tops. Give me a single reason
 why I shouldn't get some.

MUFFDIVER: Because you a fool.

EXT. PUB. DAY.

*The two friends are on the street and they know a lot of people.
The black kids outside the pub greet them.* CLINT *calls out to a girl
in the street.*

CLINT: Hey Yvonne, wha' 'appenin'? Wanna buy any E? Any
 bush? What about a pair of shorts?
 *(And he pulls a pair of shorts out of nowhere. She shakes
 her head, laughing.)*

EXT. SHOE SHOP. DAY.

Then CLINT *is standing outside a shoe shop. He's trying on a strong
black boot which he's taken down from a display. He does a little
dance wearing the one new boot. It fits and he's celebrating. The
shop assistant, a young white-faced girl in black, her long hair
standing straight up, watches him suspiciously.* CLINT *delicately puts
the shoe back.* MUFFDIVER *is in the background.*

EXT. STREET. DAY.

Later, CLINT *and* MUFFDIVER *walking quickly, heading towards a
squat that's been recommended to them.*

MUFFDIVER: Fuck me? Fuck me, why, for fuck's sake?

CLINT: Because what's my life doing?

MUFFDIVER: Clint—

CLINT: It's coming together. I can make it without you.

MUFFDIVER: Yeah, sure, where's the shoes?

CLINT: You can't put me down, because the shoe is due.

MUFFDIVER: Yeah, like my arse is due. You got no money for shoes.

CLINT: I'll work for you until Tuesday.

MUFFDIVER: No. You don't even work for me now.

CLINT: What?

MUFFDIVER: You're not professional.

CLINT: And there's my new home. Our office suite. It's ready for business occupation, right? We're swinging over there now, yeah? It's a palace you said—

MUFFDIVER: Yeah, I said.

CLINT: I had to sleep out last night, Muffdiver.

MUFFDIVER: There's Headley.

EXT. STREET. DAY.

They look across the street where HEADLEY *is walking along, a TV interviewer with her, a cameraman and sound guy in front of her. She talks eloquently about the area, indicating people and shops. As the crew moves backwards, out of a doorway comes the black tramp in rags, lumbering into shot.*

They stop shooting. HEADLEY *sees* CLINT *and* MUFFDIVER *and indicates for them to come over.*

CLINT: I don't wanna see her.

MUFFDIVER: She's business, man.

CLINT: She's always wanting.

MUFFDIVER: She's drug business, man.

(MUFFDIVER *leads* CLINT *into the gallery.*)

INT. GALLERY. DAY.

MUFFDIVER: Let's look at some artwork for the new place.

(CLINT *and* MUFFDIVER *have joined a gallery opening. Young smart people holding glasses. Wealthy attractive people.*

MUFFDIVER *looks at all this with much interest and envy.*
CLINT *and* MUFFDIVER *mingle.* CLINT *takes a drink from
a passing tray and hands one to* MUFFDIVER.
MUFFDIVER, *cool and distant, doesn't take much notice of*
CLINT, *who's always going on at him.)*

CLINT. This squat, we're not going to be let down. Is it definite?
I can't be a waiter and sleep in the gutter.

MUFFDIVER: What about Sylvie? Is she definite?

CLINT: What? *(He's amazed.)* With you? With Sylvie? You?

MUFFDIVER: Don't keep saying her name like that. How d'you
know Sylvie anyway?

CLINT: Sylvie. I've known her so long I can remember when she
didn't drink.

MUFFDIVER: How come I haven't seen her before, then?
(A woman is beside MUFFDIVER, *looking for a light.* CLINT
*steals a gold lighter from the table and lights the cigarette.
He puts the lighter in* MUFFDIVER's *pocket.)*

CLINT: Sylvie was in the drug rehab.

MUFFDIVER: But she's back on. *(Pause. He can't tear his eyes away
from the surroundings.)* These people. Tsa-Tsa. They got
clothes, cars, houses—

CLINT: Shoes.

MUFFDIVER: Maisonettes. Everything.
*(*MUFFDIVER *walks decisively out of the place, as if he's
decided what he must do with his life from now on.* CLINT,
*as always the deputy, walks out behind him, stealing a
bottle of champagne and putting it under his jacket as he
goes.)*

EXT. BACK OF SQUAT. DAY.

CLINT *and* MUFFDIVER *stand at the back of a five storey London
House, looking up at the rear of the building.*

MUFFDIVER: Tom-Tom said it's a whole luxury place. The owner's done a runner—he's some big criminal. We've probably got three months of total mod-cons.

CLINT: Great, total con-mods.

MUFFDIVER: Okay, in through the window.

(CLINT *removes his jacket. As he does so, he talks to the world in general.*)

CLINT: The shoe is due. The new shoe is overdue. *(To* MUFFDIVER.*)* Which floor?

MUFFDIVER: Top.

(CLINT *vacillates, moves backwards.* MUFFDIVER *grabs him and shoves him towards the building.*)

I'll keep a sharp look out!

Cut to:

EXT. BACK TO SQUAT. DAY.

Now CLINT *is clambering up the drainpipe, about half-way up the side of the tall building. Very dangerous.* CLINT *hears a popping noise and looks down to see* MUFFDIVER *swigging from a bottle of champagne.* MUFFDIVER *gives him the thumbs-up and indicates for him to continue upwards.*

Cut to:

EXT. BACK OF SQUAT. DAY.

CLINT *has climbed up to the floor below the top one, and is clinging perilously to the drainpipe. From his point of view we get a high view over London. Then he turns back to the face of the building and looks into a large room.*

INT. SUFI CENTRE. DAY.

This is the Sufi Centre. About twenty people holding hands in a circle and moving slowly clockwise. In the middle of the circle are four people whirling and chanting as they move.

The Sufi whirlers are all white, apart from two black girls. Mostly it's young hippyish women in casual clothes.

Outside the circle is DR BUBBA, *an Indian, instructing them what to do and clouting a drum which he holds under his arm. An old man, whirling, wearing a bow-tie, opens his eyes and sees* CLINT *suspended outside the window. He does a double-take. Then he accepts that he is having a vision and he puts his hands together and acknowledges* CLINT *as an angel, since* CLINT *has, from his point of view, developed wings.*

EXT. BACK OF SQUAT. DAY.
CLINT *scrambles upwards.*
Cut to:

EXT. BACK OF SQUAT. DAY.
CLINT *is right at the top of the house, but the drainpipe is starting to come away from the wall.* CLINT *tries frantically to grab at things but there's nothing near by. He holds on to a grating for a few seconds but it pulls out of the wall and crashes to the ground, just missing* MUFFDIVER *who yells angrily up at* CLINT.
CLINT *looks down. He feels certain he's going to die. He is terrified. He knows he can't climb down the broken drainpipe.*
CLINT: Help me Muffdiver, *help me man!*
   (*He manages to look down at* MUFFDIVER *standing there.*
   MUFFDIVER *genuinely distressed and confused.*)
MUFFDIVER: What can I do?
CLINT: Call the police!
   (CLINT *watches* MUFFDIVER *who takes a few paces away, but returns and indicates complete helplessness.*)
Cut to:

EXT. BACK OF SQUAT. DAY.
CLINT *has grabbed another pipe above the window frame. He pulls himself up and swings around the side of the building, where there's a balcony. He clambers on to the balcony. The glass doors to the*

flat are locked. He smashes one of the windows with a brick, cutting himself. But he lands on the leopard-skin carpet, covered in blood.

INT. LIVING ROOM OF SQUAT. DAY.

CLINT, *cut and bleeding, walks around the squat, wiping the blood off himself with a white towel.*

The squat has clearly been burgled a few times: the TV and stereo ripped out, and records and clothes and rubbish strewn about the place.

CLINT *walks from room to room, taking in the thick carpets, glass tables (cracked or smashed), and broken pin-ball machine. The living room is a big space. There is a bar but all the bottles are empty or smashed.*

CLINT, *as he walks about, is more and more pleased with what he sees, grunting and whistling his approval.*

INT. SQUAT. BEDROOM. DAY.

CLINT *in the master bedroom, lying on the bed.*

He discovers switches beside the bed which operate the curtains; these move furiously back and forth. He enjoys this for a while. Then he fiddles with the lights in the room, which go off and on, dimming and brightening. He's really like a child now, unable to believe his good fortune.

Finally he hits another button and a huge TV cabinet opens. A shelf comes out, on which there's a plate of rotting food.

Cut to:

INT. CLINT'S BEDROOM. DAY.

Now CLINT *is trying to open the main wardrobe in the room, but it is locked. He kicks it open: it gives.*

He touches the console beside the bed to stop the lights going on and off. The room is semi-dark, the light red. He opens the wardrobe cautiously. As it opens the wardrobe lights up, to reveal an illuminated row of vulgar shoes and boots belonging to a spiv: leopard-

skin and crocodile shoes, *flashy boots with spurs, cowboy boots, etc.*

When he's taken all this in, CLINT *removes his own boots and selects a pair of shoes to wear, like someone choosing a chocolate from a full box. He tries them but it's a struggle; they're too small, they'll never fit. He tries walking in them but he falls over, laughing. None of them fit.*

INT./ EXT. BACK OF SQUAT. DAY.

CLINT *shouts out of the window to* MUFFDIVER *waiting impatiently below.*

CLINT: Yo!

MUFFDIVER: What's it like?

CLINT: Round up the posse!

    (MUFFDIVER *is ecstatic. Under his breath, to himself, as a celebration, he mutters.*)

EXT. FRONT OF SQUAT. BUILDING. DAY.

MUFFDIVER: Round up the fucking posse! Tsa-Tsa!

EXT. STREET. DAY.

MUFFDIVER *hurries through the streets, pleased. As he goes, he sees* BIKE. *Indicates for* BIKE *to go over to him.* BIKE *cycles along beside him.*

MUFFDIVER: Found us a place to live.

    (BIKE *hits the horn on his bike in acknowledgement.*)

EXT. DINER/STREET. DAY.

Outside the diner, SYLVIE *and a middle-aged man, not extravagantly dressed or posh, have just left the place.* SYLVIE *looks quite smart. She smiles and talks animatedly.* MUFFDIVER *stops, then follows them. The man waves at a cab. They both get in.* MUFFDIVER *suddenly decides to start chasing the cab. It stops at traffic lights.* MUFFDIVER *is looking in the window: the guy has his hand up* SYLVIE's *skirt. The cab moves away.*

SYLVIE *pulls down the window.* MUFFDIVER *runs beside the cab.*

MUFFDIVER: *(Through window)* We've got a place. 14 Whitehall
  Gardens. Top flat. OK.
  (He smiles at the guy.
  Stay with SYLVIE *in the cab a few seconds. The guy looks*
  at her. She puts her head back and laughs.)

EXT. DOORWAY/SCAFFOLDING. DAY.

BURNS *standing in a doorway, his possessions around him. He's*
always cheerful, despite everything. MUFFDIVER *goes to him.* BURNS
gives him money. MUFFDIVER *is surprised by the amount.*

MUFFDIVER: How you doing Burns—clubs busy?

BURNS: Long weekend, big demand in the clubs up West. I could
  easily shift a couple of hundred through the bouncers—I
  know them all, I got most of them their jobs. Have you got
  it?

MUFFDIVER: More? Fuck it. I'm really short of supplies right now.

BURNS: By the way, I've had the word. Mr G's ready to see you.

MUFFDIVER: Yeah, I heard. We need him, now.

BURNS: Where shall I tell him to come?

MUFFDIVER: I've found the premises. I've got us a luxury business
  base.

BURNS: For all of us?

MUFFDIVER: Yeah, you'll have your own room. Burns, your posse
  needs you. *(Pause.)* How's your stomach?

BURNS: Making noises.

INT. LIVING ROOM OF SQUAT. DAY.

Later that day. MUFFDIVER *and* CLINT *have taken possession of the*
squat and moved their gear in. CLINT *is wrapped in the leopard-*
skin carpets and wearing a cowboy hat.

MUFFDIVER *is pacing, really wound up.*

CLINT: I did good, right, in getting this place? Muff?

MUFFDIVER: Yeah. Didn't I say I'd take care of you? Who needs shoes with these carpets? I have to stop myself—

CLINT: What?

MUFFDIVER: Feeling too happy. In case it don't last. We can really do something here.

CLINT: You mean parties?

MUFFDIVER: I mean as a business base. And I could kiss her here. This is just the venue . . . for a first kiss.

CLINT: Sylvie won't even turn up.

MUFFDIVER: She'll come. (*Pause.*) She's desperate.

(*Now we see the posse walk in through the door one by one, carrying their ragged possessions.* BIKE *comes in apprehensively, with nothing but his bicycle.* BURNS *is a Scotsman, unemployed, fiftyish.* TOM-TOM, *a white Rasta, late thirties, a junkie.*)

BURNS: (*To* CLINT) Home!

CLINT: Yeah!

Cut to:

INT. LIVING ROOM OF SQUAT. DAY.

They're unpacking their things and admiring the squat. They choose rooms for themselves and lay out their sleeping bags. BURNS *is changing the locks on the door and he chats away to* TOM-TOM *who's laying out his stuff in a corner of the room.*

Then SYLVIE *walks in through the door. She is carrying a trumpet and some other belongings over her shoulder.*

MUFFDIVER: You need a room here Sylvie. Only the best for you.

BURNS: Yeah, only the best.

(SYLVIE *looks around.*)

MUFFDIVER: We're gonna fix it up and everything, aren't we Burns? Furniture. Hot water.

TOM-TOM: Cold water, even.

SYLVIE: Where's little Clint? Has he got his clothes on?

MUFFDIVER: How about a spliff? Bike, roll Sylvie a spliff.

(BIKE *scuttles off across the squat.*)

TOM-TOM: Give us a toot.

(*She plays a long sad note on the trumpet.* BURNS *looks at the others approvingly.* MUFFDIVER *watches her, utterly entranced.*

He's never been in love like this before.

He thinks for a moment, then he rushes into Clint's room.)

INT. CLINT'S ROOM. DAY.

CLINT, *absorbed in his own world, isn't aware that* SYLVIE's *arrived. He's sitting on the bed with two pairs of boots from the wardrobe. He's trying, with a knife, to cut around the toe so they fit.*

MUFFDIVER *shoves him off the bed and then prods the mattress energetically, testing it. He also whacks the buttons on the console beside the bed. The 'effects' go crazy.*

MUFFDIVER: This is good. Total theatre, man.

CLINT: Look at these shoes. I'm on my way. Walking.

(MUFFDIVER *makes a face.*)

They're for work, not for best.

MUFFDIVER: What work? You dealing for someone else?

CLINT: In the diner. They're pretty. Except they don't fit.

(MUFFDIVER *looks at the room in a businesslike manner. But still finds it difficult to broach the subject on his mind.*)

MUFFDIVER: So what exactly is happening here?

CLINT: Oh fucking no. This is exclusively my room.

MUFFDIVER: Yeah, granted. But there's one drawback.

CLINT: There's no drawback.

MUFFDIVER: Listen to me.

CLINT: I climbed the drainpipe!

MUFFDIVER: It's a double room. That interests me.

CLINT: Tsa-Tsa. But does it interest the other person?

MUFFDIVER: Yeah. It does. It interests them.

CLINT: My arse it interests. What other person is it?

(We see, but they do not, SYLVIE *in the room.)*

There's no other person. I'm the only other person you got.

MUFFDIVER: I love her. I'm addicted to her.

(They turn and SYLVIE *is standing in the doorway.* MUFF-DIVER *is embarrassed, but continues, shyly, gently.)*

How would you like this room?

(He pummels the bed histrionically while activating the lights. The TV shoots out of the wall, with the old dinner still intact on the panel.)

SYLVIE: My god. Shoe heaven.

CLINT: Yeah, they're only for work, not for best.

SYLVIE: Will that man really give you a job?

CLINT: Yeah—

*(*MUFFDIVER *activates the curtains to distract her.)*

SYLVIE: *(To* CLINT*)* Clint's settled in here—aren't you, little mouse?

CLINT: *(Sarcastic)* But wouldn't this suit you? Nice duvet, nice mattress, nice Muffdiver on top of you—

*(*SYLVIE *laughs.* MUFFDIVER *is furious, glares at* CLINT *and throws a shoe at him.* SYLVIE *indicates for* MUFFDIVER *to go to her. When he does, she puts her arms around him and kisses him. She indicates to* CLINT *to go to her. She does the same to him. Then she gently pushes the two of them together, encouraging them to hold each other.)*

INT. LIVING ROOM OF SQUAT. DAY.

Later that day. BURNS *and* CLINT *together.* CLINT *is getting the practical* BURNS *to cut open the toes of an especially vulgar pair of red cowboy boots covered in metal studs—using a big knife.*
SYLVIE *over the other side of the room practices the trumpet.*
BIKE *is fixing his bicycle.*
TOM-TOM *is asleep on the floor, on his back, music-box beside him.*

The door to another room is open and MUFFDIVER *is hurrying about with his possessions, settling in.*

BURNS: *(Working and eating)* You sure this is what you want, Clint boy?

CLINT: Burns, the point is moot. I'm going to wear the boot. *(Pause.)* Ol' Muffdiver is starting to get pretty heavy with people. He wasn't always like that, was he? He was sweet.

BURNS: You knew each other at school, right?

INT. MUFFDIVER'S ROOM. DAY.

This room, which he's moving into, is small and virtually empty, except for several tailor's dummies on stands. Slightly eerie.

MUFFDIVER *has put out two sleeping bags, side by side. Now he's adjusting the pillows, etc. He's unpacked his things neatly.*

INT. LIVING ROOM OF SQUAT. DAY.

CLINT: *(To* BURNS*)* There was this day, Burns, man. Me an' Muffdiver stole some LSD from someone at school. And there was another boy who wanted acid badly. So Muff got this stuff and went to him and sold it for a lot of money. I remember, we were in the school cloakroom and he had this money in his hand and his whole face brightened up like I'd never seen it before. He thought he could do anything. I reckon he wanted his whole life to be like that moment.

BURNS: Listen, Clint, these boots . . . Well try 'em on.

(CLINT *puts on the boots, with his bare toes sticking out through the end.*)

CLINT: Great. Thanks Burns, I really appreciate it.

BURNS: Why don't you just buy a cheap pair? Are you sure they're right for restaurant work?

CLINT: Clint is skint.

BURNS: It might rain.

(CLINT *pulls the boots off. There are two plastic bags beside* BURNS, *in which he keeps sandwiches and food.* CLINT

*empties the bags neatly, shakes out the crumbs and puts
the bags over his feet. He puts on the boots again, and
stands there clicking his heels together.)*

CLINT: Ole! Ready for the street.

BURNS: What you gonna sell on the street? Has he given you
something?

CLINT: No. I gotta ask him now. Then I'm out sellin' for the last
time. Then I'll buy a new pair. The new shoes are due, the
shoes—

(They watch as MUFFDIVER *calls* SYLVIE.)

MUFFDIVER: Sylvie, Sylvie.

INT. MUFFDIVER'S BEDROOM. DAY.

SYLVIE *and* MUFFDIVER. *He is apprehensive . . . but determined.
His clothes on one dummy, hers on another.*

SYLVIE: All your little things . . . laid out neat and tidy. *(Pause.)*
And my things too.

*(*MUFFDIVER *opens his hand to show her a bag of smack.)*

SYLVIE: Do you take smack?

MUFFDIVER: *(Slightly amused)* But Clint does, off and on. *(Pre-
tentious.)* I prefer drugs of illusion. *(Pause.)* Kiss.
(He goes to kiss her. She retreats.)
Don't. Just try me out.

INT. LIVING ROOM. DAY.

Later, in the living room, the whole posse there. CLINT *and* MUFF-
DIVER *having a serious and loud argument.*

MUFFDIVER: No, man, that's not possible—

CLINT: Please, Muffdiver, give me thirty.

MUFFDIVER: Fucking thirty! *(To the others)* Hey, Tom-Tom, Bike,
what's he saying to me? He's saying give him thirty!

CLINT: *(Appealing to the others)* Yeah, that's all. Sylvie.

BURNS: What's the lad want?

TOM-TOM: Thirty Es and As to sell tonight. No chance.

MUFFDIVER: *(To* CLINT*)* Come on, man, you jerk off now. I can't take you seriously as a salesman.

CLINT: Thirty Ecstasy, thirty acid, and some ME-35. Sale or return. I'm shit-hot reliable. An A-1 salesman, like everyone here. You know what it's for. The footwear is there, in the shop waiting for me.

MUFFDIVER: Yeah, Mr Poet, last time I leaned forward with you, you took half the stuff yourself and gave away the rest.

*(*MUFFDIVER *starts to look down at* CLINT*'s feet, and pulls up his trouser bottoms to reveal the red cowboy boots with the toes in plastic bags sticking out at the end. He invites everyone to look.)*

Hey, hey . . .

(The others move in closer. SYLVIE *puts her hand in her mouth to stop herself laughing.* BURNS *is annoyed by their mirth. But* CLINT *doesn't lose his dignity.)*

CLINT: Yeah, a good price for me, a good price for you, that's how I get the new shoe.

SYLVIE: *(Appealing)* Muffdiver—

CLINT: You haven't had the childhood I been through. Messages from there are still reaching me. Sexually abused. My father shooting me up with H when I was thirteen—

MUFFDIVER: Exactly my point.

CLINT: What?

MUFFDIVER: You not used to paying for it.

CLINT: Then he got murdered—

BURNS: You gonna get murdered, son. People looking for you with iron bars.

CLINT: Children's homes, probation officers, trials, beatings, shit, shit.

MUFFDIVER: Yeah, Yeah.

CLINT: All I want is to get my life started!

*(*BIKE, TOM-TOM *and* MUFFDIVER *laugh.)*

INT. STAIRS/HALLWAY/BOOT ROOM/SUFI CENTRE. DAY.

CLINT *and* MUFFDIVER *walk slowly downstairs,* MUFFDIVER *with his arm around him.* CLINT *is looking very down.*

MUFFDIVER: I lose my temper, man. You know me. I'm nervous about Sylvie. I want her so much. When I look at her I can't understand why she isn't mine. *(Pause.)* Here's the stuff you wanted to sell.

(And he gives him the Es and As.)

CLINT: I knew you'd come through.

(Now they stop at the open door of the Sufi Centre. Curious, they wander in.)

Look, look.

(A group of people are sitting cross-legged on the floor. A guided meditation is taking place. DR BUBBA *leads them through it.)*

DR BUBBA: *(To group)* Now you're relaxed, let's concentrate on breathing. Count your breaths in and out. One, two, three. Slowly, slowly, from the stomach. You are not, I say not, I repeat not, blowing up a balloon. This is to slow us down. This enables us to see our lives clearly for a few minutes.

(When CLINT *turns to look at* MUFFDIVER *he sees him leaving.* CLINT *closes his eyes, takes a breath, smiles to himself relaxedly and puts the drugs in his pocket. When he does take a squint he sees a row of shoes. This is deeply pleasing to him.*

He chooses an excellent pair of shoes and, removing the cowboy boots, tries them on. They fit. Bliss.

He is creeping out of the door in his new shoes, blowing kisses at them, when DR BUBBA *is behind him.)*

DR BUBBA: You are in love with those shoes?

*(*CLINT *continues walking away.)*

Do they fit?

*(*CLINT *finally stops and turns to face* DR BUBBA.*)*

I am your neighbour, Dr Bubba. This morning, why didn't
you come in through the front door? *(Pause.)* Let's see. Are
they not a little floppy, my boy? You need a size less, I
imagine. Lift up. Lift up, if you please.
(DR BUBBA removes CLINT's new trainers from his feet.)
Now, let's look here. *(At the row of shoes.)* Mr Runcipher—
asleep over there—
*(We see Mr Runcipher swaying and sleeping instead of
meditating.)*
—has a smaller foot and kinder nature. You poor boy.
*(But CLINT hurriedly puts the cowboy boots back on, minus
plastic bags.)*
CLINT: No, no, it's OK, thanks a lot, don't worry—
(A shot of DR BUBBA's sandal next to CLINT's foot.)
DR BUBBA: But look, my foot and yours are entirely equal. Clearly
you favour the exposed toe. Latest fashion? May I give you
my sandal?
CLINT: Do you have strange powers, Dr Bubba?
DR BUBBA: If I had strange powers, what would you want me to
do for you?

EXT. STREET. DAY.
CLINT *in the street, swallowing pills. He stands and watches people
as they walk by, looking for potential customers, nodding and hiss-
ing at potential buyers. He's determined and singleminded.*
We see BIKE *down the street from him, looking out checking the
area, occasionally signalling to* CLINT.
Cut to:

EXT. STREET. DAY.
CLINT *in a doorway, taking money from a middle-class white girl
and giving her the stuff.*
BIKE *is in the background.*

INT. LIFT. DAY.

CLINT *in the lift of a filthy West London Tower block. Two dirty fifteen-year-olds, one white, one black, are in the lift with him. The* WHITE KID *has a cut-up face: chains of stitches.*

WHITE KID: Show us the gear, Mr Eastwood.

CLINT: *(Distracted)* Show me the money.

(The black kid pulls out a knife. CLINT, *now quite stoned, looks at them and laughs. They look down at his feet and start to laugh.)*

EXT. STREET NR HI-TECH BAR. DAY.

A couple of TOURISTS, *a German man and woman, with rucksacks, are wandering distractedly in the street. The street* DEALERS, *one by one, spot them, and practically sprint towards them.*

DEALER ONE: Germans . . .

DEALER TWO: Tourists . . .

DEALER THREE: Free money.

*(*CLINT *shoves them aside.)*

CLINT: They're my beauties.

Cut to:

EXT. STREET NR HI-TECH BAR. DAY.

CLINT *with the* TOURISTS. *They're fascinated by his spiel . . . and his hands all over them, cajoling, wheedling, charming.*

CLINT: *(Picking up a rucksack)* And if you're looking for a cheap hotel . . . and you say you are. How much are you paying? *(Amazed.)* You're being destroyed. Your little Aryan faces are being ripped off. Let me help you. We're all young people.

TOURIST WOMAN: Are you a hotelier?

CLINT: Yes, yes I am. Eastwood House, a hostel for young people in need. This place will cool you.

TOURIST MAN: But there is heating, Mr Eastwood?

CLINT: Underfloor heating, yeah.

EXT. STREET NR DINER. DAY.

CLINT *with a* BUYER, *a young suited man on the street, near the diner. They talk urgently and quickly. This is* CLINT *in his selling routine. He is professional and convincing, good at this, having done it many times before. He spots the* BUYER *on the street, eye contact: then he goes to him, leading him into a doorway or sidestreet. He really knows how to hustle without frightening the guy.*

CLINT: Yeah, what d'you want? Hash? No. E? Tabs? E, yeah? I've got some good E, burgers not capsules. The purest form. This stuff will chill you man. Just tip it on your tongue. Taste the fizz. Yeah?

BUYER: How much?

CLINT: Twenty. These are going quickly. How many? Ten? I can do a reduced price for ten. Yeah, going for that?

BUYER: Three.

CLINT: Yeah, little rave? You'll buzz on these. They're the best on the street. Just gimme the money, that's sixty, and you hang right there.

BUYER: Where you going?

CLINT: Five minutes. Two and a half. I can't carry the stuff round with me at great personal risk. Would you?

(The BUYER *is reluctant.* CLINT *hardens.)*

CLINT: You've seen me about. I'm on this corner every night. If you're not satisfied I'll refund your money.

(The BUYER *gives him the money.* CLINT *backs away, and then splits quickly.)*

EXT. STREET OUTSIDE DINER. DAY.

Minutes later. CLINT *has walked round to the diner. He watches the waiters keenly. He's also looking for* HEMINGWAY.

Finally he spots him, talking to the barman who's making a line of gloriously coloured cocktails. CLINT *raises his arm in extravagant greeting.* HEMINGWAY *waves at him and nods gravely.* CLINT *points down at his feet, indicating that the present shoes are shit but that the future is promising.*

He looks at MELANIE *and she smiles at him.*

Outside diner a man walks up by CLINT's *side. It's the* BUYER. *His eyes travel to the* BUYER's *angry face.* CLINT *is very agitated.*

BUYER: *(Sneering)* Where's my cool E—to chill me, chill me?
  (CLINT *gives it to him.*)

EXT./INT. HI-TECH BAR. DAY.

CLINT *enters bar counting his money in the revolving doorway of a seedy hi-tech bar in the area. A notice saying:* NO DRUGS IN THIS ESTABLISHMENT. *Open dealing going on. A guy under the notice, carving up a lump of hash on the table.*

An old black man stands and sings drunkenly, accompanied by someone in the corner on keyboard.

Big dealers in dark glasses sit around with their women.

A cluster of rent boys, some in make-up, twittering around. A couple of women prostitutes, junkies with them. A handful of transvestites, all arguing and chattering.

CLINT *speaks to several people as he walks through to the bar.*

CLINT: Wanting? Wanting? Wanting?

RENT BOY: Not from you, dear.

Cut to:

INT. HI-TECH BAR. DAY.

CLINT *is clutching drinks, crisps and cigarettes which he puts down.*

TOM-TOM, SYLVIE *and* FAULKNER *are sitting at the table.*

TOM-TOM: *(Pleased with the drinks)* Hey, this is good.

CLINT: Yeah, why not?

SYLVIE: *(Kissing him)* Generous.

CLINT: What's that on your cheek? *(He looks at her.)* It's OK, I
  thought you were developing a second nose. Hi Faulkner.
  (FAULKNER *insists on kissing him.*)

(To them all) I tell you, I had a good day at the office, I mean it. I can be a sweet dealer when I put my mind to it.

SYLVIE: We did good too, shopping for the squat.

TOM-TOM: And not an item paid for.

(TOM-TOM has a new suitcase beside him which he opens. The four of them pull out telephones, teapots, ornaments, cutlery, lamps, etc. As they look through it SYLVIE sees CLINT scratching his face and pulls his hand down.)

FAULKNER: Oh yuk, yuk.

CLINT: I'm on fire. I wanna tear my arms off and smash them on the table.

SYLVIE: How come?

CLINT: I'm kicking.

SYLVIE: Can't they take you into the rehab?

CLINT: They already threw me out.

SYLVIE: For what?

CLINT: Drug-taking.

(They laugh. SYLVIE pulls a sporty cap with ear-flaps and an adjustable peak out of the suitcase and gives it to CLINT.)

SYLVIE: Here.

FAULKNER: Oh yeah.

CLINT: Is this really for me then?

(She and FAULKNER help him put it on—a big procedure, accompanied by posing and clapping and laughter.
From across the bar CLINT is watched by a middle-aged black guy.)

SYLVIE: Thought it would suit you.

FAULKNER: Not quite. Put yourself in my hands.

(FAULKNER readjusts the cap.)

Better.

SYLVIE: Isn't he a sweetie?

TOM-TOM: Not bad for a derelict, for a disaster.

(Among friends, CLINT sits back like a rent boy and puts

his feet on the table, forgetting the state of his boots, which people notice. Goes into a stoned reverie.)

FAULKNER: Clint's so good-looking, apart from the feet and the skin disease. Oh find me a man, someone. Had one today?

CLINT: We're looking after her now.

FAULKNER: Christ. The thing is, Sylvie, people don't realize what hard work it is sucking cock for a living. What a skill and trade it is, like bricklaying. The public think, oh five minutes jaw work and there you are, tax-free millions. But it's dirty, risky and exhausting, your little head bobbing up and down for hours on end. I'm getting a proper job.

CLINT: I don't wanna hear about it. I'm getting a proper job.

FAULKNER: *(Laughs)* It's only prostitution by other means.

CLINT: *(Quietly, to* SYLVIE*)* Can I see you?

SYLVIE: You're seeing me now.

CLINT: We should do something cultural together. *(Pause.)* You always liked me.

SYLVIE: I do, I do.

CLINT: You won't stay with Muffdiver. He doesn't know that yet. You've made him fall in love with you. It's not a feeling he's accustomed to. Then you'll let him down.

(She looks at him, surprised by his cruelty.)

SYLVIE: Stop it.

CLINT: What d'you want, Sylvie?

SYLVIE: What you got? *(Pause.)* You've got to stick with him. He's the only one who knows what's going on.

(The black guy taps CLINT *on the shoulder.* CLINT *turns. The guy indicates another black guy, who gets up and takes* CLINT *out into the street.* CLINT *turns to look at* SYLVIE *as he goes.* SYLVIE *and* TOM-TOM *start to pack up their things.)*

Mr G. Tonight?

TOM-TOM: *(To* SYLVIE*)* Yeah, we better get on with it. You didn't tell Clint?

(She shakes her head.)

You tell that boy something and it goes no further than Europe.

EXT. STREET/ELECTRIC CINEMA. DUSK.

A BLACK GIRL, *early twenties, a nanny, takes* CLINT *by the arm and leads him through the streets, throwing away his new cap in disgust.*

Past the Electric Cinema, a few people outside. The GIRL *walks briskly, and* CLINT *tries to keep up with her.*

CLINT: Headley want to see me? She in a good mood? What's on at the pictures?

GIRL: *La Dolce Vita.*

CLINT: What's that?

(The GIRL *gives him a contemptuous look.)*

INT. HEADLEY'S FLAT. EVENING.

Weird music. The atmosphere a mixture of hi-tech late 1980s and hippy eclectic. Indian and African things. Much third-worldism. We are in the living room. Three LITERARY TYPES *talking, a man and two young women, laughing, drinking, all expensively dressed. Various snacks on the table. Beer, wine, champagne.*

CLINT *breaks away from the* GIRL *and takes some salmon from the table.*

LITERARY MAN: And are you a writer too?

CLINT: Yeah. I'm putting down my story. It's pretty sickening, you know. *(To* GIRL.*)* Tell Headley I'll wait here for her. *(To* LITERARY MAN.*)* Wanna deal with something real for a change?

GIRL: You come on.

(And she pulls CLINT *away.)*

INT. HEADLEY'S STUDY. EVENING.

HEADLEY *is a tall, strong, imposing professor and writer. She is not the type to listen much to others. Her mood can swing from the hard to the sentimental pretty quickly.*

Anyhow, for the time being she ignores CLINT, *who tiptoes around, nervous of her and not wanting to be there at all.*

HEADLEY *is, at the moment, with a woman and baby.* HEADLEY *is pulling clothes out of a cupboard for both child and mother.* HEADLEY *talks continuously.*

HEADLEY: Why do I have to help them? Doesn't the fucking state do anything? I'm not a fucking doctor am I?

(She stares straight at CLINT, *who recoils and turns away moodily.)*

I'm just strong and rich, that's all. So these people come to me every day because they know I'm too guilty and weak to refuse them.

(She talks to the baby in good Spanish, then gives the woman a gorgeous string of beads, pressing them on the unresisting woman.)

They're Indian, from Mexico. Sell them if you like.

(The woman goes, backwards. HEADLEY *looks at her with contempt, then sits with her head in her hands.)*

CLINT: *(After a pause.)* Headley, I'm here.

HEADLEY: I know, dear, I can hear you scratching.

(Put out, CLINT *goes to the birdcage and prods the bird.)*

CLINT: How are you, parrot-face? Want some bush to get outta your face?

(He fishes some bush out of his bag and gives it to the bird.)

HEADLEY: It's a toucan. Cyrano. I require that bush, Clint. I intend to get very high.

CLINT: *(Approaching her)* Headley, man, this stuff is fucking steep.

HEADLEY: *(Noticing his boots)* Don't stamp dog-shit into my Persian rug.

CLINT: You haven't got a better pair of shoes by any chance? You know, lying around. They're dear.

HEADLEY: Buy some. You street dealers earn more than I do. Or does that other boy, the rough one, Bill Sykes, control you? *(She looks at him. He's not answering these kind of questions. He goes round the rug and puts the bush on the table. She makes a note on a piece of paper.)*

CLINT: What you writing? About F. Scott Fitzgerald's books?

HEADLEY: Something about the representation of black women in film. Women noir?

CLINT: Yeah? Oh Headley, you really know how to enjoy yourself.
(HEADLEY slaps her knee as if summoning a dog or a baby. CLINT starts to get even more nervous.)
No, Headley, I better get going, you know. I've gotta get some shoes lined up for my job.

HEADLEY: You want to eat, don't you? Here.
(And she pulls him towards her.)

Cut to:

INT. HEADLEY'S STUDY. EVENING.
CLINT *is sitting on* HEADLEY's *knee. She touches his face, hair, hands, partly out of affection, partly out of disinterested love, and partly it is medical examination. Then she cuddles him, saying:*
HEADLEY: 'Thus is his cheek the map of days outworn
When Beauty lived and died as flowers do now.'
(CLINT stares into the distance.)

INT. HEADLEY'S LIVING ROOM. NIGHT.
A little later. The living room of Headley's flat. It is darker now. The three LITERARY TYPES *are present, eating, drinking and laughing, prior to going out for the evening.*

CLINT *is sitting across the room with a plate of food on his knee, eating eagerly.*
One of the LITERARY TYPES *has removed her high heels and waves them at* CLINT *as he eats. He glances up at her and then continues to eat, ignoring this shit.*
LITERARY WOMAN: Let him wear my shoes, they'll suit him.
  (HEADLEY *walks up and down, mainly addressing* CLINT.)
LITERARY MAN: Don't go on, Headley.
HEADLEY: There are crimes that people commit against others. Of course. But there are, to me, more intriguing crimes, the ones that people commit against themselves. These puzzle me, especially as I get older and wish to live to a hundred and fifty. What do I love? *(She indicates the room.)* My garden.
  (The LITERARY MAN *has filled the* LITERARY WOMAN'*s shoe with champagne and now drinks from it.*
  HEADLEY *hits a button on the CD. We hear Allegri's Miserere Mei.)*
  Jugged hare. The Beatles. But what could you say, Clint? What do you love? Drugs.
  (And she laughs scornfully. CLINT *is, by now, bent over, dinner on his lap, half off the chair. He looks up at her. She drags thoughtfully on her joint.)*
  No one need make you bleed. You'll do it to yourself.
  *(*CLINT *is angry with her. But he can't speak. He puts his food down, and falls over on to his knees, crawls a bit, and finally walks and runs out.)*

EXT. STREET NR DINER. NIGHT.
The music continues. CLINT *has left* HEADLEY'*s place. Now he relaxes and perks up as he walks past the diner. Two waitresses are outside, including* MELANIE. *He's about to strike up conversation with her when he spots* HEMINGWAY.
Cut to:

EXT. DINER. NIGHT.

MELANIE *watches* CLINT *go. He steps into a puddle, soaking the exposed toe.*

Cut to:

EXT. STREET NR OFF-LICENCE. NIGHT.

Further up the street CLINT *sees* BURNS *coming out of an off-licence carrying bottles of beer.*

He walks on. Further up he sees BIKE *on his bicycle, riding without hands, carrying booze and food. He cycles past* CLINT, *not noticing him. Maybe this is a hallucination and* CLINT *accepts it equably.*

INT. SQUAT. NIGHT.

CLINT *enters the flat and sees there's no one in. He wanders around until he sees the* TOURISTS *sitting leaning against their rucksacks, with a picnic spread out in front of them.*

CLINT: So you got in all right?

TOURIST WOMAN: Which is our room?

CLINT: Err . . . this way.

> (CLINT *leads them upstairs into Burns's room, which is, naturally, full of his stuff. There are photographs of his children, his handyman's gear, clothes, etc.)*

> The rent, s'vous plait.

TOURIST WOMAN: Now, Mr Eastwood?

CLINT: Yeah, on the button and no travellers' cheques accepted.

TOURIST MAN: But this is someone else's room.

CLINT: This? *(He shoves some of Burns's gear aside.)* Burns is moving out tonight. Make yourself comfortable. I'm just going to have a sleep, then I'm going out to buy some shoes, for work, not for best.

(The TOURIST MAN *counts out the money.)*

INT. SQUAT. MUFFDIVER'S ROOM. NIGHT.

CLINT *goes into Muffdiver's room—sees Muffdiver's and Sylvie's stuff side by side, which surprises and hurts him. He goes through Muffdiver's things, finding nothing of interest but a knife.*

He gropes through Sylvie's things and finds three pairs of old ballet shoes that would have fitted a child, a kid and a teenager. He puts them back.

Also amongst her things he finds a number of literary paperbacks: Jean Rhys, Willa Cather, Jane Bowles, Jayne Anne Phillips. Plus several full notebooks of her own writing. He flicks through the pages, which are densely written.

At the door, on his way out, he has a brainwave. He goes to the dummies and puts his hand up inside one of them. He takes most of Muffdiver's stash of money, leaving a few quid behind, out of generosity. He is very pleased with this.

EXT. ROOF OF SQUAT. NIGHT.

CLINT *puts most of the money under a brick on the roof, taking a little for himself.*

INT. CLINT'S BEDROOM. NIGHT.

A couple of hours later. CLINT *has crashed out on his bed, eyes open, staring at the ceiling. The curtains move slowly back and forth, billowing in the wind. He hears noises from outside: chanting from the Sufi Centre below mixed with noises from the living room in a hallucinogenic blend. He gets up.*

INT. LIVING ROOM OF SQUAT. NIGHT.

CLINT *opens the door on to an odd scene. A hallucination, the only time in this film. And only for a few seconds.*

He sees SYLVIE *wearing a ballerina's tutu and dancing.* BURNS *is dressed as Father Christmas.* BIKE, *in a yellow jersey and cycling shorts, is suspended from the ceiling on his bicycle with a tray of cocaine across the handlebars.*

TOM-TOM *is playing the guitar dressed as Keith Richards.*

There is music. The entire scene seems to be taking place in a snowstorm.

CLINT *blinks several times and the scene returns to normal. Even then it is a pretty odd scene.*

BIKE, BURNS *and* TOM-TOM *are frantically fixing the place up.*

BURNS *is installing the two table lamps which* SYLVIE *and* TOM-TOM *stole that afternoon. (Obviously, in the room, until now, there is only an overhead light or some other arrangement.)*

SYLVIE *is preparing drinks for later.*

TOM-TOM *is arranging crisps.*

BIKE *is washing up.*

SYLVIE: Were you there all the time?

   (TOM-TOM *hands him a dishcloth and a pile of plates.*)

TOM-TOM: Get wiping, man.

CLINT: Wipe your own arse.

SYLVIE: Mr G's coming to see Muffdiver.

CLINT: What for?

TOM-TOM: (*Indicating plates*) I thought you were interested in restaurant work.

   (CLINT *gives him a dirty look.* TOM-TOM *regards him resentfully.*)

SYLVIE: (*Going to the trouble to explain*) Mr G's the top man, you know that. Sign on with him and you don't have any drug-flow problems.

   (CLINT *wipes the plates, making sure* TOM-TOM *sees him.*)

SYLVIE: (*To* CLINT) Muff's gonna do a big buy. Keep us all going for weeks.

CLINT: Which we gotta sell on the street.

SYLVIE: Yeah, it's work for all of us.

(Making sure TOM-TOM *is watching,* CLINT *throws one of the plates in the air and catches it on the end of his finger and twirls it around dramatically and impressively, nodding at* TOM-TOM.

Now MUFFDIVER *hurries into the room in businesslike mood. He takes everything in quickly. Everyone working away satisfactorily, except* CLINT, *with a plate whirling on his finger.)*

MUFFDIVER: Great. Good, everyone. *(Snaps finger at* CLINT.*)* You. *(To her)* Sylvie. Boardroom.

(He jabs at BIKE. BIKE *looks at him eagerly, ready to respond.* MUFFDIVER *nods.* BIKE *obviously knows what to do.)*

INT. LANDING. NIGHT. BIKE *gets a pot of tea for three set out on a tray from dumb waiter and goes into Clint's room.*

INT. CLINT'S ROOM. NIGHT.

MUFFDIVER, SYLVIE *and* CLINT *in the room.* CLINT *moves in and out of consciousness, resentful, confused.* MUFFDIVER *excited. He chops out a line of coke for himself.*

MUFFDIVER: This is an executive meeting—of the top executives of Muffdiver, Sylvie and Clint Eastwood Limited, PLC.

SYLVIE: What's PLC?

MUFFDIVER: Posse Limited Company.

(BIKE, like a servant, is handing out the tea. CLINT *tries to talk.)*

MUFFDIVER: You wanna speak? Right. Bike.

(BIKE takes out a notebook and pencil. Meanwhile MUFF-DIVER *snorts up the coke, looks up and listens.)*

CLINT: You always in charge of everything.

MUFFDIVER: Yeah, I got the initiative. But it's the three of us— three business partners—doing this shit together.

CLINT: Doing what, though? What? What? What?

MUFFDIVER: Tonight, it's tonight, we're going big. This posse can deal, E, A, M-25, M-26—to the whole district. We got the contacts, the premises, the staff. The market's expanding, you know it is. Supply and demand, those cats out there can't get high enough. Course, there can't be any weak links. Weak links have to be taken care of. *(He stares at* CLINT.*)*

SYLVIE: Sounds good.

MUFFDIVER: Yeah? Say yeah.

CLINT: You can't boss Clint around. It don't suit me. Gotta go my own way.

SYLVIE: *(Gently to* CLINT*)* Let's give it a chance. Let's get somewhere, all of us. Think of all the shoes you'll be able to buy. In two years you can buy your own shoe shop.

MUFFDIVER: Right. Mr G'll be here in a minute. Let's make a good impression. Meeting's adjourned.

INT. LIVING ROOM. NIGHT.

MUFFDIVER *is inspecting the posse in a line-up.*

MUFFDIVER: Bike, don't slow things down. Burns, how's the special cool lighting going?

BURNS: It going.

(He touches a crumb off BURNS's *face. He inspects* CLINT's *shoes, etc.)*

MUFFDIVER: Right. Tom-Tom, you used to be a Master chef . . . If they want drinks . . . Got any ice? *(Panicking.)* Mr G's used to the best.

(The lights have already flicked during the line-up. Then the lights go completely.)

Burns, fix the fucking lights, man!

EXT. FRONT OF SQUAT BUILDING. NIGHT.

The lights BURNS *has fixed up, chintzy little things, are flicking on and off.*

Cheering.

BURNS *tries to fix the lights.*
The front door bell rings in the living room.
The two German TOURISTS *walk in.*

TOURIST WOMAN: Mr Eastwood—

TOURIST MAN: Mr Eastwood, the lights in our room are extinguishing onwards and offwards.

TOM-TOM: What room?

TOURIST MAN: Mr Eastwood has rented us a room upstairs. He said we could chill out. It's cool.

(BURNS *looks at* CLINT.)

BURNS: Yeah?

(MUFFDIVER *is confused. He goes to the German* TOURIST MAN *and holds out his hand.*)

MUFFDIVER: Mr G?

TOURIST MAN: Mr Wolf. Please to meet you.

INT. HALL OF HOUSE. RIGHT.
MR G *and his posse have come up the hallway and are now by the Sufi Centre.* MR G *and the others look suspiciously into the Sufi Centre.*

INT. LIVING ROOM OF SQUAT. NIGHT.
(Same time.)

MUFFDIVER: Who are these people?

TOURIST MAN: Mr Eastwood, the landlord here—

BURNS: Mr Eastwood the landlord? *(To them.)* You sleeping in my room?

TOURIST WOMAN: It was rented to us. How do you say it? All in?

(TOM-TOM *and* SYLVIE *restrain* BURNS *as he struggles to get* CLINT.)

INT. SUFI CENTRE. NIGHT.
Meanwhile, downstairs, DR BUBBA *rises and goes forward to greet* MR G *and Mr G's* ASSISTANTS.

DR BUBBA: Please, you are all welcome. Remove your shoes.

(MUFFDIVER *rushes downstairs into the Sufi Centre, behind*
MR G, *and sees the indignity he is about to suffer.*
Meanwhile the German TOURISTS *are coming down the*
stairs, turning to the group.)

TOURISTS: Don't stay in this place.

(MUFFDIVER *is virtually bent over double, so grovelling is he.*
MR G *turns and sees him.*

MUFFDIVER *gestures him and his posse out of the place,*
tripping over meditators as he goes.)

MUFFDIVER: Mr G, you can't choose your neighbours, can you?
Come upstairs for some refreshment and sorry. Sorry.

INT. LIVING ROOM OF SQUAT. NIGHT.

MUFFDIVER *leads* MR G *and his posse into the room. He has a smart*
young black ASSISTANT *with him and two young women, one black,*
one white.

MUFFDIVER *brings them in and they stand there waiting for* MR G
to sit down. The girls talk to each other.

Then the black woman goes to BIKE*'s bicycle and takes it.*

TOM-TOM: Mr G, Mrs G.

MUFFDIVER: Welcome, welcome.

(TOM-TOM *nods at* BIKE. *The woman climbs on to the bike*
and honks the horn. MR G *grins for the first time. We can*
see that BIKE *is becoming very anxious and is about to*
react. MUFFDIVER *glares at him.*

BURNS *is still furious with* CLINT *about the* TOURISTS *and*
surreptitiously tries to whack him.

MUFFDIVER *glares at* BURNS.)

MUFFDIVER: Burns!

(MR G *finally sits down. His posse sits down, the black girl*
on Bike's bike.

SYLVIE *offers them all peanuts.*)

Cut to:

INT. SQUAT LIVING ROOM. NIGHT.

MUFFDIVER—*and this is one of his specialities—is doing conjuring tricks for* MR G. *He wears a cape and top-hat. Behind,* SYLVIE, *who has dressed up rather pathetically, plays the trumpet.*

MUFFDIVER *pulls balls out of his mouth, strings of handkerchiefs out of the white girl's ear, etc.*

MUFFDIVER: Is it real or is it false? No one wants too much reality, we all know that.

    (MR G *has been looking around at the place with much curiosity.*)

MR G: When have I been here before?

ASSISTANT: It's Jimmy's place.

CLINT: He's lending it to us.

ASSISTANT: Really?

    (*To end the act* MR G *nods at* MUFFDIVER. *It's over.* MUFF-DIVER *bows.*

    MUFFDIVER *indicates to* TOM-TOM. TOM-TOM *takes charge.*)

TOM-TOM: This way, please, if you don't mind. Just for a few minutes, to ensure privacy. Let's go through, I mean up.

INT. SQUAT LANDING. NIGHT.

Everyone filing out of the squat. CLINT *moaning and cursing as they go,* BIKE *protectively carrying his bicycle.*

BURNS: (*German accent*) A word, Mr Eastwood the landlord.

INT. LIVING ROOM OF SQUAT. NIGHT.

MR G *and his* ASSISTANT *and* MUFFDIVER *sit in serious conference, drinking. The* ASSISTANT *has his briefcase open, listening to* MUFF-DIVER *as he puts his proposal.*

EXT. ROOF. NIGHT.

The others, including MR G's *girls, are on the roof of the squat.* BIKE *sits looking through the bars of his bicycle at everyone, especially* CLINT, *who he's happy to see with* SYLVIE.

CLINT *takes* SYLVIE'*s hand and leads her to the edge of the roof.*
His hand is over the brick (where he concealed the money) as he
talks.

CLINT: I made some money today. I wanted to give you some.

SYLVIE: Oh no. What about your shoes?

CLINT: I'll take care of that tomorrow. And start work the next
day. I'm pretty confident about things, Sylvie.

SYLVIE: *(Takes the money)* Thanks, Clint. Thanks.

CLINT: Top of the world. I need to get out of London. Let's go
. . . Let's go to the countryside tomorrow, yeah? I know a
good place where there's not too many farmers. What
d'you say?

(She nods at him.)

INT. SQUAT LIVING ROOM. NIGHT.

MUFFDIVER *and* MR G *and his* ASSISTANT *in heavy conference.*

ASSISTANT: Everything seems agreed then. Give us the upfront
investment now, as arranged. The delivery of everything
you've ordered will be in two days.

MUFFDIVER: *(Excited)* And, Mr G, both of you, I tell you, I've
got the best on-the-street salesmen in the area. My people are
hand-trained. Dealing's no longer for amateurs. I want to get
a smooth home-delivery service started. Like in Chicago—
'Hash-to-go', 'Call-a-snort', 'Dial-a-spliff'. Bikes, mopeds, a
courier service.

ASSISTANT: Hand-trained, you say.

MUFFDIVER: Yeah. *(Loses confidence.)* Yeah.

MR G: Hand-trained by whom?

MUFFDIVER: By me, Mr G.

MR G *and his* ASSISTANT *look at each other.* MUFFDIVER
gets up.)

INT. MUFFDIVER'S BEDROOM. NIGHT.

We see MUFFDIVER'*s confident, smug face as he walks towards the*
tailor's dummy in the bedroom.

EXT. ROOF. NIGHT.

The others on the roof. We see CLINT's *face, eyes closed, breathing deeply, looking up at the sky.* BURNS *eating a huge sandwich.* TOM-TOM *just sitting there.*

INT. MUFFDIVER'S ROOM. NIGHT.

We see MUFFDIVER's *hand reaching into the back of the dummy.* *We see him pulling some money out. Counts it; realizes it's not all there; gets agitated; counts it again; searches again. Searches the room for money. Finally gives up. Is furious.*

INT. STAIRS OF SQUAT. NIGHT.

MUFFDIVER *tells* MR G *that the money has gone and he can't pay him.* MUFFDIVER *is speechless. The sad and comic sight of him telling them the money's gone and them rising in irritation to leave. The others come back into the room, the women going out with* MR G. *Mr G's* ASSISTANT *just turns and points at* MUFFDIVER.

INT. STAIRS OF SQUAT. NIGHT.

Rest of troup stand watching MR G *leaving. We reverse on to* MUFFDIVER's *face as everyone is filing past him.*

INT. LIVING ROOM OF SQUAT. NIGHT.

MR G *and his posse have gone.* MUFFDIVER *is running around the room, screaming, attempting to smash everything, as they try to stop him.* BURNS *keeps grabbing at him. The others are hunting around, under chairs, carpets, etc., for the purloined money.* CLINT *searches especially hard.*

MUFFDIVER: Where's my fucking money, you fucking bastards, where is it, who's got it? I'll kill you for humiliating me! Mr G thinks I'm a total jerk-off and idiot fool prick total arsehole, Jesus! Search, search, you useless bastards! Who's got it?
    (*He grabs* BURNS *by the throat, pulling a knife on him.*)
MUFFDIVER: You desperate old man, it must be you!
CLINT: Muffdiver, man—

(He turns to CLINT.*)*

MUFFDIVER: So it was you!

TOM-TOM: Bike's brother was in here too at one point.

SYLVIE: And the tourists.

BURNS: *(German accent, laughing)* Yes it was them. Mr Eastwood
the landlord.

> *(*MUFFDIVER *sinks down in despair. The posse look at each
> other, some laughing.* SYLVIE *goes to him, reaching down
> and touching him.* CLINT *watches her. She looks up at him.)*

CLINT: Tomorrow, yeah? You an' me.

MUFFDIVER'S BEDROOM. NIGHT.

MUFFDIVER *stands naked at the window of his room, trying to fix
old sheets or dirty curtains to the window frame. He's banging away
with hammer and nails and keeps hitting his thumb. The wind and
rain blow through the window.*

*When he's done this he sits in bed. He counts the money he still
has and counts the tabs and capsules and 'burgers' he has in his
possession. We then see that* SYLVIE *is there in the room with him.
With great dignity she has put her things out on a packing case.
She cleans her face with cotton wool. She moisturizes her face with
care and combs her hair.*

MUFFDIVER *looks at his drugs and money and then at her. At first
he doesn't catch her eye. They then look at each other. Apprehension
on his face.*

She goes to him.

*From outside, through this scene, we hear the others playing rhyth-
mically on cans and trumpet and other homemade instruments. It's
a loud, hypnotic sound, getting faster and faster.*

INT. LIVING ROOM OF SQUAT. NIGHT.

*The men—*CLINT, BURNS, TOM-TOM—*on the floor in the living
room.* BIKE *sitting beside his bicycle.*

The door to Muffdiver's room is ajar. Human noises are heard.

CLINT *glances nervously at the door. He has Sylvie's trumpet at his lips, giving it a toot now and again.*

BURNS *watches* CLINT *and sees how disappointed and yet hopeful he is.*

TOM-TOM: *(To* BURNS*)* What's your real trade then?

BURNS: Electrician, me. This line of work isn't something I thought I'd get into when I was young, bodyguarding someone called Muffdiver, walking round with LSD strapped to me scrotum. Eh Bike?

*(*BIKE *opens his mouth to speak but some inner grief prevents him. They all look at him in anticipation but nothing comes.*

CLINT *toots on the trumpet,* BURNS *taps an empty Coke tin with a pencil,* TOM-TOM *drums on his knees. They grin at each other.)*

INT. SQUAT. MORNING.

EXT. MORNING. CLINT *has got up early. He's finished making sandwiches. He pops a couple of tomatoes into a bag.* TOM-TOM *is asleep on the floor.* BIKE *also asleep, next to his bicycle.*

To his surprise CLINT *also sees* FAULKNER *asleep on the floor, covered in other people's clothes, a pair of high heels beside him, a dress flung over a chair.*

FAULKNER: Going somewhere?

CLINT: Tsa-Tsa—bit of fresh country air up our nostrils.

FAULKNER: All of you?

CLINT: No way.

Cut to:

INT. SQUAT LIVING ROOM. DAY.

The others are stirring now. CLINT *squats down and waits at the far side of the room.* BIKE *and* TOM-TOM *are moving about.*

Finally, MUFFDIVER *emerges from his room, in leopard-skin print bathrobe, looks around, greets his posse, kisses* FAULKNER's *hand and goes to* CLINT.

MUFFDIVER: Sleep all right?

> (CLINT *nods.*)
>
> Tsa-Tsa, you look good anyway. Combed your hair too.
> *(He grabs* CLINT's *sandwich bag, looks inside and pulls out a mouldy-looking tomato.)*
> What's this?
> *(He notices* CLINT *is holding a rolled-up towel.)*
> Going to the seaside?
> (CLINT *shrugs.*)
> Was it you? Tell me.

CLINT: No, man.

MUFFDIVER: Don't go anywhere today. I wanna talk about my night with Sylvie. It was the best night I ever had—ever. Don't be like that, Clint, I still like talking to you.

> *(Not getting any response,* MUFFDIVER *goes off.)*

INT. MUFFDIVER'S BEDROOM. DAY.

CLINT *slowly opens the door to Muffdiver's bedroom.* SYLVIE *is lying in bed, facing away from him. He holds his sandwich bag.*

SYLVIE: There are some days when you just know you're never gonna get up.

> (CLINT *squatting behind her, strokes her shoulders, neck and face.*)

CLINT: We still on?

SYLVIE: What? Oh, it's you.

CLINT: For the outing. You said.

SYLVIE: What?

> *(They look at each other. Now* MUFFDIVER *is behind them.)*

MUFFDIVER: What's he doing? *(To* CLINT.) What you want in here?

CLINT: I'm calling a board meeting.

MUFFDIVER: You're up to something. The shoe is through.

(MUFFDIVER *starts to throw him out. They fight.*)

CLINT: Fuck you!

SYLVIE: Stop it, you silly boys! *(To* MUFFDIVER*)* We were just going out for the day, to the countryside. That's all!

MUFFDIVER: Tsa-Tsa, so why don't we all catch a bit of the seaside then? Get out of the filth.

SYLVIE: But we are the filth, dear. Clint's got a place he fancies.

CLINT: No I haven't.

MUFFDIVER: Yeah? Where is it?

CLINT: I can't go. I gotta buy some shoes today. I start work tomorrow morning.

MUFFDIVER: Right then. We're on. It's a good idea to get out, with Mr G angry with us and all.

(MUFFDIVER *goes to the door, shouts out.*) Tom-Tom, fancy a trip?

INT. MUFFDIVER'S BEDROOM. DAY.

SYLVIE *goes to* CLINT *as* MUFFDIVER *organizes the posse.*

SYLVIE: You look dirty.

CLINT: Thanks.

SYLVIE: I should wash you.

CLINT: You wouldn't.

SYLVIE: I should give you a bath. Come on, Clint.

CLINT: Now?

SYLVIE: Before we go.

INT. BATHROOM. DAY.

The bathroom is a large, dirty room which was once intended to be luxurious and decadent. A big kidney-shaped bath, with a shelf for sitting on.

SYLVIE *has run the water and is testing it with her elbow. She turns and laughs with* CLINT. *He stands there awkwardly. She grabs his belt and pulls down his trousers. They struggle. He becomes serious.*

CLINT: What are you doing to me, Sylvie?
Cut to:

INT. BATHROOM. DAY.
CLINT *is in the bath washing his hair with shampoo, as she opens a beer.*
CLINT: Whatever you do, don't look at me.
  (But she looks at him, smiling.)
  Why are you looking like that?
SYLVIE: Don't be afraid of me.
CLINT: *(Holds his arms out)* Look at me.
SYLVIE: You're a beautiful boy.
CLINT: But you wouldn't want to hold my hand, would you?
  (She washes his hair.)
  I'd like to talk to you.
SYLVIE: What would you say, baby?
CLINT: I'd want to know where you've been. I'd love to know where you come from. Describe your mum and dad.
SYLVIE: People who . . . it's incredible . . . the police should stop certain people having children.
CLINT: I hate people who blame their parents for everything.
SYLVIE: So do I.
  (MUFFDIVER *comes into the bathroom and sits down. They look at him nervously but he is abstracted.)*
SYLVIE: *(Embarrassed)* A bath meeting.
Cut to:

INT. BATHROOM. DAY.
We see MUFFDIVER *taking his clothes off. The three of them in the bath.* SYLVIE *between* CLINT *and* MUFFDIVER. MUFFDIVER *subdued, dreaming.*
CLINT: *(To* SYLVIE, *of* MUFFDIVER*)* I like him when he's like this.
SYLVIE: Stoned, or thinking about his money.

(SYLVIE *and* CLINT *laugh at this.* CLINT *imitates Muffdiver's rage of the previous evening, taking off his voice.*)
CLINT: 'Where's my fucking money, you fucking bastards . . .'
(Pause.) Where the same blood. *(To him.)* I could touch you,
I could. And you could kill me. *(To her.)* He could just wipe
me out. Maybe he should. I make him feel soft. He hates
anyone who does that to him. Even you. I wonder why he
wants to be so hard.
(She looks at him in surprise.
He quickly gets out of the bath. SYLVIE *sits there and
shivers.* CLINT *holds out an old overcoat for her to get
into.*)
Mum, don't get cold.

EXT. OUTSIDE FRONT OF SQUAT. DAY.
*The posse bundle out of squat, in holiday mood. They've all at-
tempted to dress up for the occasion. They pass* DR BUBBA *standing
on his balcony, in an elegant white robe, amusedly watching them
and casually eating a piece of toast.*
TOM-TOM: *(Mocking)* Om! Om! Om! *(To* BURNS.*)* I've been
through all that. Been through it, man!
*(*CLINT *is behind them, the last down the stairs, less cheerful
than the rest, seeing as* MUFFDIVER's *ruined his day by
bringing the whole posse with him.* CLINT *is horrified by*
TOM-TOM's *mockery of* DR BUBBA. CLINT *puts his hands
together respectfully and bows at* DR BUBBA.*)*

EXT. RAILWAY STATION. DAY.
*The posse at Victoria Station running down the platform for a train.
They carry pizzas and beers and* TOM-TOM *has a big beat-box with
him.* BURNS *and* CLINT *carry a crate of beer.*
*They eventually crash into the compartment of the train, out of
breath, laughing.*
The guard blows his whistle. The train starts off from the station.

EXT. COUNTRY STATION. DAY.

The posse coming out of a little country station in Kent. They are regarded strangely by passers-by who stop and stare as they stand blinking in the fresh air. CLINT *spots a bus coming and starts off towards it.*

MUFFDIVER *puts on his dark glasses.*

INT./EXT. BUS. DAY.

The posse climb up to the top deck of a country bus, BIKE *having difficulty getting his bicycle up the stairs.* BURNS *helps him.* SYLVIE *rushes to the front.* TOM-TOM *and* CLINT *fight to sit with her,* CLINT *winning, being the more determined.*

He turns around to cheer and celebrate but MUFFDIVER *is sitting right behind him.*

Cut to:

INT. BUS. DAY.

The bus speeds through country lanes and suddenly breaks spectacularly out into open countryside. Cheering.

BURNS: *(Eating)* This is the life.

    (CLINT *shouts at people in the street.*)

CLINT: Get down you leather queens!

EXT. COUNTRYSIDE. DAY.

The posse are now standing in open countryside, a little bewildered, looking lost. They turn to CLINT, *who's the only one with any idea of where they are.*

Two local kids, a boy and girl of about fifteen or sixteen, stand looking shyly at them, these London weirdos, in admiration. This is everything they want to be when they grow up, as cool, bizarre and clearly living in freedom.

TOM-TOM *waves to them like a rock star greeting his fans.*

TOM-TOM: Elmore James. Chuck Berry. The Lightnin'—

    (CLINT *starts off towards the kids.*)

CLINT: Hey, yo, wanna buy something? Need some Ecstasy? Acid? Ice?

(BURNS *grabs him.* BIKE *is laughing.* MUFFDIVER *looks at him steadily, neither critically nor with affection but trying to work out what's going through his mind. Does* CLINT *really want this job? And why has he brought them to this place?*

BIKE *cycles off down the lane.*

CLINT *steps over a stile into a field.* TOM-TOM *and* BURNS *follow him.* SYLVIE *takes* MUFFDIVER'*s arm and tries to guide him over the stile. He won't go over it.)*

SYLVIE: What's the matter?

MUFFDIVER: My boots. (*And he indicates his superb boots which he refuses to get dirty.*)

EXT. COUNTRYSIDE. DAY.

The posse walking through a wood. They're in a cheerful mood— and drinking. Music from TOM-TOM'*s beat-box.* BURNS *hides behind a tree and jumps out on* BIKE, *making donkey noises.*

MUFFDIVER *bends over to try and clean his boots, which are already muddy.*

The two local kids follow them through the wood, intrigued.

CLINT: *(To* BIKE) Fancy some country grass?

(BIKE *takes a spliff.* CLINT *takes one himself.* CLINT *offers one to* TOM-TOM. TOM-TOM *waves him away.*)

This country grass will fly you into the eternal moment.

TOM-TOM: Talk about something else. Foliage. Tree bark. Ten years I've been a junkie and I can tell you, druggies are boring, small-minded and stupid. The people are enough to put you off taking the stuff. Don't you know anything else?

CLINT: I want to, Tom-Tom.

(MUFFDIVER *takes* SYLVIE'*s arm.*)

EXT. POND IN WOOD. DAY.

They walk beside a large pond deep in the woods, watched by the two local kids from across the other side. TOM-TOM *wading in the water by himself, talking to himself.*

TOM-TOM: Otis Redding. *(Pause.)* Marvin Gaye. *(Pause.)* Smokey. Smokey Robinson.

(Still in dark glasses, MUFFDIVER *suddenly tries to shove* BURNS, *who's watching* TOM-TOM, *into the water. He gives him a hard shove but* BURNS *is immovable, as he munches another pizza.)*

BURNS: *(Without turning)* I bet you were a real fucking bully at school.

*(*TOM-TOM *wades out further.)*

TOM-TOM: Sam Cooke. Bob Marley. Aretha.

EXT. COUNTRYSIDE. DAY.

Later. They all walk along a high ridge with a view down to a cottage. In the garden LILY *is hanging out some washing. She has a little boy with her, aged seven or eight.* BURNS *is on the bike,* BIKE *himself besides* BURNS. TOM-TOM *and* MUFFDIVER *together,* MUFFDIVER *nodding as* TOM-TOM *goes on with his list.* SYLVIE *and* CLINT *together, watched by* MUFFDIVER.

CLINT: *(To* SYLVIE*)* Six months I'd been at the rehab. As a reward, not a punishment, as a reward, they send us on this outward bound shit. We're trudging up a mountain, ten deviants, with four social workers and all.

TOM-TOM: *(Off camera)* J. J. Cale.

CLINT: I've done something wrong and no one's allowed to talk to me. Suddenly I see this carpet of mushrooms, magic mushrooms. They're everywhere, just growing out the earth. I'm behind a tree gobbling them down. Soon the mountain's breathing and the trees are dancing and the sky is swirling with energy and atoms. And I can see the people are sly and cunning and ignorant. I can see that the people who won't let anyone talk to me are in love with power and cruelty. They don't love me. And I know what I want to do. Get back to London and be with the only people for me, having adventures.

TOM-TOM: Phil Spector.

MUFFDIVER: (*Looking at* CLINT) Where's he going . . . with my money?

(*And* CLINT *is running down the hill towards the cottage, making Red Indian whooping calls.*)

SYLVIE: I think he's spotted a new pair of shoes.

EXT. OUTSIDE COTTAGE. DAY.

From LILY's *point of view we see the posse, with* CLINT *running down the hill, coming towards her.* BIKE *cycles down the hill.* SYLVIE *dances down the hill.*

LILY *is a damaged, nervous woman, smoking constantly, early forties, been through a lot. The cottage has only recently been bought and is in the process of being done up.*

The posse, seen from the house, are a higgedly-piggedly bunch, threatening and risible at the same time.

LILY *examines them closely. She becomes tense and then joyful.*

EXT. FIELD. DAY.

LILY *walks and runs towards them.*

LILY: Is it you? Yeah, it would be, it is you!

(*She goes to kiss* CLINT *but* CLINT *holds back, not going to her. We look at* SYLVIE *looking at them, puzzled.*)

CLINT: These are my friends. And this is Sylvie.

LILY: Hallo Muff.

Cut to:

EXT. FRONT OF COTTAGE. DAY.

Minutes later, they're all walking towards the cottage, LILY *with her arm around* CLINT.

LILY: *(To* BIKE*)* We've only had the house a few months. *(Indicating* CLINT.*)* I expect he wants to have a look. *(Pause.)* My boy's come back.

(She turns to look at MUFFDIVER *who is snogging with* SYLVIE *as they walk.* BURNS *very interested in the house, striding towards it.)*

INT. LILY'S HOUSE/KITCHEN. DAY.

LILY *is putting the kettle on. She is with* CLINT. *The others have gone through into the parlour.*

LILY: Don't take this the wrong way—but you haven't come to ask for anything have you?

CLINT: Mum, I've got money.

LILY: Why, what have you and Muff been doing? I can guess.

CLINT: No. Here.

(He gives her the head he stole from Headley's room.)

LILY: Thanks. It's dead.

CLINT: It's Japanese. I always bring you something. *(Pause.)* I want a photograph of Dad. Have you still got that one of the three of us?

LILY: I'll have to look for it.

CLINT: Why, haven't you kept much from our old house?

LILY: Some.

INT. PARLOUR. DAY.

While LILY *and* CLINT *are in the kitchen, the others have gone through into the parlour,* BIKE *carrying his bicycle of course,* TOM-TOM *soaked,* BURNS *trying to organize them, and* SYLVIE *upset and trying to get heroin out of an irritable* MUFFDIVER. *She pleads with him.*

LILY *and* CLINT *come through with tea.*

LILY *(To* BIKE.*)* Wouldn't you like to leave that machine outside?

BURNS: He takes it everywhere with him.

LILY: Well, tell him to wipe his tyres.

(BIKE *wipes his tyres on the doormat.*)

Hallo Muff.

MUFFDIVER: Hallo Lily.

BURNS: There's a cracking fire through there—mind if Tom-Tom
gets his clothes off in front of it?

LILY: No, no. My husband'll be back in a minute.

BURNS: How much did you pay for the place, love?

LILY: Dunno.

INT. LILY'S HOUSE. DAY.

LILY *is showing them the house. It's been a run down place which
she and* STONE *are doing up.* BURNS *touches walls, examines wood-
work, electrics, etc.* LILY *perks up at* BURNS's *interest but keeps
looking nervously at* CLINT.

Cuts to:

INT. LILY'S HOUSE/VARIOUS ROOMS. DAY.

Another room, more finished?

*A huge framed poster of Elvis. The only other ornamentation in
this room is Elvis paraphernalia—good stuff, well presented, not
too tacky.*

A photograph of STONE *dressed as Presley which* BIKE *examines
and poses as, trying to make* CLINT *laugh—which he doesn't.*

LILY *explaining to* TOM-TOM *what they're doing with the cottage.*

BURNS, CLINT *and* SYLVIE *looking on.*

CLINT: Stone'll be back soon. Not my dad—Mum's new husband.
Stoneface.

LILY: Don't you start. He's not new. Eight years we've been together. *(To* MUFFDIVER.*)* I wish I'd known you were coming,
Muff.

MUFFDIVER: I wish I'd known, Lily. I thought I was going to the seaside. Clint, why didn't you say you wanted to see your mum?

CLINT: Stone—on Saturdays he dresses up as Elvis.

BURNS: I used to do that.

CLINT: Stone hates my guts.

LILY: Have you come home for a slap? Look at the mud on your feet.

BURNS: When did you get this place?

LILY: We got it a year ago. It was derelict. We've saved it.

BURNS: I bet you're right proud of yourself.

LILY: We've given it all our love and attention.

CLINT: I'm going to have a shower.

BURNS: They haven't got any books.

TOM-TOM: Music says everything I want to know. This place has music. Listen.

BURNS: I wish I had a house.

INT. KITCHEN. DAY.

Later. LILY *goes into the kitchen and finds* SYLVIE *going through the medicine cupboard, restless and agitated.*

LILY: Headache, love?

> (SYLVIE *shakes her head.*)

> Need something else?

> (LILY *gives her a Valium from her handbag.* LILY *knocks over an open jar of honey that spreads like an opening flower across the table.*)

LILY: He'll murder me.

SYLVIE: Come on.

> (*They clear it up together.*)

SYLVIE: Lily, he's a sweetheart.

LILY: Is he? Yes he is, my little Clint.

SYLVIE: Why—

LILY: His dad was addicted to everything, you name it, and violent. What he did to me. Someone chopped him up. Good job. What a life—I thought it was over. Then I moved into John Stone's. You should know, I'll tell you, he loves me. He has me three times a day. Sometimes more. You can't say fairer than that. There's no heaven and no god, is there?

SYLVIE: I have to ask. When you went to John Stones's why didn't you take Clint with you?

LILY: You saying I'd just leave my boy? Stone took him in too. He was kind to him. And what did Clint do? He puked in bed. He shouted names at Stone's friends in the Territorial Army. He injected himself and nearly died. The day came. Sylvie, I had to choose.

SYLVIE: Between your son and your lover.

EXT. OUTSIDE LILY'S HOUSE. DAY.
John STONE, *middle-aged, owns a second-hand shop selling porn, guns and knives. His dog sits beside him in his car, a pink Cadillac. He's turned into the yard of his cottage to see* BIKE *doing wheelies. Further away, sitting on a wall, are the two local kids, watching with juvenile interest as* BIKE *performs for them.* BIKE *stops when* STONE *turns up.*
STONE, *cool, grim, gets out of the car with his dog and walks past* BIKE *ignoring him.*

INT. KITCHEN. DAY.
Through the window LILY *sees* STONE *coming towards the house. She is nervous.*

LILY: Here he comes now. Please go and calm them all down for me.

    (SYLVIE *leaves the kitchen.*)
Cut to:

INT. KITCHEN. DAY.

John STONE *comes into the kitchen. He steps unwittingly into a pool of honey which has been overlooked. She looks at him worriedly and then goes to kiss him.*

STONE: Lily. It's all right.

LILY: Let's have a drink.

(She pours two large Scotches.)

INT. UPSTAIRS CORRIDOR OF COTTAGE. DAY.

MUFFDIVER *walks along the top corridor of Stone's house, past a bedroom in which he glimpses* SYLVIE *standing with her back to the door, combing her hair. He goes in and gives her a bag of smack. Another room is the bathroom and* MUFFDIVER *sees his friend* CLINT *leaning against the sink and staring at himself in the mirror. They look at each other in the mirror.*

The last room is Stone's study, a large room. MUFFDIVER *opens the door slowly. The room is full of weapons mounted on the wall: rifles, handguns, antique guns, old swords and daggers.*

The room is also a shrine to Elvis, with Elvis gear everywhere. The room's major item is an Elvis costume, beautifully made, obviously Stone's, mounted on a dummy.

MUFFDIVER *is fascinated by all this stuff and moves further into the room, taking down a dagger and a gun.*

He tries on Stone's Elvis jacket and looks at himself in the full-length mirror, posing with the gun and dagger.

MUFFDIVER: Somebody.

INT. KITCHEN. DAY.

STONE *and* LILY *in the kitchen*

STONE: What's that blackie doing in the yard, love? *(Pause.)* Has your boy come back? For good—or what? What do you want to do with him? Is he the same? Is he?

(She gets up. She gestures in distress.)

INT. STONE'S LIVING ROOM. DAY.

STONE *goes into the living room where* TOM-TOM *is fiddling with the piano.* STONE *goes to him.*

STONE: How you keeping?

TOM-TOM: Not well. You?

> (TOM-TOM *plays 'Are You Lonesome Tonight' and* LILY *starts to hum the melody.* STONE *moves snakily, as Presley, impressed by* TOM-TOM's *playing. As* LILY *hums and* TOM-TOM *plays* STONE *does the speaking section of the song, with* BIKE *looking through the window behind him.* BIKE *laughs and urges* TOM-TOM *on. He catches* STONE's *eye.* STONE *gives him a look. Now, as this continues, water starts dripping through the ceiling on to* STONE's *head. He notices. Looks up. And dashes out of the room.)*

INT. ROOM IN THE COTTAGE. DAY.

STONE *dashes through into another room where* BURNS's *fat carcass is laid out on the sofa, watching TV, a beer and a plate of sandwiches in front of him. As* STONE *dashes through the room to the opposite door,* BURNS *gets up with a sandwich clenched between his teeth, knocking the beer over.*

Cut to:

INT. STAIRCASE/ROOM. DAY.

STONE *is going upstairs quickly.*

STONE *is on the top floor of the house. Now he shoves the door of the bedroom and sees* SYLVIE *with her jeans around her knees injecting herself in the crotch.*

In the corridor once more he sees, at the far end, MUFFDIVER *standing guiltily outside the door of* STONE's *study wearing his Elvis jacket.*

STONE *jerks his thumbs at him, indicating that he should take it off and get out.* MUFFDIVER *moves.*

Now STONE *bursts into the bathroom and pulls back the shower curtain.* CLINT *is in the shower.*

STONE: Get outta there, boy, the water's coming through.

>   (CLINT *jumps out.* STONE *turns off the water, getting wet himself, and several tiles fall off the wall.*)

CLINT: Must have been stuck up by a moron.

STONE: Jesus. Jesus.

>   (STONE *starts throwing the tiles on the floor.* CLINT *is not frightened yet and continues to dry himself, not concealing himself and eczema-scarred body.* STONE *is shocked rather than hostile.*)

Someone shove you in an acid bath?

CLINT: I got a job, Stone.

>   (STONE *goes slowly towards* CLINT. CLINT *retreats.* STONE *reaches out to touch him.*)

STONE: What kind of strange little boy are you?

CLINT: Don't you touch me.

STONE: Still using shit, Clint? Don't even reply, you're an addict and therefore a complete liar.

>   (*Now* SYLVIE *is at the door behind them, not seen by* STONE.)

Your mother loves you but what you done but break her heart?

CLINT: Have I?

STONE: Apologize to her.

>   (SYLVIE, *laughing at* STONE, *comes into the room towards him, not in the least scared.*)

SYLVIE: Oh mister. Mister.

>   (*She goes to* CLINT *and helps him up, holding him.*)

STONE: You're smart, girlie. What you doing with these bad boys? You're above them.

SYLVIE: Me? I'm not above no one.

INT. LIVING ROOM OF COTTAGE. DAY.

All the posse present now, in the living room.

LILY *and* BIKE *come into the room carrying tea and biscuits. The atmosphere is no longer relaxed, as it was when they first came into the cottage. They look at each other expectantly, as if to say: 'Should we leave?'*

MUFFDIVER *and* SYLVIE *lie on the sofa together, whispering and playing with each other.*

CLINT *stands there drying his hair after the shower, hurt and disturbed, looking to* MUFFDIVER *for support.* MUFFDIVER *ignores him.*

BURNS *sits forward in an armchair, worried, as always, about all the others.*

TOM-TOM *is at the piano, tinkling a melancholy tune.*

LILY *pours the tea and* BIKE *hands it around to the others.*

LILY: *(To* BIKE*)* There's a good boy.

> Now STONE *comes into the room and stands there, looking at the posse individually, puzzled, as if trying to work out how the posse came to be this way, this loathsome.*
>
> BIKE *hands tea to* BURNS. BURNS *puts his tea down immediately. He's made a decision after seeing* STONE*'s face.)*

BURNS: Let's get off then.

STONE: I've said nothing.

BURNS: I can smell . . . *(and he sniffs)* contempt.

STONE: *(Parodying* BURNS*'s sniffing)* I'm getting it too. From you. You think everything respectable I've built up with my hands somehow belongs to bums like you. That I don't deserve it. That I've stolen it. I haven't. You people—

BURNS: Here we go.

STONE: You listen for once to someone who isn't stoned, who can speak the English language, fat man. You only desire to be . . . what you are now. This. The lazy dregs of society. *(Glancing at* MUFFDIVER.*)* And superior. But none of you know fuck-all. That boy for instance. *(He indicates* CLINT.*)* I know him. Absolutely useless. He knows nothing about nothing. He can't do fuck-all.

BURNS: *(Shaking his head furiously)* No! There is intelligence—

STONE: You're slaves of sensation, just slaves—

BURNS: Your way of life, that's slavery, habit, repetition—

STONE: Without will or strength or determination. You'll always take the easy way.

SYLVIE: If only you know, Mr Stone, how hard it is when you're out of tune with the straight world and what strength and determination you need when you've got nothing. On the street . . .

STONE: To tell the truth, girlie, I pity you. I pity people who don't know the purpose that real work gives you.

BURNS: I can wire a house. I can install a shower.

CLINT: *(To LILY, of STONE)* More than he can.

STONE: *(Looking scornfully at SYLVIE)* I saw you upstairs. Addiction is the most pathetic and wretched thing.

(TOM-TOM has hung his head during this. MUFFDIVER tries to catch his eye. Tension is rising all round. MUFFDIVER shows TOM-TOM the knife. TOM-TOM laughs wryly.)

Because you think you can be happy by sticking a needle in you. You're yellow cowards, afraid of life.

SYLVIE: *(To LILY)* Lily, when I look at your man, Stone, I think: that person will never understand anything about other people's hearts. *(Indicates CLINT)* Whereas he loves . . .

LILY: *(Shouts)* No, that's a lie. Stone loves! He loves me! *(To STONE.)* Yes?

STONE: *(To SYLVIE)* If you want to die, go and do it in a corner and don't commit no crimes on ordinary people.

(STONE spits on the floor. MUFFDIVER, who's been preparing himself throughout this, hurls himself at STONE with his knife. But STONE's a fighter. MUFFDIVER and STONE struggle, LILY screaming, everyone yelling. The knife

eventually falls from MUFFDIVER'*s hand.* TOM-TOM *picks it up.*
And BURNS *holds* STONE. SYLVIE *and* CLINT *hold* MUFF-
DIVER.
    BIKE *turns away.)*
BIKE: *(To* TOM-TOM*)* I don't think they'll ask us back.

INT. KITCHEN. DAY.
BURNS, BIKE, TOM-TOM, SYLVIE *and* MUFFDIVER *going out through
the kitchen door.* CLINT, *last, about to follow them, when he spots
a pair of shoes parked in the corner of the kitchen, sitting on
newspaper, freshly cleaned. He quickly removes his boots and puts
on the good shoes, carefully putting the old pair in their place.*
CLINT: The shoe is overdue.
    (Now he goes through into the hall.)
    Mum.
    *(At the top of the stairs he sees the little boy, now in py-
jamas and old dressing gown, coming slowly downstairs.
    At the top of the stairs is* LILY, *preoccupied.)*
LILY: I'm just coming.

EXT. FIELD. AFTERNOON.
The posse moves off across the field, SYLVIE *being given a piggy-
back by* BURNS.
Now LILY *runs after them, carrying the shoes that* CLINT *left behind.
She stops and shouts, running until she catches up with* CLINT.
Seeing this, MUFFDIVER *has the others continue, into the distance.*
LILY: *(Breathless)* Stay, stay. Stone says . . . it's OK.
CLINT: Tomorrow I start work, Mum.
LILY: Whose shoes are those? You left yours. *(She looks down.)*
    Oh no, give them back.
    (He shakes his head.)
    He'll take it out on me. You can't do it! Clint! Thief!

(She throws the old pair at him.)

TOM-TOM: Elvis Aaron Presley.

(And Stone is standing there dressed as Elvis, with a Rott-weiler.)

EXT. COUNTRY STREET. LATE AFTERNOON.

An old hippy is coming out of a house with guitar cases, putting them in the back of a big van—watched from across the road by the posse.

MUFFDIVER *looks at* CLINT. CLINT *goes over to the hippy.*

Cut to:

EXT. COUNTRY STREET. LATE AFTERNOON.

The van pulls away with them all sitting in the back. We watch this event from the point of view of the two local kids, deeply in awe of the entire event.

Then the van is gone. Music from the beat-box hangs in the air for a while, then silence; desolation. The local kids turn away.

EXT. OUTSIDE THE DINER. NIGHT.

Doors of the van burst open. BIKE *cycles out of the van. The others tumble out after him. The hippy's van draws away. The posse on the pavement, dispersing in different directions.*

CLINT *standing outside the diner, watching, ready to wave. He spots* MELANIE. *But at the table she is serving at, he sees Mr G's black* ASSISTANT *and Mr G's two women friends eating and laughing.*

Now FAULKNER *crosses the road with one rent boyfriend.*

FAULKNER: So you're back, Marco Polo. Jesus. Phew. You're dead meat, man. All of you.

CLINT: Mr G? He not bothered about us. He amused.

FAULKNER: Not Mr G. Mr Gangster whose place you're squatting. He's heard about it. He's very angry about you sitting on his toilet. He's coming over.

*(*CLINT *hurries away after the posse.)*

EXT. OUTSIDE THE SHOE SHOP. NIGHT.

CLINT *hurries past the shoe shop.* BUSY BEE *in the doorway starts to unpack his paltry belongings and make himself comfortable for the night.*

BUSY BEE: Where's my jumper?

INT. HALLWAY/SUFI CENTRE. NIGHT.

CLINT *stands outside the Sufi Centre, watching the chanting and revolving. He catches* DR BUBBA's *eye and is about to go to him. But* SYLVIE *carrying groceries, is behind him.*

SYLVIE: What a fabulous man, Dr Bubba.

CLINT: But what are they doing, these people? What do they want?

SYLVIE: I talked to one of them. They chant and meditate to get serene. To clear their heads. They want to stop wanting all the time and start really living.

CLINT: Yeah?

(They remove their shoes and practically dash to join the group. They join the circle and revolve, CLINT *looking pretty awkward. The others smile and encourage him. He watches* SYLVIE. *After a good whirl, as the circle gets smaller and smaller, they stop, and separate, in a circle.)*

DR BUBBA: What do you all feel, if you don't mind? Let us compare calmnesses.

(There are several replies from the group: 'Yes, calm . . . happy . . . OK . . . tired . . . not religious. Not spiritual'. Then it's CLINT's *turn. They look at him.)*

CLINT: Sexy . . . Just . . . sexy.

(People freeze, not knowing how to take this. They look at DR BUBBA. DR BUBBA *starts to bend forward and straighten, bend and straighten.)*

SYLVIE: *(To someone in group)* He all right?

PERSON IN GROUP: Dr Bubba is doing his laughing meditation.
Cut to:

INT. SUFI CENTRE. NIGHT.
SYLVIE *putting on her shoes.* CLINT *looking for his shoes.*
CLINT: Hey, some bloodclot's swiped my shoes! Hey, yo, Dr
   Bubba, man!
   (*But* DR BUBBA *is talking to someone else.*)
   Where are they! Give them back!
SYLVIE: The shoe has flew!
   (CLINT *starts to smash the place up, throwing things
   around.*)
CLINT: Where are they! Where are they!
   (DR BUBBA *comes across and removes his own shoes, Indian
   chappals. Very flimsy sandals. He gives them to* CLINT *who
   is very distressed.* CLINT *takes them resentfully.*)

INT. LIVING ROOM OF SQUAT. NIGHT.
CLINT *standing in the living room barefoot, waving the sandals
about.* BURNS *lying on the floor with* BIKE *in his arms.*
CLINT: Look, look!
BURNS: I'm so happy, so fucking happy.

INT. SQUAT BATHROOM. NIGHT.
SYLVIE *is alone in the bathroom. She tries to shut the broken door.
She has cotton wool and a bottle of disinfectant. And a razor blade.
She rolls up her sleeve and slowly, carefully, as if she's done this
before—the dark scars are visible—cuts herself. She cuts herself
five times until the blood comes. She watches herself in the mirror.
She bathes each cut.*

INT./ EXT. OUTSIDE BATHROOM DOOR. NIGHT.
SYLVIE *comes out of the bathroom.* CLINT *is outside, waiting for
her. She is not certain if he's seen her.*

CLINT: Sylvie, what are you doing?

SYLVIE: Don't follow me round.

CLINT: Where are you going now, then?

SYLVIE: Muffdiver's taking me out.

CLINT: Let's go out for a drink first. It's only a few hours before
I start work. How about a quick drink?

(She looks at him and finally relents. He is pleased.)

INT. HI-TECH BAR. NIGHT.

CLINT *and* SYLVIE *go into the hi-tech bar with* BIKE, *minus his bike
for a change. The place is pretty full.*

TOM-TOM *is at the bar. A* BLACK DWARF *springs around, collecting
glasses. As usual, as* CLINT *comes in numerous people talk to him,
saying 'Buyin', sellin', got any M-25?' etc.*

CLINT: I'm retired. In a new business. Got a day job.

*(*CLINT *and* SYLVIE *push through the crowd. Then* CLINT
steps in a puddle of beer, wetting his feet and cursing.)

BLACK DWARF: *(Laughing)* You wanna get some new shoes,
innit?

Cut to:

INT. HI-TECH BAR. NIGHT.

CLINT *has got them drinks.* SYLVIE *is sitting down, beside* FAULK-
NER.

SYLVIE: You love him—

CLINT: I mean it, you an' me, we've got to finish with him. We
mustn't get dependent.

SYLVIE: But we need him. Look at us, people like us, wasted
trash—

CLINT: Yes, he'll take us down.

SYLVIE: We can't do nothing for ourselves. He's a sparky little
kid with a dream.

CLINT: Of money, only. Powerful people, they're the worst, they
always want to take you over.

FAULKNER: Oh stop it you two.

(CLINT *stares at her. Kisses her cheek. She sighs. He gets on his knees and under the table, between her legs.*)

FAULKNER: Is he?

(SYLVIE *nods*)

When he's finished, ask him to do me.

(*The camera on* SYLVIE'*s face.* FAULKNER *dabs her forehead with his handkerchief.*)

Cut to:

INT. HI-TECH BAR. NIGHT.

Under the table. We see CLINT *on his knees with his head under* SYLVIE'*s skirt. As he withdraws for a breather, he notices* FAULKNER'*s excellent shoes which, unlike the rest of him today, are entirely conventional.*

Now SYLVIE *kicks* CLINT *to continue, which he does, while at the same time he's clumsily putting one sandalled foot beside* FAULKNER'*s.*

FAULKNER: Lick my top-caps baby. (*To* SYLVIE.) Clearly no shoe is safe in this boy's company.

CLINT: Can I borrow them, Faulkner, just for the day?

FAULKNER: No you can't.

(*But there's a struggle under the table as* CLINT *frantically tries to wrench* FAULKNER'*s shoes off, and* FAULKNER *tries to get rid of him.* SYLVIE *laughing.*)

Help me, help me!

(*We see* BURNS *and* TOM-TOM *looking at this from across the bar and laughing approvingly.*

BURNS *turns as five or six policemen come into the bar through two entrances.*

As CLINT *comes out from under the table a pint of beer tips off the table and down his back. He gets up quickly, very pissed off, and sees what's happening.*)

CLINT: Oh no, oh Christ, what's happening? They can't arrest me, not now. I'm only a waiter.

SYLVIE: Get rid of your stuff!

(He stands there petrified, looking around.)

Clint!

(Meanwhile everyone in the place reacts fast. They know what to do. We see this in comic detail: people dropping their drugs on the floor; others swallow theirs; a white man, standing beside TOM-TOM, drops his stuff into TOM-TOM's pocket, even as TOM-TOM drops his own stuff on the floor.

We see feet kicking stuff under tables. One man pops his shit out of the window. Someone else throws a lump of dope in the air and catches it in his mouth.

FAULKNER punches CLINT in the balls.

SYLVIE grabs CLINT and holds him, going through his pockets, finding his stuff and throwing it on the floor, kicking it under a table into a corner.)

EXT. OUTSIDE THE HI-TECH BAR IN THE STREET. NIGHT.

This isn't a major bust. Two police cars, a couple of arrests. People drifting away.

CLINT and SYLVIE stand to one side, having seen it all before.

TOM-TOM is being hauled off by the police.

CLINT: *(To TOM-TOM)* Sid Vicious.

(CLINT cracks up laughing. SYLVIE nudges him and they see MUFFDIVER across the street, dressed up, looking very smart.)

MUFFDIVER: *(To SYLVIE)* Hi baby. Tsa-Tsa.

SYLVIE: Yeah, look at you, it's nice.

(MUFFDIVER takes CLINT to one side.)

MUFFDIVER: I'm taking Sylvie out for a bit of grub and then to a little rave. So give me the money you owe me for the hundred and give me the ones you haven't sold.

(CLINT *goes through his pockets.*)

(*Sarcastic.*) Thanks for the day out, man. (*He looks at* CLINT *and is sorry for his sarcasm.*) No.

(CLINT *gives him money.*)

CLINT: I had to get rid of the rest of the stuff in there. (*Pause.*) I won't be working for you no more, Muff, man. I start work tomorrow.

MUFFDIVER *looks down at* CLINT's *sandals. Does a double-take. Looks at him sympathetically.*)

MUFFDIVER: I'll never let something as bad as that happen to you.

CLINT: Have a good evening.

(*He walks away, crying.* MUFFDIVER *yells after him.*)

MUFFDIVER: I won't let them do it to you, I promise, Clint, I won't!

EXT. SQUAT BUILDING. NIGHT.

CLINT *walking back to the squat. Outside the house several cars are parked on the pavement. A* HEAVY *is throwing out the dummies from Muffdiver's room.*

CLINT *sees the black tramp dressed in rags walking towards him.*

CLINT *runs towards the house.*

INT. HALLWAY/SUFI CENTRE. NIGHT.

CLINT *walks upstairs past the door of the Sufi Centre.* DR BUBBA, *who's been waiting to catch him, comes out.*

DR BUBBA: Remain down here for some time. Some men are looking for you boys, courtesy of the previous occupant. They don't love you.

(*As* CLINT *looks up the stairs, the posse's gear is being thrown out of the door.* BIKE *suddenly flies down the stairs and is thrown out. He struggles with the* HEAVY *but is ejected, his bicycle thrown down after him.*

The HEAVY *turns and glares at* CLINT.)

HEAVY: This squat is closed. You Muffdiver?

CLINT: *(Aggressive)* Why?

HEAVY: Someone's looking for him.

DR BUBBA: *(About* CLINT*)* This young man is my personal assistant.
(*The* HEAVY *looks at him and goes. From the top of the
stairs we hear* BURNS *complaining, arguing and fighting
with the* HEAVIES.

CLINT *quickly dives back into* DR BUBBA's *place, which is
deserted at this time.*

DR BUBBA *watches him walking nervously around the place.
He watches him go to the window, open it, and look up
at the drainpipe up which he originally entered the house.
He starts to climb out of the window.* DR BUBBA *restrains
him.*)
Stay here.

CLINT: I had some money for shoes stashed up there. I've gotta
get it.

DR BUBBA: They won't let you up, boy. And you must warn your
other friends. Don't come back here. Go. Go.

EXT. FRONT OF SQUAT BUILDING. NIGHT.

CLINT *is walking quickly away from the squat—backwards. He
watches the* HEAVIES *throwing the posse's belongings out into the
street.*

BURNS *is picking up some of the things and putting them into a
supermarket trolley. The* HEAVY *shoves* BURNS *hard and pushes the
trolley over.*

CLINT *talks to himself as he turns and runs.*

EXT. DINER. NIGHT.

CLINT *walks to the diner and looks in through the window. He
sees* MUFFDIVER *and* SYLVIE *sitting at a table eating and talking
amicably, drinking wine.*

CLINT *watches them. He can't decide whether to go in or not. He's about to step inside when he sees* HEMINGWAY *putting his coat on and preparing to leave.* MELANIE *is also putting her coat on.*

CLINT *conceals himself as the two of them come out,* MELANIE *putting her arm through* HEMINGWAY'*s once they're outside. They go.* CLINT *watches them.*

He turns and BUSY BEE *whose jumper he nicked is standing beside him.*

BUSY BEE: Where's my jumper?

    (Instinctively, CLINT *turns and runs.)*

INT. HEADLEY'S FLAT. NIGHT.

CLINT *is in the hall of Headley's flat, trying to get past her.*

CLINT: Let me in, Headley.

    (He's in a terrible state, exhausted and wretched.)

HEADLEY: But yesterday you ran out, all independent.

CLINT: Just for a little while.

HEADLEY: To hide from the law. What a gas. Gimme some more of that bush then.

CLINT: I swear I got nothing, Headley.

HEADLEY: What's the point of you then? Got your bloody shoes?

    (She looks at him, in a pitiful state. Then down at his ridiculous sandals and wet feet.)

    What happened to you?

CLINT: It's a long story, Headley.

INT. HEADLEY'S STUDY. NIGHT.

HEADLEY *lies face down on her sofa.* CLINT *is brusquely instructed to rub her back.* CLINT *sits over her arse.*

HEADLEY: Ummm . . . yes. There, right, down a bit, harder, move those fingers. Knead my cheeks, darling.

CLINT: I'm not going no further.

HEADLEY: Hey. Don't you need the money?

    (We should play this off CLINT'*s face; the humiliation, the calculation, the wild thinking and then, with the* MAN'S

VOICE, CLINT's *fear of being beaten up. Suddenly there's an American* MAN'S VOICE *outside and hard knocking on the door.)*

MAN'S VOICE: Headley.

*(*CLINT *is terrified and looks around for a window to escape through.)*

HEADLEY: How are you, dear? *(To* CLINT.*)* Don't stop now.

MAN'S VOICE: Am I allowed to come in?

HEADLEY: Goodness, no, I'm not quite ready for you.

MAN'S VOICE: All right if I take a shower then?

(Pause. The MAN *goes.* CLINT *gets up.)*

HEADLEY: Stay, stay.

CLINT: I'm not getting into nothing weird. I've been sexually abused before. And I'm starting work tomorrow. I've only got tonight to find a pair of shoes—or get some money to buy some tomorrow evening. Give us some dosh, Headley.

HEADLEY: But you haven't earned it.

CLINT: I beg you, Headley, give us thirty quid, thirty fucking quid, that's all. Give me the money, Headley!

INT. HEADLEY'S FLAT. NIGHT.

CLINT *walks quickly through Headley's flat. He sees the man's clothes flung over a chair. But of course he doesn't know they belong to* HEMINGWAY.

Beside the chair is a pair of boots, American boots, tough and colourful and easily distinguishable. The best boots he's seen so far.

CLINT *quickly removes his own Indian chappals and examines these American boots, caressing and sniffing and holding them. He's about to put them on when the door from the shower opens.*

CLINT *scarpers, quickly.*

Cut to:

INT. HEADLEY'S FLAT. NIGHT.

HEMINGWAY *comes out of the shower, a towel wrapped around him. He looks down and sees a pair of knackered Indian sandals where his own splendid boots were.*

HEMINGWAY: Headley! Headley! God dammit!

EXT. SHOE SHOP. NIGHT.

CLINT *prepares to sleep in the doorway of the shoe shop. A couple of other people are already there, including* BUSY BEE *whose jumper he nicked.*

The others have blankets and rudimentary pillows and stuff, while CLINT *has virtually nothing but an old coat, which he pulls around himself, his feet, with the magnificent boots, sticking out.* CLINT *spits in his hand and cleans the boots.*

CLINT: Tsa-Tsa.

EXT. STREET/NOTTING HILL TUBE. MORNING.

The rush hour. Well-dressed, motivated and employed people dash around. CLINT, *eager to join the employed world, moves in and out of the crowd, feeling self-conscious about his wretchedness. Across the street* BURNS *sees him and calls out.*

BURNS: Clint!

> (*He tries to get through the traffic to* CLINT *but* CLINT *fails to hear him and moves off quickly.*)

EXT. STREET NR TUBE AREA. MORNING.

CLINT *walking in another part of Notting Hill.* BURNS *has finally caught up with him.*

BURNS: Listen. Christ.

> (BURNS *just grabs him and pulls him off the street.*)
> Come on. This way.

CLINT: Burns, man, I got a job waiting for me. Right now this minute.

BURNS: You're with me, little boy, yes you are.

CLINT: No! What are you doing?

(*But* BURNS *is strong.*)

BURNS: We're going to see the boss, my wee man. And wipe your
feet too.

EXT/INT. HOTEL. DAY.

BURNS *drags* CLINT *through the doors of a seedy hotel in the area.*

INT. HOTEL ROOM. DAY.

BURNS *drags* CLINT *into a hotel room, shuts the door and leaves
him standing there, a little bewildered.*

MUFFDIVER *and* SYLVIE *are in the room, quite panicky,* MUFFDIVER
stuffing things into a small bag. SYLVIE *is getting changed into her
Gothess gear.*

*The two of them look different, older perhaps, more involved with
each other. Still, the atmosphere is tense.*

Once more CLINT *feels excluded, but confident about his future.*

SYLVIE *and* MUFFDIVER *are warmer towards him than they've ever
been, which disconcerts him.*

CLINT: What are you two playing at?

MUFFDIVER: The owner of that squat is looking at us. It's a fact
he's very pissed off. So we're going to chill out.

SYLVIE: You should make moves too.

MUFFDIVER: We'll meet somewhere in a few days. We'll rendez-
vous. In Portsmouth.

CLINT: Portsmouth?

SYLVIE: It's for your sake, baby.

(*Now* MUFFDIVER *puts a long black wig on.* SYLVIE *hands
him a black leather studded jacket.*)

MUFFDIVER: I'm disguising myself as Goth in order to leave town
without trouble. Sylvie's going as a Gothess.

(*He glances in the mirror at himself. A touch of vanity.*
CLINT *can't help laughing at him.*)

CLINT: Yeah, Mr Goth, and I'm starting work in ten minutes time. *(Points.)* Look man, the shoes has come true.

SYLVIE: Sit down. We've got you a birthday present.

> (MUFFDIVER *hands him a plastic bag. To his delight* CLINT *pulls out a pair of huge DMs.)*

CLINT: *(To them both)* Thank you. Thanks.

SYLVIE: You're escaping as a skinhead, Clint.

> (*She runs her hands through his hair, kisses his cheeks and pulls out a pair of scissors. She starts to cut his hair, cutting out a big lump.*)

CLINT: No! I gotta go. See you!

> (*He struggles. She tries to hold him.*)

MUFFDIVER: Be cool, Clint, brother. Put the boots on and get your hair off.

> (MUFFDIVER *tries to remove* CLINT'*s boots and replace them with the DMs.*)

CLINT: *(Distressed)* No, you be cool, man. Christ. Sylvie. Christ. Sylvie—I loved you and everything. Both of you. What are you doing? I loved you.

> (*And* CLINT *backs away towards the door, trying to stop crying.*)

MUFFDIVER: Clint!

SYLVIE: No! Stay!

> (*And* CLINT *dashes out of the door.*)

EXT. STREET. DAY.

CLINT *hurries towards the diner, upset, and trying to fix his hair. He stops and tries to look at himself in a mirror on one of the market stalls to see if the missing hank of hair is noticeable. He sees that it is.*

Walking through the market he steals a cap from a stall he's passing.

BIKE *stops beside him and shouts at him to stop.*

Then he hurries on, only stopping to check his shoes and adjust the hat. He's ready for HEMINGWAY.

INT. DINER. DAY.

The diner is crowded. The two SMART WOMEN *are there, and they recognize Clint. Waiters fly about, including* MELANIE, *who smiles at* CLINT. *Behind the bar the flashy barman mixes fantastic cocktails.*

CLINT: *(To* MELANIE*)* Is Mr Hemingway here?

MELANIE: He expecting you?

CLINT: Oh yeah, Melanie. Tsa-Tsa.

Cut to:

INT. DINER. DAY.

CLINT *desperately trying to arrange himself.* HEMINGWAY *emerges.*

CLINT: Here I am, you know, Mr Hemingway, this is me as arranged. The job hasn't gone to another?

  *(*HEMINGWAY *smiles and shakes his head.)*

HEMINGWAY: Let's have a look at you.

CLINT: *(Turning around).* You know I'm counting on this gig.

  *(*HEMINGWAY*'s eyes start at the top of* CLINT*'s body and move slowly downwards. During this process of examination* CLINT *looks out of the window of the diner and sees* MUFFDIVER, *in full heavy Goth gear, standing outside.) With him, also disguised, is* SYLVIE, *with black lipstick, eyeshadow, etc., in long black velvet clothes.*

  MUFFDIVER *knocks on the window and indicates for him to come out.*

  MELANIE *looks at them and at* CLINT. CLINT *looks away. Then* MUFFDIVER *and* SYLVIE *walk on.*

  Now HEMINGWAY*'s eyes continue. At last he takes in the shoes. And suddenly looks up to* CLINT*'s face. He looks down to the boots again, and once more up at* CLINT.

  CLINT *smiles broadly, happily, his smile spreading across the screen.)*

CLINT: Whaddya say, Mr Hemingway—the boot is cute, right? The boot is a hoot, yeah?

INT. TRAIN. DAY.

MUFFDIVER *is standing in the corridor of a train as it rushes through the English countryside. He is proud, disdainful, and still dressed as a Black Sabbath man.*

SYLVIE *has her head out the window, hair blowing.*

From her point of view we see the countryside rushing away.

EXT. TRAIN IN STATION. DAY.

The train has stopped in a station. MUFFDIVER *is now sitting in a seat, looking out of the window. Some of Sylvie's belongings are in the seat next to him. The train starts to move away from the platform. He looks out of the window and sees* SYLVIE *on the platform, walking away from him. She turns and waves. He gets up and gesticulates, but the train is moving away. It is too late. He turns to see her take off her vampire wig and throw it away.*

INT. DINER. DAY.

CLINT, *in waiter's gear, subserviently stands by a table, two smart white men in suits are deciding what to eat.* CLINT *has his pad at the ready. As the end titles roll, we see* CLINT *in the restaurant, putting plates down, removing others, running around. Freeze frame on his face.*

END

Eight
Arms to
Hold
You

Eight
Arms to
Hold
You

One day at school—an all-boys comprehensive on the border between London and Kent—our music teacher told us that John Lennon and Paul McCartney didn't actually write those famous Beatles songs we loved so much.

It was 1968 and I was thirteen. For the first time in music appreciation classes we were to listen to the Beatles—'She's Leaving Home', with the bass turned off. The previous week, after some Brahms, we'd been allowed to hear an Elton John record, again bassless. For Mr Hogg, our music and religious instruction teacher, the bass guitar 'obscured' the music. But hearing anything by the Beatles at school was uplifting, an act so unusually liberal it was confusing.

Mr Hogg prised open the lid of the school 'stereophonic equipment', which was kept in a big, dark wooden box and wheeled around the premises by the much-abused war-wounded caretaker. Hogg put on 'She's Leaving Home' without introduction, but as soon as it began he started his Beatles analysis.

What he said was devastating, though it was put simply, as if he were stating the obvious. These were the facts: Lennon and McCartney could not possibly have written the songs ascribed to them; it was a con—we should not be taken in by the 'Beatles', they were only front-men.

Those of us who weren't irritated by his prattling through the tune were giggling. Certainly, for a change, most of us were listening to teacher. I was perplexed. Why would anyone want to think anything so ludicrous? What was really behind this idea?

'Who did write the Beatles' songs, then, sir?' someone asked bravely. And Paul McCartney sang:

> We struggled hard all our lives to get by,
> She's leaving home after living alone,
> For so many years.

Mr Hogg told us that Brian Epstein and George Martin wrote the Lennon/McCartney songs. The Fabs only played on the records—if they did anything at all. (Hogg doubted whether their hands had actually touched the instruments.) 'Real musicians were playing on those records,' he said. Then he put the record back in its famous sleeve and changed the subject.

But I worried about Hogg's theory for days; on several occasions I was tempted to buttonhole him in the corridor and discuss it further. The more I dwelt on it alone, the more it revealed. The Mopheads couldn't even read music—how could they be geniuses?

It was unbearable to Mr Hogg that four young men without significant education could be the bearers of such talent and critical acclaim. But then Hogg had a somewhat holy attitude to culture. 'He's cultured,' he'd say of someone, the antonym of 'He's common.' Culture, even popular culture—folk-singing, for instance—was something you put on a special face for, after years of wearisome study. Culture involved a particular twitching of the nose, a faraway look (into the sublime), and a fruity pursing of the lips. Hogg knew. There was, too, a sartorial vocabulary of knowingness, with leather patches sewn on to the elbows of shiny, rancid jackets.

Obviously this was not something the Beatles had been born into. Nor had they acquired it in any recognized academy or university. No, in their early twenties, the Fabs made culture again and again, without effort, even as they mugged and winked at the cameras like schoolboys.

Sitting in my bedroom listening to the Beatles on a Grundig reel-to-reel tape-recorder, I began to see that to admit to the Beatles' genius would devastate Hogg. It would take too much else away with it. The songs that were so perfect and about recognizable common feelings—'She Loves You', 'Please, Please Me', 'I Wanna Hold Your Hand'—were all written by Brian Epstein and George Martin because the Beatles were only boys like us: ignorant, bad-mannered and rude; boys who'd never, in a just world, do anything interesting with their lives. This implicit belief, or form of contempt, was not abstract. We felt and sometimes recognised—and Hogg's attitude towards the Beatles exemplified this—that our teachers had no respect for us as people capable of learning, of finding the world compelling and wanting to know it.

The Beatles would also be difficult for Hogg to swallow because for him there was a hierarchy among the arts. At the top were stationed classical music and poetry, beside the literary novel and great painting. In the middle would be not-so-good examples of these forms. At the bottom of the list, and scarcely considered art forms at all, were films ('the pictures'), television and, finally, the most derided—pop music.

But in that post-modern dawn—the mid-1960s—I like to think that Hogg was starting to experience cultural vertigo—which was why he worried about the Beatles in the first place. He thought he knew what culture was, what counted in history, what had weight, and what you needed to know to be educated. These things were not relative, not a question of taste or decision. Notions of objectivity did exist; there were criteria and Hogg knew what the criteria were. Or at least he thought he did. But that particular form of certainty, of intellectual authority, along with many other forms of authority, was shifting. People didn't know where they were any more.

Not that you could ignore the Beatles even if you wanted to. Those rockers in suits were unique in English popular music, bigger than anyone had been before. What a pleasure it was to swing past Buckingham Palace in the bus knowing the Queen was indoors, in her slippers, watching her favourite film, *Yellow Submarine*, and humming along to 'Eleanor Rigby'. ('All the lonely people . . .')

The Beatles couldn't be as easily dismissed as the Rolling Stones, who often seemed like an ersatz American group, especially when Mick Jagger started to sing with an American accent. But the Beatles' music was supernaturally beautiful and it was English music. In it you could hear cheeky music-hall songs and send-ups, pub ballads and, more importantly, hymns. The Fabs had the voices and looks of choirboys, and their talent was so broad they could do anything—love songs, comic songs, kids' songs and song-alongs for football crowds (at White Hart Lane, Tottenham Hotspurs' ground, we sang: 'Here, there and every-fucking-where, Jimmy Greaves, Jimmy Greaves'). They could do rock 'n' roll too, though they tended to parody it, having mastered it early on.

One lunch-time in the school library, not long after the incident with Hogg, I came across a copy of *Life* magazine which included hefty extracts from Hunter Davies's biography of the Beatles, the first major book about them and their childhood. It was soon stolen from the library and passed around the school, a contemporary 'Lives of the Saints'. (On the curriculum we were required to read Gerald Durrell and C. S. Forester, but we had our own books, which we discussed, just as we exchanged and discussed records. We liked *Candy, Lord of the Flies*, James Bond, Mervyn Peake, *Sex Manners for Men* and *Skinhead*, among other things.)

Finally my parents bought the biography for my birthday. It was the first hardback I possessed and, pretending to be sick, I took the day off school to read it, with long breaks between chapters to prolong the pleasure. But *The Beatles* didn't satisfy me as I'd imagined it would. It wasn't like listening to *Revolver*, for instance, after which you felt fulfilled and uplifted. The book disturbed and intoxicated me; it made me feel restless and dissatisfied with my life. After reading about the Beatles' achievements I began to think I didn't expect enough of myself, that none of us at school did really. In two years we'd start work; soon after that we'd get married and buy a small house nearby. The form of life was decided before it was properly begun.

To my surprise it turned out that the Fabs were lower-middleclass provincial boys; neither rich nor poor, their music didn't come out of hardship and nor were they culturally privileged. Lennon was rough, but it wasn't poverty that made him hardedged. The Liverpool Institute, attended by Paul and George, was a good grammar school. McCartney's father had been well enough off for Paul and his brother Michael to have piano lessons. Later, his father bought him a guitar.

We had no life guides or role models among politicians, military types or religious figures, or even film stars for that matter, as our parents did. Footballers and pop stars were the revered figures of my generation and the Beatles, more than anyone, were exemplary for countless young people. If coming from the wrong class restricts your sense of what you can be, then none of us thought we'd become doctors, lawyers, scientists, politicians. We were scheduled to be clerks, civil servants, insurance managers and travel agents.

Not that leading some kind of creative life was entirely impossible. In the mid-1960s the media was starting to grow. There
was a demand for designers, graphic artists and the like. In our
art lessons we designed toothpaste boxes and record sleeves to
prepare for the possibility of going to art school. Art schools were
very highly regarded among the kids; they were known to be
anarchic places, the sources of British pop art, numerous pop
groups and the generators of such luminaries as Pete Townshend,
Keith Richards, Ray Davies and John Lennon. Along with the
Royal Court and the drama corridor of the BBC, the art schools
were the most important post-war British cultural institution, and
some lucky kids escaped into them. Once, I ran away from school
to spend the day at the local art college. In the corridors where
they sat cross-legged on the floor, the kids had dishevelled hair
and paint-splattered clothes. A band was rehearsing in the dining
hall. They liked being there so much they stayed till midnight.
Round the back entrance there were condoms in the grass.

But these kids were destined to be commercial artists, which
was, at least, 'proper work'. Commercial art was OK but anything
that veered too closely towards pure art caused embarrassment;
it was pretentious. Even education fell into this trap. When, later,
I went to college, our neighbours would turn in their furry slippers
and housecoats to stare and tut-tut to each other as I walked
down the street in my Army-surplus greatcoat, carrying a pile of
library books. I like to think it was the books rather than the coat
they were objecting to—the idea that they were financing my
uselessness through their taxes. Surely nurturing my brain could
be of no possible benefit to the world; it would only render me
more argumentative—create an intelligentsia and you're only producing criticism for the future.

(For some reason I've been long under the impression that this
hatred for education is a specifically English tendency. I've never
imagined the Scots, Irish or Welsh, and certainly no immigrant

group, hating the idea of elevation through the mind in quite the same way. Anyhow, it would be a couple of decades before the combined neighbours of south-east England could take their revenge on education via their collective embodiment—Thatcher.)

I could, then, at least have been training to be an apprentice. But, unfortunately for the neighbours, we had seen *A Hard Day's Night* at Bromley Odeon. Along with our mothers, we screamed all through it, fingers stuck in our ears. And afterwards we didn't know what to do with ourselves, where to go, how to exorcize this passion the Beatles had stoked up. The ordinary wasn't enough; we couldn't accept only the everyday now! We desired ecstasy, the extraordinary, magnificence—today!

For most, this pleasure lasted only a few hours and then faded. But for others it opened a door to the sort of life that might, one day, be lived. And so the Beatles came to represent opportunity and possibility. They were careers officers, a myth for us to live by, a light for us to follow.

How could this be? How was it that of all the groups to emerge from that great pop period the Beatles were the most dangerous, the most threatening, the most subversive? Until they met Dylan and, later, dropped acid, the Beatles wore matching suits and wrote harmless love songs offering little ambiguity and no call to rebellion. They lacked Elvis's sexuality, Dylan's introspection and Jagger's surly menace. And yet . . . and yet—this is the thing—everything about the Beatles represented pleasure, and for the provincial and suburban young, pleasure was only the outcome and justification of work. Pleasure was work's reward and it occurred only at weekends and after work.

But when you looked at *A Hard Day's Night* or *Help*, it was clear that those four boys were having the time of their life: the films radiated freedom and good times. In them there was no sign of the long, slow accumulation of security and status, the year-after-year movement towards satisfaction, that we were expected to ask of life. Without conscience, duty or concern for the future, everything about the Beatles spoke of enjoyment, abandon and attention to the needs of the self. The Beatles became heroes to the young because they were not deferential: no authority had broken their spirit; they were confident and funny; they answered back; no one put them down. It was this independence, creativity and earning-power that worried Hogg about the Beatles. Their naïve hedonism and dazzling accomplishments were too para-doxical. For Hogg to wholeheartedly approve of them was like saying crime paid. But to dismiss the new world of the 1960s was to admit to being old and out of touch.

There was one final strategy that the defenders of the straight world developed at this time. It was a common stand-by of the neighbours. They argued that the talent of such groups was shal-low. The easy money would soon be spent, squandered on objects the groups would be too jejune to appreciate. These musicians couldn't think about the future. What fools they were to forfeit the possibility of a secure job for the pleasure of having teenagers worship them for six months.

This sneering 'anyone-can-do-it' attitude to the Beatles wasn't necessarily a bad thing. Anyone could have a group—and they did. But it was obvious from early on that the Beatles were not a two-hit group like the Merseybeats or Freddie and the Dreamers. And around the time that Hogg was worrying about the author-ship of 'I Saw Her Standing There' and turning down the bass on 'She's Leaving Home', just as he was getting himself used to them, the Beatles were doing something that had never been done before. They were writing songs about drugs, songs that could be fully comprehended only by people who took drugs, songs designed to be enjoyed all the more if you were stoned when you listened to them.

And Paul McCartney had admitted to using drugs, specifically LSD. This news was very shocking then. For me, the only asso-

ciation that drugs conjured up was of skinny Chinese junkies in
squalid opium dens and morphine addicts in B movies; there had
also been the wife in *Long Day's Journey into Night*. What were
the Mopheads doing to themselves? Where were they taking us?

On Peter Blake's cover for *Sgt Pepper*, between Sir Robert Peel
and Terry Southern, is an ex-Etonian novelist mentioned in *Remembrance of Things Past* and considered by Proust to be a
genius—Aldous Huxley. Huxley first took mescalin in 1953,
twelve years before the Beatles used LSD. He took psychedelic
drugs eleven times, including on his death bed, when his wife
injected him with LSD. During his first trip Huxley felt himself
turning into four bamboo chairs. As the folds of his gray flannel
trousers became 'charged with is-ness' the world became a compelling, unpredictable, living and breathing organism. In this
transfigured universe Huxley realized both his fear of and need
for the 'marvellous'; one of the soul's principal appetites was for
'transcendence'. In an alienated, routine world ruled by habit, the
urge for escape, for euphoria, for heightened sensation, cannot
be denied.
    Despite his enthusiasm for LSD, when Huxley took psilocybin
with Timothy Leary at Harvard he was alarmed by Leary's ideas
about the wider use of psychedelic drugs. He thought Leary was
an 'ass' and felt that LSD, if it were to be widely tried at all,
should be given to the cultural élite—to artists, psychologists,
philosophers and writers. It was important that psychedelic drugs
be used seriously, primarily as aids to contemplation. Certainly
they changed nothing in the world, being 'incompatible with action and even with the will to action'. Huxley was especially
nervous about the aphrodisiac qualities of LSD and wrote to
Leary: 'I strongly urge you not to let the sexual cat out of the
bag. We've stirred up enough trouble suggesting that drugs can
stimulate aesthetic and religious experience.'

But there was nothing Huxley could do to keep the 'cat' in the bag. In 1961 Leary gave LSD to Allen Ginsberg, who became convinced the drug contained the possibilities for political change. Four years later the Beatles met Ginsberg through Bob Dylan. At his own birthday party Ginsberg was naked apart from a pair of underpants on his head and a 'do not disturb' sign tied to his penis. Later, Lennon was to learn a lot from Ginsberg's style of self-exhibition as protest, but on this occasion he shrank from Ginsberg, saying: 'You don't do that in front of the birds!'

Throughout the second half of the 1960s the Beatles functioned as that rare but necessary and important channel, popularizers of esoteric ideas—about mysticism, about different forms of political involvement and about drugs. Many of these ideas originated with Huxley. The Beatles could seduce the world partly because of their innocence. They were, basically, good boys who became bad boys. And when they became bad boys, they took a lot of people with them.

Lennon claimed to have 'tripped' hundreds of times, and he was just the sort to become interested in unusual states of mind. LSD creates euphoria and suspends inhibition; it may make us aware of life's intense flavour. In the tripper's escalation of awareness, the memory is stimulated too. Lennon knew the source of his art was the past, and his acid songs were full of melancholy, self-examination and regret. It's no surprise that *Sgt Pepper*, which at one time was to include 'Strawberry Fields' and 'Penny Lane', was originally intended to be an album of songs about Lennon and McCartney's Liverpool childhood.

Soon the Beatles started to wear clothes designed to be read by people who were stoned. God knows how much 'is-ness' Huxley would have felt had he seen John Lennon in 1967, when he was reportedly wearing a green flower-patterned shirt, red cord trousers, yellow socks and a sporran in which he carried his loose change and keys. These weren't the cheap but hip adaptations of

work clothes that young males had worn since the late 1940s—
Levi jackets and jeans, sneakers, work boots or DMs, baseball
caps, leather jackets—democratic styles practical for work. The
Beatles had rejected this conception of work. Like Baudelairean
dandies they could afford to dress ironically and effeminately, for
each other, for fun, beyond the constraints of the ordinary. Step-
ping out into that struggling post-war world steeped in memories
of recent devastation and fear—the war was closer to them than
Sgt Pepper is to me today—wearing shimmering bandsman's out-
fits, crushed velvet, peach-coloured silk and long hair, their clothes
were gloriously non-functional, identifying their creativity and the
pleasures of drug-taking.

By 1966 the Beatles behaved as if they spoke directly to the
whole world. This was not a mistake: they were at the centre of
life for millions of young people in the West. And certainly they're
the only mere pop group you could remove from history and
suggest that culturally, without them, things would have been
significantly different. All this meant that what they did was in-
fluential and important. At this time, before people were aware
of the power of the media, the social changes the Beatles sanctioned had happened practically before anyone noticed. Musicians
have always been involved with drugs, but the Beatles were the
first to parade their particular drug-use—marijuana and LSD—
publicly and without shame. They never claimed, as musicians do
now—when found out—that drugs were a 'problem' for them.
And unlike the Rolling Stones, they were never humiliated for
drug-taking or turned into outlaws. There's a story that at a bust
at Keith Richard's house in 1968, before the police went in they
waited for George Harrison to leave. The Beatles made taking
drugs seem an enjoyable, fashionable and liberating experience:
like them, you would see and feel in ways you hadn't imagined
possible. Their endorsement, far more than that of any other
group or individual, removed drugs from their sub-cultural, avant-

garde and generally squalid associations, making them part of
mainstream youth activity. Since then, illegal drugs have accompanied music, fashion and dance as part of what is to be young
in the West.

Allen Ginsberg called the Beatles 'the paradigm of the age', and
they were indeed condemned to live out their period in all its
foolishness, extremity and commendable idealism. Countless pre-
occupations of the time were expressed through the Fabs. Even
Apple Corps was a characteristic 1960s notion: an attempt to run
a business venture in an informal, creative and non-materialistic
way.

Whatever they did and however it went wrong, the Beatles
were always on top of things musically, and perhaps it is this,
paradoxically, that made their end inevitable. The loss of control
that psychedelic drugs can involve, the political anger of the 1960s
and its anti-authoritarian violence, the foolishness and inau-
thenticity of being pop stars at all, rarely violates the highly finished surface of their music. Songs like 'Revolution' and 'Helter
Skelter' attempt to express unstructured or deeply felt passions,
but the Beatles are too controlled to let their music fray. It never
felt as though the band was going to disintegrate through sheer
force of feeling, as with Hendrix, the Who or the Velvet Underground. Their ability was so extensive that all madness could be
contained within a song. Even 'Strawberry Fields' and 'I Am the
Walrus' are finally engineered and controlled. The exception is
'Revolution No. 9', which Lennon had to fight to keep on the
White Album; he wanted to smash through the organization and
accomplished form of his pop music. But Lennon had to leave
the Beatles to continue in that direction and it wasn't until his
first solo album that he was able to strip away the Beatle frippery
for the raw feeling he was after.

At least, Lennon wanted to do this. In the 1970s, the liberation tendencies of the 1960s bifurcated into two streams—hedonism, self-aggrandisement and decay, represented by the Stones; and serious politics and self-exploration, represented by Lennon. He continued to be actively involved in the obsessions of the time, both as initiate and leader, which is what makes him the central cultural figure of the age, as Brecht was, for instance, in the 1930s and 1940s.

But to continue to develop Lennon had to leave the containment of the Beatles and move to America. He had to break up the Beatles to continue to lead an interesting life.

I heard a tape the other day of a John Lennon interview. What struck me, what took me back irresistibly, was realizing how much I loved his voice and how inextricably bound up it was with my own growing up. It was a voice I must have heard almost everyday for years, on television, radio or record. It was more exceptional then than it is now, not being the voice of the BBC or of southern England, or of a politician; it was neither emollient nor instructing, it was direct and very hip. It pleased without trying to. Lennon's voice continues to intrigue me, and not just for nostalgic reasons, perhaps because of the range of what it says. It's a strong but cruel and harsh voice; not one you'd want to hear putting you down. It's naughty, vastly melancholic and knowing too, full of self-doubt, self-confidence and humour. It's expressive, charming and sensual; there's little concealment in it, as there is in George Harrison's voice, for example. It is aggressive and combative but the violence in it is attractive since it seems to emerge out of a passionate involvement with the world. It's the voice of someone who is alive in both feeling and mind; it comes from someone who has understood his own experience and knows his value.

The only other public voice I know that represents so much, that seems to have spoken relentlessly to me for years, bringing with it a whole view of life—though from the dark side—is that of Margaret Thatcher. When she made her 'St Francis of Assisi' speech outside 10 Downing Street after winning the 1979 General Election, I laughed aloud at the voice alone. It was impenetrable to me that anyone could have voted for a sound that was so cold, so pompous, so clearly insincere, ridiculous and generally absurd.

In this same voice, and speaking of her childhood, Thatcher once said that she felt that 'To pursue pleasure for its own sake was wrong'.

In retrospect it isn't surprising that the 1980s *mélange* of liberal economics and Thatcher's pre-war Methodist priggishness would embody a reaction to the pleasure-seeking of the 1960s and 1970s, as if people felt ashamed, guilty and angry about having gone too far, as if they'd enjoyed themselves too much. The greatest surprise was had by the Left—the ideological left rather than the Labour Party—which believed it had, during the 1970s, made immeasureable progress since *Sgt Pepper*, penetrating the media and the Labour Party, the universities and the law, fanning out and reinforcing itself in various organizations like the gay, black and women's movements. The 1960s was a romantic period and Lennon a great romantic hero, both as poet and political icon. Few thought that what he represented would all end so quickly and easily, that the Left would simply hand over the moral advantage and their established positions in the country as if they hadn't fought for them initially.

Thatcher's trope against feeling was a resurrection of control, a repudiation of the sensual, of self-indulgence in any form, self-exploration and the messiness of non-productive creativity, often specifically targeted against the 'permissive' 1960s. Thatcher's colleague Norman Tebbit characterized this suburban view of the Beatles period with excellent vehemence, calling it: 'The insufferable, smug, sanctimonious, naïve, guilt-ridden, wet, pink orthodoxy of that sunset home of that third-rate decade, the 60s.'

The amusing thing is that Thatcher's attempt to convert Britain to an American-style business-based society has failed. It is not something that could possibly have taken in such a complacent and divided land, especially one lacking a self-help culture. Only the immigrants in Britain have it: they have much to fight for and much to gain through being entrepreneurial. But it's as if no one else can be bothered—they're too mature to fall for such ideas.

Ironically, the glory, or, let us say, the substantial achievements of Britain in its ungracious decline, has been its art. There is here a tradition of culture dissent (or argument or cussedness) caused by the disaffections and resentments endemic in a class-bound society, which fed the best fiction of the 1960s, the theatre of the 1960s and 1970s, and the cinema of the early 1980s. But principally and more prolifically, reaching a world-wide audience and being innovative and challenging, there is the production of pop music—the richest cultural form of post-war Britain. Ryszard Kapuscinski in 'Shah of Shahs' quotes a Tehran carpet salesman: 'What have we given the world? We have given poetry, the miniature, and carpets. As you can see, these are all useless things from the productive viewpoint. But it is through such things that we have expressed our true selves.'

The Beatles are the godhead of British pop, the hallmark of excellence in song-writing and, as importantly, in the interweaving of music and life. They set the agenda for what was possible in pop music after them. And Lennon, especially, in refusing to be a career pop star and dissociating himself from the politics of his time, saw, in the 1970s, pop becoming explicitly involved in social issues. In 1976 Eric Clapton interrupted a concert he was giving in Birmingham to make a speech in support of Enoch Powell. The incident led to the setting up of Rock Against Racism. Using pop music as an instrument of solidarity, as resistance and propaganda, it was an effective movement against the National Front at a time when official politics—the Labour Party—were incapable of taking direct action around immediate street issues. And punk too, of course, emerged partly out of the unemployment, enervation and lack of direction of the mid-1970s.

During the 1980s, Thatcherism discredited such disinterested and unprofitable professions as teaching, and yet failed to implant a forging culture of self-help. Today, as then, few British people believe that nothing will be denied them if only they work hard enough, as many Americans, for instance, appear to believe. Most British know for a fact that, whatever they do, they can't crash through the constraints of the class system and all the prejudices and instincts for exclusion that it contains. But pop music is the one area in which this belief in mobility, reward and opportunity does exist.

Fortunately the British school system can be incompetent, liberal and so devoid of self-belief that it lacks the conviction to . crush the creativity of young people, which does, therefore, continue to flourish in the interestices of authority, in the school corridor and after four o'clock, as it were. The crucial thing is to have education that doesn't stamp out the desire to learn, that attempts to educate while the instincts of young people—which desire to be stimulated but in very particular things, like sport, pop music and television—flower in spite of the teacher's requirement to educate. The sort of education that Thatcherism needed as a base—hard-line, conformist, medicinal, providing soldiers for the trenches of business wars and not education for its own sake—is actually against the tone or feeling of an England that is not naturally competitive, not being desperate enough, though desperate conditions were beginning to be created.

Since Hogg first played 'She's Leaving Home', the media has expanded unimaginably, but pop music remains one area accessible to all, both for spectators and, especially, for participants. The cinema is too expensive, the novel too refined and exclusive, the theatre too poor and middle-class, and television too complicated and rigid. Music is simpler to get into. And pop musicians never have to ask themselves—in the way that writers, for instance, constantly have to—who is my audience, who am I writing for and what am I trying to say? It is art for their own sakes, and art which connects with a substantial audience hungry for a new product, an audience which is, by now, soaked in the history of pop music and is sophisticated, responsive and knowledgeable.

And so there has been in Britian since the mid-1960s a stream of fantastically accomplished music, encompassing punk and New Wave, northern soul, reggae, hip-hop, rap, acid jazz and house. The Left, in its puritanical way, has frequently dismissed pop as capitalist pap, preferring folk and other 'traditional' music. But it is pop that has spoken of ordinary experience with far more precision, real knowledge and wit than, say, British fiction of the equivalent period. And you can't dance to fiction.

In the 1980s, during Thatcher's 'permanent revolution', there was much talk of identity, race, nationality, history and, naturally, culture. Pop music, which has bound young people together more than anything else, was usually left out. But this tradition of joyous and lively music created by kids from state schools, kids from whom little was expected, has made a form of self-awareness, entertainment and effective criticism that deserves to be acknowledged and applauded but never institutionalized. But then that is up to the bands and doesn't look like happening, pop music being a rebellious form in itself if it is to be any good. And the Beatles, the most likely candidates ever for institutionalization, finally repudiated that particular death through the good sense of John Lennon, who gave back his MBE, climbed inside a white bag and wrote 'Cold Turkey'.